# Thrall

## Richard Beauchamp

GRENDEL PRESS

Thrall
Copyright © 2024 Richard Beauchamp
All rights reserved.

This is a work of fiction.
Any names, characters, places, and events are products of the author's imagination and are used fictitiously. Any resemblance to persons living or dead is coincidental. Any opinions expressed are those of the characters and should not be confused with the author's. No part of this book may be reproduced in any form or by any means, electronic or mechanical. This includes storage and retrieval systems without written permission from the author, with the exception of brief quotations in reviews.

Published 2024
ISBN: 978-1-960534-23-1 (Paperback)
ASIN: B0DL8YR8RL (eBook)

Written by Richard Beauchamp
Interior illustrations by Michael Harper
Cover by Matthew Revert
Edited by LL Garland

Published by Grendel Press LLC
www.grendelpress.com

AUTHOR'S NOTE: The events that take place in this novel depict scenes of racism and contain offensive language including racial slurs. The views, verbiage, and actions depicted in this book are not shared by the author or publisher. Reader discretion advised.

# PROLOGUE

"Mee-maw, Mee-maw, come look!" Dawn said, her squeaky little voice brimming with excitement. She tugged on the hem of Analetta's smock while the old woman she diced potatoes, cursing her stiff knuckles.

"Not now, child. Mee-maw must feed you. Mee-maw cook." Analetta did not pause in her metronomic slicing. Her voice was flat with distraction as she ignored the pain in her hands, gnarled like oak knots. These damn foggy excuses for mountains and their constant humidity played hell on her joints. She missed the dry cold of her homelands. She missed much about her homelands. Better than this place of feigned piety and genuine ignorance a thousandfold.

"But Mee-maw, there's a ghost coming up the hill, a real-life ghost!" Dawn insisted.

"Go bother Mother about it," she said, nodding a head towards Philipa, who sat by the hearth, nursing Eliza, or trying to. The baby was colicky and prone to fits, and her glistening spittle-flecked lips squirmed around the swollen nipple, attempting to spit it out.

"Oh, give it a rest, child, *please,*" Philipa groaned from her rarely vacated roost by the fireplace. Analetta smirked at the tiredness in her voice. Like she had any right to be tired. She was just a fat-titted sow; her only jobs to feed her newborn and loaf around, sighing in a perpetual state of exasperation. Analetta was the one who cooked and cleaned and kept the fire going while the men went off to the mines. *She* was the man of the house when the men were gone.

"It's true! There's a ghost coming up the hill!" Anne said, joining her sister at the window, their little dark brown mops of hair bopping up and down in excitement.

"*Dumnezeule,*" Analetta sighed, putting her knife down. She wiped her hands on her apron, trudged to the window, her wrinkled forehead furrowed with concern.

"None of that hill-speak now. You know what Liam said," Philipa said, from her place by the hearth.

"I'll speak how I want in my own house, little *fata,*" Analetta said, with a dismissive wave of her red, swollen hand. In that moment, she hated the entrepreneurial spirit of her son. All the Coldona men were cursed with it, with that need to outrun their heritage, to obtain the wealth that was always lorded over them by their bosses and handlers. *Gypsies,* the Americans called them. Analetta learned early on this was *not* a term of endearment.

The bitter thought-stream that flooded her mind burned up like kindling when she saw that there was indeed a ghost coming up the hill. Two ghosts, actually, on horseback, both carrying torches. The spit dried up in Analetta's mouth when she saw the peaked hoods and the red crosses embroidered upon their right shoulders. Not just ghosts, but harbingers of death.

"Philipa, get the girls together. Shoes on. Get ready to leave." Analetta approached the door.

"What? What're you going on about old woman? I—"

"*Now!*" Analetta hissed as she went through the door and slammed it behind her.

The riders approached at an unhurried canter, faceless and inhuman behind their cloaks. Analetta had heard of these men of the white cloak.

Terrorizers of the dark-skinned people this country had so recently seen as property and had so recently torn itself apart over their claim to enslave them. Those of the burning crosses and silly little Christian chants.

She took Liam's squirrel rifle off the skinning table and aimed it at the nearest rider.

"State your business," she said, her accent thicker with the fear. Analetta hated that she sounded more like a scared girl than a stern, salt of the earth woman.

"Come to rid the hills of your kind, you old bitch," the bare-handed rider said. "We knowed it was you who poisoned the town. Got our babies sick and our men unfit to work."

Analetta laughed, then loaded a cartridge into the chamber. She knew how to use the gun, her son made sure of that.

"You blame everyone but you for pigheadedness. We had nothing to do with what your little town is going through. Your own incompetence brought that," she said. "Leave this place."

"Or what? Gonna plink us with that popgun? Gonna use that got damn hill folk magic on us? Don't think we don't know you're one of them. Medicine woman. Witch doctor. We heard stories," the other rider said, circling the small house. A torch sputtered in his dark-gloved hand.

"Stories. *Provestiri,*" she said with a thin grin and spat on the ground.

"There she goes, speakin' that infernal tongue!" the gloved rider said.

"No magic responsible for *here*. For *this,*" Analetta pointed at the ground with the barrel of the gun. "*You* do that. *You* blast mountain, poison water. Not us. My Liam? He smart. He know how to do job. You? Dumb pighead man," she said. "No magic here. But will be if you keep—"

A deep rumbling shook the earth beneath their feet. A flock of starlings took flight from the surrounding hillside and darkened the sky in their murmuration.

Wood crackled as fire met tinder. The gloved rider had tossed his torch on the tar paper roof while she was distracted. Despite the humidity, the roof took to fire like a kindling box.

"*No!*" Analetta whirled around to fire at the bare-handed rider, but he had already closed on her. He knocked the gun out of her hands with the torch, then tossed the flaming club into the woodpile. Freshly seasoned poplar, painstakingly cut by Analetta's own hands to see them through the winter. She grabbed for the rifle slung on her attacker's saddle, but the gloved rider shoved her away with a foot as he passed again. Muffled screams came from within their humble little shack, built by hand by her and her son.

"Best go get them babies 'fore they roast alive!" the gloved rider said with a cackle. Another boom, another charge going off very close by. As their cabin burned, Liam and his sons were down in the earth, doing their best to make a fortune and seek that mythical status out of poverty that the Coldona family had sought their whole life.

"You hear that? Sounds like them foreign roaches gettin' buried down below! Bastard and his sons can rot in hell." The bare-handed rider's words faded behind her as Analetta burst through the door.

The house was filling with smoke. She scrabbled for the children but couldn't see through the burning tears in her eyes. The door slammed shut behind her.

"Mee-maw!" someone, it sounded like Dawn, screamed.

"*Copeiii Mei!*" Analetta screamed, forgetting her English in her panic.

"May you all rot in Hell!" came a voice from outside. Analetta grabbed the nearest child, her tears making the squirming body she grabbed anomalous as she tried to see through the smoke. She ran for the door, putting her shoulder into it. The thick oak door did not give. Laughter cackled outside. Again, she threw her body against the door despite the throbbing ache in her shoulder, but something was blocking it.

A full, throaty scream pierced the air. A grown woman's howl of pain. Analetta spun to find her Philipa ablaze. The ceiling had caved in, dropping pounds of burning tar paper. The young mother flung herself to the floor, Eliza still attached, smothering the baby as she rolled and flailed and set the floorboards alight, flames burning away her once luscious black hair.

Analetta grabbed the heavy oak cutting board she'd just been dicing potatoes on and hurled it at the window on the eastern wall. The glass shattered outwards, and she went to it, a squirming, coughing Dawn in tow. She tried to clear away the many jagged shards that would slice them to ribbons if they attempted to crawl through it.

If it weren't for the children, she would've just dived through it herself. Righteous anger made her immune to the pain. Deep in her bones, she'd known this was coming. Everywhere they went, it was the same.

A rifle barrel appeared through the ragged pane just as she made to push Dawn through.

"No ma'am!" the bare-handed rider barked. The barrel belched a brief flash of light. Analetta felt the hand of God punch her in the left shoulder. Her arm immediately went numb, and she cried out indignantly as she dropped Dawn.

"Mee-maw! Mee-maw!" the child screamed, before the smoke cut her off, turning her cries into deep, hacking coughs.

In one last burst of fear-driven adrenaline, Analetta Coldona hurled herself at the thick wooden door, but it was no use. Her shoulder bones shattered as easily as the window, and the old woman screamed. She had painstakingly carved the *proteja* into that very same door. A sigil of protection, it was supposed to guard her and her kin. It was supposed to make this cabin a safe place.

But this safe place now burned and crackled and roared around her, transforming itself into a prison. Anne sprawled passed out in the corner, oblivious to the roaring blaze that inched towards her like a feral animal stalking a potential meal. Analetta watched the little girl's feet blister and burn as flames began to lick at them.

Analetta screamed once more as she understood that history would always repeat itself. The realization smacked into her like a brick to the face. She remembered the voyage across the ocean from Europe, the roughness of the sea and the stink of their living quarters. She remembered the way customs had frowned reading their name aloud, as if they just *knew* what they were, who they were. The suspicious looks from the townsfolk when they first arrived. The battles for land claims. Liam's fights with the foreman.

The warnings were all there. Analetta should've known. But just once, she'd allowed herself hope. So foolish. There was a reason it was called the Coldona Curse. Curses can't be outrun.

Analetta had sworn she would never unleash it. She would never be like her ancestors who used that ancient poison to enact revenge on those who brought them suffering. Because suffering only beget more suffering. It was her ancestors, her grandmother and her mother before her, that had learned to infuse the Coldona Curse with strong blood magic, to bring about that insidious plague with an incantation spell.

As she watched her grandchildren burn, as she heard the maniacal laughter of those ignorant men over the roar of the flames, she knew the time had come. If they could not find peace even in these remote hills, then she would blight this land with the same fear and agony and biblical annihilation that the Coldona name had carried with it for hundreds of years.

They wanted to blame their misfortunes on magic? Then, by God, she would show them what happens when you kick the hornet's nest.

Analetta stood tall, closing her eyes against the burning smoke. She shirked off her smoldering smock, ignoring the pain in her shoulder. Against the flames, a wraith-like body was revealed, cords of muscle obscured by folds and dewlaps of time-worn flesh. The kitchen knife was in her hand. She dragged it across her palm. She had to be quick, had to complete the incantation before the smoke got to her.

"I'm sorry, Liam," she said, letting the blood pool in her palm, her infernal ink. "*Fie ca ei să sufere veșnic!*" she screamed as she began to paint the sigil for invocation onto her knobby breastbone, her flesh the canvas, her blood the paint. "*Fie ca ei să sufere veșnic!*" she yelled again, her voice growing croaky with the smoke. Over and over, she repeated the phrase, until the intricate six staved sigil was completed, and Analetta's veiny, gnarled feet left the smoking floorboards. She said it once more, her voice modulating an octave lower, before her body glowed blood red.

The two men were rendered silent by the tableau before them. The sigil on the door began to glow a deep, ruby red. The ground shook beneath their feet, a sustained, wavering tremor wholly divorced from the TNT blasts deep underground that had shaken these hills for years. The horses bucked their bewildered riders from their saddles and galloped to parts unknown.

A few seconds later, just as they got to their feet, they were promptly deposited back on their rear ends as the house exploded with a *whoomph*. From that searing fireball of splintering wood blossomed something unfathomable, consuming the two men in its wake.

Burning planks and charred body parts rained from the sky. Those in the town below saw what appeared to be a red meteor explode upwards from the site of the burning home. It flew high in the sky before sharply arcing downward, towards the Doefield Mine tract. Far below that blasted ground, the last of the Coldona line were buried under tons of dolomite and galena.

A secondary tremor shook the town, and those who bore witness to this horrifying display thought it another earthquake, the New Madrid fault line reawakening. But the ground stopped its tremors as soon as the scintillating red orb disappeared.

Deep below ground, through miles of karst, into the hollowed bowels of these highlands, something stirred beneath the newly churned rubble.

# PART ONE
# INTERLOPER(S)

M.HARREN

# Chapter 1

Lou studied the serpentine asphalt unspooling ahead of him, unwilling to admit what everyone else surely thought.

"You sure you know where you're going?" Jessie asked from the back, voice thick with heavy indica.

"Yep, these fucking backroads all eventually lead around and go back to the same place," Lou said from the pilot's seat. His red eyes shifted from the winding unpainted blacktop to his phone screen, where his GPS told him he was in the middle of a bright green field some ten miles away from their actual position. He wouldn't admit they were lost though. He was the designated country boy of this ragtag group of assholes. Wasn't about to be made a fool of, even if his familiar homebase was in the Kentucky part of the Appalachians, and not this shithole backwater part of Missouri.

"Shoulda just went through the checkpoint, man. Flexed your rights on those fucking pigs," Geoff said from his shotgunner's position. "Fourth and fifth amendment, baby. No search without probable cause."

He passed the crumbling roach back to Jessie, who shook her head. The glazed look on her face betrayed her baby tolerance compared to everyone else in the band. Allen wasn't even smoking. He was passed out in the third-row seat, his snores more abrasive than Geoff's 5150 with the gain past midnight.

Lou laughed, shaking his head.

"Shit, man, that might've worked with your white ass. You seen the amount of Dixie flag truck decals we passed? I bet ten to one every one of those highway patrol boys drops hard Rs at the dinner table. Plus, they woulda smelled the grass for a mile." Lou cranked the volume knob on the in-dash. "Just shut up and enjoy the ride."

Ever since the tour began someone always had their iPod jacked into the aux, everything from grindcore to grunge playing at a barely audible level, more background ambiance than anything. Mastodon's "Blood and Thunder" played through the shitty old van system, but they were all too deafened from tonight's show to really give a shit. For a while, they all lapsed into a comfortable silence. The motion of the van, the gentle susurration of tires on blacktop, and the general encompassing thickness of the night lent a cozy, insular quality to the atmosphere. This was always how it was after a show, everyone coming down from the adrenaline high of performing. Whoever wasn't the DD for the night was usually coming down off many other things, interstate travel lulling them into a weed-augmented sleep. Just the four of them against the whole fuckin' world.

Lou focused on the road, trying to keep a mental gridwork in his head of where he was in relation to the interstate many miles behind him. He knew they'd eventually come across some backwater town that would lead to a small interstate metropolis further down the road, like how all these Midwest rural townships were. At least that's how Kentucky was, once you got away from the mountains.

Lou liked driving. He trusted his piloting of the Shaggin' Wagon far more than that of his band members. Mostly because he was the only one who didn't like to drive stoned to the bone (just a hit or two to get him in the zone). Not to mention his short-lived stint driving trucks with his daddy before he decided to take his passion for thumping four strings and try to make a living at it. For him, the act of driving in itself was meditative. When the wheels were rolling and the night was thick around you like it was now, it almost felt as if he were some transitory being. Just flying through time and space the way quantum matter does, fluid and insignificant. The world around him nothing but an ephemeral blur.

The road kept going, turning steep and winding as they entered the Ozark foothills. He hadn't seen another vehicle for some fifteen minutes, but, given their location and the fact it was well past midnight, it wasn't so unusual. Lou was glad for the isolation. He let his mind wander free as the van coasted along the winding road, instinct guiding them to some bum fuck backwoods burg like a divining rod to water.

"Those sound guys at Delmar need to get their shit together," Jessie said, her mind always on stage. "Could barely hear Lou or Geoff through the monitors. Guy even had the audacity to act all huffy when I asked him to fix the stage mix. Fuckin' weekend warrior sound guys... We need our *own*." Her brain constantly worked in terms of measures, bars, and phrases, her hands constantly air drumming to imaginary riffs.

"I thought it sounded great," Geoff said. He pulled down the passenger side visor mirror and began to roll another joint in the weak light.

"Motherfucker, as long as you can hear *yourself* you think it sounds great." Lou's eyes flitted to his side mirror. Headlights had rounded the curve a quarter mile back and were growing closer. "Yo, put that shit up. Could be a good ol' boy." The headlights gained on them. He noticed Geoff glance towards his side mirror and give a dismissive shrug.

"Fuck him, just some redneck on a booze cruise, I bet," Geoff said, continuing to sprinkle the sticky weed into the Zig-Zag he had taco'd up between two fingers.

Within thirty seconds the car had eaten up the road between them and was on their ass. Except it wasn't a car, it was a truck. Lou could tell from the high-sitting headlights. The rumble of a powerful engine unrestrained by an absent muffler snarled like some apex predator even through the music and the van's interior. Lou was nearly blinded as twin suns shone in his side mirrors, the truck apparently having enough wattage in his hi-beams to signal for fucking Batman.

"What the fuck!" Lou squinted and sped up, wanting to put some space between him and the dickhead in his jacked-up ride.

"Je-sus, just pull over and let this asshole pass," Geoff grumbled, slitting his eyes against the glare. Lou's stoned retinas felt like they were witnessing a solar flare.

Lou was in the process of flipping on his blinker when the van's steering wheel suddenly lurched in his hands. Their trailer canted hard to the right. The truck had kissed its bumper. Amps, guitar cases, and drums crashed around inside the trailer.

"Did he just fucking hit us?" Jessie said, the haze from her voice clearing up rapidly.

"Huh? 'S going on?" Allen's head poked up from the very back.

No one answered him. The truck nudged the trailer again, and Lou felt the van jerk in his hands just as they were rounding an L curve. Tires squealed and the van shuddered. Lou suddenly had *that* scene from Deliverance in his mind, the ass-fucking scene with the hillbilly and the chubby one from the group. That image quickly transitioned to a montage of all the Rebel flag stickers he'd seen since arriving in this hellish state. Every mile they travelled south since their show in Saint Louis was like heading back in time.

Lou slammed the gas to the floorboard. The Econoline 450's overworked and often overheated V8 engine groaned in protest as he decided right then and there he wasn't stopping. They were in the middle of fucking nowhere, and this asshole had the room to pass if he really wanted to. No, the driver *wanted* them to stop. What better place to enact some crazy inbred white people shit than the side of a dark country road? Hell no, he was going to give this dickhead a run for his money.

"Hey man, what.... What are you doing?" Geoff pushed his feet against the foot well and grasped the oh shit handle on the van's ceiling.

"Let him pass, Lou!" Jessie said as the van worked its way up to sixty. Every member of Blasphemer was thrown about in their seats as Lou took the next turn fast enough to almost flip the goddamned thing.

"Stop this fucking van, Lou. They wanna fuck around, I'll make sure they find out." Allen cracked his thick bull's neck in anticipation of violence, the sleep gone from his voice.

"Nope, these guys came out of nowhere, had room to pass and they didn't take it," Lou shouted, his voice tight. "They're fucking ramming us, man, they want us to stop. I'm not letting anyone in this van get buttfucked against their will!" Lou gritted his teeth as he found a straightaway and punched it.

"*What?*" Jessie and Geoff screamed simultaneously as the truck slammed on its brakes and skidded to a stop, growing rapidly smaller in their rear-view mirror.

"The fuck? They're—" Lou began, then Geoff screamed, a finger with weed residue clinging to it jabbing forward.

"LOU!"

Lou peeled his eyes from the side mirror and saw the black strip in the road right before it disappeared under them. The van bucked and shuddered like a wounded animal, and Lou heard muffled explosions of tires coming apart. The steering wheel suddenly became possessed in his hands. Everything took a hard leaning turn to the right, and then Lou's screaming throat was on fire as he felt the van begin to roll.

When Lou came to, he was vaguely aware of his body being pulled, of limbs being tugged free. He was also aware of his throbbing head, which felt like he'd let Jessie use it as a practice pad for her double bass pedal. He smelled piss, the sharp tang of gasoline, the sickly-sweet odor of transmission fluid, and another smell. An odor he'd only ever associated with his dad's shed in the backyard, where bucks were strung up, exsanguinated and processed for the family freezer: exposed innards, the old penny smell of fresh blood.

"The fuck..." he groaned as he managed to peel open one eye. The van sat on its right side, resembling a great metal whale, beached indignantly on the side of the road. Broken glass and dark stains covered the county highway. The trailer was an unrecognizable mess of metal and fiberglass in a blast of the remains of various instruments, from Jessie's drums to his bass cabs, strewn about the surrounding woods and road.

Someone moaned. Lou thought it might've been Geoff, off somewhere coming out of his own daze. Lou groaned and pulled at whoever was dragging him across the road. He tried to move his legs but found he couldn't, the lower half of his body hung like so much dead meat from his waist.

"He's wigglin' like a worm, Roy." An unfamiliar voice thick with hick-speak sounded over Lou's head. He felt a boot nail him in the ribs and the whole right side of his body exploded with pain.

"There, that oughta still 'im."

"What about the others? I think I seen a girl in there. Must've been hurled out somewhere."

"Sheeeit, git your pecker outta your ass, boy. Could be the governor's daughter or something for all we know. Ain't no one gonna miss *this* greasy turd."

Someone laughed as Lou was tossed into the hard metal bed of a pickup truck. He tried to yell, but the pain had a vise on his lungs. Each breath he took he had to fight for. Lou thought that adrenaline was supposed to numb this shit, like in the movies. But besides his legs, he felt *everything*. He had no idea the human body could endure this much pain. The night sky filled his eyes, a solid puffy wall of slate gray clouds.

"You sure we can't take just one more of 'em? He might need them."

"Nope, we been here too long as it is. Besides, look at that one, smeared all over the road. One of 'em will be along soon enough to clean house. I think I hear someone comin'. Let's get on. He'll be plenty happy with this."

*Motherfucking Ku-Klux-Klan, man... fuck,* were Lou's last thoughts before he lost the battle with his consciousness, only faintly feeling the truck engine rumble under his body.

# Chapter 2

E VER SINCE SHE WAS little, Jessie Lamont wished she could fly. She'd once broken her ankle jumping off her foster parents' (thankfully) one story ranch house, flapping handmade papier-mâché wings as fast as her little arms would allow. Despite the trauma that ensued—her overprotective suburban-neurotic foster parents screaming their lungs off at her on the way to the ER, her ankle becoming a bright hot flare of pain—the thing that stuck most vivid to her was that brief moment where she floated, yes, *floated,* in the air. Her body seemed frozen in the air. Her childlike sense of wonder stretched out that instant into a delicious dilation and let her languish in the weightlessness.

The only thing to ever come close to that experience was her first time trying DMT, that rocketing-through-the-void feeling when you finally breakthrough into the fifth dimension. But now, she *was* flying, literally. One minute she was half-floating on the bench seat that had permanently accumulated the musky aroma of ball sweat since the 'Devastation Across the Nation" tour started, letting the potent sour diesel ease her aching arms and legs, the next, some asshole came in from out of the ether and was ruining the vibe. Lou was yelling something about ass-fucking, and then they were rolling. Jessie had time to imagine this is what Geoff's guitar picks felt like when they took a ride in the washing machine. And then she was being flung out the square portal of the van's busted side window, her body seeming to fit perfectly through the jagged void, *nothing but net, baby.*

Jessie had just enough mental wherewithal to try and grab onto the window's edge as her body shot through it and out into the world. But this only resulted in her being slingshotted from the van as it rolled, and then time was slowing down again, just like that time on the roof. Mild déjà vu came over her as she was once again weightless, once more flying, but instead of manicured green lawn and the blue plastic swimming pool she was aiming for, it was country blacktop, which then became dark forest.

She was aware of being thrown into the trees. Stiff limbs jabbed into her body, as if she was hitting every tree branch that ever existed while she plummeted back to earth.

Then the earth slammed up to meet her, and she smacked into the ground hard, face and chest taking most of the impact. As she hit the ground, Jessie felt it happen between heartbeats, the impact just right. She ripped in a great gust of air, inhaling wet leaves and bits of dirt, before her lungs seized up with her heart. Her whole body went numb, her heartbeat shocked into a stuttering, polyrhythmic cadence that made bright white stars explode across her vision.

Jessie tried to breathe and found she couldn't. It was like her brain had disconnected from her body. She was vaguely aware of her fingers spasming and clutching forest detritus, but she hadn't the faintest control over it. Her heart continued to beat in that erratic stop-start rhythm, the seconds between beats becoming longer, the beats themselves more erratic. Darkness began to seep in around her eyes. A million miles away, a motor slowly idled past, a loud snarling beast that coughed to a stop just behind her. Car doors slammed shut. Men whose voices were thick with backwoods drawl. The agonized squeal of a bent car door being pried open. The dragging of cloth and shoes against asphalt. Lou somewhere up there, groaning, his deep baritone unmistakable. Terror cut through her brain fog as she realized it had to be the people from the truck. The ones who made them crash.

Car doors slammed shut again. The vehicle snarled to life once more before slowly fading away. Then it was only the forest sounds. The scream of cicadas and crickets, sounding almost like the feedback from Allen's amp through her ringing ears, before that faded too. She understood in some abstract way they had taken Lou, these interlopers from the dark. She needed to understand how and why this was happening, but her mind was too focused on the immediacy of survival.

She was aware of a darkness enveloping her, but through the vanta-black veil she detected a red, pulsing aura, like a torch sputtering in the distance of a deepest night. The ruby glow drew closer, bringing with it a tidal pull towards something terrible, something awful.

Though Jessie wasn't entirely sure if she was alive or dead, she fought to get away from this encroaching red orb. She felt her soul being pulled away to erode in its aura, like some colossal black hole slowly sucking away at a nearby star.

Just when she couldn't resist it anymore, just when she was sure she would be consumed by this scarlet cloud, lightning struck. Thunder cracked. Jessie's world exploded with a most intense light, one that shone with the brilliance of a thousand suns. The orb evaporated instantly, all was nothing but white, until slowly, darkness faded in again, but this time it was the earthly darkness of night.

Jessie's whole body tingled as if every inch of her flesh had been numbed with circulation loss. Pins and needles flooded in everywhere. She heard a great, wet ripping noise and realized it was herself, gasping, gulping air. Her heart beat slow but hard in her chest, each pulsation a mule kick against her ribs.

Slowly, the contours of a face came to her. Bright artificial light stabbed at her eyes, and as they adjusted, she saw a golden corona of hair enveloping the figure.

Jessie was not religious, in fact probably the most militantly atheist of everyone in Blasphemer. But for a moment, she had to wonder if it was an angel staring down at her.

"Oh, my sweet Jesus, yes. Come back to me, girl, come back, honey," the voice said, tremulous. A soft hand cradled Jessie's head, and she saw she was at the border of the forest, the shoulder of highway a steep grade to her left.

"What..." Jessie breathed, blinking, tasting bitter earthy grit in her mouth. She spat, then coughed, and with that cough, her vision flashed with stars again and she put a hand to her aching chest. "Ow..." she groaned.

"Easy, honey. You were... you were going into cardiac arrest, I think. Had to do some serious CPR on you. You got some sprained ribs. But Christ, I think you'll live," said the woman with a shaky laugh.

For a long moment Jessie just lay there, coming back to her body by degrees. Her whole chest and abdominal area were one big bruise, and she had to force herself to take quick, shallow breaths. Anything deep and it felt like someone was sticking her with a million prison shivs.

"Can you sit up for me, honey?" the woman asked, then with the greatest of care, raised Jessie to a sitting position. "Okay?"

"Yeah..." Jessie said, looking at her full-on now. Her heart gave a quick stutter with the movement before returning to its normal pace. The woman was in her forties or fifties, middle-aged, but still strikingly beautiful. Piercing blue eyes set into a symmetrical face that was equal parts rugged and sensual.

"Alright, let's see if we can get you to your feet." The woman slowly helped Jessie stand up. The world tilted off its axis for a second, her legs trembling, but the woman's strong arms held her in place until she gained control.

"I'm... I'm good," Jessie said, not wanting the woman to let go. She found strength and comfort in that embrace. Whoever this woman was,

Jessie felt a surge of conflicting feelings towards her. First there was this unexplainable feeling that this woman was a pure, good human being. She radiated warmth and protection, and Jessie's frazzled mind needed both in that instant. On the heels of that, however, was the kneejerk reflex of marrow deep distrust garnered by years of parental abandonment and unstable childhood environments. Jessie didn't know which one to trust.

Together, they climbed their way up to the road. Jessie thought she was going to pass out from the effort. Her heart gave a quick shudder-beat before resuming its normal rhythm when she saw the wreckage before her. The van lay on its side, the trailer an amalgam of shredded metal, and its contents, their livelihood, strewn about the road in splinters and shards like the eviscerated innards of some great beast.

Then her attention fell on a pair of legs sticking out from under the van, ending in the ratty checkered slip-ons that Allen always wore.

"Allen," Jessie gasped, and staggered towards the van, her own bodily trauma forgotten. She saw that the rest of Allen's body was not attached, there was simply a ragged red stump of torso a few inches above his jeans. The gleam of white spinal column jutted up among the gray and red ropes of his inner plumbing where the van had ripped him in half. Jessie felt the world begin to spin and backed up a few feet, falling to her knees. Her stomach roiled like she was on the ass end of a three-day booze bender, and she vomited, sobbing at the same time. Each abdominal contraction hurt like hell. Each heave of her gut brought with it those million stabbing blades of pain in her ribs, but she couldn't stop herself. For at least five minutes, she lost control of her body again, until she felt that soft hand on her back, and it was like a switch flipped.

Jessie choked off the last of her bile-tinged dry heaving, wiped her mouth, and forced herself to look away from the remains of her vocalist.

She became vaguely aware of someone screaming, the sound muffled but nearby.

"HELP ME! JESUS FUCKING CHRIST PLEASEEEE!"

It was a high-pitched, hysterical voice, so raw with fear and agony that Jessie wasn't sure who was yelling. Then she remembered Lou, the drivers who came before, the memories coming to her in blurred snapshots. There was just so much to take in, her mind reeled.

Jessie could see the woman clearer now, the headlights of her vehicle hardening the details. She watched her climb awkwardly up the side of the van, using its undercarriage as a makeshift ladder. Though the woman was middle-aged, lean muscle pulled taught against the shoulders of her flannel, her exposed forearms corded with sinew.

"He's trapped. I'm gonna need your help, darlin'," she said, taking out a folding pocketknife as she wrenched open the driver's door and lowered herself inside. Dazedly, Jessie climbed the side of the van, ignoring the scraping ache in her mid-section, smelling the various mechanical fluids that bled from the van the same way Allen's insides leaked from his sundered half. She thought she was going to vomit again but bit it back. A life was depending on her. Jessie looked down into the twisted portal of the driver-side door. The woman stood over Geoff, cutting away his seat belt, his right arm held out at an impossible angle.

"Oh fuck," Jessie muttered under her breath as she saw his once-straight forearm, always vascular from his years of shredding arpeggios and jerking himself off with guitar solos. It was now L-shaped. A white nub of bone poked out a few inches above his wrist. Geoff screamed again as he fell from the passenger seat, freed from his seat belt.

"Alright, honey, listen to me. I gotta get you out of here, and it's gonna hurt something fierce pulling you up, but you just gotta bear with us, okay?" The woman tried to reorient Geoff's body to a sitting position. He was sobbing and rambling about his arm, and the sight of him hysterical like that cut through Jessie's haze as she reached down.

"Alright, stick your good arm out for her to grab, and I'm going to hoist you up from the bottom," the woman said. She proceeded to get him awkwardly to his feet in the cramped space. Jessie saw that thankfully his legs weren't injured, weren't separated from his body like Allen's. As he reached out to grasp her hand, she made the mistake of looking into the back of the van, where the missing half of Allen's body was hanging half out the window, sprays of red and—

"Honey! Focus now, help me," the woman snapped. Jessie blinked, swallowing hard as she grabbed Geoff's good hand and pulled, while their benefactor helped push him up from underneath. He moaned as they slowly extricated him from the wreck, until finally he lay splayed out on the van's side, like a beach bum suntanning on a lounger. Geoff was gasping, his whole body soaked and reeking of sweat. A moment later, the woman was out of the wreck too, and together they helped Geoff down onto the ground, his right arm dangling like a rubber prosthetic.

"We need to call the police! This guy... He tried to run us off the road... They took Lou, they fucking took Lou!" Jessie began to shout, her mental haze finally lifting. The sheer horror of the situation began to wash over her, her heart once again palpitating. She clawed at her pants for her cellphone, but when she pulled it out the screen was shattered, a phantasmagorical display of pixels. The device was destroyed.

"I don't know how to tell you this, honey, but you all picked a real bad spot to wreck," the woman said. "You're straddling the county line between Dolvin and Carter. Ain't no signal out here till you get to Carter."

"Then take us to the fucking hospital! Or something, Jesus Christ, Jesus, I—" Jessie was beginning to hyper ventilate. "They took Lou, they—"

Strong, firm hands gripped her shoulders. The woman looked at her with intense cerulean eyes, her face shiny with sweat.

"Listen to me, honey, the nearest thing we got for a hospital is Saint Francis, and that's about an hour away. I got my med bag with me, let me do what I can and then we'll head into town to call the authorities.

He's losing blood and I'm pretty sure you're in v-fib." She disappeared into her car before returning with a big duffel bag.

"My fucking arm... I'll never play again. I'll never play again, man. Goddamnit, it fucking *hurts*..." Geoff moaned.

The woman motioned for the two to get off the side of the road. "Come on over here. People like to fly down this thing half drunk." She pulled out a high-end first aid kit from her bag, along with an assortment of other medical devices.

"Who... Who are you? You a doctor or something?" Jessie asked as the woman pulled out a roll of duct tape, a narrow plastic board and a small wooden dowel.

"Or something, you could say that. Veterinarian," she said with a thin smile as she approached Geoff, who leaned against her car, his face gone ashen with shock.

# Chapter 3

THE GOOD THING ABOUT being the only livestock-certified veterinarian in a county full of farmers and horse ranchers was that the business was steady and the pay was good. The kicker was that Susannah was pretty much on call 24-7. It would have to stay that way until she had her apprentice Elizabeth, a smart young girl from Mizzou's agricultural and livestock program, up to snuff and could trust her with some of the more difficult procedures. Until then, she had to contend with the urgent late-night calls from people like the Kurtzes, who bred Akhal-Tekes and Clydesdales to sell to rich doctors and lawyers.

"Miss Paige, you gotta come quick. Them goddamn coyotes came back tonight, got one of the foals again. Swear to Christ, I'm 'bout to go back into them woods and shoot every last one of them—"

"How bad is it, Billy?" Susannah had asked, biting back the irritation in her voice. She'd just gotten snug into bed, a paperback from Saint John's pharmacy bookmarked in her lap.

The Kurtz property was on the very southern end of Carter County, a thirty-minute drive at the least. Sighing as she got off the phone, she'd gotten dressed, told Buckie (who gave her the saddest case of puppy dog eyes she'd ever seen) that she'd be back soon, and prayed she had enough gas in the Explorer to make the drive.

It was bad alright. The pack of mongrels had somehow jumped the ten-foot fence surrounding the foal stable that kept the young horses separate from their mothers at night to avoid being trampled in the event something stirred them up into a panic. The coyotes cornered one of the Clydesdales and tore it up good, killing one and maiming another. The beasts had managed to take a few good bites out of the surviving foal before Billy heard the commotion and chased them off with his shotgun. He'd never actually seen the coyotes in person, they were always too damn quick to run off, but besides cougars, there was no other animal out there (that he knew of) that could perform such brutal hit and run attacks. Susannah had agreed with the boy.

After an hour of intense triage, it was obvious the surviving horse wasn't going to make it. Susannah told Billy his options after assuring him that trying to keep the horse alive would only prolong its suffering, and they decided on an overdose of tranquilizer to send the beautiful animal off peacefully. Afterward, it had taken ten minutes or more to rinse off the horse blood that covered her arms up to the elbows.

Susannah had driven back six hundred dollars richer, half tempted to take the interstate to shave off some time but hadn't wanted to risk getting pulled over, her exhaustion mistaken for inebriation. She was dog-tired. Having to put down such a large, graceful animal had drained her mentally as it always did, and she knew, with it being Memorial Day weekend, the highway patrol would be out thicker than flies on a cow patty. The nearby Arkansas border wouldn't help, either. She had decided to take the backroad way home, which in the daytime would greet Susannah with a picturesque view of the verdant low mountains she loved.

Now, she half wondered if it had been fate, or perhaps God's plan that had made her change her mind at the last minute and take the backroad way home. Susannah instructed the boy with the mangled arm to bite down on the wooden dowel. He was quickly going the color of catfish belly.

"I ain't gonna lie to you... Geoff, is it? This is gonna hurt bad, honey. But we need to get this arm set ASAP. The trauma surgeon can do the rest when we get there," she said, thankful it was a clean break. Even failed med students could set a transverse fracture. She tugged lightly at the spasming hand to stretch it out ever so slightly so she could get the two bones to connect once more. She worked as quickly and smoothly as possible, instructing the young woman to hold the man down as she did so. With a sharp but precise jerk, the bone slid back into the skin and the arm was straightened.

Susannah hoped the poor boy would just pass out from the pain, but he screamed like a bobcat in heat and bucked like a rabid mule, nearly reducing the dowel to splinters before finally losing consciousness. She taped his arm to the crude splint and applied the same antiseptic solution she'd used on the injured Clydesdale to the break site. The boy lay against her car while she tended to the young woman, cleaning all the wood splinters and dirt out of the shallow gashes along her flanks with a saline solution. Mostly superficial injuries. What worried her was the young lady's heartbeat, which, as she put two fingers to the girl's throat, felt like the uneven threadiness of a heart arrhythmia. Judging by the myriad tattoos and piercings adorning the red-haired girl's body, she didn't think the girl was religious at all. A shame, because she should be thanking God Susannah got to her when she did. She'd been going into cardiac arrest when she found her. Though she was stable now, Susannah could tell she was going into shock once she started ranting. Some insane story about someone running off with one of their friends.

Not only that, but Susannah had gotten a flash.

When she'd first touched the girl—flipped her over from her stomach to her back, pulling out the dirt and leaf litter clogging her mouth and throat—it came. A razorblade. A feeling of complete, eviscerating hopelessness. She could piece together from the crash site that this woman was a musician, probably lived a fast and loose bohemian lifestyle. But that flash let Susannah know there was something black and poisonous under that tough veneer.

*Flashes.* That's what her mother had called them. The Paige family had been touched with all form of second sight for generations. Her grandmother had premonitions, could see the day someone died. Her mother could sense illness within people. Nothing so eloquent as "Hey, you got cancer, honey," when shaking someone's hand, but an abstract feeling of rot, or entropy, from the person emitting the flash.

With Susannah, it wasn't anything so refined, or helpful. It came sporadically. Sometimes she wouldn't have a flash for years. Sometimes she'd have three in a week. Susannah didn't know what she saw with her flashes. It was always random, so out of context with the strangers she touched that she didn't know what to make of them. Shaking an insurance salesman's hands and seeing a stillborn infant clutched in his shaking arms as he sobbed. Hands brushing when exchanging cash with a client, and suddenly having a vivid flashbulb memory of that person being sexually assaulted as a teenager. It seemed Susannah only picked up on others' hellish misery. Whether it was one of God's many ways of testing her or not, she wished she could do without it.

It seemed to be happening more often lately, as it did when she was stressed. She tried not to think about the images she saw from the girl as she splinted the poor man's arm. The electric current that seemed to rip through her and into the girl as she performed desperate CPR. It had been one of the most intense flashes of her life. Not just flashbulb memories seared into her brain, it was if Susannah absorbed something from this young lady, and in turn, Jessie had taken something from Susannah. Some sort of esoteric exchange that left her feeling lightheaded and woozy for the briefest of moments before adrenaline took over as the girl began to breathe on her own. And just as suddenly, she had known the girl's name was Jessie Lamont.

Basic field triage done, they loaded the unconscious man into the backseat of her Explorer, and the young lady flopped into the shotgun seat. Susannah headed back towards Carter. She was dog-tired as the adrenaline from coming upon the crash site wore off, but she was determined to see this through, to help these poor kids.

"Now... you said you heard someone pull up before?" she asked cautiously of Jessie, who stared out into the unending scenery of forest and blacktop. The girl seemed a bit calmer now, perhaps more of her wits about her. However, Susannah was unnerved when Jessie faced her, her words clear, her conviction unwavering.

"Lady... I'm telling you, someone tried to run us off the fucking road. Rammed us from behind... then there was something in the road, a spike strip or something. When I was laying in the woods, I heard those same guys pull up. I heard them take Lou. One of them... I heard one of them say the name Roy."

Susannah's gut tightened and a shiver tried to work its way up her spine.

"Wait... you said Roy? You *sure* one of them used that name?"

"Yes, absolutely." Jessie met her gaze. "Why?"

"I just... it's important you remember. For the police. They'll need all the information they can get," she said, her mouth going dry.

They passed through Carter, which had exactly three stoplights, two gas stations, a smattering of fast-food joints and the usual inventory of locally owned stores that provided the basic needs of its populace. Susannah gripped the steering wheel tighter, telling herself this little girl must've had her brain scrambled from the wreck. But then again, she saw the tires on that van. All four of them plus the trailer tires were blown out, and there was nothing in the road to show what'd caused such destruction.

*Roy... No way... There's just no way...* she thought, passing through Carter as quickly as they had entered it. Saint Francis was in Dolvin, which was another thirty minutes down Route Y, the one state highway that connected all of these little burgs to the interstate. She thought of Daniel, who was always within arm's reach of her thoughts, no matter how unrelated the subject matter.

Daniel, who loved fishing and cars and working on engines. Daniel, who'd gladly taken the job at Roy Langan's auto body shop so he could get some hands-on experience with cars. Daniel, who'd worked at Roy's garage for a year, it being the last place he'd been seen leaving before going missing. Daniel, the reason she'd taken to inconspicuously touching as many people in town as she could. Just to find anything, perhaps a small glimpse of what had happened to him, but instead was only cursed with random images of trauma and suffering.

Daniel, her son.

# Chapter 4

IT WAS ALMOST THREE in the morning when they pulled into the parking lot of Saint Francis Emergency. Not quite a full-sized hospital, more of an upgraded 24-hour walk-in clinic with a direct line to air-vac if needed. After getting a tired-looking nurse to help them get the unconscious Geoff into a wheelchair, they checked both him and Jessie in.

Susannah sat in the waiting room and mentally processed everything that had happened in the last three hours. She felt synapses misfiring and her eyes were gritty with lack of sleep.

After an hour, a doctor came back with Jessie, a pill bottle in her hands.

"Excuse me miss, are you... uh... her mother?" the doctor asked.

Susannah shook her head.

"No, it's um... a long story," Susannah said, too exhausted to explain how the girl came into her life.

"Oh, well, okay. Just thought you should know you saved her life with that CPR. We had to perform an ablation to get her heart back to normal rhythm. Miss Lamont here suffered something called R-on-T phenomenon. Basically, blunt force trauma can temporarily stop the heart. She'll be okay, but I strongly advise against any strenuous activity for the next two weeks. We're sending her home with some beta-blockers to help keep her heart rhythm in check. Mr. Richards will need to stay overnight, however. There are signs of infection in his break site, so we're going to keep him and make sure the antibiotics take." He nodded curtly to both of them and left.

Jessie turned to Susannah. "I need to use your phone. Please..."

She nodded and put her phone in the girl's quivering hands. After repeating her story to the dispatcher on the other end of the line, Jessie told them about Allen being dead, then gave a thorough description of the missing man, Louis Springer.

"Tall, African American, dreadlocks down to his butt, and a face full of metal," Jessie shouted at the receiver. She huffed and yelled, "*Fuck you!*" into the phone before shoving it back into Susannah's hands. The girl collapsed into one of the waiting room chairs and began to sob.

"We should've just taken the goddamned interstate... What the fuck is even happening?" she said. Susannah risked breaching boundaries and put a soothing hand on her heaving shoulder. Jessie flinched, then yielded to the touch. Susannah braced for another flash, but mercifully, it didn't come.

"What'd they say?" she asked softly.

"They can't do anything about it until tomorrow. Doing their stupid fucking sobriety campaign on the interstate, said all the sheriffs were tied up at the moment. Said they're going to check out the crash site, send a coroner out there tonight, but that was it. Don't you guys have local police?" The girl looked up at Susannah with a desperation that made her soul ache. Susannah saw herself in those eyes, knew exactly the despair this young lady felt. She was in this exact tumultuous state a year ago, when her boy inexplicably went missing, and it seemed everyone who was at liberty to help her was busy doing other, more important things.

"I'm afraid we don't. These unincorporated townships don't have enough funding for their own police force. Best we got is county sheriffs.

Two to be exact," she said. *And neither one of them are worth a squirt of hot piss*, she thought.

"Jesus... I don't even know what I'm supposed to do. I barely have any money. I can't afford a motel. I need to call our tour manager. I need to call Lou's wife... and Allen's parents... God, this is so fucked," Jessie said, her voice trembling and on the verge of becoming a sob. The young woman's face disappeared into her hands as a heavy sigh escaped her. Susannah tried not to let the string of profanities get to her, understanding this woman's hysterical shock.

"Listen, honey, you can stay with me. First thing tomorrow morning I'll get the sheriff out to my house to take your statement. I'll make sure they send the coroner out for your... friend. You can use my phone to call whoever, but I think you need to get some sleep, Jessie. You've been through a lot. Come on. I gave the nurse my number for this Geoff fella. They'll call with updates," she said. Jessie looked up at her, confused.

"Why are you helping me? I'm no one to you. I appreciate your offer, but you've done enough already. You saved my fucking life. Thanks for that, thanks for everything, really, but I need to just—"

"Honey, what you need is sleep, and a shower if I'm to speak frankly. You've just endured an extremely traumatic experience. You need rest. Please, come home with me. I couldn't call myself a true Catholic if I turned away someone in need."

Susannah drove the thirty minutes back to her little ranch house off Possum Holler Lane, where she led Jessie, almost catatonic now, into the quiet, dark house. Without resistance, the girl let Susannah guide her to the soft, oversized sectional that Harold insisted they buy even though they never had enough guests over to properly use the darn thing.

Jessie was asleep by the time Susannah returned with a pillow and blanket. She knew that deep, dreamless sleep the poor girl was experiencing. More a period of her overtaxed mind shutting down than actual rest. A state closer to a coma than sleep. The brain's most basic coping mechanism. Susannah had had many such nights like that. Where she just shut down. Beyond sleep, but not quite death.

She put the blanket over the dirt and blood-smeared girl, seeing those many long, straight scars blending in with the new wounds, gently propping her head up and moving sweaty auburn hair out of the way for the pillow.

*Dear God, what have you gotten me into? Is this a sign?* she thought, looking across the living room to one of the many framed photos of her family. Harold (who was currently on the river for a two-week stretch) slung a burly arm around Daniel, his smile radiant, the only kind he had. The two of them held up a whopper of a blue cat they'd pulled out of Table Rock Lake.

Daniel was one of many who'd gone missing over the past few years, and for a town the size of Carter, that was an anomaly.

And now there was *this*.

# CHAPTER 5

TWICE LOU TRIED TO raise himself up to a sitting position, hoping to flag down a passing car from the back of the truck. But his arms felt like fragile toothpicks, his back screamed in agony with every pothole or rut the truck's shitty suspension jolted over. Instead, he lay there, going in and out of consciousness. When he saw headlights coming from the opposite lane, Lou screamed as loud as he could, putting Allen and his infamous guttural vocals to shame. But then the center panel of the truck's rear window slid open, and a revolver held by a greasy hand snaked its way out, the black eye of the barrel staring in his general direction.

"Best keep ya mouth shut, *boy*," said a voice from the truck's interior.

Lou kept his mouth shut.

It wasn't until they'd veered off onto a rough gravel road that he came fully awake. His agonized body shoved around that rusted metal prison, twice landing on the spike strip mat they'd thrown in the back with him. He couldn't help but scream as the pointed jacks dug into his hip and side as the truck shuddered and jolted up the rough mountain tract.

"What the fuck!" he yelled. By the time the truck jerked to a stop, Lou's arms and legs were twitching, uncontrollable spasms of pain shooting through him. He knew his back was broken; knew he was probably paralyzed. He accepted this fact with numb resignation as truck doors slammed shut, then the tailgate squealed as it was lowered. "Please…" he begged the two men towering over him. He smelled failing deodorant and engine grease coming off them. "You Klan assholes don't understand. I'm only half black, okay? I was just passing through, I—"

The men began to guffaw like donkeys with loud, stupid laughter.

"You hear that, Tate? This boy thinks we're the KKK," the man on the right said. He knelt next to Lou, a sweaty, gaunt face with patchy stubble, greasy brown hair pulled back in a messy ponytail. "We may be hillbillies, but give us some credit, son. We picked you because the cops… now *they's* racist. They hear of a black fella, excuse me, *half black* fella gone missing up in these hills, they ain't gonna give a hot greasy shit about that. We ain't Klansmen son, but by the end of the night you gonna wish we was," he said with a grin. "Get him by his ankles, Tate, I'll get his pits."

Lou's mind floundered for context, for an explanation. If these two inbred neanderthals weren't Klan, then what the hell were they doing kidnapping him?

Lou screamed in pain as the two men hoisted him up and out of the truck bed. His head lolled around. He was in some shitty driveway, a corrugated metal shack off to the left, a row of derelict cars surrounded by tall grass. To Lou's right was a house that looked like it'd been built during the Dust Bowl, mismatched wood paneling and windows gone filmy to the point of being opaque, etched by time. It looked like a strong breeze might flatten it.

A single overhead floodlight lit their surroundings, and he heard the whisper of moth wings and the light *bonk* of cicadas bashing their heads against the bulb. It was the only sound besides the men's strained breathing.

"Hold on a second, Roy." Tate huffed. He was heavy-set compared to his partner, bald scalp glistening with the floodlight. His face scrunched up as he shoved his hands into the small of his back. When he leaned back, his spine crackled, producing a groan from his slack, wet mouth. "Sumbitch is heavy, we oughta stick him in the 'barrow."

"Oh, you lazy piece of shit. It ain't that far," Roy said, but disappeared all the same, walking off to the right. Lou turned and saw him pushing an old wheelbarrow, the rusty axle making a metallic keening sound.

"Please, whoever you are, you don't gotta do this. I got a baby girl at home, man. People are gonna ask questions. My bandmates, they'll have seen you drive off with me. Please..." Lou hated that he was begging. He was raised in rough country, his daddy taught him how to fight, taught him to kick the shit out of the billy-bob rednecks at school who called him a porch monkey behind his back. The ones that slipped folded up pieces of paper in his locker showing a shittily-drawn cartoon of him in a hangman's noose. Daddy raised him to never take shit from anyone. But he was taking the shit now, and there wasn't a goddamned thing he could do about it, except try to reason with these fucking weirdos.

He almost passed out as they dropped him into the giant metal bowl of the wheelbarrow, a thousand red hot daggers shooting from the small of his back up to his neck. They turned him around and began to head towards the thicket of dogwood and poplar trees that lined the property. One of the men produced a flashlight and pointed it towards a narrow trail that cut through the woods. Lou watched helplessly as they pushed him through thick spiderwebs and thicker spiders that had made the trail their home.

"You think Daddy will take him? He's got a point, Roy. You know daddy ain't never took to the colored folks," Tate said as they went deeper into the woods.

"Sheeeit, you think he's gonna care about that, being the... you know, the way he is now? He's *gotta* take the sumbitch. Or he can starve. He ain't in a position to be picky," Roy said.

"You heard him though, last time. When it took us awhile to get the last one, he said one of these days he'd just *get* one of us. Said he got tired of waitin' sometimes." Lou detected fear in the man's voice.

"He bluffin', baby brother. He'd never do that to his own sons. 'Sides, he can't leave the property. He needs us." Roy tried to feign indifference, but Lou could detect the tremor in his voice too. He sensed a palpable tension between these two, even through his haze of pain. A great anticipation, a giddy fear that spread to him like contagion.

Janel, his wife, always said he was an empath. He acted like a tough, stoic bastard on the outside, the metalhead rockabilly getup only accentuating this, but underneath that veneer of badassery was a sensitive, insightful man. He cued in on people's emotions, sometimes without wanting to. Lou had felt the ubiquitous anguish of the grieving parents whenever he saw mass shootings on the TV. Felt the rage from the chanting crowd of protesters outside a police station when yet another person of color was gunned down under suspicious circumstances.

It was a blessing and a curse. Some days he woke up feeling anguish or anxiety and had no rhyme or reason to feel so, wondering if he was picking up on someone's nearby emotions or if this was his own. Lou was tuned into emotion the way a bloodhound tuned into a scent trail. It helped with the ladies at least. He was insightful and this augmenting his flirting skills, he knew when he was wanted and when he wasn't, knew how to back off just enough to not appear thirsty. It was how he got Janel, after all.

Asshole-puckering fear is what he felt now. Sensed it from both men as they went deeper into the woods, the flashlight revealing dense viridian walls of leaves and bushes encroaching from either side of the trail. He smelled a variety of lush forest scents—wild lavender and juniper. But these sweet scents were undercut with something sharp and pungent. It made Lou's eyes water and tickled his brain with its familiarity.

Soon the terrain sloped upward, and the men had to abandon the wheelbarrow as it became near impossible to push it up the ridge.

*Where the fuck are we going?* Lou thought as they proceeded to carry him, his mind too bogged down with pain to think. All he knew was they spoke of their daddy like he was some kind of cannibal. *Just fucking great.* He didn't know which fate was worse: Being burned alive on a cross surrounded by a bunch of racist assholes or being eaten alive by a crazy one. He almost wanted to laugh with hopelessness.

All because he didn't want to go through a sobriety check point.

Eventually they came to a plateau, the ridge evening out to a flat meadow. Lou caught glimpses of his surroundings as the flashlight erratically cut through the woods, the one named Roy clamping it between his teeth as they crab-walked with him between them. The pain must've been making Lou hallucinate, or maybe breaking his back had released all the built-up psychedelics in his body from his early days being a gun for hire bassist and being in a constant haze of acid and shrooms. Lou had heard from some of the oldheads he bought his acid from how they got flashbacks sometimes if they popped their back too hard. Swore all them feel-good chemicals got stored up in your spinal fluid or something.

In the snatches of the flashlight beam he saw dozens of small, crooked crosses lining the wall of trees bordering the meadow. All painted eggshell white. Everywhere the flashlight's beam played across, he saw them. Mostly uniform in size with slight variations that let you know they were painstakingly handmade.

"Okay, okay, gotta stop," Tate panted and dropped Lou's ankles.

Black speckles washed across Lou's vision, agony erupting all over his body. Roy continued to hold him by the armpits. "Come on, you fat sack of shit. We're so close," he huffed. Lou half considered elbowing this skinny dickhead right in the ribs, or maybe go for a ball shot, but it wouldn't do any good. His legs hung uselessly from his body, all he could manage was a feeble twitch of his toes, but even that took monumental effort. Instead, he just let himself be held, trying to think of what was missing from this bizarre scene. As Lou got his wind back, he realized what was surrounding them: total silence. A pregnant, heavy quiet wholly at odds with the dense woodland that surrounded the men.

It was almost June, and they were in the middle of a dense forest. The Ozarks should be roaring with life. Crickets, coyotes, cicadas, the normal chorus of animal sounds were completely absent in these woods, just the strained breathing from these two men. Lou knew from his daddy that the only time the forest went quiet like that was when something big and mean was making its way through. Only apex predators commanded the silence of the forest on their approach.

Tate took up his end of Lou's dead weight and they began again, proceeding towards a sheer cliff wall, at the base of which was a gaping cave entrance. The sight of that black maw in the limestone made him sick to his stomach. The fear he felt was all his own now. Absolutely nothing good came out of places like that. He struggled and squirmed in Roy's arms, not caring if it was futile. His lizard brain was screaming for him to fight, now that flight wasn't an option.

The two men dumped him just outside the cave entrance. Roy shone the flashlight into the cave, a tunneling entrance that went deep, far beyond the shine of the light. Roy stuck two fingers in his mouth and let out a high, shrill whistle. They waited, in a heavy silence anticipating what was to come out of the cave. Nothing happened for three or four minutes, long enough for whole epochs to pass as Lou's terror drug out the interminable moment. The skinny man whistled again. The tension must've gotten to Tate as well. The big man made a small, almost imperceptible sound of terror in the back of his throat, something like a puppy whine. Lou wondered if the guy was touched or something.

"Hey, Daddy! We got one for ya!" Roy bellowed. Then, a shuffling scuttle sounded from deep within the cave, the pat of bare feet on stone, the reverberating aural quality lessening as it grew closer.

"He's comin', he's comin'!" Tate whispered, swallowing thickly before shutting off the flashlight. They sat in near-perfect dark. Lou blinked several times to let his eyes adjust to the blackness. Suffocating anxiety flooded him, being both blind and paralyzed, as he heard something approach from the cave. With glacial slowness, the world around him dissolved from pure black to dark, monochromatic gray as he got his night eyes. The faint glow from the moon in the overcast sky, the border of trees, the vast slate face of the cliff wall—one by one his surroundings came back to him.

The faintest trace of movement flitted in the mouth of the cave, a barely discernable silhouette inching closer. A smell wafted up to meet Lou's nose. Unwashed man flesh, a primal stink so bad it rivaled the monkey exhibits at the zoo. Then, a deep, phlegmy inhalation, like a snuffling pig.

"D-Daddy..." Tate breathed, his voice high-pitched and squeaky. He almost sounded like a child now, his voice keening into a soprano register. Roy remained dead silent.

The snuffling grew louder. Great, raw inhalations of wind through a corrupted sinus tract.

"Wass' wrong with 'im?" The voice was deep and ragged. "Smells... wrong..."

Lou almost yelped as the figure scuttled forward, reminding him of the wolf spiders that used to dart for cover like lightning when he turned on the lights in his dad's barn. Except this was no wolf spider. The man, if that's what he was, was standing only three or four feet away from Lou now, a pale silhouette against the night. The men behind him took a step back.

Lou squinted and saw finer details. The man was naked, hunched over, the smell emanating off him in waves so strong it nearly made Lou retch. His ghostly silhouette resembled an imp more than a man, the way he crouched, the way his bulbous head twitched from side to side.

"Smells wrong," the man-thing snarled. "Brought me a got damn… *negro*?" It spat this last word out. "Hell, even normal negroes don't smell like this one," it hissed, that awful snuffling sound very close to Lou's face now, like a pig scenting the air.

"Goddamnit, we risked our *necks* for this one," Roy began, and time skipped forward. One moment the imp-thing was crouching before Lou, the next it was out of sight, rushing past him. He heard Roy cry out, a croaking gurgle. "You… sumbitch, we—"

"Now you listen to me, boy. Listen *good,*" the imp said, his voice going even lower in register. Lou tried to crane his neck, but doing so caused another bolt of pain to shoot through him. He heard the creak of muscles flexing. Roy choked, and Tate began to whine again. "I may be starving, but I ain't gonna eat me no goddamned negro. Not one that smells like that anyway. He nothin' but gristle and shit. Smells like he's been eatin' grass his whole life, smells like a goddamn cow," It, or… he, spoke slowly, each pause in his word punctuated by a gurgling groan from Roy. "You got six days before the eclipse. I can feel it, the planets lining up. If y'all ain't got a proper supper for me by then, well… ain't no tellin' what I'm… no, *we*… are apt to do."

With that, a body thudded back to earth. Roy started coughing and wheezing. Lou thought it sounded like their father had lifted the man by the throat, but that was impossible. The man—that imp-shaped man with the weird voice—was tiny, diminutive. *Meth, it's gotta be meth. They say Missouri is the meth capital of the world. This dude has done iced himself to the point of insanity, thinks he's a fucking caveman.*

"Daddy, please, we worked hard to get this one, we—"

Lou heard a gasp, and watched from the corner of his eye as the thing was right on Tate, hands bunched into those overalls.

"Excuses. I kept you alive this long 'cause I thought you'd take care of me. Six days, boys. You have no idea what's at stake. You just gotta keep us… me, fed a little longer. But *this?* Goddamn…" Their patriarch hissed and disappeared back into the cave with that same viper quickness, that same skipping-forward of time. One second, he's here, the next he's over there, some kind of terrible magic trick.

"What we gonna do, Roy? I don't wanna keep doing this. He's getting' worse..." Tate began to sob. It was an ugly, despicable sound. Though he loathed these men something fierce, Lou couldn't help but pity them—or at least Tate—just a bit. Lou began to understand this situation was not what it seemed. He may not be the only hostage here.

Roy walked over, wheezing. The authoritative pistol shot of hand meeting cheek cut off Tate's cries.

"Get your—get your... fuckin' shit together, Tate," Roy panted, in between grunts of pain. "Quit crying like a goddamned baby. Not like you got nothing to worry about. It's *me* he takes it out on. We just gotta... fatten him up is all. We know what daddy likes. If not we'll just... Hell, I don't know." Roy's grimy fingers rasped against the stubble on his face. "We'll... We'll figure it out, okay? We always do, don't we, baby brother. I said *don't we, baby brother?*" Roy shook Tate by the shoulders. "Now come on, help me carry this sack of shit to the shed. Gots me a plan."

# CHAPTER 6

E VEN THOUGH THEY WERE here to help, Jessie's chest tightened and her pulse quickened at the sight of the patrol car pulling up the driveway. Spending most of her life being a drifter-punk and going through foster homes the way her biological dad went through Coors Light, she'd had her share of run-ins with the police. Most of them were never good. The instinctual fight-or-flight response tickled her lizard brain when she saw the words COUNTY SHERIFF.

"They're here," Jessie called. Her eyes flashed from the window to the large brass cross above the old TV, Jesus hanging forlornly upon it. One of many choices of décor that allowed Jessie to paint the mental picture of a homespun Christian woman who may have been just a smidge obsessed. Christian imagery festooned much of the house. Susannah appeared a moment later from the kitchen, holding a cup of steaming coffee, dressed in jeans and a Bass Pro tank top, her golden hair hung loosely in a ponytail.

"How're you feeling, honey?" Susannah gave her an appraising look, as if making sure she was all there.

"Still sore, but I'm good I think." Sore was an understatement, but Jessie knew what she had to do.

"Alright, then. Let's *do* this. I'll warn you... Charles Baumgartner can be a mite unpleasant to deal with sometimes." Susannah took a deep breath and opened the front door, a solemn look on her face, as if preparing herself. As if it were *her* having to give a statement. As if it were *her* who was going to try and enlist these cops to look for her best friends in a strange land.

Jessie followed her out the door in an oversized shirt, SAINT BETH'S FIRST EPISCOPAL CHURCH printed on it, along with flannel pajama pants whose cloth drawstrings she had to draw all the way tight for them to stay around her waist. Just like a kid. Susannah had cobbled together the ridiculous outfit after insisting on Jessie showering and getting out of her torn and dirty clothes. The woman herself oozed an aura of warm matriarchy, the way she gently commanded Jessie. Not only that, but she felt a profound but distant connection to this woman. As she showered, Jessie thought of that darkness, the pulsing red, and what she realized now must've been a near-death experience. The shock when Susannah touched her. Like she had inherited something from her with that simple touch.

The events of last night felt more like some fucked up distant dream, and Jessie, ever grounded in pragmatism and rationale, applied a psychological approach to the whole situation. She told herself since she'd never known her own mother, she had tuned into Susannah's motherly air the way she tuned into the pocket of a beat. Imprinting, or whatever the psychologists called it. Whatever the reason, she found herself instantly liking the woman, even if she exuded fundamentalist Christian out the wazoo. She hadn't tried to preach to Jessie yet, at least, and she had the gut feeling the woman never would.

They stepped out onto the porch just as two men got out of the white and gold sheriff's Charger. Jessie was viscerally aware of her battered appearance. She'd finally gotten a chance to look at herself in the mirror this morning. Even though she'd swallowed two of Susanna's aspirin, she looked just like she felt—like a banana in the bottom of a shopping cart, bruised and vulnerable. Her right eye was nearly swollen shut, her lips puffy from being split open. Somehow, she'd managed to not knock out any teeth during her meteoric descent to earth, so there was that, at least.

"Miss Paige," the driver said. He was tall, thick in the shoulders and gut, like a high school lineman who was on the downward bell curve of his glory years. He tipped his Stetson as he approached, taking off the aviators to reveal emotionless hazel eyes. "Thanks for putting this meeting together."

His partner—a man whose physique and face were as unremarkable as the non-playable characters in Allen's stupid RPG games—sidled up beside him.

"Sure hope this gathering is under better circumstances than the last time we saw each other, Miss Paige." The sheriff glared at the woman, and Jessie sensed a lot of baggage between these two.

"Sheriff Baumgartner. Can't say it's necessarily good, but it's this young lady here who needs your help, not me." Susannah put a gentle hand on Jessie's shoulder.

"Ah yes... you're the one who called last night about the van that overturned off County Road 345?" Baumgartner consulted a notepad he had kept tucked in his shirt pocket. "'98 Ford Econoline with a trailer full of music equipment? You reported a supposed corpse on the scene?"

Jessie's throat grew thick. *Not a corpse, a human fucking being.* "Supposed?"

"We got the road crew out to clear the van, and we didn't find no body. Lot of blood. Some guts. No body though," the sheriff said flatly. Susannah and Jessie looked at each other.

"Sheriff, there was a man torn in half at that scene. I know, 'cause I helped rescue the other one," Susannah said.

"Well, we didn't see one. You know, we got coyotes thick out here, even the odd black bear. Maybe—"

"Oh, Jesus fuck—" Jessie's ribs constricted around her heart like a python. She clasped a hand to her mouth, not sure if she was going to throw up or sob. She struggled to do neither, determined to keep her composure in front of these two men.

"There was a dead body out there, Charles. A human being. You—"

"That's *Sheriff* to you, goddamnit. Now, we put that in the report, alright? Not much else we can do about that. As far as everything else, let's see here..." He looked over his pad. His partner only stood there, a vacuous gaze on his face. He seemed to be eyeing Jessie, though her baggy clothes obscured anything that might even be remotely seductive about her body. Still, she drew in on herself, feeling the coffee she drank earlier crawl up her throat.

"—Sorry to say, most of the equipment we found was trashed. Most of that mess was hauled off to the county dump."

At this, Jessie felt a pang of grief, not only for Allen and his horrible death, but for their instruments, their livelihood. It'd taken her four years working as a line cook at a shitty interstate Burger Zone to buy her DW kit. It was her pride and joy. She'd spent hours behind that kit, honing her craft.

"You also mentioned something about a fella being... *abducted?*" The sheriff raised one bushy eyebrow.

"That's right, sir." Jessie forced herself to spit out the *sir*. She saw the way he was looking at her—the doubt, the mild contempt. She managed to choke out an abridged version of last night's events, sans the weed smoking. It was her fourth time having to tell this story. She was feeling like she was reciting the memory of some terrible nightmare.

"Well, you sure you weren't just stoned out of your gourd on goblin grass and maybe *hallucinated* that boy of yours getting taken?" The sheriff addressed Jessie as if she were a frightened child who thought the pile of clothes in her bedroom closet was the boogeyman. His deputy, finally altering his facial expression with a shit-eating grin, produced a plush green zip-up bag. Jessie had gotten it from a cute smoke shop down in Laredo on their last Dixie Line tour. JEZIE'S GOODZ was Sharpied into the fabric.

"You *are* Jessie Lamont, right? Would this be yours?" the sheriff asked. Jessie's lips moved, struggling to form words that never came.

"Charlie," Susannah interjected, stepping forward, "What the hell does that have to do with—"

"Stay out of this, Suze. You should be lucky I came out here at all, after that ridiculous hogwash with your son. Bringing my goddamn daughter into it. For being such a pious Christian woman, you're awfully prone to libel. Now, Miss Lamont—" Charles Baumgartner took a defiant step forward, "How's about *you* tell *me* about this lovely little grab bag of delights you have here. Or the half ounce of marijuana we found in the center console of the van?" he asked.

In a well-rehearsed routine, Baumgartner and the unnamed deputy closed in on Jessie like a pack of coyotes converging on a lone deer. The bloodstained Ziploc bag full of Afghan Kush sequestered away in an evidence bag was held out by Baumgartner. The deputy had unzipped the plush bag and there were Jessie's bowl, her one hitter, a few crumpled rolling papers and the small blob of hash folded up in wax paper.

"Technically weed is legal here, but with the amount you got, and the fact there's a deadly crash involved, you're looking at a DUI at least, possibly vehicular manslaughter." the deputy said with a smirk.

"That's right, Deputy Anderson. I'm thinking 4-5 months in county lockup and a year of probation unless you got yourself an excellent lawyer. Maybe more if we find out it was *you* who was driving the van. Driving stoned is the same as driving drunk." Baumgartner tilted his head to the side. "Now, I want you to be real honest with me, lady, 'cause—"

"Are you fucking kidding me?" Jessie exploded. Here she was, thinking she wouldn't have to keep her guard up, that maybe these country bumpkin assholes would help her, unlike the inner-city dickheads in

Memphis who took any excuse to give her a thorough pat search, hands too curious, smiles too big. Rage flooded her now, and she wasn't sure she could contain it.

Fuck the good girl act. "My friend just fucking *died* right before my eyes. The one who *was* driving the van, his name is Lou Springer, someone took him. My other friend is sitting in the hospital. There are lives in danger here, and this, *this* is what you come at me with? My friend is *missing*, probably abducted by some inbred fucking hillbillies, and you're coming at me about *weed*?" she said, suddenly right in the sheriff's face. She tried to snatch the weed from the sheriff's hands, but he held it above his head.

"Ma'am, I suggest you take a step back and calm yourself before Deputy Anderson over here feels the need to taser you on account of you being all belligerent." The calmness in his voice belied the smile of a man lusting for conflict. He *wanted* this to escalate.

A gentle but firm hand settled on Jessie's shoulder.

"Take a deep breath, sweetheart," Susannah said from behind, gently pulling her back.

"Now, I don't mean to appear insensitive. I understand, young lady, you've gone through quite a traumatic event. That being said, I can't find myself feeling all too sympathetic for a band of Satan-worshipping heathens. You see, I ran IDs on you and the other occupants of the van, those I could find, anyway. I found out about your little rock band. You know about this girl's band, Susannah? Call themselves *Blasphemer*. Ain't that something? So, this little merry band of hedonistic hellraisers comes idling along in *my* county, a quiet, good Christian community, mind you, and then *you* cause all this ruckus, talking about abduction and road traps. Hurling wild accusations. Stirring shit. Could be a work truck dropped a nail-studded two by four off the back of his tailgate, and the driver, *whoever* that may be, may have been too stoned to slow down in time. Could be—"

"She mentioned hearing the name Roy, Sheriff. One of the guys who ran off with this boy. Said she heard it clear as day. You think *that's* a coincidence?" Susannah interjected. The sheriff rolled his eyes hard enough to put most angsty teenagers to shame and let out an exasperated sigh.

"Oh, for heaven's sake, not this brouhaha again. No more of this Langan shit. Roy Langan ain't got nothing to do with this. Ain't had nothing to do with your son either. Roy Langan is a two-bit meth head who can only count as high as his fingers allow and not some criminal mastermind, just like his brain-dead brother. Did you get a look at these two fellas, Miss Lamont? Can you give me a description at all?"

"...No..." Jessie suddenly felt very stupid, like a dumb, insecure little girl. She fought the insane urge to cower behind this woman whom she'd met only yesterday. God, this was fucking *insane.* She should be in the Memphis House of Blues sound-checking her drums right now. She should be running through warm-ups with Lou. She should be giving Allen a high five as he checked his vocals and his guttural roar shook the venue.

"Well then, I—"

"Sheriff, if you're not going to help this woman, then I'm gonna kindly ask you to get the Hell off my property," Susannah said.

During the course of Jessie's shouting, a dog had started barking somewhere in the large fenced-in backyard. Jessie saw Buckie, a blonde border collie, whom she'd made acquaintance with in her deep fugue-like sleep, having come up and squeezed his way onto the couch beside her in the night. He was the most peaceful-looking, beautiful animal she'd ever seen. But now, his snout crinkled up in a snarl, sensing his master's distress. Jessie wished the dog wasn't restrained, wished the animal would tear across the yard and bite this power-tripping asshole right in the jewels.

"Alright, alright." The sheriff shook his head, putting away the weed and motioning for his deputy to get back in the car. "Here's what I'm gonna do. I'm gonna go talk to your friend at the hospital, a Mr.... uh, George?"

"Geoff, G-E-O-F-F, pronounced Jeff," Jessie spat out. "His name is Geoff Richards."

"Right, I'll see if this uh, Mr. Richards can corroborate anything you've just said. And I'll see if we can put some facts together. As far as this Lou Springer fella goes, I can put out a BOLO, see if anyone has seen him. You said he's colored, right?"

"African American, yes," Jessie said through clenched teeth. *Colored? Seriously?*

"Right, well, he should be easy to spot. We ain't got many of them up here, do we, Deputy Anderson?"

"No, sir."

"If he's around, someone should spot him. I'm gonna hold off on that missing person's report though, 'til I can talk to your buddy. You don't want to see me again if I found out you been wasting state resources on a snipe hunt," the sheriff said, and turned to get back in his cruiser. "We'll be in touch. Little lady, you'll just wanna sit tight for a while. Don't be running off nowhere. Somebody's gotta take the fall for these drugs,"

Jessie couldn't believe what she was hearing. Her friend was dead, Lou was MIA, and even after she hammered this home, this guy was hounding her about a fucking *plant.* "What about Allen?" Jessie asked.

"If we hear reports of a mutilated body being found out in the National Park, you'll be the first to know," Baumgartner said, slamming the car door shut.

"Lordy be." Susannah let out a breath as the two men drove off. She put a hand to her chest and looked down at the ground as if expecting to find some valuable answer to life's problems buried in the dirt. She then looked up at Jessie, her face no longer showing that warm, open motherly concern. "Is it... true? What he said about that... Satanic stuff?" Jessie swallowed, feeling a pit of abyssal despair open up in her gut at the thought that the one friendly face she'd met out here in this rural purgatory would soon turn on her.

"We don't actually worship Satan, okay? We're all agnostic or atheist, but not Satan-worshippers. We just... it's an act. The label told us to play it up. Be edgy, have an image, all that. I... I don't believe in anything in particular, but I respect others' beliefs. I know you're a woman of God and I respect that. It's not like he says." Jessie knew she was rambling but didn't want to offend this sweet woman who had opened her doors for a complete stranger, who more than likely saved her life. Someone who acted more like a true Christian than all the evangelical dickheads she'd had to deal with on the street corners of Memphis, shouting about salvation and the damned and the end of the world.

Susannah nodded slowly but didn't seem entirely convinced.

"He truly is an unpleasant man, that Baumgartner. He wears a cross under his Kevlar vest but he's as Christian as them evangelists who spit nonsense on the TV and live in mansions. All preach and no practice... Lordy be, what a mess." Susannah headed back towards the house.

"Not that it's any of my affair, but it sounds like you and him have some unresolved business." Jessie had noted the rude familiarity with which Sheriff Baumgartner conducted himself, the way Susannah so brashly referred to him by his first name. Something about her son.

"Come on inside, honey, and I'll make it your business too. My gut tells me there's something big going on in this little county, and you just became a part of it, for better or worse."

# Chapter 7

"You think maybe... we was just a smidge hard on them?" Anderson asked as the Charger shot down US Highway 61, merging onto Y, and on to Dolvin. Baumgartner let the Charger climb up to seventy and switched on the cruise control. The faster he went, the better he could think.

"Maybe just a little bit, but not much. You're new here, so I'll cut you some slack, but there's some bad blood between me and that Paige woman. All that shit with her son happened before you were hired. She showed an ugly side then. Tried to drag my daughter into it. You don't fucking do that." Baumgartner took a pinch out of his can of dip and tucked it between lip and gum. It wasn't the poison he wanted, but it would do for now.

"She thinks you killed her son or something?" Anderson asked, as he took out the small glob of hash that had been folded up in the wax paper and smelled it. He gave a nod of approval before tucking it into his shirt pocket.

"Nah. She's hung up on this Langan fella. Her son worked for him. Or them, I should say."

"Hell, you talking about Langan Bros. Automotive? That garage off Main Street?" Anderson asked.

"Yep, the very same. 'Cept before it was Langan Bros., it was just their daddy, Virgil. He was this county's sole mechanic. Raised them boys on carburetors and transmissions from the time they'd graduated from shitting their britches. Then they had that accident, car fell on the boys in the shop. Damn near neutered Roy, and Tate... well, he's all Forrest Gump now. Suze's boy, Daniel, went missing 'bout a year and a half ago. He was working at the garage around that time, last place he was seen was leaving there. Susannah got it in her mind that the Langan boys killed him or disappeared him or something. It probably never crossed that poor woman's mind that maybe he just got up and ran off. Fled to the west to be a hippie or something. Who knows? But I know the Langans didn't kill him. They had no reason to. I think she knows that deep down inside too. She blamed me since I couldn't provide any answers that suited her."

"But what's that gotta do with your daughter? Didn't know you had one. Don't ever speak of—"

"She ran off," the sheriff said. "It's got nothing to do with that whole clusterfuck."

That's what he told himself anyway. It made sense. Baumgartner was a hellraiser in his youth. The chemical cocktail of hormones made him engage in his fair share of dumbassery. But his lil' Viv? Christ almighty, that girl was like the Tasmanian Devil in them cartoons, a whirling dervish of chaos. Caught selling drugs at school. Getting into fights. Coming home with a new tattoo or piercing every week. Listening to that God-awful screaming music just like Blasphemer. Then to top it all off, his wife comes to him all mild-mannered-like one day, tells him that she caught Viv in bed with another girl.

That was the breaking point for Charles. He was raised Southern Baptist. Southern Baptists didn't ken to homosexuality. His wife tried to get him to be understanding, that this was normal, that she was experimenting, and even if she wasn't, was it really so bad?

"Look at it this way, at least she won't be getting knocked up anytime soon," Chelsea had said behind a timid smile, the one she gave when she was handing him a pile of shit dressed up in a bouquet of roses. Like it was all just some innocent little thing.

Last he saw of Vivian (she even hated her name, said it sounded like a *boomer name*, whatever the hell that meant), she was slamming the door in his face and giving him the finger. That was two years ago. Not a phone call or a text message since. He told himself she was out on the West Coast, probably a smelly muff-diving hippie somewhere in San Francisco. He kept believing it even after they found her car, abandoned on the side of 72 some ten miles up the road, with a good bit of her personal belongings still in it.

Chels tried to get him to open an investigation. He said no. Threw around phrases like nepotism and county resources. Told her she was going to make him look like a fool if he opened up this whole case and it turned out to be nothing.

Shortly thereafter, Chelsea left too.

"...Oh. Uhm, alright." Anderson broke the silence when it stretched out long enough it was clear the sheriff had no more to say on the matter.

He debated telling Anderson about the other pieces of this long, complicated puzzle. About the other missing people around Carter. About how Virgil Langan was a goddamn good meth cook. How he'd struck a deal with ol' Virgil after pulling him over one night with enough pure white ice to get half the state high. Charles, being a connoisseur himself, had decided to work the game. He got free product and turned a blind eye to Virgil's cooking. In return, the old meth cook snitched on the competition, letting Baumgartner bust a selection of small shake n' bake operations so it looked like he was doing his job. What'd they call that? Quid pro quo?

Charles's daddy, who was Carter County Sheriff for almost twenty years, had taught him the importance of forming valuable relationships as a lawman. Being as isolated as they were, a Carter County deputy couldn't rely on backup the same as the state highway boys did or the city police. That changed only slightly with the advent of technology and long wave CBs, but even today, backup could be anywhere from an hour to two hours away in the backwater boonies where cell reception was spotty and many of the roads unmarked. So, the lawmen around here had to learn to adapt, to know when to pick their fights, and which ones to turn their backs on.

"The overzealous ones, the ones with no friends, are the ones who end up shot in the back in a shallow ditch somewhere... That, or they just plumb burnout and eat the gun," his daddy had said. "We're an ins'lar community, and it's our place to know our people, earn their trust. Find the ones with their hands deep in the soil and have a solid working relationship with them. 'Cause, you make enemies with them... you're done."

Indeed, Baumgartner was just following in the footsteps of his daddy and *his* daddy before him. Back in the day, it was allowing the moonshine runners to run their hooch all over the hills in exchange for letting the sheriff bust a dummy still or two to keep the teetotalers happy. Fast forward seventy-five years, now it was methamphetamine, which Baumgartner had taken a fierce liking to. Being the only competent lawman out here, he'd needed something to keep him going. Something that helped him burn the midnight oil when case reports stacked up and people like Susannah Paige harangued him, trying to turn the whole goddamn community against him. Stirring up such a goddamn fuss even his wife left him, though that relationship was already skating on thin ice.

Baumgartner debated telling Anderson all this. He was still a rookie, but he'd soon have to be initiated into the ways of backcountry justice. They did things differently out here, and he'd have to get with the program soon enough. But the whole Langan business was still a little tender to be poking at.

It was a damn shame Virgil got too big for his britches. He remembered the day when the feds were called in because one of Virgil's distributors flipped on him. Not long after, when Baumgartner had tipped him off about the federal warrants coming down on his head, there was an explosion. It had set a hundred acres of Ozark wilderness afire starting up near the Salem plateau. The charred remains of the meth lab were found tucked deep in the woods, a few miles north of the Langan property, and Virgil Langan had been presumed dead. No body was ever found though, neither at the site of the explosion, nor at the Langan residence. All ten acres had been thoroughly searched, and... nothing.

That's because the sheriff had done the Langans an *awful* big favor.

Baumgartner recalled the cave that sat on the edge of the Langan property as they headed towards the hospital. It was the only place the feds hadn't looked. After the USGS made topographical readings of the area, it was discovered that the Langans had been living atop uncharted subterranean territory. That wasn't uncommon, as this part of the state was famous for one of the largest unexplored cave systems in the world. The thought of going underground into caves no one had ever tried to explore had made his asshole pucker up tight with fear. Even as a grown man he'd remembered the stories about the Carter caves.

Wives' tales, told on playgrounds by goosing children and next to simmering stove tops by chiding mothers, discouraging their children from wandering off into the hills. Stories about why the mining companies had pulled up stakes after fifty years of digging, even though there was plenty of galena left to mine. About the men stuck down there after the enormous cave-in back in '48, thirty miners trapped deep in the earth. About how unstable the ground was out in that patch of no man's land between Carter and Salem. An infamous honeycomb of sinkholes, where the ground could swallow you whole easy as a bucket mouth bass gullets a worm.

The Langan brothers, Roy and Tate, had the right to refuse the geologists and policemen who wanted to search the cave, as it was an auxiliary part of their property the warrant didn't cover. And refuse they did. Virgil Langan was thought deceased, so the feds shrugged their shoulders and went back to Jefferson City. By all accounts, their backwoods boogeyman was dead.

It was a shame those Langan brothers couldn't cook like their daddy though.

Damn shame.

# CHAPTER 8

I T WAS CLEAR THE boy was doped to the gills. His green eyes were glassy, and his long hair was plastered to his head with fever sweat. Baumgartner thought his face resembled that of a cow chewing cud, content and passive. He was a skeleton of a man, veiny arms covered in tattoos, the right forearm in a cast.

"Just tell us what you can remember, son," Anderson said, his face more approachable, more jovial than Baumgartner's hard visage. Charles thought they could cobble together a mighty fine good cop/bad cop routine if they worked like this more often.

"Fuckin' asshole tried to ram us off the road, man." Geoff Richards's voice was breathy, but full of conviction. "One minute, we're driving to our next show, next we were being rammed. I saw the spike strip ahead of us. They set a trap for us, dude. Set us up." As the blood pressure alarm beeped, Baumgartner figured recalling the event gave the kid an adrenaline dump. That was the sign of someone telling the truth.

"But why were you out in the middle of nowhere?" Baumgartner interjected. "Memphis is a straight shot from I-55. Y'all weren't trying to avoid the checkpoints, by chance?" The sheriff drilled the doped-out punk with the full heat of his gaze. Geoff wasn't an idiot though; he narrowed his eyes.

"The fuck is this, huh? Why you asking about that? Someone took my fucking *friend,* officer. Someone made us wreck into—"

"Easy, son. We're just wanting to get to the bottom of what happened. It's just... we gotta make sure y'all's stories match up. You know, on account of the narcotics found in the vehicle," Anderson said softly.

"Narcotics?" Richards said with a squint. Then his face went pale, as understanding dawned on him. He swallowed with an audible click. "I don't know shit about no drugs, man. All I know is some psychos made us flip and took my friend."

"You get a look at 'em?" Baumgartner prayed this boy didn't see a damned thing. He was staring down the wall of an incoming shit storm. What the boy said next would mean the difference between getting slammed by a category five or contending with a light drizzle.

"Yeah. One was just a normal lookin' redneck fuck. The other was big. Fuckin' butterball," Geoff said. "Smelled like shit too."

Anderson and Baumgartner looked at each other from across the hospital bed.

They would've asked for a written statement, but the boy's left-handed writing was chicken scratch. He consented to have his testimony recorded instead.

Someone had forced them onto a spike strip, that much was undeniable. The bluff about the nail-studded two by four he used on the girl... Charles knew that was bullshit. He saw those tires when he went to investigate the wreck. They looked the same as the deflated husks on the rims of so many Dodge Neons and Ford Tauruses behind the wire. Typical drug dealer rides that awaited processing back at the impound lot, tires shredded all to hell by blackjack strips in high-speed pursuits.

If that much was true, then he had to assume that the part about the duo running off with that black feller was true as well. Two men who fit the Langan brothers' description to a T. Category 5. Hurricane Langan was about to make landfall.

"Ain't that one Langan kinda big in the waist? Taint or something, his name is," Anderson said as they got back in the car.

"*Tate*, yeah... that boy is a thick one." Baumgartner sighed as he started the Charger up. He was, in his mind anyway, a responsible meth user. Never used on the job, except in the mornings to wake himself up. Didn't go on four-day binges and get psychosis like the rest of them tweakers did. As he sat in the driver's seat, though, his mind's wheels spinning gravel and going nowhere, he badly wished for a hit. *Badly.* His body felt full of tv static, his skin getting gooseflesh as his nerves screamed for just one clarifying hit of that enlightening, harsh smoke.

"And they do have a pretty loud truck. That big ol' murdered out 2500. Pulled Roy over a few months ago about the window tint on it." Anderson was looking at Baumgartner now, waiting.

Charles could feel the gaze on him as he gripped the wheel. Oh yes, just one hit of the ice. Get his synapses firing, help him figure out the best way to skin this particular cat.

"Yep," the sheriff said, more to himself than his deputy. He was thinking of the seven other people who'd gone missing since Virgil Langan's magic disappearing act. These things happened in isolated places where people lived off the land and the land itself had many holes and hollers one could fall into. But the frequency they were happening lately... Even Baumgartner, going full ostrich with his head in the sand, couldn't deny the oddity of it.

There was the Paige boy, David or Donald... no, Daniel. That Susannah Paige raised a big fuss about it, which he knew he couldn't fault her for. He'd be mighty upset too if his only son (if he had a son) went missing. Baumgartner made sure to reinforce in his own mind that Vivian *wasn't* missing. Nor was Daniel. Kids ran off. It's just what happens sometimes. Kids stuck in these rural backwaters dream of the great world beyond, not realizing it was just as shitty out there as it was down here in the boonies.

But Susannah just couldn't get it through her goddamn head. Took ads out on billboards. JUSTICE FOR DANIEL and MAKE THE CARTER COUNTY SHERIFFS OFFICE DO THEIR JOB. She had started social media campaigns, pushing for investigations to be opened up. The woman spearheaded an online crusade that to this day gave him migraines. The sheriff's office had to temporarily shut down their humble website, even taking the sheriff's work email off the directory. Their inboxes and query portals had been flooded with strangers from all over the world telling Baumgartner to quit being a sack of shit and do his job.

Except he *was* doing his job, goddamnit.

He thought of Vivian's middle finger raised behind her. The painted black nail catching the early morning sunlight, her purple hair shining, almost iridescent. She didn't even look at him as she left. Some days that fact still reddened his ass. Two years, not so much as a goddamn phone call. How long could someone stay mad? How long—

"Sheriff?"

Baumgartner blinked, realizing he'd lapsed into a haze, white-knuckling the steering wheel.

"You hear me?" Anderson asked. " I said maybe we should go out there, you know, just touch base with the brothers."

"Yeah, I reckon we should." The bones in Baumgartner's wrist popped as he squeezed the steering wheel as hard as he could. He didn't want to go out to that property, to that cave again.

None of the bodies had ever been found—*She never called*—and the caves were the only place they didn't look—*Her car was right in the center of*—all those disappearances happened within a few miles of the Langan property.

Christ almighty, he wanted this sleeping dog to remain snoozing, but he aimed his Charger towards the Langan residence all the same. He had an obligation to his people, to keep them safe, even if that meant stirring up a real nasty crockpot of shit stew.

*You're just too chickenshit to wanna know the truth. What if she didn't run away? What if—*

The souped-up engine roared. He felt Anderson giving him the side-eye, but he wisely kept his mouth shut.

# Chapter 9

L OU, NEARLY DELIRIOUS, TRIED to imagine the hottest venue they'd ever played, if only to take his mind off the real-life nightmare he was living out. There was the dive bar down in Louisiana they played during their first tour—The Pissin' Gator. It was just outside of Alexandria and catered to rock 'n' roll and metal acts. The night of their show, the venue's A/C went out. In the middle of a soupy Louisiana summer night.

The place had been so humid with perspiration from sweating Cajuns and the dense swamp that bordered the gravel parking lot condensation dripped off the walls and onto everything. By the end of their set *everything* was wet, like they'd all been misted from a sprinkler during the entire show. Lou remembered how pissed Geoff was. Their de facto guitar tech, he had to reset the truss rods on all their guitars and basses, the humidity warping their instrument necks to an almost comical bow.

But compared to this goddamn tool shed, The Pissin' Gator may as well have been a meat freezer. They'd placed him in a corner of the shed with a yellowed pillow and a couple burlap grain sacks for bedding. His wrists had been thoroughly duct taped together, though he was sweating so much he could've worked his way out of them if he had found the strength. The brothers were kind enough to hook up an old, whining oscillating fan in one corner of the work shed, but all that did was push the hot, swampy air around.

Almost worse than the heat was the smell. His body reeked of old and new sweat. The shallow hole they'd dug in the dirt floor where he was allowed to piss and shit (with assistance from Tweedledee and Tweedledum, who checked on him every couple of hours) hummed with all manner of flying insect. Mostly shit-smeared flies that found his face as appetizing as his bodily waste. The heat had baked the stench into something physical and insidious, a poisonous effluvium so potent it probably violated the Geneva Convention. His shame intensified with the miasma that hung in the hot air. Lou had been reduced to nothing more than a farm animal, a pig wallowing in his own mess. It didn't help his captors had to stand by while he noisily emptied his bowels and dribbled tea-colored piss into the hole, the two of them bitching about the stink all the while. Humiliation paired with self-disgust so deep it etched into his soul. Lou knew if, and that was a big fucking *if*, he made it out of this alive, some serious therapy was in his future.

It seemed he'd gone through all seven stages of grief during his 24-hour interim in the shed. Guilt at having put the rest of the band members' lives in danger because of his dumb last-minute decision. For abandoning his daughter and Janel, both of whom were expecting a phone call from him any minute now. He always let them know when he had finished yet another long drive in one piece. Rage at these men and their weird fucking cannibal dad for kidnapping him and making him endure this bizarre torture. If he got out of this alive, he was never crossing Missouri state lines again. If he flew, he'd pay the pilot out of his own pocket to circumvent this godforsaken place.

Lou hadn't quite worked his way to acceptance when the rickety shed door opened, and the two men appeared. One of them made a retching noise.

"Jesus fuckin' Christ, we shoulda just let him use the outhouse," Roy croaked. "Smells worse than a goddamn ruptured septic tank in here."

The two men, with shirts over their noses, dragged Lou out into the sunlight. After being cooped up in the dark, dank shed, he was blinded for several seconds as ephemeral needles stabbed his corneas. It was perhaps ten or fifteen degrees cooler out here, still hot, but not sauna hot. He thought perhaps they were going to kill him now, since their racist cave dweller dad apparently didn't want to eat him. It surprised him to find he had no urge to make peace with God. He'd heard of this phenomenon in a lot of the books he read on agnosticism and documentaries on religion. How even the most devout atheists, faced with impending death, find themselves accepting God in their witching hour, hoping for absolution and a chance at the great hereafter. Yet, as Louis saw his imminent end, he found no deity. He acquiesced instead to whatever void came after this mortality. If there *was* some great celestial entity in the sky kicking his feet up on the recliner and enjoying the shit show, he mentally told the big man to go fuck himself.

To his surprise and confusion, however, he saw not an old shotgun or some other backwoods executioner's tool, but sustenance, laid out on one of the many stumps spread sporadically throughout the property. A grease-stained McDonald's bag, and a large drink sweating through its plastic container. The physical need to gulp it down almost hurt more than his back, which had mercifully gone numb at some point in the night.

"Listen boy, you're gonna eat all this here, alright?" Roy said to Lou, then wheeled on Tate. "Make sure he eats it all, especially the milkshake. You know daddy has... *had* a sweet tooth."

"Oh... okay." Tate had been staring at the ground, his eyes looking everywhere but Lou. In that moment, Lou caught a palpable dichotomy between these two, yin and yang of the most fucked up order. Even in his heat-exhausted, agonized state, he felt the rift between them. He could exploit this if he played his cards right. Roy suddenly came over, clapping Tate in the head.

"Hey, you hear me, boy? I said make sure he eats it. Not you, *piggy*," Roy poked him hard in his stomach. Tate's lip began to tremble. Roy sighed, then put his forehead to his brother's. "I'm sorry, I didn't mean that. Just... listen to me. We only got to do this a little longer. I got me a plan, okay? We just gotta endure the shit a little longer. Okay, baby brother?" Roy's voice switched to something high and sweet. Lou had a clear picture of the manipulative dynamic.

"Yeah, okay," Tate said, so quiet Lou almost couldn't even hear him.

"Alright then. I'm gonna go back in the house and call Billy, tell him we're both gonna be a little late, and to go ahead and open up the garage without us. Sundays are usually slower than molasses, anyway. Now remember, don't you go eatin' none of that. That's all for him," Roy jabbed his brother's gut once more before walking into the house. For a moment Tate only stood there, hands thrust deep into the pockets of his grease-stained denim overalls.

"Please. The milkshake." Lou's voice was ragged, the thought of that creamy coldness hitting his throat almost making him want to weep. Tate swallowed thickly and reached for the shake, which already had a straw in it. His hand trembled as he held it out to Lou, who slurped greedily at the blessedly cool, half-melted ice cream. Though he was only vegetarian, not nearly as militantly vegan as Jessie (though even she had been sliding back recently) and the others in Blasphemer, who abhorred *all* animal products, Lou tried to stay away from dairy if he could. It fucked his sinuses up and gave him the shits, but he knew he was far past the guiding needle of some first-world morality compass. His contrived convictions about the world had dribbled out of him, along with everything else, to ferment in that fucking shed.

Tears stung his eyes, and a bubble lodged in his throat making it almost impossible to swallow as the thick, but cool—*god, so fucking cool*—shake slid down his gullet. Each gulp of the sweet, icy nectar was like ambrosia from the gods. He knew he should slow down but didn't care about the inevitable cramps and violent shits to come. His Adam's apple bobbed something fierce as he drank, cherishing the tingle that spread throughout his body with each swallow, a cold cramping ball forming in his stomach. Then the brain freeze jammed an icepick through his left eye and up into his brain. He ripped his lips away from the straw, eyes twitching, lips smacking.

"I'm sorry, mister. It wasn't supposed to be like this..." Tate's voice quavered like a scolded child. Tears began to mix with the sweat on those red, round cheeks of his. Lou coughed, his mouth thick with shake residue, and then cleared his throat.

"It doesn't have to be. You can still make things right, man. Just drop me off near a gas station or something, I won't say nothing. Just wanna get home, man. I got a baby girl, dude, a *daughter*. Her name's Lateria. All you've done so far is rescue me from a wreck. So far as I'm concerned, we're even," Lou said. He saw those tiny mole-like eyes squeeze shut.

"No... You don't get it, mister. Our daddy... our poppa. He needs you. Needs to eat. He ain't right. I know that, but he's our daddy!" Tate used his free hand to wipe away the tears.

"Fuck your dad, man. Your dad's gone crazy. Was he a meth head or something? I heard of meth heads going crazy, staying up for eight days at a time and—"

"SHUT UP! Don't talk about him like that!" Tate roared. The pudgy hand holding the milkshake closed into a fist. The cup crinkled and the lid popped off, white nectar spilling over the sweaty hand. Lou watched with profound sadness as the creamy confection dribbled to the ground. For a maddening second, he considered licking it off Tate's hand and had to stop himself from doing just that.

"Alright man, we're cool, we're cool. I won't diss your pops, I'm just sayin'—" Lou eyed the spilled milkshake, grieving for it like the death of a close family member. "I need a doctor man. My back is broke. You take me somewhere and I can get some help, I won't say nothing, I promise." Lou struggled to keep his voice soft, that gentle sort of lulling voice he used on Janel after a good hour or two of lovemaking, thick with hope and kindness and sincerity. Lou saw the crucifix dangling in front of the overalls and part of him wanted to laugh at the absurdity of it all, but he didn't. He had to give his best Oscar-winning performance if he was going to get out of this alive. "You're a man of God, right? Do the good Christian thing, Tate."

"You don't understand. He's sick. When he went into them caves, all burned up and running from the law, he came back sick. We went looking for him down there, and we saw... *things*." Tate put the milkshake on the stump and took out the Big Mac, unfolding its yellow wrapper. Tate held the burger out to his captive. Lou's stomach roiled with need as he saw the grease dripping off the meat, and the special sauce slowly oozing down the patties and bun. Even before he was vegetarian, he used to hate McDonald's, but that was before he knew what true starvation felt like.

"Listen, can you please undo my hands? I ain't going nowhere man, I can't fuckin' walk and y'all live in the middle of bumfuck, it's not like I got anywhere I *can* go. I don't wanna be fed like a baby. You already reduced me to less of a man keeping me in that goddamn shed. Please, if you're not gonna let me go, at least let me eat like a man. I won't try nothing stupid." Lou was trying for a compromise. Tate looked at him, beady eyes searching for the truth, the way his daughter Lateria used to look at him when he'd 'steal her nose' with his thumb. When she was young enough to fall for that shit, that is. That sort of naive curiosity only an infant has. Lou gave him his best open book stare. Tate swallowed, looked back at the house, then at him, then at the house again.

*Yes, you fucking pig-eyed motherfucker, get my hands free so I can wring that canned ham neck of yours.*

Tate pulled out a folding pocketknife, and suddenly, a pang of hope. *A little closer*, Lou's mind screamed. Just as he started to unfold the blade, they both heard the distant crunch of tires on gravel, and Tate's eyes went wide. As he fumbled to put the pocketknife away, Roy exploded from the house.

"Goddamn sheriff comin', come on!" he screamed, running at them.

"Oh hell," Tate groaned. They picked Lou up and half ran towards the shed, the heavier brother tripping, nearly dropping him only a foot from the shed. Lou started to yell, screaming as loud as he could, but they hurled him into the fetid shed. He landed flat on his back. The pain was breathtaking, tearing from him a scream that ebbed to a whimpering croak as his vision went gray. A wave of lava climbed his fractured spine and into the base of his skull. Everything from the waist down tingled with stabbing sensations. Roy looked around frantically and found an old oil-stained rag. He shoved it into Lou's gaping mouth before he could find his voice. His lips stretched around the dirty rag in a silent scream.

"You even so much as cut a fart in here while we're talking, and I'll come in here, stick your head down in that hole, and make you bob for turds, you understand?" Roy's voice was all venom as he grabbed Lou by his dreads, turning his head toward the fly-rimmed hole. He remembered how indignant he had felt when Tate's sweaty arms held him over it, keeping him from falling into his own lake of filth.

Lou nodded, halfway out of it with pain. With that, Roy let him go. They were just out the door, Roy locking it behind him, as he heard the car pull up.

# Chapter 10

S USANNAH FELT MILDLY UNHINGED showing Jessie the large, detailed map of Missouri that hung in her study. Several red circles marked the southeastern portion of the state, surrounding the geographical boundary of Carter County in a rough oblong circle. Pinned to the map were newspaper articles, several of which screamed MISSING PERSON. She had never shown anyone her little project before, not even Harold. *Especially* not Harold, who was every bit the stoic, salt of the earth man who despised scandal. He never liked being the center of attention and had abandoned his wife's fervent crusade once the whole town came to Baumgartner's defense.

At first, still grieving over Daniel's disappearance, he'd supported her desperate inquisition. Both of them needed to find an outlet for their bereavement, to assign blame to the inept law enforcement tasked with finding him. Eventually, Harold learned to move on, to accept that their son might've just run off. Baumgartner, eager for a truce, had sat down with the man over a few beers at Blue Springs Lake and must've had a good, long, man-to-man with him. But Susannah just couldn't accept that.

Having just graduated from high school, Daniel was insistent about becoming a race car driver. He raved night and day about car performance specs, racer names, and more. Unlike most children who start off wanting to be an astronaut or a veterinarian, only to let time and society crush their dreams into something more realistic, Daniel held fast to one day driving rally circuits or the Formula 500.

More than a few discussions got heated between Daniel and his parents. Susannah wanted him to at least audit a few classes over at Dolvin Community College. Just some kind of backup, in case this world, always cruel and unforgiving, robbed him of his aspirations. Harold wanted him to go to the Vo-Tech school and learn a trade. The world needed more mechanics and carpenters, not Dale Earnhardts. There'd been arguments, yes, but Daniel wasn't the type to just get up and run off. He just *wasn't*.

"Holy shit," Jessie said as she sipped coffee and stared in disbelief at the fastidious detailing of disappearances. It was the first thing she'd said since Susannah sat her down in her small office, where Harold assumed she scrapbooked, or read, or pursued newer hobbies outside of her vet practice. Jessie pointed at the wildly shaped red border comprising the county, and within it a small red asterisk that had been scratched into the map so aggressively that it almost tore through the thick laminated cardstock. "What is that?"

"The Langan property. Look, their house is smack in the middle of all these disappearances." Susannah jabbed a finger at the red asterisk, then swallowed back the rant on the Langans that wanted to explode out of her. She'd spent the last two hours apprising Jessie of her obsession with the disappearances, the secret hobby she worked on day and night. During the two-week interims Harold had been on the tugboats, floating the Missouri and Mississippi rivers, his mind didn't have to wonder at the broader possibilities of his son's disappearance. Her mother's heart could bear no such luxury.

"Johnathan Lambert and Peter Galin went missing two and a half years ago. One was a well-known hunter in the town, the other an old coot who used to roam the hills for morels and mushrooms. Neither likely to get lost in the woods. Then, there was Cecil Deevers, an out-of-town college student who came to float the Current River during the summer. Cecil was on a solo float out on the river. Last anyone saw her was right here, at Shank's Bend."

Susannah was bent over a different map spread on the coffee table. Her eyes drilled into the blown-up map of the Tri-County area showing all the waterways that passed through from the Current to the Black River, in addition to the county line, the national forest, and the town of Carter itself. She pointed out where the Mark Twain National Forest boundary was almost catty-corner to the Langans' land. Shank's Bend was a sharp dip in the river that meandered, almost oxbow style, into the border of Langan property. The two red circles marking Shank's Bend and the Langan place were only about ten miles apart.

Susannah's voice grew ragged as she went on. She felt herself getting worked up, the mild adrenaline rush of finally telling someone, showing them how all the pieces fit. She imagined Daniel as the biggest piece in a puzzle that was half completed. She prayed what happened with Jessie and her unfortunate band members would help put a few more pieces into place.

"Most of these folks hunted and foraged around the Black River, which cuts right through Mark Twain. Lot of cave mouths and de-commissioned mine shafts out that way. Park rangers blocked 'em off to keep kids out. The official stories tried to paint them all as death by misadventure. But if you knew those folks, well, you'd know that was a bunch of bull." Susannah forced herself to stop for a moment, letting her fingers anxiously comb through her hair. She looked at Jessie before going on. The girl wouldn't meet her gaze, her face a granite slate of blankness. It was the same look Harold gave her the one time she dared show him the very tip of this vast, submerged iceberg. That look had been enough for her to clamp her mouth shut. But not with Jessie. She would forge on, regardless of her mounting doubts.

"Then, there was the Walters couple." Susannah got up and straightened out with a crackle of her spine followed with a sigh. She grabbed a hybrid topographical map. It showed hydrology tables and aquifers for all of Carter County, at the center of which was a large, circular body of water labeled BLUE SPRINGS LAKE.

"Do you know what a stovepipe lake is, honey?" she asked Jessie.

The girl had been sitting mute the whole while, a world-class poker face painted on. She blinked, and Susannah figured she'd lapsed into a daze absorbing all this info. A sudden pang of doubt stabbed at Susannah. Regret at having vomited out all this information to a virtual stranger. God, Jessie probably thought she was insane. Still, she couldn't stop herself now. *In for a penny, in for a pound.*

"Uhm... no. Can't say I do." Jessie took a long swig of her coffee. Susannah almost stopped, sensing the mounting incredulity from the young girl, but decided to press on anyway. She *had* to see the whole picture, or it just wouldn't add up.

"Well, that's what Blue Springs is. Besides the caves, it's our only tourist attraction. The Walters family lived in a little cabin out there. Used to have a beautiful Golden Retriever named Roxy I treated. Anyway, they went missing about three months after Peter. Both of them. Janine and William used to compete in triathlons together. They were about my age. Probably would've outlived us all if they hadn't gone missing."

Susannah forced herself to slow down. She was rambling on, but couldn't, wouldn't stop. "Anyway, official story was, they spilled their little sailboat out in the lake, got sucked down into the stovepipe. Blue Springs is one of the few lakes in the country with an undercurrent. You can thank the mining companies and their blunders for that. But these were Ironman competing folks, Jessie. Both probably could go toe-to-toe with Olympic swimmers." Susannah had to stop and catch her breath. Recalling these deaths, their circumstances, it reinvigorated her need to search for her son. It reignited the simmering rage she felt towards Baumgartner and all the dismissive men who had the audacity to shrug her off as some kind of crazy, bereaved woman. The urge to jump into her car right then and there and start canvasing cave entrances was so strong she was starting to tremble. She realized her heart was pounding and forced herself to take a deep breath before reaching the end of her manic presentation.

"I don't—" Jessie began, but Susannah put a hand up, intent on finishing this. She had to.

"Then there was the geologist, David Parker. He was a USGS specialist who was based out of Mizzou. He'd come out here to map the rest of the cave systems that connects between Carter and Lordell. Hundreds of miles unmapped, uncharted. It's so dangerous down there though, the land's all gumbo from the deep extraction lead mining. Sinkholes and ceiling collapses galore. Baumgartner tried to spin it off as death by misadventure, just like the others. But all of Parker's sonar and mapping equipment was still in the car, which was abandoned off Route 72. Same as the sheriff's daughter, though he won't dare admit she got taken. He tells himself she ran off, but... both of their cars were found within a mile of what used to be the Doefield mine. The entrance is still there. It's gated off, sure, but that wouldn't stop someone who's really determined. Don't you see, Jessie?"

Susannah returned to the map. All the disappearances had been plotted out in a rough circle engulfing the Langan property on all sides. Jessie's face changed in a way that was hard to read, and once more Susannah felt embarrassment and regret at unloading this frantic conspiracy-laden lecture on Jessie. Susannah, now growing red-faced and exasperated, went on. She had set something in motion here and had to see it through.

"My son worked for the Langans, fixing cars. He was last seen leaving their shop. You wanna know their names? Tate and *Roy* Langan," Susannah said, holding herself now, the trembling getting worse. What if Jessie thought she was just some insane conspiracy theorist connecting abstract dots to a broader picture? But she wasn't crazy. *She wasn't.*

"Jesus..." Jessie's eyes flitted between the maps. Susannah prayed the young woman could connect the dots like she did. How couldn't she? It was all there. Anyone with half a brain could put the pieces together and see something was profoundly wrong with all this... couldn't they?

"Mind you, this all started happening right after the big forest fire. Explosion at Virgil Langan's meth lab. They never found his body... supposedly," Susannah said, but she didn't have the energy to go on about the Langan patriarch's mysterious death. That was a whole other can of worms entirely.

"You probably think I'm crazy, don't you? I'm sure you just want to go home, not thrust into this crazy crap."

"No, I just... it's a lot to take in. So much has happened in the last twenty-four hours. I'm supposed to be in Memphis right now tuning drums and practicing blast beats. Instead, I'm sitting in a house in a place I've never heard of, discovering that what happened last night wasn't just a random hate crime, but, uhm... might be the work of a serial killer? Think I need more coffee." Jessie stood up and headed towards the kitchen. Susannah followed, desperate for a fresh jolt of caffeine.

She had vomited words for the last two hours and felt equal parts embarrassment and relief. So much mental pressure had been accumulating within her. Susannah hadn't realized how far down the rabbit hole she'd gone until it all came pouring out of her in a frantic gush.

Susannah's brain now felt the way her stomach did after voiding a spoiled meal—empty and full of relief. She had never thought the day would come where she would have a valid reason to share her findings with someone, *anyone*, but here was this strange young woman. Under normal circumstances, Susannah would have never associated with Jessie, a tattooed, atheist drug user, who probably looked at churches the same way Susannah looked at heavy metal concerts. Only something as absurd as a murder conspiracy could bring the two together.

Now more than ever, she felt a conviction that God had thrust this street-punk, hedonistic, foul-mouthed girl into her life. Yet at the same time, Susannah realized she might've just scared off the one girl who could help bring attention to this case. They'd known each other for a little over twenty-four hours, and she's just info-bombed Jessie with her deepest secret. Jessie had a life that expanded far beyond the geological boundaries of Carter County. She probably longed to return to it, escaping this madness.

Despite her "Carter Disappearances 101" presentation, there were things she'd held back. Things Susannah knew would make her sound crazy if the long-winded lecture she'd just spewed out hadn't done the job. Like the gift, or curse, of the touch. How the flashes she sometimes received weren't just from people. Sometimes she got them from touching objects of great significance to their owners. She was the one who'd found Vivian Baumgartner's car, recognizing the Miata from the Lordell High School parking lot. Susannah had gotten out, looked into the car, and touched the door handle. Then it happened.

Fear. Pain. The distinct musk of a dirty, unwashed man. It had lasted all of two seconds but had slammed into her like a freight train. She called Charles, let him know what she'd found, but who could she tell about her... what were they, visions? Hallucinations?

Then, of course, there was Virgil Langan's death. Everyone in Carter knew he and Charlie had been thick as thieves. She knew, she just *knew* that family of greasy bastards had something to do with all this. But that was all speculation and intuition, what men like Charles Baumgartner liked to call hysteria, their favorite catch-all for women who made a fuss around here. Or, in Charlie's succinct words, a 'hysterical, do-nothing horse doctor with too much time on her hands and a bitch streak as long as the Mississippi'. Still, she had to wonder if the detailed monologue she'd just gone on was enough for Jessie to think Susannah was hysterical too.

"You know, I can arrange for you to get a bus ride home, get you back to... wherever you're from. Baumgartner spouted all that nonsense with the drugs, but he has no legal ground to keep you here. I wouldn't be offended if you wanted to leave this crazy place immediately," Susannah said.

She felt mildly ashamed at the exhilaration that suddenly coursed through her. The advent of this young woman, her bandmate's disappearance, they could be the catalysts that finally set into motion a proper investigation into the Langans. Susannah desperately wanted Jessie to stay but wouldn't stop her if she wanted to go home.

"You don't understand. I don't really have a home. Let's just say my upbringing was... chaotic. It wasn't until I joined Blasphemer that I'd finally found people who accepted me for who I was. The road is my home, as cliché as that sounds. But it just got destroyed by a couple of assholes, and now I have good reason to suspect they wrecked your home too, in a manner of speaking. What am I going to do? Go back to that shitty apartment I can't afford to live in by myself? Surrounded by Allen's records and his posters and all the stuff that reminds me of him? No, I'm staying. I'm making sure we find Lou *and* Allen because I don't think that sheriff really gives a shit if they're found or not. I just... I don't understand why. Why would these Langan people randomly start killing folks after their dad died, or disappeared, or whatever?"

That was the million-dollar question, wasn't it? *Why?* It was what kept Susannah up more nights than not. What caused her to float away during lovemaking with Harold, driving her to fake it just to get him off her so she could go back to it. Back to wondering and pontificating and theorizing. It was the question that had her taking more nightcaps from Harold's whiskey collection than was probably healthy. Often, she had to anesthetize her brain and muddle her thoughts just long enough to try to sleep.

"That's the thing I've been trying to figure out. Motive. I've known the Langans for years. We all sort of knew Virgil was cooking meth, but unfortunately, that's not uncommon up here. Other than that, they were just a poor, white trash family that kept to themselves and ran their automotive shop. Used to be a prominent mining family, but a few deals went bust. Fast forward half a decade, and now they are... what they are. People only started disappearing after Virgil did. Why?"

"Maybe they went crazy with grief, just sort of snapped and started killing people," Jessie said, stirring creamer into her coffee. Her eyes widened, then she pointed with her spoon. "But they didn't chop the cars. You said their dad cooked meth, right? Maybe they just... hell, I don't know. It's too planned out to be compulsive if it's every couple of months, like you said. And you said they never found the bodies. Like, *any* of them?"

Susannah nodded. "That's right. And there's only one place they didn't look..." The coffee went rancid in her stomach at the thought. Her poor, sweet Daniel rotting somewhere down in a cave. Susannah recalled how, in a frenzy, she'd begun touching everything he'd ever cherished. His lacrosse helmet. His AutoTrader magazines. Hoping for another brief flash of insight like with Vivian's car. But there was nothing.

"Are those caves really that dangerous? I mean, so long as you have some rope and guide markers to keep yourself on the right track..."

"You don't understand," Susannah said, remembering what her granddad had told her about the mines. He was an ordinance engineer for Doefield Mine #3, Carter's biggest mine and single source of employment for the whole county. *We blasted out so much dolomite, the entire plateau up here became like fine china. God help us if the New Madrid Fault ever throws another shit-kicker. Reckon damn near the whole town would fall into the earth.*

"The ground down there is unstable. You so much as slip and fall on your butt, you could bring down an entire section of cavern with you. It's not just a matter of getting lost, it's a matter of the earth itself waiting to eat you whole. Not only that..." Susannah debated telling the rest. The wild, fantastical side of her father's stories of the mines. "I guess there's some kind of gas down there that makes men hallucinate. A lot of them talked about seeing demons down in the main shafts. Monsters, imps, hearing screams coming from the caves during a full moon. They blamed it all on this Romani family that lived up in the hills and tried their hand at mining, said they had a member of the family who was a witch or some such. It got where Doefield had to shut down the mine because they couldn't find anyone willing to work it anymore. And that was before the EPA forced them out anyway... safety violations."

"Well, if there's even a chance those fu—freaking hillbillies took Lou down there, I'm putting on my spelunking hat and going after him."

Susannah glimpsed the fire in Jessie's eyes, and her heart ached for just a moment. She saw herself in those eyes, the young girl's unwavering tenacity making her feel braver than she was. *You're a fifty-three-year-old veterinarian with arthritis in one hip, let's not get ahead of ourselves.* Her phone vibrated in her pocket. It was the clinic. She'd been so caught up in this Langan business she had almost forgot she was scheduled to work today.

"Elizabeth? Crap, I'm so sorry, slept through my alarm. I'll be there soon, I just—" she began, but her intern cut her off. Something she never, *ever* did. The tension in the young girl's voice shot anxiety through her.

"Miss Paige, you need to get down here immediately. There's an emergency. It's the Gutweins. Their cattle." Elizabeth sounded like she was on the edge of a nervous breakdown.

"What about their cattle, honey?" Susannah's mind was doing a complete 180. Thoughts of insidious caverns and inbred meth dealers evaporated as professionalism took over.

"They got a few that survived, but they're all tore up. Just... get down here, *please.*" Something crashed in the background before the line went dead.

"What is it?" Jessie asked.

Susannah realized her anxiety must've shown on her face.

"Work emergency. Listen, I need to go. Make yourself at home, there's plenty to eat. If you feel up to it, you can go back in the study, look over everything I have. Maybe you'll see something I can't. Computer is in there too, if you want to use it." she said, slipping on her shoes and shoulder bag. Buckie, sensing Susannah's sudden franticness, stood up from his doggy bed. His snores had emanated softly from the corner during their conversation. Now, he whined and followed her around as she collected her things. She kneeled and gave him a quick kiss on the forehead. "If I'm not back by six, can you feed Buckie here?"

"Sure thing. After everything you've done for me, it's the least I can do," Jessie replied, scratching the dog behind his fluffy ears. Susannah used the distraction to make her way out the door, wondering what kind of mess she was about to walk into.

*The Gutweins only live ten minutes down the road from the Kurtz ranch.* She thought of the Kurtzs' slaughtered foal as she started the Explorer. There had been a marked increase in the number of livestock kill offs recently, hadn't there? Susannah shook her head. *Now* she was getting into conspiracy mode. She had to snap out of it. It sounded like a whirlwind waited for her down at the clinic.

"—and featuring country music star Heath Gunderson. That's this weekend at the Lordell County Fairgrounds. Come for the music, stay for the eclipse! I can tell you folks, Lordell is probably the best place in the whole county to see it. It's gonna be a good time, bring the kids and—"

Susannah switched the radio over to her gospel station and sped out of the driveway, kicking up gravel. There was a sensation of things falling into place now. Like when she had heard Jessie mention the name Roy for the first time. A firm feeling came over her that something terrible was about to befall them all. The fire in Jessie's eyes came to her again, and Susannah prayed she wouldn't have to endure this harrowing journey alone.

# CHAPTER 11

C HARLES NOTED THAT THE place had sure gone to shit since Virgil passed. The yard was a cluttered graveyard of scabrous, rust flecked cars and parts. Engine blocks and piles of scrap littered the property like carcasses in a killing field. The shack they called home looked like it'd aged thirty years in the two or so since he'd been out here. The only thing that looked new was their truck, a big Dodge 2500 with a four-inch lift, offroad tires, and tint that made looking inside impossible. Their pride and joy, that truck, and probably the thing that was going to get them in trouble. The sun was just setting by the time they'd pulled up; deep red rupturing over the hills as if the sky itself were hemorrhaging. The fading light glinted off the truck's blue paint job, the only thing on this entire piece of land that wasn't rust covered.

He found the brothers standing around in the driveway, shooting the shit, or appearing to. Baumgartner's bullshit detector, well-honed through years of being a county sheriff, was going off as he watched the two men trying way too hard to seem like they'd been in the middle of banal conversation. Roy shot the two lawmen a mildly annoyed glance as they got out of the cruiser. The big boy, Tate, looked at the ground and scuffed a boot in the dirt as if he'd just gotten caught pulling his pud and didn't want to admit it.

"Sheriff Baumgartner. Long time no see," Roy said as the officers closed the distance.

"Roy, Tate. How you boys been?" The sheriff looked at the truck as he spoke. It was parked in profile to him, but he thought he could see a bit of chrome rubbed off the front bumper. The brush guard in front looked dented, ever so slightly, like they'd rear-ended someone.

Or like maybe they'd tried to run someone off the road.

"Oh, you know, just trying to make an honest living. Working that garage. Changing oil and rotating tires, trying to get out from under Pa's shadow," Roy said.

"Is that so? No more of that *fine* Langan methamphetamine spreading like the plague over my county, huh?" Baumgartner asked with a smile.

"No... no, sir," Tate said.

"Well, that's good, cause y'all can't cook for shit." Baumgartner noticed Anderson giving him a perplexed look out of the corner of his eye, but he ignored it. "Listen, as much as I'd love to stop and chew the cud with you boys, I came out here to touch base. See, some folks got ran off the road about fifteen miles up yonder, by Route Y. Happened just last night." Baumgartner pointed east. He stared closely at Tate as he spoke. Roy took after his daddy when it came to being a snake in the grass, but the big one was a few pennies short of a paper dollar. If either of them were going to give themselves away, it would be Tate.

"Run off the road? Well, that's a *damn* shame, Sheriff. You know how these mountain roads are, though. Don't watch where you're going and—"

"No, Roy. Someone *ran* them off the road. Used a spike strip to make 'em flip. Pretty complex setup. The people who survived said it was a big ol' truck that did the job. Big ol' *loud* truck. Like that one sitting right there." Baumgartner nodded towards the Dodge.

"Well hell, we don't know nothing 'bout that, do we Tate? What time was this, Sheriff?" Roy asked, acting genuinely flummoxed.

"Close to midnight." Baumgartner's eyes never left Tate's down-turned face. The boy must've felt that iron gaze on him. His canned ham fists were shoved deep into his overall pockets, where they squirmed like two things alive and agitated. Roy kept his gaze on the two men though, arms calmly by his sides.

"That's the thing, sir. Me and Tate were at the shop late last night, had this damn Subaru, transmission just wouldn't budge. Took us two, plus Willy Colefield to get the damn thing out. Piece of shit imports. People need to buy American." Roy shook his head. "Didn't get home 'til... what, 2 am last night, huh, Tate?"

"Yeah... sounds 'bout right," Tate mumbled.

"We call this Willy fella right quick, he gonna confirm that?" Anderson piped up.

"Sheeeit, he oughta. He was under the damn thing with me, almost got his thumb taken off! It was gonna be the fuckin' GTO all over again. Wasn't gonna lose my other ball for that sumbitch," Roy laughed. Tate forced a chuckle that sounded as authentic as a Hollywood laugh track.

"You know, Sheriff, I was actually getting ready to call you," Roy said. His brother looked up at that, confused. Roy glanced back at him, a silent bit of communication passing between them. Tate blinked and nodded. "See, we got us some trespassers up here."

"Trespassers?" Baumgartner raised one eyebrow. He spat a brown stream of chaw a few feet in front of Tate who stared at it as if it were the most interesting thing he'd ever seen. "Go on."

"Yep, couple of ol' boys set up a goddamn trailer 'bout a mile back yonder." Roy hitched his thumb behind him. Baumgartner saw the thicket of white oak and dogwood surrounding the property. A narrow path bisected the trees, like a part in the Devil's hair. He knew where that trail led and did not want to go down it. "We think it might be a shake and bake operation. And we don't want that shit anywhere near us, do we, Tate?"

"No sir," Tate said robotically.

Anderson and Baumgartner exchanged glances.

"You telling me someone set up a *meth lab* on the property of the most well-known crank cookers this side of the Missouri River?" Baumgartner put his hands on his hips. He smelled bullshit, but he couldn't think of any reason the Langans would have to make up such a dumbass story. It basically gave him permission to go deeper into the guts of their property.

"Yessir, seen 'em coming and going all times of night. Hell, bet they're out there right now, cooking that shit up. Rumor has it my daddy left a bunch of cookin' caches throughout the woods here when he was runnin' crank. Reckon they found some an' started up." Roy shook his head with incredulity.

"And that ain't got *nothing* to do with you two?" the sheriff asked. Roy shook his head again, reached into the neck of his shirt. Baumgartner unclasped the clip on his holster in reflex. He watched as Roy brought out a thick silver crucifix hanging from his neck. The sheriff's hand didn't move from the walnut grip of his gun.

"No sir, me and Tate here, we found uhselves God. We're clean, Sheriff, I know that may be hard to believe, but we is," Roy insisted, walking towards the thicket. "Come on now, I'll show you where them bastards set up shop. Best get out there before it gets dark." He pointed towards the sky. It was fading from salmon pink to rose purple as the sun hid behind the foothills. Baumgartner swallowed, then looked over at Anderson.

"Go on, see what this dipshit is hollering about. Keep that gun out though, boy," he told Anderson. "I'm gonna have a chat with Tate here, while you all go investigate." He saw Tate's eyes flare wide for a moment before he swallowed, blinked, then went on staring down at the brown streak of dip spit on their driveway where the sheriff had deposited it.

Anderson nodded, proceeding forward. His Glock 19 was out, pointed at the ground, the barrel-mounted light clicked on.

"You go on ahead of me and don't try no funny business. I got me an itchy trigger finger," Anderson warned.

"What's the matter, boy?" the sheriff said. "You look like someone just shot your dog and pissed in your Cheerios." Tate continued to look everywhere that wasn't Baumgartner's eyes. It was just them now, and he hoped the Langan boy felt the heat on his neck. The sheriff continued staring at him.

"Nothin' sir, just tired is all. Like Roy said, we was up late last night, working on that car."

"Yeah... he says a lot, don't he?"

"I reckon."

"You know me and your daddy used to be pretty good friends. I remember when you all had that accident. GTO, wasn't it?"

"I, I reckon," Tate swallowed. Baumgartner could hear the click in his throat.

"Yeah, heavy sumbitch, that was before they started putting fiberglass and plastic bullshit in all these cars. Fuckin' thing was a two-ton torpedo of American muscle. Shame what happened. You remember anything of that day?"

"No sir. Just remember wakin' up in the hospital, my head all bandaged up. And Roy, he was gimp for a while." Tate's voice sounded shallow at the recollection.

"That's right. Ol' Roy ain't gonna be a daddy anytime soon, huh?" The sheriff laughed.

"Reckon not."

Baumgartner remembered the accident well. He'd just been sworn in as sheriff, and it was his job to interview Virgil to find out what happened. This was before their little deal had been made. He'd been showing the boys how to change the oil filter on the GTO, and the old man said that sumbitch had been on there tight. Took a lot of finagling, he'd said. Tate was directly under the car, while Roy was half out, the jack between his legs. According to Virgil, the jack slipped and part of the axle kissed Tate's head like a mother sending her child to bed. Though the doctors had managed to add a plate, rebuilding his skull, a studious observer could still see the slight indentation and a pale line of scar tissue from his left ear to the back of his head. Then there was Roy, whose pelvis had been crushed, his groin mangled. He was wheelchair bound for three years before he could walk again. Moves with an arthritic limp to this day.

It was unclear just how much of his manhood the doctors were able to save. Roy didn't talk about it much.

"Used to be, you'd ride with your daddy, back in the day when he'd meet up with me. Always his favorite son. You knew what was going on then, didn't you? Bet you helped your daddy cook that meth up. Shoulda paid more attention to his recipe. You all coulda had a good thing going. Reckon your memory problems prolly got in the way of that though, huh?" Baumgartner eased the pressure onto Tate, slowly bringing the pot to a boil.

"I don't want to be like my daddy. Not no more. I just wanna work on cars is all, sir." Tate scuffed a boot on the ground. Baumgartner was about to say something else, when a muffled crash came from inside the little tool shed on the edge of the property. Tate's head shot up, and he looked back towards it, blinking.

"The hell was that?" Baumgartner took a step towards the shed. He switched on his big Maglite, illuminating a horde of flies buzzing around the structure. A faint whiff of something foul came from that direction. His hand was once again on his gun.

"Oh, it's just uh… just the damn raccoons. We've got 'em bad this summer, sir. Roy ain't burning the garbage like he's supposed to." Tate shuffled towards the shed, putting his ample bulk between the sheriff and the small wooden building.

"The fuck kinda garbage you got in there? Smells like a goddamn heap of twice baked cow patties or something." The sheriff crinkled his nose. Indeed, he knew the smell of human shit. He'd had to do his fair share of wellness checks on older folks who lived way out in the hills, alone. People who'd died in their trailers and sat for days in their own mess before someone thought to go check on them. The miasma radiating from the shed had the distinct, sulfurous quality of rot to it.

"Oh, fish guts… and stuff. W-we caught us a heap of trout on the Jack's Fork a few days ago. Forgot to burn the innards after we cleaned 'em." Tate was wiping at the sweat that dotted his large forehead.

"Well, why don't I help you get rid of them 'coons real quick? Sounds like they're still inside. Least I can do, bothering you all this late." The sheriff took another step towards the shed where the odor grew stronger. Yes, definitely human shit, not fish guts.

"No, we oughta not. Think they got the rabies. They been acting all crazy. You don't wanna mess with them, Sheriff." It sure was muggy out, but poor Tate looked like a two-dollar whore in a Catholic confessional. Baumgartner focused the Maglite on the boy, his round face strained and glistening.

"Tate, look at me, boy. I said *look at me.*" Baumgartner's voice took on that well-trained authoritarian hardness. Tate squinted into the light. "I need you to start telling me the truth. Right now. You and your brother are about to be in an entire world of shit, but I know Roy. He's the schemer, not you. I know you got your brains scrambled, but I also know he uses you. You be honest with me, and I'll remember that when the Judge is roasting you like a pig on a spit. What's in the shed, Tate?"

Tate's upper lip trembled; his scraggly blonde mustache plastered to his teeth. He opened his mouth and was about to say something when a high-pitched whistle came from the woods. Two shrill ululations, like a signal of some sort.

"Now what the fuck was *that*?" A second later, there was a commotion. Branches breaking far off, then a sharp, familiar sound. The unmistakable *crack* of Anderson's pistol firing, from deep behind the trees. Once—then after a few seconds' pause, three more shots in quick succession. Distant shouting soon followed.

Baumgartner whipped out his gun, a flat-black Colt Python. An antique compared to the standard issue Glock, but it was his daddy's gun. It didn't jam and the walnut grip fit his hand like he was born holding it. Plus, its size had an authoritative power that made people stop what they were doing. The enormous bore .357 barrel had a habit of paralyzing even the surliest meth head. Tate's eyes grew to the size of boiled eggs at the sight of the large black barrel trained on him.

Charles pinned the flashlight with his armpit and reached for the radio with his free hand. "Anderson, report!"

The radio remained silent. "Deputy Anderson, goddamnit!" he yelled into the radio. Still nothing, but he could hear bodies moving fast through dense woods, the crack and rustle of limbs and leaves being trampled, coming towards them. "Sonofabitch, don't you move boy, or I swear to God I'll ventilate what little brains you got left in that noggin," he told Tate, who froze with his hands up. Baumgartner plunged into the dense woods, his asshole puckered tight with the anticipation of conflict.

Limbs and switches tugged at him as he ran through the forest, the foliage so dense it was like swimming through molasses. Baumgartner shouted for Anderson again, stopped to listen for the trampling of sticks and leaves. He tried to look everywhere at once as the bugs made kamikaze dives into his flashlight. Dozens of limbs and branches shot fractal shadows across the verdant foliage in the wavering glow. Sweat stung his eyes, but he kept them open, looking for his deputy.

"Sheriff!" a weak, gurgling voice cried out. Charles whipped the light around to his right, saw the flash of a tan uniform, a bright smear of red. Anderson raced towards him, then froze, a hand to his neck. Blood seeped out between his fingers at a steady pace. Anderson's eyes rolled wild, feral. "Bit... me. Fuckin' *bit* me! Bit me, Sheriff!" His voice was ragged from the hole in his neck.

Baumgartner wanted to ask, *what, what in God's name fucking bit you?* And for a split second, he thought of Tate and the rabid raccoons. He almost laughed but choked it back and wrapped a steadying arm around Anderson.

"Come on, boy, walk with me now." Baumgartner was trying to half-carry him along, wishing he hadn't given up the weights. In high school, he could deadlift four hundred pounds easy. Could've fireman-carried Anderson to the car, like a real hero, but he knew trying that now would cause a slipped disc and a hernia at the very least. If it wasn't for the meth, he'd be as big as Tate. Together, they half-shambled back towards the Langan property. Baumgartner could feel and smell Anderson's life leaking out of him.

Tate stood right where Charles left him, his eyes bulging as he saw Anderson, who had a sheen of blood coating the left side of his body. The big man's frame did not move, but his head swiveled like a barn owl. He trailed the two officers back to the cruiser where Baumgartner ripped off his uniform top and held it to Anderson's throat.

"Just like that, keep pressure on it for me." Baumgartner put his hand over Anderson's, helping him apply pressure. The deputy looked at him hard for a moment. When their eyes met, the fear Baumgartner saw in the man's gaze made frost form in the base of his spine and work its way up his neck.

"He bit me, the crazy sumbitch bit me, he—" Anderson was rambling, but Baumgartner ignored him, reaching across the seat to his radio. He hated calling in an emergency over the CB like this, but he knew without looking at his phone there would be zero bars out here. He called in Dolvin County dispatch because they were the closest, but even then, there was no guarantee of when the EMTs would get there.

"I need Medical to 141 Oak Hill Drive, Carter Township. We got an officer down, serious injuries."

The dispatcher calmly informed him medical transport would take at least thirty minutes. There'd been a four-car pile-up on I-55, and the state boys had called all surrounding counties to help.

"GODDAMNIT! What about air evac?".

Same story. The one AirMed helicopter that serviced the county was flying towards Saint Louis as they spoke to take one driver to the trauma ward.

Baumgartner flung the CB radio hard against the dash. His body trembled with indecision before he realized it would take him at most twenty minutes to drive to Dolvin himself, maybe a little less if he *really* gunned it. Tate stood frozen in the Charger's headlights, only blinking when Baumgartner clicked them to hi-beams and revved the engine. These goddamn brothers were to blame for all this, and he didn't have time to hunt Roy down in those woods. Hell, that's probably what Roy wanted all along, get them separated, get them lost out there.

He got out and leveled his gun at Tate.

"Get your ass in here, boy, you're coming with me!" Tate didn't move for a second, shock making his vacuous gaze even more stupid looking.

Baumgartner drew back the hammer on the Python, the click loud enough to sound over the hum of the idling V8. "Did I stutter?" Tate blinked like someone had just spat in his face before running towards the Charger. Charles swung open the back door, then slammed it behind Tate after he'd shoved his bulk into the back of the cruiser.

With everyone in, the sheriff peeled out of the driveway, turning on his jackpot lights. The Charger burst onto the highway and roared up to eighty, then ninety.

"What was it, Anderson? Talk to me, son." Baumgartner's eyes never left the road as he spoke.

"Was... was a man... Fucking, fucking monster. Man..." The deputy's voice grew weaker. The sheriff took his eyes off the road to nudge Anderson.

"Hey! Don't you go to sleep on me, you sumbitch! Keep them eyes open, now." His hands slipped on the bloody steering wheel. The Charger fishtailed sickeningly on the road before he corrected it.

"Am I.... am I under arrest, Sh—" Tate began from the back seat.

"You're gonna be *dead* if you don't keep your fuckin' fat mouth shut!" Charles's eyes shot to the rearview mirror. "You knew what would get him, didn't you? Ain't no fuckin' raccoons out there. You and Roy planned this, you goddamned sons of bitches." Their world became a winding blur of green and gray, the blacktop snaking away underneath them, the souped-up V8 roaring.

A gurgling croak sounded from the passenger seat. Anderson slumped over, his hand falling away from the ragged hole in his throat. Blood poured freely down his shoulder and dripped onto the center console of the Charger.

"FUCK!" For the first time since he was a boy, Baumgartner felt genuine panic. He might've literally put the pedal to the metal on a straightaway of Route Y, if he hadn't seen the illuminated white sign. *CARTER 24-HOUR ANIMAL CLINIC.*

Anderson would be dead by the time he got to Dolvin. The man had already lost several pints of blood. The sheriff knew these folks weren't actual doctors, but surely they had to have *something* there to close a gaping flesh wound. The Charger's tires squealed like a thing tortured as he cut hard to the left. Baumgartner over-corrected. The vehicle drifted into the square patch of gravel parking lot, almost clipping Susannah Paige's Explorer.

# Chapter 12

IN ALL HER YEARS of running the vet clinic, Susannah had never seen so much carnage. The minute she pulled into the parking lot and saw the large cattle trailer hitched to the Gutweins' truck she knew she was in for a nightmare. She hopped out of the Explorer and jogged past the trailer, the once silver interior spattered with blood and dripping red onto the gravel parking lot. Susannah didn't bother going through the front. Instead, she ran around to the side where they had the large, prefabricated shelter meant to house up to six livestock-sized animals.

All she had to do was follow the smell of blood and the pungent tang of ruptured intestines. She came around the corner to find Elizabeth kneeling down next to a hurt cow. James Thomas and another vet worker, Sierra Davidson, helped the Gutweins with another animal that was thrashing violently, one stall over. The first cow was lying on its side, several tubes coming from its snout, kicking its hooves out sporadically while Elizabeth was hunched over the animal. The bewildered girl's arms were covered up to the elbow in blood, her red hair hanging in messy strands from an unraveling bun. She was doing her best to suture up a large wound in the cow's abdomen that exposed the stomach cavity. Elizabeth cried out in frustration as one loop of intestine squirmed out, popping the sutures.

Elizabeth looked up when she saw her mentor. "Oh, thank the Lord."

Without a word, Susannah crouched next to her, grabbed a wide-barrel syringe of irrigation saline, and began rinsing the intestines of dirt and waste before working them slowly back into the hot cavity of its body. She heard the frenetic sounds of hooves drumming against the aluminum walls, the agonized lowing of a bull in great distress, but these quickly faded away. Susannah shuddered violently as a flash slammed her senses.

Teeth. Unlike any animal she'd ever seen before. Screeching whose genus could not be identified by sound. Sheer animal terror from the cow. It was the first time she'd ever gotten a flash from an animal.

Susannah snapped out of it, realizing Elizabeth was looking at her in panic.

"Honey, didn't you try and anesthetize these—"

"We tried, Miss Paige, but it wouldn't take!" Elizabeth said, almost in tears as she worked re-suturing the ragged flaps of skin. Susannah felt like she was handling a bucketful of oily snakes as she struggled to keep the cow's plumbing in long enough for the girl to close the wound. Once she could take her hands out, she would pinch the remaining flesh shut while Elizabeth tied the last stitches.

"Wouldn't take? What—"

A woman cried out a few feet away, followed by a loud crash. The cow the others were trying to mend planted a huge hoof into the aluminum divider, denting it an inch from Susannah's head.

"We gave this one two full epidurals of lidocaine-ketamine, and she's still kicking. I don't know what's happening, Miss Paige, it doesn't make sense!" Elizabeth said. *She's just about to reach her breaking point*, Susannah thought. She must've misheard the girl. Two full L/K epidurals were enough to put a one-ton elephant into a coma, let alone a six-hundred-pound Holstein. Susannah moved around the legs to face the animal. Its eyes were half-lidded, blood-tinged snot and drool leaking from its flared nostrils and gaping mouth. The old girl was digging her hooves lazily into gravel, carving deep furrows in the earth. She wasn't as feisty as the one next door, even so, she shouldn't be feisty *at all.*

Susannah ran over to the next stall and found Miss Gutwein, a heavy-set woman in her fifties, planted on her butt. Her husband cradled one of her legs delicately, and Susannah asked if they thought it was broken.

"I don't know, goddamnit, I just know it hurts!" Janice Gutwein yelled. James and Sierra stood some five feet back from the animal, who was tangled up in a surgery harness.

"What in heaven's name happened to these cows?" Susannah tried to keep her composure, but good God, *this* was not what she needed right now.

"We don't know. Got up this morning just before dawn to go fill the troughs and heard them screaming. Went to go get Larry, and *this* half-drunk dipshit comes running with his Bushmaster. I didn't see anything 'cept some shapes moving off towards the woods, but Larry here... Jesus, honey, help me up!" Janice was smacking her husband in the shoulder. Susannah got on the other side and helped hoist her to a standing position. "Think he just bruised it, but Lord *almighty,* it hurts." Janice hiked up her dress to show the bright purple beginnings of a bruised hoof print on her upper thigh.

"I swear, it was a goddamn chupacabra or something. Weren't no coyote or puma," Larry said. Susannah could smell the 'shine and sweat coming through his pores, clocked his bloodshot eyes.

"Ain't no goddamn chupacabras up here, Larry. This ain't fuckin' *Mexico,* you worthless drunk," Janice cried. The cow continued to buck and snort, more innards spilling from the thing as it thrashed, its gaping stomach wound growing in size the more it moved.

"Miss Paige, I swear, we hit the vein right and everything. These cows got enough anesthesia to knock out an entire herd. I don't know what's going on." Sierra was holding up an empty syringe to corroborate her claim, chest heaving.

"I'm telling you, it was something on two feet! Ran off like a monkey, it did," Larry said. Susannah went over to the next stall and saw one animal laying limp, a freshly deposited cow patty lazily oozing from its behind.

"Looks like you dosed this one right, at least." Susannah was already running back towards the clinic to get more lidocaine.

"No... That one just... died," Elizabeth said.

Mind reeling, Susannah raced back with three large syringes of their strongest anesthesia. She was violating several protocols, but they were far past protocol at this point. The Gutweins continued arguing about what mutilated their animals, while the three vet techs stood around looking helpless and confused. Susannah bit the cap off one syringe as she approached the first cow, stuck a finger to its neck, feeling the weak pulse of its carotid. She jammed the needle and depressed all 200 CCs of tranquilizer into the poor thing's blood stream with both hands. As she pressed down the plunger, the hooves slowed their determined digging. A low, gurgling mewl escaped from the cow before it finally stilled.

The next one was trickier, all caught up in the harness, standing on its back hooves. It thrashed around like a bull-sized marionette with an epileptic puppeteer. The poor thing trampled its own innards, frothing blood and looking around crazily. Elizabeth was vomiting a few stalls over, unable to bear witness to the tragic sight.

Susannah shook her head in defeat, handed Sierra the syringes, and ran off to her car.

"Hey, where are you goin'?" Larry bellowed, not wanting to be left alone with an enraged wife and the dregs of his ailing cattle.

It took her less than a minute to run to her car and come back, a Marlin .22lr in her hands. This was the part of the job she dreaded, but long ago she'd learned the concept of ethics when it came to her work. She only used the gun for emergencies, when the animal was an imminent danger to those around it, or if it was on the loose and had a communicable disease. Susannah had learned to recognize a deep, instinctual feeling, a sudden pang in her gut, that told her when an animal was simply too far gone to be saved and keeping it alive any longer would only serve to prolong its suffering. She'd gotten that pang just now.

Susannah walked back in the stall, sighted the barrel on the creature in the harness, and waited for its head to come to a stop.

"The hell you doin'? That's a four thousand dollar—"

The small-caliber rifle popped like a firecracker, cutting off Janice Gutwein with a cracking *snap*. Susannah was a damn good shot after years of having Harold take her down to the range and had planted a .22 round right between the cow's eyes. "Your four grand cow would have died of sepsis by the time I pushed her guts back... in..." Susannah trailed off. There should've been a brief, violent spasm, followed by a slackening of the whole body.

The spasm came with a vengeance, hurling the creature's entire body against the stall wall with a force that caused the entire shelter to shudder. Blood spurted from its forehead, convincing Susannah that the skull wasn't just grazed. How was it still *moving*? She'd chosen the .22 for its neatness when it came to doing the job, leaving a nice little two-centimeter entry wound. But it hadn't been enough. The cow let out an enraged bellow. Good Lord, the sound, the sight. Susannah wanted it to be over, but it just went on struggling, a one-act circus show from Hell as it continued to slip and dance on its own inner plumbing.

"Stop! Just make it stop!" Elizabeth's voice was barely heard over the chaotic sounds coming from the surgery harness.

Susannah came to a sudden realization. Hot lava coursed through her bowels. She raised the gun to the cow's bobbing head and emptied the rest of the seven-shot magazine into the thing's skull, desperate for this madness to end. By the time the rifle's trigger clicked empty, its head was a ruin of exposed bone and gristle. Finally, like a car running on fumes, the creature's movements slowed to a stop, the weight of its body gently swaying in the harness, bloody foam dripping lazily from its mouth.

"You just... you just killed my—" Larry began, but Susannah was moving fast, ignoring them.

"Elizabeth, Sierra, James, wash your hands, immediately. Either of you get blood on you?" she snapped at the Gutwein's, both of whom looked perplexed, shocked. Besides the shiner on Janice's thigh, they both looked clean. She quickly moved from them, shepherding her small crew towards the cleaning stations in the clinic, her heart thundering in her chest.

"What is it, Miss Paige?" James asked as they each went to one of the sinks, dousing their arms and legs in medical grade disinfectant.

"We need to get a blood sample from each cow and send it off to Mizzou or Wash-U immediately. Don't wanna scare anyone, but it may be something like rabies." Susannah worked a dense, pink-tinged lather up to her forearms. She scrubbed hard, the industrial-strength paste making her skin tighten.

"Oh, Jesus... oh shit, man. Rabies?" James said. In that moment, the bright-faced college boy seemed to age a decade with fright, scrubbing frantically at his arms.

"Look for any abrasions or nicks on your skin when you're done, even if it's just a small paper cut. Let me get the Gutweins squared away, and I'll call the hospital about getting rabies shots ready." Susannah rinsed herself off. She tried not to think about the unpleasant possibilities awaiting them. These poor college kids were simply doing their best to earn school credits.

"Well hell, can I take it home and process it? Use the meat, at least?" Larry pointed at one of the ruined cows.

"No, I would strongly advise against that. These cows were acting in a way I haven't seen before, and that foam... I think whatever it was that attacked your cattle may have been rabid. That, or some mutation of mad cow disease," Susannah said.

"Rabid? But they just got bit this morning. That shit takes weeks to get 'em acting all crazy." Janice's eyes shone more with fear than doubt.

"I know, I just... I don't know what else it could be. Something was *very* wrong with your cattle, Mrs. Gutwein, that's all I know."

"Listen, I'm telling you what I saw. I know I hit the bottle too much, but that don't mean I was hallucinatin'. They ran on *two* legs, like men." Larry pantomimed an awkward scuttling run.

"Alright, Larry." Susannah sighed, too tired to argue with the drunk. She remembered the image that had come into her mind, those teeth. "That doesn't change what's happened here. Listen, I'll waive my normal fee if you'll lend me your front-loader so I can deliver this thing to the crematorium after the head is removed for testing. We need to keep these two separated, though, move 'em all the way down to the end stalls," Susannah said, hitching her thumb towards the small concrete building off to the side of the clinic. She had built the crematorium out of sight of the main building, with its brutalist architectural style. The exposed concrete and the black soot pipe chimney was at odds with the cheery "your animal is safe here" atmosphere Susannah hoped to cultivate.

"Oh, what... help you do your *goddamn* job after you just slaughtered one of my goddamn cows? Yeah, sure." Janice shook her head. In that moment, Susannah could've strangled her. Of all her clients, the Gutweins were her least favorite. For one thing, she was almost positive they ran a gelding mill on their property, and for another, she was pretty sure Janice beat on her husband. He was a foolish old lush, but that just wasn't right. Didn't help that the big woman liked to take the Lord's name in vain as often as a child asked for candy.

"Come on, Janice, there's nothing else to do about it. We may as well help." Larry was pulling her along.

The two of them drove off, the trailer leaving a dark trail of blood on the drive and highway behind them. Susannah knew it would take them an hour or two to swap out and bring the front-loader down, so she devoted the time to gathering herself. She directed Sierra and Elizabeth to collect blood cultures from the two unconscious cattle, but only after donning full biohazard gear.

As she waited, she sat in one corner of the clinic, massaging her temples. Now more than ever, she wished Harold was here, holding her in those tree-trunk arms of his, the smell of Old Spice and fresh perspiration calming her. She sent him a text, knowing he was probably on a part of the river with no cell signal, and told him to call her next chance he got. His soothing baritone voice had gotten her through many hardships. She needed to be comforted. He may have been a man hiding behind a stern veneer of the rural stoic ideal, but regardless of his poker-faced nature, he knew how to comfort her. He knew how to love her.

By the time the Gutweins had rolled up with their front-loader, the sky had phased from bruised peach to cherry, the sun buttering the foothills to the south, and finally to deep red that eventually faded to a dark black veil as night fully claimed the valley.

They had loaded the dead cow into the bucket, and Janice brushed past to climb behind the wheel. She kicked it into life, turning the tires towards the crematorium. Larry reached up to hoist himself into the other seat, then stopped dead and pointed past Susannah.

"The hell?" he said.

All three of them looked towards the highway and saw the red and blue swirl of police lights rocketing towards them. Then, with a screech of tires, the cruiser skidded to the left, kicking up a wall of gravel dust as it flew into the parking lot sideways. When the roof lights clicked off and the cloud fell away, the only spots of color to be seen on the vehicle were dark red handprints streaked across the passenger side window.

Susannah surprised herself when she saw who got out of the Charger. A word slipped out of her mouth she hadn't said since she was a teenager.

"You've gotta be fucking kidding me."

# Chapter 13

B AUMGARTNER WAS OUT OF the car and making his way around to the other side before he could see clearly, sweat stinging his eyes as it poured down his face. Ignoring the burning, he whipped open the door to the back seat.

"Help me with him, you goddamn water buffalo!" he shouted at Tate, who was struggling to squeeze out of the car. The sheriff moved to the passenger door and was pulling the unconscious Anderson out by the time Tate had extricated himself. Together, they hauled the limp, blood-caked rag doll towards the waiting crowd of people.

Baumgartner stopped when he saw the Gutweins, a couple he'd had to sort out more than once in the domestic dispute department over the years, and his old thorn Susannah, looking stricken, maybe even shell-shocked. He stared at the various red smears leading from the back of the building. A whiff of something he caught on the high wind almost made him forget what he was there for. The place smelled like a slaughterhouse.

"Sheriff?" What in God's name—"

"This man needs help, Suze. Please, bury the hatchet just this once, and get this man closed up," he said, almost panting.

"Charles, I'm a veterinarian! This man needs a *hospital*!" Susannah nearly screamed, shocked by the extent of the damage. Baumgartner shifted his grip, turning Anderson towards him. His deputy was paler than a winter crappie and dark arterial blood continued to seep below his slack-jawed face.

"Yeah, well, Dolvin is fifteen minutes away, and Anderson needs help *now*. Can't you just... I don't know, sew him up or something?" Baumgartner was close to begging.

Susannah pulled a glove from her back pocket, snapped it on, and reached out to feel the man's cheek. She stretched it back to press a finger against an exposed bit of gum, then put a bare one under his nostrils. "Capillary refill is bad, thready pulse... he's barely breathing." The deputy shivered violently, then muttered something.

"What was that, buddy?" Baumgartner asked, not realizing how affectionate his voice had gotten, like he really cared for this man. He supposed he did.

"He's going into shock. Jesus Christ, just... come on." Susannah threw open the doors to her clinic.

Baumgartner followed, his prisoner helping transport the barely conscious Anderson into the building. Tate's head craned towards the discarded biohazard suits as they walked in, muttering something under his breath. The sheriff couldn't decipher it and he didn't care. They hauled Anderson's limp body onto a metal operating table like a sack of wet goose down.

"Give me some space. Charles, you keep trying the air evac. I can try and get him stabilized, but I'm telling you, this man needs an actual *hospital*." Susannah's voice was tremulous but firm as she flew around the clinic, grabbing gauze, various bottles filled with antiseptics, and other stuff the sheriff didn't recognize. He obeyed, calling the dispatch extension from his phone, requesting an update from County. Same bullshit as earlier.

Baumgartner watched Susannah wince at the throat wound, his own stomach sick at the sight of it. It was worse than he had realized, seeing it fully exposed under the harsh clinic lights. His deputy's neck had been reduced to ragged flaps of gristle, black lines of corruption curling over the edges, spreading onto his chest and shoulders like some form of blood poisoning. *Jesus Christ, what the hell did that to him?*

"Did you see what got him, Sheriff?" Larry Gutwein's voice behind him made Baumgartner flinch as if he'd been struck. He had been so focused on the sight of Anderson's wound, he almost shit himself, having forgotten all about the others in the clinic with him.

"What? I... no, I didn't," he said with irritation, taking a step away from Gutwein, who had ambled up uncomfortably close to him and smelled like a whiskey-soaked ash tray.

"What happened to him? What'd y'all—"

"Police business, Larry, now go *fuck off* somewhere!" Baumgartner snapped, his nerves wrung tighter than bridge cables. The last thing he wanted to do was deal with *this* pathetic drunk. Sorry excuse for a man couldn't even keep his damn wife in line.

"Come on, let's get out of this nuthouse." Janice dragged her husband away by the arm. They had only gotten a few steps when a surprised gasp came from the table.

Susannah had backed away from the operating table slightly, penlight in hand. She'd been in the middle of applying what triage she could, starting by examining the pupils in Anderson's eyes. A semi-translucent pink lake surrounded his head where she'd flushed the wound with antiseptic. Susannah moved to wrap his throat in gauze when the man hitched up violently, then stilled once more. Baumgartner saw the chest had become flat... unmoving. The eyes had an almost serene peace to them.

"Anderson?" he asked.

"I think that might've been a... a death spasm," Susannah's voice was flat. She put two fingers to the portion of his throat not flayed open, and for a long moment she stood like that, occasionally moving the fingers around, looking for a pulse. Everyone in the room froze, the Gutweins included, all of them staring at the table and waiting.

Eventually, Susannah sighed and shook her head.

"Do you know if this man was of the faith, Charles? Maybe I can say a word or two," she asked softly, from over her shoulder.

"I-I-I don't know," Baumgartner stared down at the ground, ashamed. He should know such things.

A small voice piped up from the corner of the clinic. "He... He ain't dead."

They all turned to Tate, his enormous hands once again burying themselves in his overalls. He had said it plainly, as a matter of fact, not as someone in the throes of bereavement, denying they'd lost their loved one.

"What'd you say?" Baumgartner asked, but another small gasp drew his attention back to the table.

Susannah had her large silver crucifix necklace out, holding it in one hand. In the other, she reverently made the sign of the cross, moving her lips in prayer. She stopped in the middle of the ritual as the body began to twitch. Minutely at first, little finger twitches here and there, but the eyes remained opened and staring, the unbreathing mouth agape. She slowly leaned over, Charles assumed she was listening for sounds of respiration, the cross dangling from her fist. When Susannah put her ear to Anderson's mouth, the necklace came to rest on the body's pale arm.

There came a sound of bacon fat spitting in a hot skillet. Susannah was thrown back into Baumgartner, the force almost knocking him off his feet. The rancid sizzling had stopped, replaced by something from deep within the man's ruined throat, like the hiss of an alligator.

Baumgartner heard a childlike whimper from somewhere far away as Anderson shot up from the table, his head darting around wildly.

"He ain't dead," Tate repeated softly. Anderson's twitching, jerking head swiveled in his direction.

"You... y-you fucking..." Anderson said through gritted teeth, his voice as rough as 60-grit sandpaper. He raised his arm, the one brushed by the crucifix, and stared at the blackened, bubbling spot on his flesh. "You... fucking BITCH!" he roared, and suddenly he was right in front of Susannah. Something had changed in the man's eyes. It wasn't the placid, easy-going gaze that Baumgartner knew, the one that made him so approachable compared to the sheriff. There was an icy hardness now, something feral, like a puma stuck in a trap, ready to chew its own leg off to be free.

Baumgartner didn't even realize he was raising his gun until it appeared in his hand. Muscle memory and years of training forcing his body to do what his conscious mind could not. The revolver hung, heavy and final.

Susannah flinched. The deputy whipped his head forward like a viper, then recoiled almost as instantly. She had thrust out the crucifix before her, trembling so badly she almost dropped it, then clutched it against her bosom.

"Anderson... what's going on, fella? You look a mite peaked. Talk to me." Baumgartner trained the barrel on Anderson, in disbelief that he'd pointed his weapon towards his own deputy. Even entertaining the thought of shooting a brother officer violated his very core of being. It was one of the few principles he had left.

Anderson hadn't noticed the gun. He was fixated on the crucifix. The big cross seemed to glow double in those murderous eyes of his.

"He's like Daddy now," Tate blubbered.

Baumgartner geared up for his deputy to lash out at Susannah again, but Anderson whirled towards the sound instead. He moved with impossible speed. Baumgartner reeled, gun barrel swiveling, before drawing a bead on him again. Anderson had *leaped* across the room, snarling like a goddamn tiger. Landed in a crouch. In another bounding stride, he slammed into Tate like a leopard on a gazelle. Anderson taking on a man nearly twice his size should've seen his efforts easily rebuffed. But somehow, the half-dead man had bowled Tate over onto his back. It was like watching a child kick over a sandcastle.

A high, girlish squeal rose out of Tate's mouth as the deputy clamped down hard. All Baumgartner could do was watch.

"NO! I DON'T WANNA BE LIKE DADDY, I DON'T WAN-NA—" Anderson's mouth locked on the tree trunk of Tate's forearm. The big man thrashed around to no avail.

Baumgartner moved on reflex, his mind replaying the memory of a pit bull they'd had to put down the summer before. Its owner, a piece of shit meth head who'd been working on turning it into a fighting dog, had kicked it one too many times. The dog snapped, latching onto the owner's ankle, its jaws locked against splintered bone, until death finally released it.

Baumgartner was unaware of his own actions as he closed in on Anderson. The barrel of the Python wavered in his attempt to follow the thrashing bodies. "God help me," the lawman's plea so small and quiet that only he could hear it. He felt his thumb peel back the hammer, his finger applying pressure to the trigger.

The gun screamed like a cannon blast, the acoustics of the clinic amplifying the report. Anderson jerked hard. A corona of blood splattered Pollock-esque against a laminated poster for heartworm medication.

The shot blew away a good portion of Anderson's right buttock. Bits of his uniform trousers floated in the air as the bullet tore into both flesh and fabric. Anderson shot his head up, cheeks and lips bathed in red, and sneered at Baumgartner with what the sheriff swore was casual annoyance. Like he had only clapped him in the back of the head instead of firing a hollow point into his ass. The sheriff fired again, feeling a piece of his mind tear away along with Anderson's left shoulder. Anderson whirled like he'd just taken a haymaker to the jaw. He stumbled but did not drop. Instead, he half ran, half loped out the double doors of the clinic, leaving behind a thick blood trail. Baumgartner was too shocked to take another shot.

"*I don't wanna be like my daddy I don't wanna be like my daddy I don't—*" Tate rolled on his back like a stuck turtle. He clutched the meat of his forearm, blood gushing around his thick fingers.

"I... I don't understand," Susannah said, bewildered, as she stared down at the crucifix rising and falling on her chest. She wasn't the only one breathing with ragged desperation.

Sheriff Baumgartner kicked a rogue IV caddy out of his way and strode past Mrs. Gutwein and her cowering husband, both of them gripping their mouths in shock. Just beyond them, Tate rocked on the ground, continuing to bawl. The sheriff knelt down and pressed the still-smoking barrel of the gun to his sweat-slicked forehead.

"Start talking, boy. You better start talking right goddamn now, or so help me God—" His thumb worked the hammer. Baumgartner chambered the third round, looking down the barrel into Tate's blubbering face. The emphatic *click* underlined the promise to his higher power.

# Chapter 14

J ESSIE SAT IN THE back of her benefactor's house, poring over the historical texts Susannah had piled away in her office. An archived article detailing various Superfund sites throughout the United States glowed on a nearby computer screen. Carter was on that list. Several other browser tabs covered local history and lore, particularly the "haunted cave" phenomenon surrounding Doefield Mine tract, and an apparent cave-in that happened in the 1950s, claiming the lives of some thirty men.

Prior to falling into the information vortex, she'd opened the computer to take care of what little business she could. She despised social media and generally left band marketing and promoting to Allen, who practically *lived* online. But now he was dead, Geoff was in convalescence at some podunk-ass hospital, Lou was MIA, and so, there was only her. It felt surreal, logging into this fake digital world to tell their meager, die-hard pool of fans that they would not be attending the show at the House of Blues tonight because of "unforeseen circumstances." As though it were nothing more than the van breaking down.

She emailed their tour manager Andy Samuels, who would no doubt be shitting bricks, wondering where they were. It was an archaic correspondence in this day and age of instant messaging, but she had no other means with which to contact him. She laughed looking over the wall of text. No, too absurd. He'd think she was back on pills or something. Instead, she gave an extremely abbreviated version of events, detailing a bad wreck with the van and that half the band was in the hospital. Enough for him to know they were out of the tour *completely*.

How badly she wanted all this to be just a horrible dream, one of those weird, vivid indica-induced nightmares. She wanted to be on stage. She wanted to be in the moment with her boys, beating the shit out of her drums and getting lost in the sea of aural chaos. Instead, she was in a quaint little ranch house in the middle of the woods, staring at the makings of a Netflix miniseries-worthy murder conspiracy.

Her mind once again came back to that strange moment in the void, between death and life. That aura. The pulling, like some terrible magnet. There was no tunnel of light, no life flashing before her eyes. Just darkness. The red cloud, which despite its benign appearance, had exuded a terrible insidiousness that even now, in the comfort of this country home, made Jessie break out in a cold sweat at the thought of it.

Predatory. Yes, that was the word she was looking for. The red cloud was predatory. It was hungry. It wanted to consume her essence, her very soul. But Susannah had come along, had imparted something within her. Now Jessie felt different somehow, in some fundamental, but unexplainable way.

Feeling restless but aching like she'd gotten hit by a freight train, Jessie decided to search through Susannah's medicine cabinet. She needed something a little stronger than the ibuprofen the kind lady had given her. Jessie made a point not to look at her battered face in the mirror, with those split lips and one eye swollen and purple. Jessie felt bad going through the woman's things after all she'd done, but she doubted the woman would miss a pill or two. She used to be a pill head, yes, during her early days on the road. The anxieties of touring stacked on the pressures of performing, along with her lingering mental baggage from a troubled childhood... her need was beyond the mental anesthetizing of weed as a remedy.

Oxys and hydros with a whiskey chaser were her usual poisons. She had known too many fellow musicians who'd died of heroin to ever touch that stuff. After about four years of increasingly volatile abuse, Jessie had gotten a wake-up call. One night, Lou had found her almost pulling a Janis Joplin in the van's floorboard, passed out and choking on her own vomit. No red cloud then, no darkness, just a faint sense of unawareness, of oblivion. Now, she mostly stuck to skunk, with the occasional beer or two. But she was hurting now, and for once, she wanted an opiate for its intended analgesic purposes.

She found what she was looking for, an expired bottle of 15 milligram Percocet. There were ten left out of a prescription of twelve. Susannah was probably the teetotaler type, only taking the pills when the pain absolutely necessitated it. *Excuse me for not being that disciplined*, Jessie thought. A pang of shame coursed through her, feeling sixteen again and rifling through her foster parents' stash of pharmaceuticals. Jessie took out two of the white pills, put the bottle back exactly as she'd found it, and walked into the kitchen.

Buckie watched curiously as she prepared her little cocktail. Using a butter knife, Jessie ground the pills into a fine powder and mixed it into the remainder of her coffee, wincing at the bitter, chalky aftertaste. With that done, she stared out the small kitchen window. Susannah probably stared out of it on many mornings, a verdant landscape of trees and a small pond greeting her, watching as the seasons took it from lush viridian to solemn brown and yellow. Jessie felt out of place in such cozy, homey surroundings.

She'd never felt at home anywhere besides the Shaggin' Wagon. Her foster homes always had an ephemeral transience. It was an unspoken rule that her many childhood bedrooms—featuring bare walls and scuffs from previous foster kids, stark reminders that she never had *her* room, only *a* room—were only temporary shelters until the next apathetic family took her in. But standing in this kitchen, she felt a sense of grounded, rooted coziness, of *permanence*. This was a home. A place where a family unit was grown. Holidays and birthdays were celebrated with big fanfare. A brief melancholy filled her as she sensed the palpable cohesion of the Paige family in this kitchen, which had probably seen hundreds of delicious home-cooked dinners. She had never, nor would she ever, know what such an existence would be like.

Jessie eagerly waited for the pills to kick in, feeling the tinges of an anxiety attack coming on, the horrors of the last day or two threatening to overwhelm her. She had them from time to time, not nearly as much since she started smoking, but her stash was currently in the grubby hands of that dickhead sheriff. How she craved the comforting skunky smoke and the burn in her lungs that let her body know relief was on its way. Chest tightening, nerve pulling waves seeped up, wanting to swallow her, so she headed back to the office.

Only one thing set her mind at ease besides drumming and marijuana. She'd been a voracious reader growing up, devouring fiction books like candy. Jessie had read fiction purely for the escape, losing herself in wondrous paranormal and fantasy worlds, taking solace in horror, watching characters on the page deal with insane and macabre situations that made her own miserable life a cakewalk by comparison.

Jessie hadn't realized she had passion for history until she'd gone to college on scholarship and taken the elective on a whim. Before she'd dropped out, she had indulged in her new obsession of studying the past. History, she soon found, was the ultimate salve.

Her anxiety often stemmed from one variable—the constant, unknowable future. Her past, and her present for that matter, had been so tumultuous and unpredictable that any attempt to plan for the *future* often sent her into a spiral of hyperventilation. She would fall into a pit of what-ifs, negative feedback loops that sent her heart thudding if she even attempted to think of where she would be in two months. It was like trying to predict the next time it would storm. Jessie often wondered if stability had *ever* been a part of her life, and in the end, the realization was debilitating.

She'd questioned why she had never found romance, let alone a partner to share her anxieties with. Jessie had searched for an answer everywhere, even picking up a sexual health course in college before discovering that there was a word for people like her. *Asexual*. Those who lacked carnal urges or a natural desire to really be with anyone. Learning that there were others out there like her was no comfort though. She'd experimented with both men and women, and the results were always unsatisfactory and awkward. Jessie was jealous of people who found comfort in others, in infatuation, those who could intoxicate themselves with another person in a rush of feel-good brain chemicals. It made her feel like an alien in a human body.

To study history meant to dive into a world that had already happened, to relive things that were set in stone, that could not be changed. To dive into history was to know what happened next, to know the future. It was a luxury she never had in her real life, to focus on lives that were not her own, and god, what a comfort that was.

She perused through the books on Susannah's shelf and picked one whose cover art she liked. *Rustic Tradition: A History of the Ozarks, Volume 1.* Jessie took it, along with another book—*The Lead Belt: A Complicated Legacy*—to the small futon in the corner of the office, where a window provided ample reading light. Lowering her bruised and battered body onto the futon, she felt the warming aura of the pills enfold her in a cloud of bliss. Buckie joined her as she opened the book on Ozark history, padding into the office and snuggling at her feet.

Jessie pored over the pages about the state's complex history. The isolated Shawnee and Osage tribes that resided there long ago. The hermit mountain folk who'd resisted the changing world around them. A state whose allegiance was unclear during the Civil War. Thoroughly numbed and floating in a warm opiate haze, Jessie forgot about the outside world and her dire situation of crimson clouds and missing friends. Instead, she let herself be consumed by the lore of Americana, rich and simple by turns.

The history of this place in particular was largely underground.

After learning about the geology of the ancient Ozark foothills, she picked up the book on strip mining. Eventually her reading brought her back to Carter and a mineral extraction company named Marquette Mining Company whose operations centered around the Doefield Mine.

Jessie blinked, abruptly shaken out of her haze as she came across names she recognized: *Langan, Paige, Baumgartner*. Apparently the Langans, the people who may or may not be responsible for her world imploding, used to be de facto owners of the Doefield Mine. Then, there were the Paiges, who had sat atop a large untapped deposit of galena neighboring the original Doefield tract and refused to be bought out. It turned out the families in this area had a long, embittered history. This seemed to add a whole new layer to the drama currently unfolding around Jessie.

Jessie learned about land disputes between the Langans and the Paiges. Intense battles that had been handled by one Constable Arthur Baumgartner, who was later arrested for colluding with moonshiners. Jessie had to smirk, thinking the shit apples really don't fall far from the shit tree.

As Jessie dug in, she found that tragedy follows corruption. Liam Coldona, a Romanian immigrant who had worked for the Langan mining family for years, one day struck out and started his own rival mining company. The Coldonas were branded pariahs for their gypsy heritage, and as such, his venture did not last long due to a tragic mining accident that led to the collapse. Thirty people, including the Coldonas, had died buried under the rubble.

Jessie continued her search online, eventually scrolling through all manner of archaic HTML websites and cheesy retellings of old folk tales until she came upon pertinent information: THE CARTER CAVE CALAMITY. The website's author and curator was a man named Bernie Standridge. He apparently lived in Carter and called himself a 'local historian'.

Jessie smirked at the paragraphs dripping with hyperbole, much of which went over what Susannah had told her about local superstition regarding the caves. But she was intrigued enough by the legend to wonder if it played into the current situation. She looked at Susannah's map of the disappearances. They seemed to cluster around the Langan property, which squatted on a cave system connected to the old mine entrance where that cave-in took place.

The gears of her opiate-fuzzed mind turned slowly. Anxious thoughts crowded in on this comforting murder mystery phenomenon. Miners crushed to death. Brief flashes of Allen's legs, ending with the ragged stump of spine. Wolf-men in the hills. Coyotes coming out to the wreck and carrying his torso off into the woods to be eaten. Death. The crimson cloud, sucking, consuming, pulling.

Two things happened in quick succession. First, a surging tide of guilt at being comfortable and content in this small cozy office. On the heels of that was an intense wave of restlessness, the urge to act, to move. Her whole world had just been upended, and she was sitting in this little library, stoned and self-soothing while the life she'd worked so hard to obtain shattered around her. She needed to do *something*, goddamnit. How could she keep sitting on her ass while Lou was out there?

She shot up from the futon, but before she could take a decisive action, nausea assailed her.

Darting from the futon, Jessie ran to the bathroom, where she vomited her spiked coffee in a dark, bile-laden geyser. She forced herself to take a deep breath. In through the mouth and out through the nose. Her stomach rumbled. More than anything, she needed food.

After rifling through cabinets, Jessie stumbled upon an impressive whiskey collection, some honey-wheat bread and a stack of plates. Clicking canine toenails started moving her way. A questing nose came around the corner first, curious at the sounds that meant food was coming, but Jessie had no idea where the dog food would be.

She moved to raid Susannah's refrigerator for anything edible for either of them, forcing her mind back to the Langan problem. Why take Lou and not the rest of them? Now that she had some context—that bad blood stretched between these families going back decades—Jessie connected threads between them, with herself and her friends caught in this vast, sticky web of backcountry drama.

No vegetables to be had, she grabbed a stick of butter and three cage-free (at least, according to the carton) eggs, as well as some cheddar cheese. Of all the members of Blasphemer, she was the most stringently vegan... or used to be. Lately she'd lapsed more into a lax vegetarian diet. Trying to find truly vegan options on the road was hard and often expensive, especially in out of the way places such as this. It was more out of principle and personal preference than any long-standing crusade against the meat industry, though she did have her qualms there. Even indirect animal products such as cheese and eggs were pushing it, especially after seeing Allen's remains... But Jessie wasn't in a position to be picky at the moment. She found a cast iron pan and began frying up the eggs.

Her mind's eye kept wandering to those brown bottles of booze, high-end whiskey she could never afford. Dewar's. Glenlivet. Woodford Reserve. Probably tasted miles above the bottom shelf bullshit she drank on tour. *Hey, Suze, you ever had Kentucky Gentleman?* she thought, shaking her head at the memories. How nice a numbing shot of that would be. Just enough to defuse her anxious mind, to dive deeper into numbing bliss, as the restlessness overtook her once more. Jessie resisted the urge, knowing that spiral only led downwards. She was high and still coming down from a traumatic experience. The urge to do something stupid was strong. But she needed to rest. Susannah and the doctor both told her so. But still... Nervous jitters infiltrated her high. The compulsive need to act was becoming stronger by the minute.

Buckie sat expectantly beside the oak dining table where Jessie frowned down at her sad egg sandwich. Her foster home specialty left much to be desired, but Buckie's puppy dog eyes were cranked to eleven, tongue popping out to lick his chops. She took a few bites, and though it tasted fine, her stomach was still tumultuous from the painkillers and thoughts of Allen. She tossed the rest to the dog. Buckie had scarfed it up almost before it was on the floor, tail wagging a mile a minute, human food obviously an incredibly rare treat for the dog.

Jessie stood in the kitchen, frozen by option paralysis. Guilt cut through her pleasant dope high like a lance through a boil as images of Allen's remains smeared across the road seared into her mind, refusing to leave. That hick voice talking about Lou. *He's wiggling like a worm.*

Rage dislodged the paralysis. She thought of the sheriff and his dismissive tone. She thought of Lou—sweet, compassionate Lou—who was one of the kindest, most genuine men she had ever met. He was out there somewhere, suffering, going through god knows what, while she was just lounging around, soaking up the creature comforts.

"Fuck this," she said to Buckie. He gave her an inquisitive stare as she marched back into the office.

How did people get around before the advent of cellphones and GPS? A memory came to her of one of her foster parents taking Jessie on a short road trip through the Smokies. One of her few pleasant memories from childhood. She vaguely recalled holding directions printed off from some website. What was it called?

*MapQuest*. That's right. Jessie opened up that ancient relic from her childhood, praying the website still worked. Surprisingly, it did. She looked at the big blown-up state map again, doing her best to approximate where the Langan property was in relation to the digital map on the website. She didn't have a firm address, but a drag and drop pin took her to the one residential driveway within five miles of Route 72, the road Susannah mentioned. As the printer chirped to life, Jessie stole back to the kitchen and took out one of the bottles of whiskey without thinking, then downed a fortifying gulp of Glen Livet.

As an inferno blossomed in her belly, Jessie remembered seeing a bike tucked away under the carport in Susannah's driveway. Back when she'd first moved into the city and had gotten a job at Burger Zone, she biked everywhere. Not only did it save her money from bus fares and commuter trains, it helped build up her calf muscles and leg stamina. It'd done wonders for her double kick performance. Win-win. Though it'd been months since she'd last ridden, the chemical cocktail in Jessie's system had her feeling confident enough to give the crazy idea a shot. According to the turn-by-turn directions she printed out, the Langan residence was approximately fifteen miles away. She looked at the clock on the stove as she headed out the door. 3 pm. She had maybe four hours until sunset.

As she took out the bike, Jessie once more had the absurd feeling of being a rebellious teenager, sneaking out past curfew to go to some underground metal concert. Would Susannah be mad if she came home and Jessie wasn't there, the bike missing? Maybe. Though the woman was incredibly nice, and Jessie owed her a lot, Susannah Paige wasn't her mom. And if no one else was going to help her look for her friend, she would do it her goddamn self.

The going was wobbly at first. It became evident as Jessie made her way down the gravel driveway that she was a bit more intoxicated than she'd realized. But once she got onto smooth pavement, the ride was easier. Holding up the paper directions in one hand and steering with the other, Jessie did her best to stick to the shoulder of the road, what shoulder there was anyway. But within minutes, it became clear this would not be like her urban commutes in the city. Folks in Carter County were clearly not used to having to share the road with cyclists. Blaring horns sounded as vehicles sped by her. Near misses made her red hair fly in front of her face and the printed directions threaten to fly from her hand.

"Fuck you, fucking redneck dicks!" She screamed at the litany of lifted F-250s and 2500s that roared past her with abandon, not daring to move over an inch to share the road with this non-automotive aberration. She half hoped one of the belligerent drivers would pull over and try her. The whiskey and pills stoked the rage blossoming in her chest, *full of piss and vinegar* as Lou would say. If one of these inbred shitkickers wanted to start something, she'd gladly finish it.

But none of the vehicles stopped, and soon Jessie was more focused on trying to navigate the steep slopes of the highway. Adrenaline filled her as she coasted down winding hills, picking up speed, the wind buffeting her face and drying the sweat on her skin before she reached the bottom, then had to deal with the calf-burning ordeal of biking up those same hills. God, she thought Missouri was all flat corn fields. What the hell was this shit?

Her heart pounded in her chest, occasionally missing a beat. The doctor's orders were to avoid strenuous activity for the next few weeks. Fuck the doctors. Fuck the shithead sheriff. Fuck this whole backwoods-ass county. Fuck everyone, except Lou. *I'm coming for you, man. Just hold on. I haven't given up.*

She turned off the main highway and was pedaling down a narrow county road. Jessie almost crashed several times trying to steer through the maze of potholes, beer cans, and roadkill that dotted the asphalt. It was a road just like this where her life had been upended. As the energy began to drain from her, lactic acid filling her legs, she coasted to a stop, watching the sun tickle the tops of the trees lining either side. A ROAD CLOSED sign waited up ahead. When she pedaled closer, she saw why: A huge circular crater at least fifteen feet in diameter had swallowed up blacktop and earth alike.

*Sinkhole. Fuck, Susannah was right.*

A complex surge of emotions swelled in her, threatening to make her explode until she opened her mouth.

She screamed as loud as she could. All the frustration, helplessness, and dread at her circumstances boiled over and she screamed until she felt something give in her throat and the scream dissolved into a hoarse croak.

Another wave of nausea hit her like a freight train. Jessie got off the bike, supporting herself with the handlebars as she stood by the side of the road and dry heaved. She heard the rumble of an engine approaching and straightened up, doing her best to regain her composure just as a truck slowed to a stop behind her. Flashbacks to the night before assailed her. Was this them? The shitheads who took Lou?

"Got damn, what's a pretty little thing like you doing on the side of the road? You alright sugar tits?" a husky voice called out. A gangly man with a scrubby beard leaned out the passenger side door of a Chevy S10 that looked to be held together with duct tape and willpower. His beady eyes roved over Jessie's sweaty, haggard body.

"Need to get to the Langans' place," Jessie said, her voice froggy. "You know who they are?"

Thin eyebrows shot up in curiosity. "The Langans? What the fuck you want with those two-bit turd sniffers?"

"None of your fucking business. I just need to find them." Jessie started to walk the bike, turning around to head back the way she came.

She stared at the directions, trying to make sense of the turns, realizing the website's info must've been severely outdated. Who knew how many of these roads were closed down now? She would have to make her own way. And she'd never been good at that. That was Lou's strong suit.

"Got a mouth on you, huh? Fiery little thing. I like that. Say, why don't you hop in—"

"Fuck off!" Jessie held up a middle finger.

"Oh, you uppity, huh? Teach you to talk to me like that—"

The man reached out, grabbing for Jessie's arm, but instead got a hold of the MapQuest directions and ripped them out of her hand. Jessie flailed out with a right hook. Her knuckle scraped crooked teeth. The man reached for her again, spluttering curses and spitting blood. Jessie didn't bother with the paper now. She was in fight mode, remembering what Allen had taught her. *Pivot into it. Use your hips.*

She screamed again. Fists flew blindly into a truck cab that smelled like musty armpits and spilled beer. Grimy hands snatched and pulled at her.

"Got damn! She ain't worth it, Russ!" the driver said. The truck surged forward. The gangly one, Russ, ripped out a lock of her hair, one last parting shot before the truck fishtailed in a squall of tires and smoke.

"Fuckin' crazy bitch, fuck you!" he yelled as they sped off down the road Jessie had just come down. A half empty Busch Lite can shot out of the truck in her general direction, trailing a comet's tail of beer on its descent.

Jessie just stood there, breathing hard, adrenaline dumping into her. She looked around, realizing she was in the middle of fucking nowhere with the sun going down. Alone. Her band in tatters. Her dreams shattered.

She clambered back on the bike and, with tears streaming down her face, struggled to pilot the thing down the rutted road. After the altercation and the few punches she'd landed, the final bit of steam released from the boiler of her soul. Still, fatigued beyond compare, feeling lost and scared, she pedaled on, Lou's face refusing to vacate her mind.

She returned to the highway and took the next turn without bothering to look or remember. She had no fucking clue where she was. By the time she reached another highway, this one reading Route Y, she was feeling delirious. A headache throbbed at her temples. Her legs felt like boiled noodles. The urge to abandon the bike, lay down in the ditch lining the shoulder and just die was strong. But she kept going. The sky was darkening now, and headlights washed past her. Car horns and screeching tires were the only thing keeping her from passing out over the handlebars as she swerved all over the road. Not a single person stopped to see if she was okay.

After a few more miles, she'd stopped in the road, unable to go on. When Jessie eventually looked up, fear cut through the exhaustion. The red mist surrounded her, bleeding in from everywhere, flowing through the trees and washing over the road. It throbbed in time with the thunderous beat of her heart. Soon, it was all she could see, until she heard the squeal of tires skidding on blacktop. Lights blinded her.

"Goddamnit, not again." Jessie didn't have the energy for another confrontation. She was completely, utterly spent. If Ol' Russ had decided to come back to finish the job, he'd probably succeed. Instead, she heard a car door open, followed by a familiar voice.

"Jessie, my God, is that you?"

Susannah emerged from the headlights' glare, and at the sight of her, the red mist began to evaporate. Thoughts of being scolded and chastised followed suit as Jessie took in the haggard-looking woman. Somehow, Susannah looked worse off than Jessie felt. She clocked bloodstains mixing with patches of sweat. An unhinged, harrowed look haunted Susannah's eyes. Despite Jessie's fear at Susannah's reaction to her foolish adventure, she was glad to see the woman. Susannah was the cavalry. Susannah was help. Susannah was her one ally in this backwater hellhole.

"You... look like shit," Jessie offered. It was all she could think to say before she collapsed on the side of the road.

She hoped to lose herself to oblivion, a temporary respite, but soon the red mist flooded into her subconscious. A voice spoke to her through that ethereal crimson.

*YOU ARE MINE. I WILL HAVE YOU. I WILL TAKE THAT WHICH SWEETENS YOUR SOUL THE WAY EVE TOOK THE APPLE FROM THE GARDEN OF EDEN. COME TO ME, CHILD.*

The words she heard were not in English, yet she somehow understood them perfectly.

The mist bled away. Rough stone walls hemmed her in on either side. Wails of human agony echoed off the sepulchral surroundings.

*COME TO ME.*

Something drew her deeper into the stone labyrinth.

*YOU ARE SO CLOSE.*

Deeper she went. The voice grew louder, more commanding.

*COME TO ME.*

Jessie knew she had to fight. She had to resist. But it pulled at her, a horrible sort of magnetism.

*No, I won't. Leave me alone. You can't have what's inside of me.* Jessie spoke from her soul, her words cast into the void.

*OH, BUT I WILL. COME TO ME, CHILD. LET ME TAKE WHAT IS RIGHTFULLY MINE.*

*No!*

*COME—*

# CHAPTER 15

S USANNAH HAD BEEN SO lost in her thoughts, recalling everything that had happened at the clinic that she nearly ran over the apparition slumped in the middle of the road, a bike between its legs. She slammed on her brakes. The Explorer fishtailed before coming to a stop within inches of the figure.

Familiar red hair hid the person's face. And the bike. Not just any bike. The green Trek bike Daniel used to ride obsessively until he'd gotten his license.

Puzzle pieces slowly connected in her traumatized brain, and Susannah realized who it was standing before her.

She flicked on her emergency flashers and got out, not caring who she inconvenienced as she ran over to Jessie, who muttered something before falling over and puddling on the asphalt.

Jessie came to about ten minutes after Susannah had hauled her and the bike into the SUV. She jerked awake with a small yell.

"What the fuck?" Jessie looked around dazedly, her voice hoarse. Susannah glanced over at her. Their eyes briefly met, and she let Jessie see the agitation in them.

"This is not what I need. You would not believe the day I had, Jessie. And now here you are, trying to get yourself killed. What the *hell* were you thinking? What were you even hoping to accomplish?" Susannah tried to keep the heat out of her voice, but *damnit,* she was close to her breaking point. All Jessie had to do was sit at home and convalesce.

"I was trying to save my fucking friend."

"You're in no condition to do anything except rest, young la—"

"You're not my fucking mom, Susannah." Jessie was glaring at her, ready to hurl another outburst, then shook her head and let out a deep sigh. "Look, I really appreciate everything you've done for me, seriously. But I can't just... sit at your house and watch the world go by. Lou needs me. And no one in this backwater ass town seems to give a shit about helping—"

"*I'm* trying to help you, Jessie. I understand, really, but—"

"No, you don't." Jessie shook her head, looking away.

Susannah slammed on the brakes, threw the Explorer into park and swiveled in her seat.

"Oh? You don't think I know what it's like to have a loved one go missing? You don't think I know what it's like to have every waking moment consumed with thoughts of trying to find them? Wondering if they're okay?" Her voice was building to a scream, but she couldn't stop it. "Shaming yourself for not doing more? Do you really think I don't understand what you're going through? *God damn you!*"

Susannah clapped a hand over her mouth, eyes wide as she realized what she'd just said, but the words had erupted out of her before she could stop them. A heavy silence hung between them while cars rushed by in a blare of horns and middle fingers. Jessie shrunk in her seat.

"I-I'm sorry. I didn't mean that, I just... Forget it." Jessie barely spoke above a whisper.

Neither woman said more for the rest of the drive back home.

Susannah had made a point over the last few months to avoid alcohol unless she was in a social setting. The months after Daniel's disappearance saw her lapsing into functional alcoholism, often surpassing inebriation, seeking that anesthetizing blackout state so she could sleep in peace. Anything to quell those harrowing nightmares of Daniel, stuck in a fetid, dark place, slowly being tortured, kept alive for unknown, nefarious purposes. Whiskey seemed to be the only thing that stopped them, allowing her solace in a black, dreamless oblivion. That alone was worth the hangovers, until Harold had gently called her out when he'd noticed his diminishing whiskey collection.

After what she'd endured today, Susannah figured she'd earned a bit of numbing. Her hands trembled as she poured a finger of Wild Turkey into one of Harold's tumblers and downed the drink before she even considered speaking another word to Jessie. The blowup in the car had been bad, and Susannah wanted to patch things up, *needed* things to be okay between them before she allowed herself to sleep. Things were crazy enough as is, and she had this deep gut feeling that the rebellious little hellion sitting at her kitchen counter would play a key role in finding out what happened to Daniel. In hindsight, she understood the girl's thinking. Susannah would've done the same thing in her place.

She took out a second tumbler, poured them both a finger, and slid the glass wordlessly over to Jessie, who'd been resting her head on her forearms.

"Here, kid. You look like you could use it." Susannah clinked her glass against Jessie's in a mock toast and quaffed the whiskey, cherishing the numbing burn in her belly. Jessie looked up at the whiskey, then aimed her red and sunken eyes at Susannah.

"Thanks." Jessie knocked back the liquor with the casual ease of someone well acquainted with spirits. As Susannah poured them both another shot, a cold nose nudged into her side. A high-pitched whine cut through the pregnant silence in the kitchen. Susannah knelt down and grabbed hold of Buckie, kissing his forehead and dutifully taking the kisses that wetted her cheeks.

Buckie was not one to usually give kisses, but tonight there was almost a desperation to his affection. Either he had caught the anxiety radiating off her or maybe it was the scent of stale fear sweat. She could smell it on herself beneath the stew of good old-fashioned BO, the hay-musk of livestock, and old blood.

"I know, Momma's a little high-strung right now, but I'm fine, honey," Susannah cooed to Buckie, whose knowing, golden eyes stared pleadingly at her. For a brief moment, she felt herself losing control. A sob threatened to explode from her throat, but she squeezed her eyes shut and swallowed hard. After a deep breath, she kissed the dog's forehead, then raised herself back up. Jessie's glass was held up, waiting for Susannah to toast her once more. "I think the world might be going crazy. Cheers," she said, knocking back the bourbon.

Jessie knocked hers back too. She smacked her lips and cleared her throat before speaking again.

"I'm sorry, Susannah. I'm a fucking mess. I didn't mean what I said about you not understanding. Of course you do. And god, you've done so much for me. I don't deserve your help." Jessie's voice quavered. When she reached for the bottle, Susannah didn't stop her.

"It's okay. I'm sorry I went off on you. You're right, I'm not your mom... It's just... been one hell of a day." Both women took a moment, allowing the whiskey to loosen the tension that was quickly leaving the room. Finally, Jessie spoke.

"So, uh... about that blood on your shirt." She pointed a finger at Susannah's soiled chest. "Everything okay?"

"No, honey, it isn't. It's about as far away from okay as you can get." Susannah stopped herself from grabbing the bottle to pour another shot. She sighed, then bit back a laugh, knowing if the unhinged chuckle were to wriggle free, it would devolve into something worse. With the whiskey blooming a calming blaze in her belly, she slid the bottle to Jessie. "I think I'm gonna shower and head to bed. It's been a God-awful long day." She started to unbutton her flannel.

"Hold on," Jessie poured herself another shot. "When I saw you, you looked like you'd just done two tours of duty in hell. What happened? Does it have to do with all *that* crazy shit?" she asked, hitching a thumb back towards the office.

"I honestly don't know, sweetheart." Susannah decided she needed another shot after all. This time she took it straight from the bottle, which drew a surprised, bemused grin from Jessie.

Susannah gulped the liquid fire, allowing it burn through her before taking another deep breath and let it out in a slow, controlled release. The tightening knot of tension between her shoulder blades, with its invisible coils around her ribs and stomach, unwound slightly. Her tolerance had definitely gone back to baseline since abstaining. Her whole body flushed with warmth, and she felt something akin to relaxation. She could still hear that awful growling from the cow as it trampled its own intestines, but it was growing mercifully fainter.

"Something is happening to the animals around here." She spoke more to herself than to Jessie.

"Huh?" Jessie gestured for the bottle. Susannah poured herself one more drink before sliding it across, this time making sure she sipped it instead of gulped. Jessie followed her example.

"Come on, let's go out on the deck." Susannah wanted to be out in fresh, clean air. Tumbler in tow, she flipped on the floodlights and stepped onto her back deck. She often sat out there, sipping coffee or whiskey depending on the time of day, taking part in silent meditation, often thinking of Daniel. While Jessie and the dog followed her outside, Susannah greedily inhaled the clean smells of the surrounding forest, devoid of half-digested cud, arterial blood, and strong antimicrobial soap.

They sat across from each other in mesh patio chairs. Susannah did her best to ignore the mild claustrophobia she got when peering into the woods lining her property. She'd come out here to relax, but the heavy cloak of night closing in around the cone cast by the floodlights made her feel vulnerable. A stab of fear cut through her whiskey haze. She imagined some feral, primal thing lurking just beyond the trees. Buckie bounded off into the yard, nose to the ground as he scouted out a spot to do his business.

She forced herself to relay what had happened at the clinic. The girl listened with that same impassive stare she had worn when Susannah had bared her soul in the back office. She almost laughed at one point, realizing this was taking on some messed up therapist-client dynamic.

"So that Tate Langan guy, he got bit by a *cop*?" Jessie asked.

"Yep. And acted like it was the end of the world. Never seen a man so scared in my life. He's a smidge touched in the head, but still... the Langans, they know something we don't."

"What happened to him? Tate, I mean," Jessie asked, finishing the last of her whiskey with a slurp.

"Don't know. Sheriff ran off with him at gunpoint. Poor boy was rambling on about his dad. How they had to take care of him. Baumgartner said he was gonna let him sweat it out in the jail, get some answers." Susannah shook her head.

"Listen, uh... I was reading some of those books about the area today. I didn't know the families here went back so far. You guys, the Langans, all this stuff with the mines. Does the name Coldona mean anything to you?"

Susannah had been watching Buckie, who'd frozen in the middle of doing his circling, pre-dump routine. The dog's head was cocked towards the trees, body stiffened. He usually only did that when he caught scent of a squirrel or raccoon. She looked away from him when the name came up.

"Coldona? Yeah, my daddy used to talk about them. Gypsy family..." Susannah gave Jessie the extremely abridged history of how a smart, efficient family from Romania had briefly upset the scales of an insular mining town. "Why do you ask?" Her attention returned to Buckie. His tail had stopped wagging.

"Came upon the name while I was reading, is all. Some local dude named Bernie Standridge has a website about it. Sounds like they were victims in the big cave-in." Jessie cleared her throat and started to say something else, but Susannah sighed and shook her head.

"Old Bernie. That fella sure knows how to stir the pot..." When Susannah didn't say more, Jessie forged ahead with something that had clearly been eating at the back of her mind.

"Hey, uh, this is kind of random, but—" Her voice was thick with alcohol as she began. Susannah continued staring at Buckie. The dog was about fifteen feet away, and she thought she heard the faintest trace of a growl. "—When you resuscitated me, or whatever it's called... you know, brought me back, did you feel anything? Like... I don't know. It sounds stupid but—"

Susannah was shocked Jessie would've been affected by the flash too. No one else Susannah had ever touched had known the feeling she felt. Before Susannah could reply, Buckie barked so strangely that even Jessie looked at him. Susannah told herself it was just a squirrel or a bobcat.

He was obsessed with bobcats, which they had plenty of out here in the hills. Buckie had gotten his fair share of scratches from chasing the wild, surly cats around her back forty. Now, his snout crinkled up in a snarl, his barks punctuated by growls of warning. He'd never done that before.

"Buckie?" Susannah called from the deck, suddenly standing, wavering on her feet, the whiskey going straight to her head. Deep in the woods at the border of her property, something stirred. A rustle of branches, the snap of a twig. *It's just a bobcat, you've had a traumatic day and you're seeing boogeymen that aren't there.*

"Uh... does he normally do that?" Susannah noted the fear in Jessie's voice. Though they'd both drunk their fair share of whiskey, the normally mild-mannered dog's frenzied barking had brought them to a stark awareness.

"Boy, get *back* here!" Susannah snapped. He glanced back, only for a second. His growling fell deeper into his throat but didn't stop. The terrible sound didn't mask the rustle of the leaves and brush stirring ahead of him. The dog bunched up in a pouncing position, tail between his legs. Susannah felt her bowels start to melt. A hot, cramping pressure built. She pictured the cave mouth at the very edge of her property, the one Harold had found while hunting whitetail a few years back. The realization caused her blood to run cold, but it was ridiculous. Her place was several miles out from the systems at the core of her conspiracy. But it seemed lately that everything was connected to the Doefield Mines, like the veins of a blackened leaf on an evil tree.

She imagined miles of dark, fetid tunnels snaking beneath her feet. All sorts of unholy things could use those tunnels as subterranean highways to move all over the county unbidden.

*Christ, you've had too much to drink, you—*

"Susannah, do you see that?" Jessie's eyes were dilated wide, staring at the woods transfixed, unable to blink or move.

"See what? Jesus Christ, see *what?*" Susannah rushed to the girl's side, oblivious of her own sin. She followed Jessie's unblinking gaze. The wall of white oaks and the few clutches of shortleaf pine bordering the yard looked the same as ever, except for the spaces *between*. The gaps of black bleeding amongst the branches held preternatural darkness. There was no movement anywhere else, none at all. A wicked sort of primal fear burned out whatever comfort the high-proof whiskey had brought her.

"Buckie!" she screamed, stomping her foot on the deck. The dog's muscles eased from his livid state, and he began to whine pitifully.

"You don't see it... Fuck, I'm going crazy," Jessie said, her breath coming out in a cough.

"C'mere, buddy!" Susannah's voice cracked with fear. The dog stood frozen, like a deer in the headlights, shocked out of his killing stance. Susannah caught a flicker of movement in the trees. It was enough for her resolve to break.

She ran into the house, nearly tripping over dining room chairs as she bolted for the gun safe. They kept the Glock-26, Harold's home defense pistol, on top of the safe. The one gun they didn't secure. Susannah almost dropped the clip as she inspected it, making sure it was full. The casings of the 9mm hollow points flashed in the overhead lights as she raced across the foyer and back out onto the deck.

Jessie stood with her mouth open, a stupefied look on her face. Buckie was backing away from the woods, hoarsely growling and whining intermittently. The dog's strange behavior stretched her nerves until they felt close to snapping. Then, something that could have been the shine of an eye sparked into view, reflecting the floodlights, breaking Susannah's nerve. On impulse, she brought the gun up in both hands, firing into the woods until the clip was empty, eschewing Harold's many lessons about trigger discipline and controlled fire. The strobe of the gun flash against the leaves imprinted white shapes across her sight.

It was as if the sound had blasted everything away, including their fear-tinged paralysis. Buckie flinched, finally snapping out of whatever held him to the spot. Ears flattened, head down, he dashed back to the porch as the last of the rolling echoes faded into the night.

Susannah's ears rang with a pregnant silence. But even over the tinnitus, she could tell it wasn't just her ears. The forest sounds had stopped. The usual bray of crickets and no-see-ums and owl hoots was gone. The woods collectively held its breath.

"Inside, now." Susannah yanked Jessie houseward by the meat of her arm.

The instant their flesh made contact, a crackling vision flashbulbed across her mind. A massive red cloud, the size of a coal barge. It seemed to envelope the whole property, leaving only rot behind. A split second later, it was gone. As her yard and the trees returned around her, Susannah was stunned beyond speech. She pulled the girl along, Buckie frantically pawing at the sliding glass door as she wrenched it open. As soon as they were inside, Susannah locked the door but kept the floodlights on. She looked out the window, seeing only the reflection of her own eyes. Nothing stirred outside.

# Chapter 16

"WHAT THE FUCK WAS that?" Jessie was staring out of the sliding glass door.

"That... that was what nerves, too much whiskey, and a very protective dog get you," Susannah said, taking another glug straight from the bottle. Her hands shook violently as she forced herself to put the bottle back on its shelf. "I think we both need to go to bed. Lordy be." Back inside, the invisible fist that had closed on her ribs began to dissipate. The whiskey buzz helped to calm things, but she'd lost control back there, and now she just felt foolish. *What would Harold think of me going off the handle like that? Christ, that could've been somebody's dog out there in the woods. I could've shot—*

"Seriously? You didn't feel that? Didn't see it? Your dog, he—"

"He gets excited easily," Susannah said curtly. It was all bullshit. *The truth? You're a dead-tired, overwhelmed old woman*, she thought. The trauma of the day washed over her in a heavy, invisible wave. Susannah was abruptly aware of the sweat and blood caked onto her arms, the filth of this terrible day clinging to her flesh. She needed a long, hot shower and then sleep. "I'm going to bed. You should too, I have a feeling tomorrow is gonna be even crazier." Without another word, she left Jessie to her own devices.

The dog followed her, whining, to the master bathroom, where she turned the shower as hot as she could stand it. She left Buckie, pawing pitifully at the bathroom door. Normally, she took off the silver crucifix necklace when bathing, but she could not bring herself to be separated from it. The cross was slightly larger than most cruciform necklaces you'd find, with the main staff being close to five inches long. Susannah had originally gotten it as a testament to her faith, proud to wear the large symbol of Christ when so many others hid it beneath their shirt. As the mirror fogged up, she stared at her naked reflection, at the cross that dangled from her neck, until she was a vague, flesh colored blob in the steam.

Over the dull roar of the water, she recalled the sound of bacon fat hissing in a hot skillet. Except it hadn't been bacon fat. It was the sound of a sacred symbol touching the flesh of what was once a human man. A deceased deputy, who took two .357 rounds to his body, then ran off like it was nothing.

Susannah let the womblike comfort of the shower envelop her while she scrubbed her whole body until the flesh was raw and pink. She thought of the insane things Tate Langan had said with the barrel of Baumgartner's gun to his temple, in that high-pitched child's voice. Those boys were hiding something terrible from the whole town. Things that correlated directly with the awful dreams she'd been having. Things that made so much horrible sense. He had spoken as if Virgil Langan was still alive. He had spoken of gypsies. Of curses.

*Does the name Coldona mean anything to you?*

Once upon a time, that name meant very little to Susannah Paige. A name that was sometimes spoken in passing at family reunions, something about the Lead Belt days. About how crazy those days were, the big accident, how sad it all was. But that was it.

She crawled into bed and huddled against Buckie in her bathrobe. Clutching the dog to her chest, she took solace in his soft fur and quiet grunts of relief as she cuddled him and thought of the name Coldona again. Of the rumors that pervaded the town around them. Mostly steeped in racism and fear of outsiders, sure, but Christ... it seemed like everyone agreed something bad was going on in the caves after the accident. And then, just as suddenly, folks stopped talking about it. The elder families of the town would mention the family name but bringing up 'the accident' seemed to be picking at a freshly healed scab. The Coldona name was spoken of at 4H clubs and Rotary lunches, but one old grammy or another seemed to be especially quick to change topics once the cave-in was brought up.

Susannah flinched when her cellphone rang, her nerves wound taught enough to snap. It was Harold. She blinked back tears of relief.

"Oh... honey," she said, laying on the bed, Buckie nestled into her side.

"Hey, Suze, everything alright? I got your text earlier," he shouted over a dull whine in the background. She knew he was standing somewhere down in the bowels of a tugboat, the diesel engines nearly drowning out his voice.

"Yeah, sorry, it's just... I was having a rough day, wanted to hear your voice, is all." Tears silently slipped from her eyes and fell into Buckie's fur.

"Yeah? What's going on, sugar? Talk to me."

In that moment, it took every ounce of Susannah's willpower to swallow the burning lump in her throat, to fight the urge to scream into the phone. The urge to tell him to come back here, come back now and hold her and use his broad back and strong shoulders as a buffer against the horrors of this world.

"Susannah?"

"Oh, it's nothing. Just having one of my moments, I'm fine now. I just miss you, Harold." Susannah forced herself to say this last with calm affection rather than the urgency burning deep in her chest. How could she possibly begin to tell him about what had happened to her the last few days? The thought of it made her mind ache. No, she would *not* burden her husband with such lunacy. If the world was still unraveling by the time he got home, then they would deal with it together. Otherwise, she would let him work his long hours on the river in peace. She knew that was what he needed. It was how he dealt with the grief.

"You know I wish I could, I miss you something fierce. Only two weeks left on my rotation, and then I'm all yours. We should take a trip up to Van Buren when I get home, maybe take the camper out somewhere. Go out to Tom Sauk or something." Susannah swallowed, lip trembling as she thought of how nice that would be. Her and Harold and Buckie away in the woods, away from all this madness.

"Yeah, that sounds just lovely. Listen... I know it's late, I'll let you get back to it. I was just getting ready for bed myself." If she stayed on the phone much longer, she would fall apart, though she wanted nothing more than to let his soothing baritone lull her to sleep.

"Alright... you *sure* you're okay, honey? Sounds like you been drinking." There was no accusation in Harold's voice, just gentle concern.

"Yes, honey. I'm just tired, long day at work. I love you," she said.

"And I love you, darlin'. Give Buckie a belly rub for me. Sleep well, Suze. Two more weeks, maybe one and a half if I can sweet talk my boss" he promised. She told him goodnight, and as promised, rubbed the collie's furry chest and belly. Buckie grunted softly in approval, but his tail did not wag, his body stayed stiff with tension. He had sensed something out there. But what? On top of everything else going on, what could possibly be out in those woods? She thought of the caves. Of the red cloud that suddenly burst across her vision when she touched Jessie. Never before had she gotten two flashes from the same person. Jessie was special somehow. The young girl had felt it too, when Susannah was doing CPR on her, and whatever it was had passed between them.

For a while she lay like that, holding her dog and thinking of her husband's promise. Two weeks. Things were happening fast now, she could sense it. What was her life even going to be like by then?

Susannah didn't realize she'd fallen asleep until she reached for a clock she couldn't see. She was no longer in bed, but in a cave. Bathed in red, the smell of burning flesh and old, congealed blood thick in her nostrils. She was in Hell, and she understood it long before she saw the bodies. Chained to the cavern walls, their emaciated forms trembling with hope at the sight of her.

"Kill us... please... just kill us—" one of them pleaded. They watched her through sunken eyes above lips skinned back to reveal crooked rows of blackened teeth jutting from receded gray gums. Wisps of straw hair clung to eggshell-white skulls. For once, Daniel was not among them. Or perhaps he was farther down in the cavern among this Legion of the Damned who wept blood from a thousand tiny bite marks along their bodies. Coils of black tendrils trailed away from their forms, pulsating with a terrible vitality.

A large red cloud boiled up from the bowels of the cave, coming towards her.

"Please, before he gets us, *please!*" the emaciated figure screamed, but Susannah ignored it, running from the cave, running from their pleas, their cries, wanting to be done with God's tests, wanting to be done with these horrors of the Devil.

She'd repented, she'd given herself wholly and completely to God, and yet he still put her through these harrowing trials, as if she were Job, being tested after having lost everything she held dear. *You have taken everything from me, You have forsaken me, and yet I still come to You, and yet I still worship You! What more could I possibly do to show my devotion to You?*

Susannah reached the mouth of the cave and felt the blistering warmth of a conflagration that surrounded her on all sides. Walls of fire stretched as far as the eye could see. She looked towards the encroaching clouds of a crimson sky. A ghastly visage revealed itself. Barely human, it collected itself from the mist, solidifying into something more than flesh. At first, she thought it was God, but through the roiling blanket of scarlet, the ethereal face that sneered at her seemed vaguely familiar.

"I MUST HAVE HER. SHE CAME INTO MY DOMAIN BY PURE CHANCE, AND SHE WAS MERELY ANOTHER MOR-TAL SOUL, UNTIL SHE FOUND YOUR TOUCH. YOU GAVE HER THAT WHICH IS BEYOND LIFE, AND I MUST TASTE THAT NECTAR," the voice boomed from that hideous mouth. The mist from within the throat whirled, becoming raking sand, then crys-tallizing into shards of blood-tinted glass, opening wide to receive her.

Susannah screamed until she thrashed herself awake, hollering. She took in lungfuls of air. It was all a nightmare, and the smell of Hell's smoky fires had followed her out.

# PART TWO

# ENDEMIC

M.HARPER

# Chapter 17

Lou had marked the passing of time by the rays of light crawling through narrow gaps in the wood and the pitch blackness that slowly bled in. Part of his mind understood it had only been two days since he was abducted, but the heat had baked his perception into a slow, melted thing. It felt as if he'd spent months in this hellhole, mind slowly falling apart. The dehydration, the fumes from his own broiling waste, and heat stroke combined to produce an endless, delirious fever dream. Everything around him had rotted, except his will to live.

Being a father, husband, man, human being... these things had not been forgotten. Lou worked at the restraints on his wrists for what felt like days, weeks. Focusing on this singular task distracted his mind from the misery of his shattered spine. Flares of agony shot through the blessed waves of numbness that flooded him from the waist down. His legs teased him relentlessly. They were *right there*. Nothing more than hanging, useless meat. He imagined kicking the door down, dashing down the driveway. But he couldn't even twitch a toe anymore, let alone get up and walk. Instead, he focused on his wrists. Ceaseless sweat had loosened the adhesive on his skin, and after hours of wriggling and rubbing his skin raw, he felt a spark of hope when the base layers of the tape began to yield.

His will to live was singular and obsessive. He had tasted hope when the cruiser rolled up, some sheriff that apparently knew these hillbilly fucks from way back when. Lou had thought maybe, just maybe, if he made some kind of noise, the cops would investigate. He tried to scream through the dirt-coated rag in his mouth, but that only caused him to gag on his own phlegm, and for a harrowing minute, he thought he would choke himself to death

Instead, he banged his head against the shed wall, knocking over a watering can on the shelf above him. When the sheriff came closer, his voice growing louder, hope blossomed huge and heavy in Lou's chest.

Then he heard the gunshots. Shouting, the scrambling sounds of commotion before the sheriff's car flew off, sirens blaring. Silence, a long, *long* bout of silence that grew more terrible with each passing hour, until he'd heard someone. He assumed it was one of the brothers that crunched towards the shed. The loud grumble of that stupid fucking truck started up, then that too drove off.

*They forgot about me. Left me here to die with my own shit and piss baking beside me*, he'd thought. And then, to add insult to injury, he'd felt his guts give a warning grumble. Lou felt the familiar cramping sensation gurgle its way through his bowels and knew the milkshake gamble was one he'd come up short on. He could feel the hot, loose waste pressing to escape his body, to erupt from him in spasmodic heaves, and without someone there to help, he saw the fate before him. The shack, the binding, the literal shit hole he'd been forced to sleep in, that was enough. Lou knew that if he was forced to lie in it, that would be the final straw. His mind would break then, break into a million little pieces beyond hope of fitting back together.

Lou sobbed as his bowels let go, his own hot mess pooling in his pants, stinking like death. He sat like that for a long time, groaning, feeling less than human. Anguish and rage towards his captors so deep his heart palpitated with it. And soon, darkness fell again. Left to rot in the pitch-black void, Lou's mind grew more feral as the hours went on and the shit cooled against his buttocks.

When his right wrist finally slipped free from the taped manacles, Lou felt a small glimmer of hope return. He yanked the rag out from between his lips, dragging the dried caterpillar of his tongue across the roof of his mouth. He thought of the milkshake, how fucking good it was, like pure ambrosia, even if it had led to shame. Lou decided if (no, *when,* Lou, *when* you get out of this, he reminded himself) the first thing he was doing was getting the biggest goddamn milkshake he could get his hands on, lactose intolerance be damned.

Lou was thankful for the darkness, thankful that he couldn't see the pathetic mess he'd been reduced to. He flopped onto his side and slowly, clumsily, tore his pants down and off his ankles. Flinging them as far as he could, he sat naked from the waist down, not giving a single, goddamned flying *fuck* who found him like this.

He dragged himself across the dirt floor, the liquid grinding of shattered vertebrae firing bolts of pain up his spine. The night rang with the oncoming roar of the diesel truck returning. Headlights cut through the wood slats as Lou army crawled to a corner beside the door, using the truck's high beams to navigate the cluttered mess. That way, when they finally came to check on him, he could at least have a fighting chance. Maybe trip them on their way in, get a python around one of their necks. Surprise, motherfucker.

The truck stopped. A door opened, then slammed shut. A pair of boots crunched across the gravel driveway. The glug of a full jerry can punctuated the footfalls as they headed towards the woods, towards that crazy bastard in the cave. *Into the primordial, a viridian purgatory... separating from the real world...* Jesus, Lou thought, remembering lyrics at a time like this.

He wasted no time. Using the narrow shafts of light from the truck, Lou floundered, searching for something, *anything* he could use as a weapon. Crawling around on arms gone rubbery from hours of flexing and twisting, he spotted a rusty, grimy shovel hanging off a hook at the opposite end of the shed. Hope once again flared within him. He pulled himself across the floor to the wall. His fingertips came up a few inches short of the dirt-crusted blade, and any attempt he made to sit up caused shards of agony to shoot through him, almost losing consciousness.

Lou's eyes darted over his barely illuminated surroundings, seeking anything else within reach. Dread threatened to lock his muscles up as everything lethal looking was hung up on wall pegs just out of his reach. The long, straight handle of a discarded rake caught his eye, leaning on the opposite wall. He crawled towards it, then grabbed the wooden handle, intending to use it like a bat to knock the shovel down. His return trip across the shed was taking way too long. The space seemed to grow ten feet in diameter for every foot of ground he managed to cross. Any second now the driver would come back, come back for *him*, and he'd be fucked, literally caught with his pants down.

He thought he heard shouts over the roar of blood in his ears, but they seemed far away. Then he heard bodies crashing through dense woods, shouts coming closer. Roy's distinct hillbilly bray grew louder, feral with fright.

Lou breathed for a count of ten as his vision went tunnel shaped. He forced himself to inhale the corrupt air, battling back the gray edges that pushed in from his peripheral vision, then got back to work. He jabbed the rake handle at the ancient shovel, trying to shimmy it off its hook. Lou's arm shook as he tried again and again. At first, the best he could do was thwack the spade with weak, glancing blows. Finally, he drew on his deep, blackened well of rage reserved for the entire state of Missouri and its two terrible sons. Lou swung the rake handle hard, and the-hook came loose from the moldy wall, crashing down on him with a dull, distant impact.

Lou shimmied into the vertical slits of light. The shovel had bit a nasty gash into his shin. He couldn't even feel it, this destruction of his own flesh.

"Fuckin' gnarly," he said through his panting as he grabbed his lethal tools and tossed them into the corner by the door. Just as they clattered to the ground, hurried footsteps and the crunch of branches and dried leaves grew steadily louder. "*Shit,*" he hissed under his breath, crawling as quick as he could into the corner to set up his ambush.

He heard raspy breathing as the crunch of forest detritus became the crush of gravel. Lou's heart pounded, his fight-or-flight response keying up. He was going to *fight,* goddamnit, he was going to fight tooth and fucking nail, until death. He pictured Lateria, her cute little button nose, the way she laughed when he blew raspberries on her tummy. He pictured Janel, framed in the morning light filtering in their bedroom window, angelic, serenity personified as she slept, luscious black hair splayed out in a corona around her head. He imagined Lateria and Janel having to live in a world without him, a world where men like that thing in the cave existed, a world where he wasn't around to protect them from such terrible nightmares.

He squeezed the rake handle, picturing in his mind how this was going to go. The shovel was ready at his side, its tip dark with blood. But then a gunshot, close now, tore at his resolve. Lou dared to sidle up to the wall and peer between the slats as Roy came into view, stumbling out of the woods.

The man's pale, hawkish face glistened with sweat in the light of his truck, body heaving as he ripped in breaths. Lou clocked the gun in one hand, the jerry can in the other, it's spout upturned as a few final drops of gasoline dribbled from it. Lou also saw he had on one of those LED headlamps like what his daddy wore when spending long nights working on the old farm truck. There was more rustling in the woods. Roy raised the gun.

"Fuck you!" Roy shouted, and the pistol barked once more.

Lou nearly gasped when he saw who Roy had been shouting at. The terrible imp from the cave emerged from the woods. The decrepit thing reeked of gasoline so strong it managed to cut through the mephitic wave of human waste that fermented in the shed like aging wine. It proceeded out of the woods at an unhurried pace, a hand up against the truck's lights. In the harsh, unforgiving light, Lou saw with terrible clarity just how monstrous the man truly was.

Goblin-like feet sported yellow, crooked toenails and toes blackened at the edges. The skin on the left side of the man's body, if he could truly be called that, was pink and mottled, reminding Lou of a hotdog that'd been over-nuked in a gas station microwave. The skin glistened sickly in the beam of Roy's headlight, and even from a distance Lou could hear the wet sound of the thing's breathing. Ragged, fluid, phlegmy.

"The fuck you think you're doin', Roy?" The voice was like wasp wings against sandpaper. "Where is he? Where's my boy? He in on this?"

"What the fuck's it to you? I—"

Time seemed to skip forward. One second the inhuman thing was standing at the woods' edge, the next he was holding Roy up by the throat, booted feet hovering a foot off the ground. Lou knew meth could really whack out some people, but he understood, looking at this horrible tableau of superhuman strength, something deeper was at play here.

"WHERE-ISSSS-HE?" the dad hissed.

"I... I don't know, goddamnit! He went off with that sheriff!" Roy's gurgling voice was barely audible over the idling truck engine.

The thing dropped Roy. "Get bit, did he?" he said, an old hick's tongue in a demon's mouth.

"I don't fuckin' know, why do you care? We're just your errand boys, we—"

"You have no idea what's at stake. You ain't just my fuckin' errand boys. I been working an angle. I been finding a way for us all to get out from under this. But I *need* Tate."

"Why?" Roy shouted. Indignant rage cut through the raw rasp of a recently choked throat.

Lou's eyes flicked from this father-son conflict from hell to the tree line. A faint orange glow, penumbral and almost beautiful, blossomed from the heart of the forest. And with it the smell of smoke.

"You wouldn't understand. I just need to know where he's—"

"I'm done." Roy looked like he was trying to get some composure back. But even through the narrow slit, even through the haze of his own heat-induced delirium, Lou's perceptive nature picked up on the fear cutting through the bravado. "I'm done with all this, with you. All this goddamn bullshit!"

The laugh that came from that thing's throat was more like a death rattle. Terrible, grating, atrophied vocal cords vibrated like a buzzsaw bow against a warped, de-tuned cello.

"Roy. we done been down this road, son. You ain't ever gonna be done with me. You leave me... it's gonna spread. *We're* gonna spread. Can't keep living off horse blood and raccoons. It ain't the same. But there's a way to stop it. We need Tate though, son. I *need* him."

Lou swallowed with a dry click. He didn't like the sound of that at all. The thing spoke as if he had legions of those just like him. Jesus Christ. Roy was right when he told Lou he was gonna wish they were just klansmen.

"We? Who's we?" Roy asked. The old man croaked again with laughter. It made nails on a chalkboard sound like a beautiful symphony in comparison.

The glow of the forest intensified. Through the aural haze, Lou could hear bodies moving through brush. Silhouettes flitted among the many shadows cast by trees and branches. They moved quick and with an eerie animal grace.

"You see, us Langans finally buried the hatchet with those goddamn gypsies. It was time we paid the piper... and pay I did. Now I got a plan. It's all gonna work out. But I need him. I need Tate, he's the key. You think them silly little crosses was enough to keep us here?" The Langan patriarch rasped, gesturing back towards the woods. "Don't want no attention drawn to us, boy. We stay put cause we *gotta*. I told 'em my boys would bring us what we need, that no more gotta end up like us. But there's only so many animals we can eat to hold us over. Their blood... it ain't the same as the blood from you, from people. We been good, makin' what you brought us last. But you *leave,* Roy, you gonna be unleashing Hell on this land. Tate can help though, just tell me where he is. You can help—"

"SHUT UP!" Roy screamed. "I DON'T WANNA HEAR NO MORE. I DON'T CARE! FUCK YOU. AND FUCK TATE!" Lou saw the man drop the gas can and reach for something small and metallic that glinted off the headlights. In one smooth motion, Roy flicked off the lid with his jeans. Lou used to be obsessed with collecting Zippo lighters as a teenager and recognized that telltale snick immediately. Roy brought the lighter up sharply, the ignition wheel catching on his denim. Lou knew that trick well. For every club they ever played, there was always some asshole trying to impress a girl with that same cheap gimmick.

The Zippo's flame was flickering to life and catching to the wick when Roy tossed it towards his father. The lighter's metal casing clinked off rock, landing at those abhorrent, scabrous feet. A moment later, the dull *whoomph* of flame shot upward, a lake of fire blossoming all around in a searing wave of blue and orange.

Lou was reminded of the grizzly televised scene of the Dalai Lama's calm self-immolation, the way he maintained a pose of prayer even as flames blackened his skin. The father merely stood there, a human pyre, while a blue trail of lit gas snaked back towards the tree line.

"We let you live, boy. We stayed in these caves so the Curse wouldn't spread. But the moon is coming, and these caves... they lead all over this land. If you don't feed us, if you don't work with me, we will hunt. We will spread. We will become a plague, we will—"

Roy's pistol finally spoke. Five rounds punched into the flaming monstrosity, all center mass shots. Should've been enough to take a normal human being down twice over, regardless of the amount of crank in his system.

The combination of fire and bullets must've finally been enough to either injure or scare the mysterious abomination because the next moment saw him running back into the woods, a humanoid meteor streaking between trees. But as he retreated, Lou heard a high-pitched, whining hiss, a tea kettle shriek mixed with the howl of a bobcat in heat. Despite the febrile warmth, his skin puckered with gooseflesh. It sounded like some kind of call, or signal.

Roy set his sights on the shed. After being startled out of his plan by the family drama, Lou backed away from the wall, scrambling to get into a defensive position.

Footsteps came closer, only a few feet away now. Lou breathed deeply one last time. He braced to fight for his life, forcing the strange scene and its possible implications from his mind. Instead, the truck door closed before the engine roared. The truck shot forward a few feet before stopping again. Lou's eyes shot open, not realizing he'd squeezed them shut until this deviation in his plan.

"What? No no no... come here, fucker. Come get some," he screamed, realizing he *wanted* this fight. He wanted this conflict to happen. He wanted *payback,* goddamnit.

For what felt like hours, the truck just sat there in a clanking idle. Meanwhile, the smoke grew more pungent, fighting the reek of shit for dominance in Lou's nose. Over the dull rumble of the engine, a new sound filled the night: the roar of a conflagration fast approaching. Finally, the truck door opened and slammed shut. Footsteps came right for him.

This was it, now or never.

# Chapter 18

LOU WAS NEARLY BLINDED as Roy threw the door open. The truck's high-beams burned away the darkness like the flash that comes before the nuclear mushroom cloud. Roy's silhouette flinched slightly, a grumble of disgust rising from his throat. A gagging sound echoed in the doorway before he finally seemed to gain some composure.

*Yeah, it's ripe in here, huh, you inbred fuck?*

"Where are you, boy?" Roy's voice was rough and strained. Lou knew the man was combatting the olfactory assault that Lou had long grown used to. The man stumbled forward, and Lou readied himself.

He'd tucked himself into a corner of the shed right next to the door, in one of the few remaining pockets of shadows the truck's headlights hadn't managed to burn away.

Lou readied the rake handle, making a mental note of where the shovel was. He would have to move damn fast for his plan to work. Roy took one more step. Lou shoved the wooden handle forward, tangling Roy's feet. The rake handle was ripped from his hands as Roy let out a surprised squawk and fell to the ground.

Lou grabbed for the shovel while Roy was in mid-fall. Swinging it down as hard as he could like an axe into firewood the minute Roy landed face-first in the rotten dirt floor. He got lucky when the blade came down hard on one of Roy's ankles. The impact rattled through the shovel handle. Dirt crusted blade bit through sinew and bone. The sound and the feeling of Roy's Achilles snapping was more satisfying than any sexual release. Roy screamed, and Lou screamed right along with him.

"FUCK YOU. FUCK YOU. FUCK YOU." Adrenaline flooded his body. All the aches and pains he'd endured temporarily bled away to unimportant throbs. A ray of hope was burning bright as the truck lights now. Lou was possessed by something not wholly himself as he scrabbled up those jean legs like a ferret climbing a tree. Something in his lizard brain had turned over, and the inner caveman that hoots and howls in its cage was let free.

He raised the shovel handle in his right hand. His good hand. He was going to kill this motherfucker or die trying.

"Stop! Stop, you sumbitch! Tryna help you!" Roy's strangled words came out in explosions of breath as he tried to buck Lou off. For an unknowable amount of time, they were just a grappling mess of limbs, testosterone, and adrenaline marinating in sweat and shit. But finally, Roy was on his back, and Lou smacked him with the shovel. He was attempting to angle it just right so he could thrust it down like a spear, but that was nearly impossible. Having to hold himself up with one arm, and his legs just useless dead meat while he tried to swing with the other. He managed to bring the bladed end down once, hard, into Roy's rib cage. It was a clumsy, falling jab, but Lou heard the green-branch splinter-snap of rib's cracking.

"Fucker!" Roy's voice was high and hissy with pain. He fumbled for the pistol that had fallen out of his hands as he tripped. Lou was seeing red though. He wasn't paying attention to the smaller details. The shovel wasn't just a weapon but an extension of himself now. Like talons on a hawk. He wanted to bury it in that motherfucker.

He struck at Roy's solar plexus. The shovel's crude tip struck off breastbone the way hidden rocks scrape off the blade when you're digging a hole. Lou knew he needed to slow down, get a good grip, and try to deliver a killing blow. But he was like a machine stuck in a loop. He wanted to deliver as much pain as possible.

Finally, he managed to get a solid hold on the shovel and aim it upwards. More by luck than by skill, he'd aimed for the general vicinity of Roy's head. He thrust the shovel forward, feeling it find purchase in bone and cartilage. But Lou couldn't see the damage he'd done. By then, the gun was up, and Lou had only just registered the black eye of the barrel when a flash and a cannon blast lit up his world.

# Chapter 19

Lou screamed, his vision and hearing lost in the light and thunder blasting across the walls around him. He expected death, floating through the great, ethereal tunnel towards whatever the Hell awaited after all of this. Instead, what he thought was a hornet flew past Lou's face as he lurched forward. A searing line of pain traced from his jaw to his left ear. The shovel crunched to a halt, striking something yielding, but solid. When he tried to pull it away for another swing, it wouldn't budge. Whatever it had sunk into, it was in there to stay.

His eyelids fluttered until his vision cleared enough to find the pointed edge of the spade buried in the middle of the skinny Langan's face. It had cleaved his nose clean in two. Blood pumped out of the nose and mouth in a slow, but steady torrent. The man spasmed beneath him.

Instead of yanking it free, Lou resituated, pulling himself up to rest his body weight against the handle, despite the agony it caused him.

"Fuck... YOU!" he said through clenched teeth, his voice muffled in his own ears. Lou pushed the dull blade deeper into the man's head, the high-pitched scrape of metal shearing through bone a million miles away. He kept pressing long after the spasms had stopped, the glint of steel disappearing into flesh and skull, and a peaceful, vacant look came into those unblinking eyes. Lou was determined to push the blade all the way through until it touched dirt, then an idea came to him, and he looked up into the blinding headlights of the truck.

"Inbred hillbilly fuck." Lou spat on the sundered face. Lou was faintly aware of a dull throb on his left cheek, but his body had been so bombarded by pain, the track of the bullet in his skin had been lost. In the galaxy of torment his body had endured, his brain was able to process only so much.

Slowly, he extricated himself from the shed, his bare legs leaving a bloody smear behind him as he crawled across the gravel driveway, gun in one hand, rake in the other. Using the handle to punch into the dirt, Lou dragged himself along, not wanting to think about what it was doing to his numbed manhood. He almost wept with joy when he saw the driver-side door of the truck had been left wide open.

Right then and there, he decided that maybe, *just maybe*, there might be some fucked up, benevolent, omniscient dickhead up there in the clouds, throwing the occasional schmuck like him a bone.

*Let's get out of this shit hole first, before we have a come-to-Jesus moment,* he thought, groaning as he hauled himself up into the truck. Every flexing movement of his back stabbed as if someone were administering a spinal tap on him with an 8000-volt cattle prod. Lou eased into the driver's seat, struggling not to vomit from the pain, then used every single ounce of willpower left in his system to slam the door shut. The truck was an automatic transmission, another stroke of luck. These fucking hillbillies loved their manual cars. Made them feel important like their dads or some shit when they had to shift gears. At least these particular assholes were pragmatic. He remembered Tate's obvious mental handicap and figured they had an automatic in the event the big man had to drive the truck for some reason.

He was about to put the truck into drive, using the handle of the rake as a shitty makeshift pedal control, when he saw movement in the corner of his eye. Blazing color filled the big rear-view mirrors. Lou blinked stupidly, realizing he'd been so used to the stifling heat of the shed and had been so fixated on the fight that he hadn't noticed the outside world was a few hundred degrees hotter.

Lou squirmed as he beheld the flaming walls roaring only a few hundred feet behind him, trees bursting into plumes of searing fire. He hadn't known that a tree could actually explode, and here was his paralyzed ass, a forest of live grenades all around him. Beyond the shooting sparks and cinders, something dark moved. A clutch of forms emerged from the fire. Humanoid silhouettes. They ran out like streaking meteors, trailing smoke and flame in their wake.

*This is Hell. The bastard shot me... I'm dead... I'm in fucking Hell.* Lou froze, transfixed by the shapes running towards the truck. Even as his primal brain screamed that these monsters, demons, whatever sick things existed down in the eternal suck, were coming for him, *right* for him. He could only sit there and watch, a deer in the headlights. Pain and plans of escape temporarily forgotten as they swarmed closer.

Except they didn't come for him. Not at first, anyway. One made a beeline for the shed, and the truck's hi-beams photographed it onto Lou's eyes. He saw the thing's body in terrible, vivid clarity, like a charred steak on a long-forgotten grill, but in the shape of a man. He remembered the way Roy's father calmly accepted his immolation. Lou assumed the cave-wraith had come back to exact his revenge for the attempted patricide.

The thing dragged Roy Langan's body from the shed, and even over the roar of the engine, the fire, and tinnitus from the gunshot, Lou could hear the thing's high, almost jubilant shriek. The same clarion call he'd heard earlier. A pinkish-gray maw cracked open in the charcoal briquette face, releasing an ear-piercing caterwaul and revealing jaws full of twisted, jagged protrusions, with four prominent eyeteeth, like ivory scythes. The long, high-pitched, undulating call made Allen's demonic, guttural shrieks sound like childish mewling. Finally, it fell upon the body with savage glee.

Two more walking pyres joined it, homing in on the body and scrabbling forward like starving dogs. They slipped and stumbled in their own flames and haste, excited by the frenzy of the feast. Roy's flesh sizzled and spit where their blackened mouths clamped on various parts of him. Their lips had been burned away in a permanent grin of hate. Lou looked on, watching the daggers disappear into a body already brutalized by his own hand. The fact he'd just killed another human being was lost in the tide of horror from this spectacle.

The first creature's throat bobbed the way Lou's own had when he was gulping down that milkshake. Roy's body twitched with each gulp. As they drank, the blackened, smoldering skin around the thing's body started to change.

"No fuckin' way—" Lou looked on as charred ash fell away like a snake shedding its skin. In its place, pink, glistening flesh was born, like scar tissue from a still-healing wound. The others were changing too. The fire engulfing their bodies extinguished with puffs of hissing smoke as they supped. Roy's body deflated beneath them.

An insane conclusion started to fit together in Lou's brain—*Got to be alive, got to be human to be a cannibal, this shit nowhere near that*—when something wet flicked across the glass.

A monstrous visage appeared in the driver's-side window. Lou whipped his head around to see one of the monsters up close. Its eyes had ruptured from its head from the heat, running down its charred face like spilled egg yolk on a hot stove. It banged its head savagely against the window, safety glass spider-webbing into an opaque kaleidoscope.

"Thought y'all didn't want *my* black ass!" Lou recoiled from the impact. Laughter bubbled up in his throat. He raised the Taurus and fired at the dark blob of a head, emptying the clip and squinting against the back spray of glass. For a moment, everything was white. The 9mm reports in the confined space of the truck cab blasted a repeating Emergency Broadcast System signal in his head.

Outside, the thing stumbled backwards. Forehead and cheeks sported oozing craters where the bullets had found their mark, blood spilling out to boil on its cindered flesh. It did not drop as it *should've* but stood there stupidly. Poking blackened fingers into its own head. The thing gaped at him as if in disbelief that Lou had the gall to shoot holes in its brand-new skull.

Smoke billowed into the cab and singed Lou's lungs and eyes, finally shocking his mind out of its reactionary stupor. This fight was done. It was time for flight.

With the rake handle wedged against the gas, Lou wrenched the lever into drive and the truck lurched forward sharply. His vertebrae ground together while the truck careened to and fro, rumbling into every hole in the ground. His arm weighed a thousand pounds as he struggled with the wheel, weaving madly through a dense maze of forest. *Whichever of those hog-humping Langans carved this driveway out was blind fucking drunk!* Lou thought, each bump and shudder of the truck's frame pure agony. Lou howled, unable to stop the throat-searing scream, the only release valve that kept his throbbing brain from imploding after what he'd seen.

It was impossible to brake accurately with the damn stick. He wanted nothing more than to put pedal to metal and rocket out of there, but he knew he was just as likely to wrap the big vehicle around a tree. He let the truck coast roughly down the mild grade of the driveway, trying to stay on the crooked tract until finally, *blessedly*, Lou spied blacktop.

The scream transformed into hysterical cackling as the truck raced onto the blacktop, off-road tires squealing. Lou cut the steering wheel hard left, not having a fucking clue as to where he was going. He only knew he had to get away from here, one word darting around in his brain like a trapped fox in a cage. It was the only word he could think of as he mentally replayed the image of those blackened husks drinking Roy's life force.

Fangs.

Sweet fucking Jesus, he had to be going crazy.

The road straightened out, and Lou pushed the rake handle down all the way now. The stick slipped off the gas pedal a few times before he found a good angle and jammed it in. The truck climbed up to seventy. Lou sailed past road signs and warnings without comprehending them in the blur. He only saw the speedometer, focusing his whole being on the needle, wanting to bury it deeper than those soul-suckers. He didn't register the burst of light or the horn blast until it was too late.

The big hand of the truck's rear end suddenly swung to 9 o'clock, twisting Lou's arms and hurling them into the air. His body bounced around the cab like a pinball off pneumatic bumpers. In an instant he was back in the Shaggin' Wagon with glass tinkling, the tires screeching, and metal taunting him. He feared the hellish journey was going to begin again. Roy's dead face sparkled in a cloud of flying glass, reminding him that he wasn't quite finished with the lesson. "Uh-uh, boy," it said, glittering mouth stretching, "one ticket left, can't get off this ride once it starts." Swirling crystalline eyes closed as he laughed, curling into the moons in the door of an outhouse. *Oh no, I'm not going back there, no fuckin' way, you'll have to fucking kill me before I go back into that goddamn fucking shed,* he thought as the chassis lurched and spun. His head slammed off the dashboard, and finally, mercifully, everything went dark.

# Chapter 20

S USANNAH SAT ON HER back porch, trying to savor the tranquility of her backyard. On warm summer mornings such as this, she could watch the blue jays and mockingbirds do their usual dance, or bluegill and bass pop the water on the small pond down below, chasing water skaters around for breakfast. In the peaceful beauty and bright sunlight of morning, the events of last night seemed like a distant nightmare. Looking back on the oppressive weight, the overwhelming sense of claustrophobic dread she had felt towards the curtain of shadows that draped the woods, Susannah felt even more absurd than she had in the moment. She glanced at the clutch of woods where she'd emptied the Glock, the scars of frenzied bullet marks.

The presence of smoke was almost thick enough to make her eyes water now. A visible haze painted the rising sun a deep, visceral red. Susannah had stared right at it without squinting, a great crimson eye staring into her soul. In the assuring light of day, it was easy to look back on last night and chalk it up to nerves from a traumatic workday. But there were signs that couldn't be ignored. For one thing, her nightmare from last night—her first time dreaming of conflagration—had apparently come true.

She thought at first it might've been a controlled burn on a nearby farm. But this did not smell like burning wheat chaff. This had the thick, sour smell of a forest fire. One that carried with it singed fur, burning wood and loam, and anything else that got caught in its path. She thought of her dream, how she'd plunged headlong into a lake of fire. That horrible, familiar face in a subterranean sky of blood. The strange things it said.

Susannah thought of Jessie and the eerie flash she got from her last night. The flayed cow screaming, the coils of innards spilling from its stomach. She thought of Buckie, as he came out with her this morning, *still* avoiding that side of the yard. The deputy, and the way the cross burned his skin. In light of all that, the fire seemed like a sure portent of doom.

She used to not ken to such fanatical thinking. Not like those crazy Seventh-Day Adventist folk who thought God spoke to them through the hair dryer, telling them when the world would end. But as she stared at the deep-hued, crimson dawn, she couldn't help but feel she was on the cusp of something apocalyptic, the insipient heat of fire but a harbinger of terrible things yet to come.

Susannah jumped when the phone went off in the pocket of her robe, nearly dropping her mug of coffee. She had the notion to just turn it off and continue sitting in the quiet, try and forget about last night. Feeling anxiety twist her bowels into knots, she pulled out her phone. It was Elizabeth.

Susannah groaned. A call this early meant another emergency.

"I'm sorry to keep calling you like this, Miss Paige—" Elizabeth said, no chance for Susannah to say hello. "But... my God, I don't know what's going on. It's like Hell on Earth. It's literally like Hell on—" She was interrupted by what sounded like someone slamming a hammer against a car hood, a rending metallic impact that drew a terrified squawk from Elizabeth.

"What's going on, honey?" Susannah said, making her way inside while slipping out of her robe.

"I don't know. This morning I was getting ready to fire up the incinerator like you asked me to, when I heard this fuss, and Miss Paige, that cow... it isn't dead."

"No, Elizabeth, that cow was *dead*. I checked it twice before—"

"But it isn't! It broke out of the incinerator and started acting crazy. It... went for..." she began, sobbing again at a great agonized squeal of stressing metal. It sounded like the clinic walls were caught in a tornado. "It went for the other cow, starting to... eat it. I ran back to the clinic and locked the doors behind me and, and... now they're *both* trying to get in here! I don't know how long the clinic's gonna hold. I tried calling the police, but they're all tied up, and I... OH MY GO—"

"Elizabeth! Elizabeth!" Susannah could only hear distant sobbing and a horrible sound, like an enraged bull in rutting season with no fertile fields to plow.

Buckie followed her around as she threw on the closest clean top she could find and slipped into jeans, nearly tripping in her haste.

"Jessie, honey, get up," she called, hearing only a muffled groan in response. By the time Susannah had woken up, the whiskey bottle was noticeably diminished, only an inch left in the bottle. When she'd gone to bed it'd been close to half full. The girl must have helped herself while Susannah was in bed, dreaming terrible things. That was alright. Whiskey was, after all, a damn fine painkiller, as she well knew, but she needed the girl up and awake. Whatever she was rushing in to face was beyond the natural order of things, beyond the creation or will of God. She needed help.

Out into the living room, Jessie had wound a blanket around herself with only wisps of red hair sticking out. Susannah shoved her awake, and Jessie rolled off the couch in her cloth burrito, groaning.

"What—"

Susannah ignored the girl for the time being, flinging open the gun safe.

Susannah scanned the collection of firearms she and Harold had acquired over the years. A few deer rifles and two shotguns. The .22's rack space hung empty as it was still in her car. She reached for the Browning shotgun. She'd always teased Harold about it. More powerful than a 12-gauge, the 10-gauge shotgun bordered on elephant gun territory, unnecessary for anything that lurked in the Ozark hills. But she was grateful for the huge-bored weapon now. Boxes of buckshot and deer slugs presented themselves to her. She chose the solid slugs after some deliberation. She'd seen what one of these had done to a cougar that'd been stalking their property when they first moved in. She wanted that solid, destructive stopping power today.

"You ever fired a gun, sweetheart?" Susannah asked over her shoulder.

"I... what? What's going on?" Jessie yawned and stumbled a few steps from the couch.

Susannah thrust the huge gun into the bewildered girl's hands. "Yes or no question, honey, need to know if you got my back." She stared at the two handguns on the shelf of the safe. The .38 special—Harold's gun—whose massive hollow points had more stopping power. Susannah was a better shot with the Glock, had far more practice with it, and it held more rounds, to boot. She grabbed a box of hollow points for the Glock and tucked the unloaded weapon into her waist band.

"Once. Way back. I had a few foster parents who were gun nuts and lived in a bad part of Chicago. But—"

"Alright, get your shoes on. You're about to get the gun safety lesson of your life," Susannah strode out onto the porch.

Jessie followed, red eyed and squinting in the morning sun. Susannah took the Browning, replaced it with the pistol, and spun the girl to face the small pond.

"Like this." Susannah reached around Jessie, the way Harold taught her, hands over hers to show how she needed to hold the gun. "Keep your finger off the trigger. See this switch here? That's the safety, flick it off."

Jessie did so, using her thumb. "Pull back the slide, like this." Susannah loaded a round into the chamber for her. "Now fire. Aim for the pond," she said. The bluegill and bass were about to get one hell of a wake up.

Jessie fired, the Glock jumping in her unsure hands. Mourning doves and blue jays took flight as pond water jumped up in a spray, the gun's report breaking the tranquil silence of the morning.

"Good aim, honey, but you gotta hold the darn thing." Susannah put her hands over Jessie's, arms wrapped around her and squeezing. It was an intimate moment, and absurdly, for just a second, Susannah felt a solid pang of matronly love when Jessie squared her shoulders and tightened her grip. This girl had come into her life and changed it forever, and in such a short period of time. Jessie barely knew her, but already knew more about her than Harold did, or even could.

*You're just trauma-bonding, or whatever the Psychology Today magazines call it*, she told herself, feeling a protective urge as Jessie fired twice more, her arms and face unflinching, anticipating the recoil. Both shots found the pond. It was a wide target, Susannah thought, but it would have to be good enough.

"Excellent, sweetheart. I'll teach you how to reload in the car. Come on." She ran into the house to grab the rest of the gear.

# Chapter 21

J ESSIE'S STOMACH WAS A gurgling cauldron of acidic bile. She chided herself for giving in to her old ways and tying one on last night. The pills had started wearing off, and she couldn't bear facing another night sober in that place. The anxieties of her situation had come on thick and heavy like the surrounding night. The whiskey felt too good with its blossoming heat in her belly, and that didn't help matters at all. It was that old search for oblivion.

Jessie had seen the red cloud three times now. She could no longer explain it away as some weird misfiring of her oxygen-deprived synapses when Susannah restarted her heart. It came clear as day, a red mist flowing in ethereal tendrils through the woods, consolidating into a solid cloud just above where the dog sat snarling and howling. Then there was that fucked up dream in the car. The voice beckoning to her. Jessie thought surely she was hallucinating. She'd done her share of acid and mushrooms, but differentiating between what she saw and what was real had always been easy until now.

Clearly Susannah hadn't seen it, but Buckie did. Right before Susannah had gone all Rambo and fired wildly into the woods, they had touched. Jessie had felt another brief current surge through her, and despite being blind to it, Susannah had aimed right at the scarlet mist.

As she was being pulled inside, Jessie had looked over her shoulder. The mist was dissipating but didn't leave entirely.

Jessie had been left alone by her new ally and had embraced an old one. Taking shot after shot, letting the whiskey fill her belly, she tried to get rid of the sense of being *wanted*, of being *hunted*. It seemed absurd, but that cloud seemed to be coming right for her. She felt a tidal pull towards it and feverishly avoided any opening that would've allowed the cloud to seep in: windows, keyholes. She wandered the nighttime house, checking every door was locked. Jessie couldn't stop thinking about it slipping through, the minute cracks and gaps of doors and roof opening to it, tendrils of red snaking through ventilation, bleeding down to infect her.

Through the blur of drink, her anger surged. She had come a long way, but still the demons of circumstance haunted her endlessly. Jessie had escaped from the unending litany of foster homes, a parade of apathetic faces, all blending into one uncaring homunculus. Next stop, a shitty fixed-income housing project in East Memphis, her neighbors crack addicts and drunks, families that she could never truly know, all in abject poverty. During that time, she'd spent four terrible, beaten-down years at Burger Zone before Blasphemer was big enough to tour internationally.

Her boss, a slovenly, power-hungry man named Devin Cardin, fixated on Jessie the second she started work, making crude comments, sliding his greasy bulk (which always reeked of BO) against her in the tight area of the back kitchen, his greasy fingers caressing a buttock or a breast. His poorly kempt pedo-stache had tickled the back of her neck once or twice. Jessie had ached to tell the creep to fuck right off, but she needed new gear desperately, an $1800 DW kit to be exact.

After several filed complaints, BZ corporate intervened and fired his ass. Jessie got promoted to store manager. That's when the real nightmare began. He'd sit out front of her apartment complex, lurking like an ever-present shadow.

He showed up at her work. His presence even infiltrated the digital domain. Constant friend requests from obvious throw away accounts. Nasty messages in her inbox. It only escalated from there.

Jessie and Allen found evidence of someone breaking into their apartment. Jessie discovered random articles of clothing (not just any clothes, but her favorite fucking band T-shirts) in her closet smeared with a crusty, crystalline substance that could only be dried jizz.

The small trash can she kept in the bathroom specifically for her 'feminine hygiene' products had been obviously rifled through. Jessie was one of those unfortunate women whose period hit them like a Mack truck and a flow like the Mississippi when it came. On a bad month, that little trash can could be filled up by the end of the week. That litany of discarded Tampax pads had a habit of going MIA, and just so happened to start disappearing around the time of the mystery cum stains appearing.

Devin Cardin became an omnipresent, soul sucking force. He was like a cancer slowly metastasizing in the body that was her life.

Eventually, Allen and Jessie reached their breaking point. Allen was always the first to jump into a pit and break up a fight, the first to knock out the crowd killers at their shows, and the first to come to anyone's aid. He insisted on confronting Devin. Talked Jessie up, letting her know she did not need to deal with this bullshit, and he would gladly teach the human slug a thing or two about hurt. But surprisingly, Jessie had been the one to draw first (and only) blood. The Devin situation had become so suffocating, her rage and frustration building, that one day she stormed out of the apartment, ran towards Devin's car and pulled his reeking body out, operating on pure, pent-up rage. She'd transformed into a banshee. She didn't remember much about the assault—it was a blur of pure catharsis—except that Allen eventually pulled her off the bleeding, screeching stalker, her arms windmilling and her throat raw from screaming. Devin stopped coming around, and Allen, pleasantly surprised, started tacking 'badass' onto her name.

Last night, with that hovering red mist, had felt like a hundred Devin's were peering at her from the dark tree line.

Reality slammed home as Jessie stumbled toward the car, balancing a heavy shotgun and boxes of ammo like groceries. Her ears still rang from the impromptu shooting lesson.

In the passenger seat, Jessie loaded the two fifteen-round magazines while Susannah told her about the phone call. It seemed the guns weren't going to be for show. Despite the sphincter-clenching terror she felt as they sped towards the clinic, Jessie did her best not to show it. She looked at the hard, salt-of-the-earth woman who had handled a basket of insanity with an almost Clint Eastwood-level of stoic grit, and she was determined to emulate it.

Susannah sped down Highway U. Jessie cursed aloud as she dropped the box of shotgun ammo, and almost threw up the whiskey percolating in her stomach as she leaned down to pick up the huge, red shells rolling along the floorboard. She bit back the acidic geyser in her throat and began clumsily loading the shells into the breach. The big gun was awkward to maneuver in the small SUV. Jessie could feel Susannah's wary eye on her as she did her best to handle the lethal weaponry. Something had been bothering her since last night and she couldn't hold it back any longer.

"That local guy you mentioned, Bernie Standridge, he made it sound like the Coldonas were murdered. Like maybe the town had something to do with —"

"Jesus... not this again. The Coldonas... that whole thing was an accident. That's what everyone always said."

"Yeah, well, history has a habit of getting whitewashed by the people who write it," Jessie said as she racked the slide on the shotgun, the loud *chi-clack* sounding like a final command; the gavel strike of an irate judge.

"Whatever. Point is... I highly doubt the Coldonas have anything to do with this mess."

Jessie left it at that, not wanting to push the issue. She could sense the tension radiating off Susannah and she didn't want to piss the woman off.

The smell of smoke permeated the car's interior. Buckie barked from the backseat at the occasional fire trucks as they screamed past. A deep, red haze smeared the sun's rays. It took every bit of willpower and deep breathing for Jessie to fight back the incoming panic attack that threatened to seize her like an iron fist.

She realized how badly she wanted more pills, to be back in that cozy little office, floating high on painkillers and forgetting about the current horrors of the world, lost in history and lore. As they hurtled down the road, engine roaring, she had a feeling that the van crash was just the fall of a single domino in an increasingly terrible line of events, and they were heading right into another nightmare.

Susannah's face went pale.

"What?" Jessie pressed, sensing that she was holding back something.

"There was something about last night I didn't tell you. The Tate boy... I thought he was just babbling. He said his daddy was still alive... but... Oh, Lord Jesus—" Susannah trailed off. The Explorer jounced into the gravel parking lot of the vet clinic. Jessie didn't comprehend what she was seeing at first, her hungover mind still playing catch up.

Two things that vaguely resembled cows were throwing themselves against a large, prefabricated metal outbuilding attached to the animal clinic, buckling in the blood-spattered walls. The cows shambled to a stop, then turned towards the SUV. One cow looked like it'd taken a front row seat to the business end of a shotgun, its skull a mangled heap of exposed, cratered bone and torn flesh. Their piebald coats were obscured by weeping boils and open sores that sizzled and popped in the sunlight.

Buckie was growling and snapping at the back window, his beautiful golden coat raised in bushy hackles. The one with the Swiss cheese head let out a terrible, gurgling grunt, reminding her of Allen's odd but effective vocal warm up techniques. It stumbled towards the vehicle on trembling legs. A quivering mass of crooked limbs, exposed muscle, and sinew, just fast enough for Jessie to wish she was riding in an armored war machine, a tank preferably. The other cow, despite the ragged wounds around its neck and shoulder, was in better condition. It turned in the direction of its mate, then charged the SUV like a raging bull.

Jessie had always told herself she would never scream like those dumb bimbos in horror movies, that she was a tough cut of leather from the streets. She'd seen dead bodies before. Had even been mugged at gunpoint by a crackhead. All without screaming. But Jessie found herself shrieking now, as eight hundred pounds of corrupted beef hurtled towards her.

"Hang on!" Susannah threw the Explorer in reverse. It jittered for a second, tires spinning up gravel, before finally catching traction and rocketing backwards. The Holstein's body plowed through the air where the car had been only a moment before, landing in one of the many rutted potholes with a meaty crunching sound. Bone jutted through skin as the leg snapped under its weight. Susannah reversed until she was almost to the shoulder of the highway and shoved the gearshift into Park. "Get behind the wheel. If things go south, take Buckie and get out of here," Susannah said, grabbing the shotgun from Jessie.

"What—" Jessie began, but Susannah was already out of the car, moving slowly towards the downed cow. While Jessie was scrabbling

over to the driver's seat, she heard something that sounded like a fucking howitzer going off. Through the windshield, she watched the Holy
Roller of Carter County laying waste, the barrel of her shotgun belching
fire and smoke.

# Chapter 22

*Mercy killing. This is a mercy killing,* Susannah told herself, the shotgun kicking into her shoulder like a pissed-off donkey. The cow was struggling. Its front right leg canted at a sickening angle where it'd snapped in the pothole. For once, she was grateful Harold had procrastinated about calling someone to fix the holes. She focused her fire on the head.

Whatever sick, unholy thing had taken hold of these cattle had to have invaded either the brain stem or the spinal cord for it to have forced the host to ignore such tremendous physical trauma. She didn't understand why the cow's skin was sizzling and popping like someone was dumping hot, invisible tar on it. No parasite or pathogen she knew of could cause that. Three shots in and the head was nothing more than a pulpy ruin. She put one more round in at the base of its neck, the fourth slug finally decapitating the thing.

Just as it stopped writhing, she glimpsed the one she thought she'd killed yesterday loping towards her. Its ruined jaw sported teeth that had no place in a cow's mouth. Almost all breeds of cattle had a flat row of bottom teeth, with a firm but featureless dental pad in the roof of their mouths for shredding grass into cud. *These* teeth had mutated into things wicked and jagged, with sharp little nubs poking out of the dental pad.

This terrifying sight so floored her that she stopped firing. Her brain desperately tried to make sense of this nightmare.

Gunshots shocked Susannah out of her daze. She swiveled to figure out where the shots came from. When she did, she had to cough to get her lungs working again. Jessie was re-aiming the Glock, her hands resting in the crook between the open door and the car frame. Just like the police did. It had been four shots altogether. Two hit its right flank, though they didn't seem to faze the cow at all. Though it was distracted long enough for Susannah to collect herself and aim. She stared at that unnatural mouth as it yawned open to let out a screaming bellow. A terrible sound of rage and pain. The sight of those teeth that should not be haunted her, her brain tripping over itself.

Finally, Susannah stopped fixating on its gnashing mouth and fired right into the forehead. Brain and bone exploded from the poor creature. It collapsed two feet away, the sundered brain pan leaking a stringy, obsidian goo where gray matter should've been. It boiled up into a spitting mess as soon as it spilled onto the gravel. She fired once more, this time at an angle, to prevent any back spray as she aimed to take its head off. Instead, the shot ripped a huge hole towards the base of its neck, the cow's head now only attached by a few strands of sinew and spinal cord. Susannah pulled the trigger again, but the gun clicked. Empty. The cow gave out a shudder and kicked one leg out before it stopped moving.

*Surely they have to be dead by now,* Susannah thought, but for caution's sake, still gave what was left of the bodies a wide berth, running towards the buckled frame of the door. She pulled at the handle, calling out for Elizabeth, and after a brief tug-of-war, yanked it open with a screech. Susannah found her inside, huddled in a corner of the clinic, rocking back and forth and gripping herself tightly.

"Elizabeth... it's alright, darlin'. They're dead and gone now," she said, voice muffled in her ears from gunfire. Susannah came up short, noticing the bloody smears on Elizabeth's blouse. She wasn't holding herself out of fear but was clutching an arm to her chest to stop the flow of blood. She was saying something, but Susannah couldn't hear. "Let me see," she said and tenderly, slowly, reached out a hand.

"I tried to make it stop eating her. That poor cow just sat there, and let it happen... then it got *me*... I'm gonna end up like them, aren't I? Like the cop, and those cows. Oh my God..." Elizabeth sobbed.

Susannah cringed inwardly at the sight of the wound. The creature had taken a good chunk out of her forearm, hooking a few of the prominent veins. Through the static in her ears, she thought she caught a snatch of Elizabeth's hysterical babbling. *Should've just let it kill me...*

"Hey, hey, hey, no talking like that." Susannah squeezed Elizabeth's shoulders hard. "Look at me, Elizabeth. *Look* at me."

Elizabeth's eyes were huge and desperate and brimming with tears.

"You're gonna be fine. Let me wrap this up, then I'm taking you to the hospital," she said, unsure if she was yelling or not. Everything sounded distant, like someone had shoved cotton in her ears. She found gauze and disinfectant, and went to work, realizing she'd patched up more humans than animals in the last 48 hours. Susannah reached for the bottle of flour-like coagulant. She normally used the clot activator powder to plug up gunshot wounds on hunting dogs, or when sadistic bastards took potshots at strays. Even after she'd cleaned the wound and sprinkled the powder on, the bleeding wouldn't stop. Susannah resorted to gauze packing for travel, but by the time she got Elizabeth to the car, the red compression bandage was completely soaked.

Jessie was sitting in the passenger seat, staring at the heap of slaughtered cattle with a glazed look on her face, the Glock still clutched in her hand. Buckie whimpered in the backseat, all his guard dog bravado gone, giving Susannah the most pitiful case of puppy dog eyes she'd ever seen. She opened the back door, nearly having to pry the border collie off with a crowbar as he jumped out, licking her and whining. Susannah assisted Elizabeth into the bench seat, then instructed Buckie to get back in the car, knowing the dog would take to the traumatized girl and comfort her. But to her surprise, Buckie cowered away from Elizabeth, hugging himself towards the opposite side door, casting worried glances at the girl and continuing to whimper.

*You can smell her infection, huh, boy?* Susannah thought, feeling sick to her stomach. Driving out of the parking lot, she thought of his odd performance last night. What had he sensed in the woods bordering her property?

"We're going to Dolvin Hospital, she needs a doctor ASAP," Susannah said, figuring now was not the time to make introductions. "You alright?" She looked over at Jessie, who continued staring out the window.

"Wha-what the fuck was wrong with them? They looked like they were being cooked alive. Was it... like leprosy?" Jessie's voice was a low monotone.

"I don't know, honey. We'll leave that one up to the doctors."

Susannah's phone buzzed in the center console. The screen read BAUMGARTNER.

"Oh, yeah, that asshole called twice. I didn't answer it, sorry," Jessie said distantly. Susannah wondered what in God's name it could be this time.

"What is it, Sheriff?" Her voice was tight from the smoke. She noted the slate gray column in the rearview mirror as they headed towards Dolvin and half wondered if her clinic would burn down. Her mind was too numb to worry over it.

"Just lettin' you know we found that girl's buddy. Was half naked and driving the Langans' truck. Wrecked it tearing ass out of their place. He's at Saint Francis if she wants to go see him." Baumgartner spoke fast, with an odd, clipped tone, almost robotic. Or maybe that was just the ringing in her ears. Not only that, but Susannah thought she heard something screech somewhere in the distance, as if the sheriff were within spitting distance of a banshee.

"Yeah? Well, we're headed that way anyway. Those cows—" she began, then stopped, no energy to reiterate what she'd just done. "Elizabeth got injured, we're taking her there now. I got Jessie with me. Two birds with one stone, and… all that." Susannah's eyes flitted towards the rearview mirror. Elizabeth lay curled up on Jessie's side of the car. Buckie continued to stare and keep his distance, a low growl rumbling in his throat. It was the sound he made at Harold on the rare occasion when he raised his voice to Susannah. A warning.

"You hear me, woman?" the sheriff hissed. Susannah blinked, realizing she'd spaced out.

"Sorry, Sheriff, signal is spotty. What was that?"

"Did she get bit? By one of those things?" he asked.

Susannah didn't say anything for a space of a few seconds, not wanting to answer.

"Got-*damnit*, woman, did she get bit or—"

"Yes." She did not like where this was going.

"You can't bring her there… you saw what happened to Anderson. This shit acts quick a-and it changes them. Some fucking mutant strain of rabies that goddamn Virgil got down in the caves. Tate is… well… Don't you dare bring her to that hospital. Where you at right now?" Baumgartner asked, his voice tight, mouth-breathing against the receiver. She *really* did not like the way he sounded. Then she realized what he'd said about Virgil, speaking as if the man were still alive.

"What am I supposed to do with her, Charles? And what's this about Virgil?" she asked, under her breath.

"Listen, Tate's told me some real interesting stuff. This shit's fucked, Susannah. Some real wicked shit… That little girl is a goner. You gotta do the same thing you do to a rabid dog. Put her down. Or bring her to the station and lock her up. Quarantine her or something, get the CDC out here. Somethin'. We can't handle this."

"You know I can't do that, Sheriff. She's just a girl. She needs *help.*" She whispered this last, though she didn't think Elizabeth was paying attention. The young woman moaned in the back seat, rambling about it being too bright outside. Elizabeth gripped her bite wound as she rocked, knuckles white from the pressure. She wouldn't stop talking about the light.

*Extreme sensitivity to light, often present in advanced stages of rabies,* Susannah thought robotically.

"I don't think the fucking doctors can help with this one, woman. She—"

Susannah hung up, not wanting to hear anymore. She looked at Jessie, gave her a thin smile.

"They found your friend. He's at the hospital. Finally, some good news, huh?" She tried to sound cheerful, but her voice came out hollow and fake.

"*Lou*? They found Lou?" Jessie snapped out of her dazed state. "Is he alright?"

"I don't know honey, but he's alive at least."

Susannah found herself speeding way over the speed limit, the SUV flying towards Dolvin, keeping a close eye on Elizabeth in the mirror. She wanted her out of the car as soon as possible.

*Same thing you do to a rabid dog,* he'd said, *you put it down.*

# Chapter 23

T HE SMELL OF AMMONIA and scorched metal filled Baumgartner's small office. A crackling hiss emanated sporadically from the back of the sheriff's department, mingling with the smell of blood and human sweat wafting up from the jail downstairs. But Sheriff Baumgartner's nose had long grown numb to those odors. The lighter grew hot in his hand, and so he forced himself to take a break, putting down the glass pipe whose bowled end was charred black from years of being kissed by a Bic. Each hit unearthed memories better left buried in the dirt of his subconscious.

*Vivian screamed at him. Slamming the door in his face. The middle finger raised over her shoulder as she walked to her car.*

He'd had to make the crank himself at home, his kitchen converted into a shake and bake lab complete with discarded ephedrine packets lining the counter, empty boxes of strike anywhere matches, pipe cleaner and a myriad of other gourmet ingredients. It wasn't nearly as clean as Virgil's stuff and often left him twitchy and agitated, but, by Christ, it got the job done.

Bloodshot eyes darted around his office, looking past the tendrils of gray chemical smoke that hung lazily in the air, towards the cheap brown vinyl paneling, towards the mounted white tail buck and the largemouth bass he'd caught out of Blue Springs Lake.

*This is all your fault, Charles. You drove her away, you and your god-damn need to control everything you fucking—*

Another howl screeched from below followed by the thud of an immense body slamming into the jail cell bars.

*You call yourself a man but you're just a fucking coward you're nothing but a fraud a—*

"That's right, you big bastard. Tire yourself out." Baumgartner said as he stared at the remaining baggie of crystal in his hand. The roar of blood in his ears wasn't enough to drown out the memory of his ex-wife's voice. He normally would never do something so stupid and reckless as to crank ice in his office, but the times, they were a-changing. For one thing, there was no one else in the small sheriff's department—at least not on this side of the bars. Anderson was gone, and with it being a Sunday, the in-house dispatcher was off work, the sheriff's department instead getting its calls fielded through by Dolvin County dispatch. It was just him and the few inmates currently residing in the six-cell basement jail.

With free reign of the place, and a very long, traumatic day under his belt, Charles decided to make himself at home, putting his feet up and listening as a now-feral Tate Langan thrashed against the inside of his jail cell. His whole body thrummed and tingled with the intense methamphetamine high. It'd been a while since he'd gone whole hog like this. His heart raced, perpetually on the cusp of an adrenaline rush.

"Would someone *please* shut that fuckhead up?" came the voice of Erol Brigham. The fifty-six-year-old man had recently turned himself in for raping his teenage daughter and was awaiting trial. But the Lordell County jail was at max capacity, so the Carter County Sheriff's Department agreed to hold the sick bastard for the time being. Baumgartner, thoughts darting around his head at light speed, suddenly had an idea. A wicked grin split his sweaty face.

He stood up, popped his neck from side to side to ease some of the tension that flooded his body when he was *really* flying high, and proceeded down to the jail, tucking a pinch of spearmint-flavored dip in his mouth as he went. He'd placed Tate in the cell in the very far back corner of the jail, which was down the hall and out of sight of their resident child molester. His hands flexed into fists before releasing, fingers splayed wide before balling up again and again, chords of muscle and the veins in his forearms standing out. Images of Vivian's back to him, her middle finger extended, flashed like lightning across his mind.

"The fuck is wrong with that guy, huh? He on angel dust or some shit?" Erol asked when Baumgartner appeared in front of his cell, the master key in his hand. Baumgartner flashed Erol an unhinged smile as the lock clicked. The barred door rolled back on its track with a metallic clang. Erol blinked in confusion and quickly stood, putting his hands against the wall the way he was taught when an officer was entering the cell. "What—"

"You're about to see for yourself, Mr. Brigham. Tell me, son, are you a gambling man? You like placing wagers? High stakes?" Baumgartner asked as he spun Erol around. It took every bit of his willpower not to beat this man to within an inch of his life. Charles was in the mood to destroy. He knew the moral high ground he had to stand on may as well be an anthill, but a fucking child molester? The thought made his blood boil even more.

No, he had worse things in mind for old Erol. Something far worse than a beatdown. Baumgartner cuffed the man's hands in front instead of behind his back as per the usual protocol.

"I-I don't know, man. What is this? What're you doing?" Baumgartner could hear the fear and confusion in the chomo's voice as he led him down the hall. The sheriff grinned a shark's grin as the sounds of Langan's protestations echoed louder off the painted cinderblock walls.

"What... the fuck—" Erol gasped when they rounded the corner and came within sight of Tate Langan.

# CHAPTER 24

A s Baumgartner escorted Erol Brigham to his doom, he thought back on the day's events leading up to this point. It'd been a busy morning for the sheriff. He left Susannah's animal clinic at around 1 am, after Tate Langan had given his confession of kidnapping six people with his brother Roy and "feeding" them to their dad. Tate, under the cold black gaze of the Python, was unable to give names or descriptions of any of his victims, even after the sheriff had pressed hard enough to leave a red ring on his forehead. Fears that his daughter had been one of them caused him to surrender to a brief but total bout of desperate panic. But no, they were all just people to Tate. He should ask Roy. Roy would know.

According to Tate, who told the tale in a blubbering falsetto, their father had spent some three days in a cave after Baumgartner himself deposited the badly burned and heavily bountied Virgil upon their doorstep. Baumgartner recalled that day with perfect clarity, remembered finding Virgil among the cindered wreck of his trailer. The man had reminded Baumgartner of Harvey Dent, Mr. Two-Face from the Batman comics he used to read as a kid. One side of his body was torched to hell, ear melded into a vague lump of flesh on the side of his red and puckered skull. Some of his lip and cheek had burned away to reveal the one or two blackened molars left in his mouth.

Virgil Langan had been on the verge of death when Baumgartner left the poor man with his boys. He was sure the man would die within the hour. He'd hoped to buy time for Virgil's sons to bury their father before the DEA came in and upturned the place. Seemed like the good Christian thing to do, and Baumgartner felt he owed Virgil that much. The Langans, in all their sophisticated logic, instead took their dad up to the cave at the edge of their property to hide him, leaving him with bread and water as though the man were only suffering from the flu and simply needed bed rest. To their credit, they'd endured the gaggle of feds who'd pulled up to their house in black SUVs, swat vans, and even a goddamn helicopter, without Virgil ever being found.

Three days later, when the last of the state boys left with their dicks in their hands and their asses chapped about there being no body to identify, Roy and Tate went to check on their dad. But Virgil Langan was different. Baumgartner assumed by 'different,' Tate meant he'd turned into whatever Deputy Anderson and Tate Langan himself had now transformed into—a red-eyed ape of a man whose teeth had seemed to push out of his gums and break off at the corners to turn into sharp little ivory fangs.

Susannah had wrapped Tate's arm up, but it didn't do much good. Anderson must've nicked an artery because the big man continued to bleed steadily through his bandages the entire ride out to the sheriff's department. Baumgartner was reminded of Anderson's wound, how no amount of pressure or coagulant could stop the flow.

Baumgartner left the pale and shivering Langan in the cell and went upstairs to answer a call from dispatch about a possible grand theft auto. That's where he finally learned the whereabouts of the African American feller that little girl was so worried about. The one that reminded him so much of his own little girl, all ornery and defiant.

When he'd come back down to check on Tate an hour later, hoping to get a written confession (because one given under duress with a gun to your head wasn't exactly gonna fly in court), he found the big man like *this*. Skin ashen, black spiderwebs of veins emanating from his bite wound. As soon as the sheriff was in sight of the poor bastard, Tate launched himself against the bars hard enough to set them trembling in their frame. He was a hissing, screeching thing now, reaching out through the bars, so quick that Baumgartner didn't have time to reach for his gun.

He panicked as Tate tried to pull his arm between the bars, those wicked little teeth gnashing. If the sleeve of his sheriff's uniform hadn't torn away and freed him, he knew he'd end up like Tate himself.

The sheriff might've acted a bit more rationally under different circumstances, but he was going on 24 hours with no sleep, he'd just cleared a whole bowl of Ozark ice, and goddamn, were things getting hinky around here.

"You pigheaded sumbitch!" Baumgartner had un-holstered his Python, his normally mercurial disposition now cranked to hair-trigger levels. He didn't care about due process or legality at that moment. This was *his* department, and this goddamn animal of a man wasn't going to put hands on him like that. Baumgartner was squeezing the trigger before he even realized what he was doing.

The gun's report in the small concrete space sounded more like a battleship armament. He watched, stunned, as a fist-sized hole opened up in Tate Langan's sternum. Tate flew back against the wall. Spray from the exit wound painted the eggshell-white cell wall a dark purple, almost black, and smeared like grape jam as Tate slumped against the wall and slid down to the floor. His mouth was open, those wicked teeth gnashing stupidly at the air like a gar out of water.

Dread welled up as Baumgartner realized what he'd just done. He was coming unraveled. *Some men just can't handle the pressure of the job. Some go south in the head, go way off the rails. Those are the fellers that usually eat a gun,* his father's stern voice came into his mind. When his ex-wife wasn't mentally haranguing him about his fatherly failures, his pa often came to him when he was on ice. It was Pa's firm, guiding voice that often helped guide Charles to his epiphanies and realizations. That lilting baritone was the only thing he could hear for a while as his ears rang with the report. He was about to go back upstairs to take another hit and see if the crystal could help him find a way out of this situation when Tate reached out a hand and rolled onto his side.

"You gotta be fucking kidding me."

Tate slowly, ever so slowly, crawled towards the cell door. Baumgartner remembered how he'd pegged Anderson with two shots, yet his deputy *ran* out of that clinic like the sheriff had done nothing more than plink him with a BB gun. Whatever this plague was—a disease or a parasite, and not some fuckin' gypsy curse like Tate had blabbered about—it was resilient enough to keep its host alive even through immense physical trauma.

Baumgartner remembered staying up smoking one night not long ago, planted in front of the TV, watching nature documentaries. Rapt like a toddler in a toy store. In one episode about parasites, a scientist had pulled a plump larva from the carapace of a wasp where it had latched onto the wasp's spinal cord. If the scientist hadn't intervened, the grub would've directed the wasp to fly towards its wriggling nest, where other larvae would eat the wasp alive. Its deadly stinger rendered inert. It's coopted body docile.

Yes, it had to be something like that, and with that realization came a twisted idea that burrowed itself into the sheriff's mind like that parasitic larva. In his ice-addled mind, he felt himself discovering what he thought were great scientific epiphanies, his stoned documentary 'research' enough for the sheriff to consider himself an expert on the subject. A parasite was taking over his town, and he was going to get to the root of it.

He'd proceeded to spend the next four hours conducting experiments on Tate Langan. The first idea involved the cross around his neck. He remembered the way Susannah's crucifix had burned Anderson's flesh, how incensed and disgusted it'd made the deputy, as though the crucifix weren't a run of the mill symbol of Christ, but a full page spread of the lewdest piece of pornography ever made.

Cautiously, Charles approached the cell. Tate's thick arms shot out from between the bars. The sheriff stared mesmerized at the fist-sized blackened, glistening hole in his chest, marveling that there was no weeping scarlet. It was as if someone had taken all the blood out of Tate's body and replaced it with thick, sludgy ink.

He took out his crucifix, said a silent prayer, and crept closer. Tate's face twisted in a snarl of primal rage, and he swatted at the necklace as it came within spitting distance of him. A brief sizzling sputter sounded over his hissing gasps as Tate's hand grazed the silver symbol. A small plume of smoke puffed up from the point of contact, smelling of rancid fried meat. The sheriff, emboldened by this reaction, thrust the hand holding the crucifix boldly between the bars. Tate recoiled, but not before smacking Baumgartner's fist hard enough to bust one of the knuckles.

"Son of a bitch!" The crucifix went flying across the jail cell, landing a few feet from Tate. The big man snarled at it before retreating across the room, his head darting back and forth between the necklace and the sheriff. Charles held his throbbing hand against his chest, his speed-addled mind racing. What kind of parasite hated crosses?

*Demon?* The very implication made his testicles pickle into raisins. Parasites were one thing, strange and appalling, yes, but well within the realm of scientific possibility. He'd learned of strange new creatures and bacteria found deep in cave systems around the world. Things that had evolved and mutated in startling ways given their unique isolated ecosystems, far removed from the rest of the world. God knows the miles and miles of caves that crawled underneath the Saint Francois range were isolated and vast enough for such a biological anomaly to occur.

But something supernatural, something *demonic*, would change everything. Baumgartner's mind returned to Tate's frantic testimony, about how the Langans were long cursed, had done them gypsy folk wrong, how this was their retribution. At first, Baumgartner didn't know what the big boy was talking about. Then he'd remembered a story his father had said over Thanksgiving dinner many, many moons ago.

Pa was only twenty whenever he became sheriff for Carter, back when Carter was a boomtown off the burgeoning lead industry. He often talked about how all you'd hear back in the day was explosions, from sunup to sundown as the Langans blasted the mountains for all it was worth, leaving nothing but the bald, denuded husks of knobby hills that stippled the land today.

"They sure didn't like them people from across the sea coming over and trying to take the hills for themselves. No sir," his father had said over a mouthful of mashed potatoes.

"Damn gypsies ruined ever'thing," their grandfather had piped up. Papa Baumgartner had long gone senile by then, but occasionally he had brief moments of clarity, and on this subject, he spoke clearly, candidly. "Goddamn gypsies thought they could come over here and take what was ours. Langans put a stop to that, and we helped 'em."

"We sure did, Daddy, we sure did," Charles's pa echoed with pride.

*Coldona.* The sheriff chewed on the name, trying to remember where else he'd heard it. He consulted his computer, inputting that name along with Carter County. The first thing that popped up in his search was that old fart, Bernie Standridge's GHOSTS OF THE OZARKS homepage. Bernie was a retired schoolteacher from the area who'd written a few bad horror books. When those didn't take off, he wrote his "historical" version of events about the 52' Doefield Mine collapse, along with a bunch of other drivel about mountain folk tales and Ozark culture. He made the whole town out to be a bunch of racists, crooked hill-billies and very blatantly labelled the "local constable" at that time—Charles's grandpapa—a corrupt good-for-nothing. Now he was trying his hand at metalsmithing, living way out on the outskirts of town, locally hated for his inflammatory "biography" of Carter.

"Fuck you, Bernie," Baumgartner said as he exited out, then typed the name Coldona into a search engine.

Baumgartner was breathing heavy and blinking rapidly as he cycled through ten open browser tabs, ignoring the sounds of Tate's caveman noises.

Coldona: Romani Surname. Romania: Transylvania. Transylvania: Vlad The Impaler. Dracul.

*Vampires.*

"Oh hell." Baumgartner laughed to himself, shaking his head as he got up from the computer terminal, his head spinning. Even though his mind refused to acknowledge anything even remotely having to do with vampires, he still found himself analyzing the facts: This thing spread through bites. Both Anderson and Tate abhorred the cross. Then there was the matter of those teeth.

Just in case, he took a quick trip down to the Harps supermarket in Dolvin for six cloves of garlic and a large, bronze wall-mounted depiction of Christ on the cross. Then, he picked up a four-foot-long wooden dowel rod from the Ace Hardware across the street. On the way back, he half thought about stopping at one of the many churches that lined the highway to ask for a bottle of holy water, but no, that would raise too much suspicion.

His CB radio squawked with updates about the fire spreading in the northeast section of Carter. It had grown into a collaborative effort between the Dolvin and Lordell County Fire Departments, struggling to contain the spread. The sheriff went back inside his office with his arms full of test materials, ignoring the calls from the flustered firefighters who were begging for a check-in, for more units to help on the scene.

After dumping the stuff on his desk, Baumgartner went down the hall to Tate's cell. There, he took his Cold Steel tactical folder from his pocket and began to slice up two of the cloves until the smell of garlic hung redolent and eye-watering in the air.

"Bon appétit, you goddamn mongrel."

He tossed the minced cloves through the bars. Langan's big head swiveled slowly, like a radar dish, towards the garlic which landed at his feet. His nose crinkled, but there was no dramatic repulsion like with the silver cross. Baumgartner even went so far as to plunk a piece right at Tate's cinderblock of a head to see if the garlic touching the skin would do anything.

But what used to be Tate Langan ignored the clove as it bounced off his forehead with a *thwack*, and instead reached for the sheriff again.

Feeling every bit like a man who'd lost his mind, Baumgartner charged at Tate with the heavy bronze cross, fully expecting a great spitting of frying flesh and hisses of pain from Tate, perhaps even a holy thunder and angelic choir to come out of nowhere to underscore his Christian bravery. Instead, Tate grabbed the cross from Baumgartner and threw it back at him, the baleful face of Jesus Christ soaring at him before it struck him hard in the shoulder.

"Well god fuckin' damnit!" Baumgartner grumbled. He now had more questions than answers. He tried to look at Tate's flailing hands. There was no evidence of burning or even a reddening of the skin where his sausage fingers had wrapped around the bronze staff. Yet, the big man still huddled in the corner of his jail cell, giving the small two-inch silver cross a wide berth, as if it were a tiger caged in there with him, apt to reach out and bite him the minute he drew close to it.

By the time he'd whittled down one end of the dowel to a jagged point with his knife, the sun was beginning to set outside. Satisfied with his work, he took the knife and nicked the tip of his pinky with it. A small pearl of blood welled up on the pad of his finger, then splashed to the floor.

Tate full-on screamed, hurling himself repeatedly against the barred cell, red eyes wide with an animalistic need. *Huh, Anderson was at least able to form a few words when he turned*, the sheriff noted. Tate was all hisses and gasps, like a surly pussycat cornered by animal control.

"Yeah, this whatcha want, huh buddy?" Baumgartner said, sticking his finger out within inches of Tate's flailing arms. His doughy face pressed between the bars hard enough they groaned. The sheriff could've sworn he saw the metal warp and bend ever so slightly. Baumgartner had a panicked thought that maybe Tate—strong as an ox before his transformation—would be powerful enough to pull the sliding cell door off its tract in his new feral condition. Not possible, he thought. The doors were constructed to withstand a full-on riot of prisoners trying to break free. At least that's what the contractor who'd updated the jail some ten years ago had said.

Charles clutched the makeshift spear, holding it high above his head. Tate made no sign that he'd registered the weapon. His bulging eyes stared at the sheriff's left hand, then followed the droplets of blood which continued to drip slowly from his pinky, spattering on the floor.

"That's good, stay right where you are, hoss." Charles charged forward with all his might, thrusting the wooden dowel into the black void of Tate's sternum. He felt the wooden shaft plunge into a thick, yielding mass, felt the dowel scrape bone before it gave another inch. He almost fell forward as the dowel punched through the other side of Tate Langan, spearing him clean through.

"Wooden stake through the heart... That's gotta do the trick, right?" But hope flooded out of him like diarrhea from an asshole as Tate continued to grope for him, seemingly unaware of the three-foot piece of wood jutting from his chest.

Frustrated and feeling hopeless Baumgartner grabbed the dowel and ripped it from Tate's sternum. The makeshift spear came away with a sick wet *plop*. Black sludge coated its shaft and chunks of unidentifiable viscera clung to the tip. Baumgartner made to thrust forward again, meaning to stab the bastard in the throat. But with surprising speed, Tate swerved his head out of the way and grabbed the spear, suddenly showing some hint of intelligence as the two began a tug-of-war over the weapon.

The only thing that stopped Tate from overpowering the sheriff was that his end was slick with his own mess. His thick hands soon became greased with black blood. The sheriff yanked the spear back, breathing hard, adrenaline coursing through him as he realized that if this was some kind of vampire, it wasn't the kind that wore capes and transformed into bats. All the Hollywood bullshit was just that: bullshit.

"What in the holy hell..." Erol recoiled from the sight of Tate, the thick tang of garlic in the air. "What the fuck is wrong with him? What—"

"Listen closely, Erol." Baumgartner said over the sound of Tate's hisses. "You got a choice here. I'm willing to let you go, you hear me? Let you walk right out of this jail and disappear into the great beyond, free and clear. The kicker is, though, you gotta whip out your pecker for this boy. Let him see what kinda kid-diddlin' heat you're packin' down there. Get *rightttt* up close and show him what you got. You do that, maybe let him play with your boys for a bit, and I'll let you go."

"*What?* What the fuck, man, get me out of here. I want to talk to a lawyer. I'm gonna get the ACLU on your ass, you fuckin' psycho. You—" Erol was struggling now, but he was an old man, and Baumgartner was energized by adrenaline and ice.

Baumgartner sighed and withdrew his taser. This was his last experiment, his final hypothesis, and he was going to see it through, one way or another.

"Sure about that? You really gonna forfeit freedom? You know what they do to chomos in prison, Mr. Brigham? Them boys are gonna be tenderizing you like a New York Strip. Probably gonna turn your asshole into an 'entrance only.' You really gonna—"

"*Get me the fuck out of here!*" Erol hollered as Tate grabbed at his orange scrubs, pudgy fingers plucking and pulling at the fabric, teeth audibly clacking together. "PLEASE!"

Baumgartner sighed and shook his head. The sheriff smelled urine as he drove the taser into Erol's side, making sure the child molester's kidney bore the brunt of the shock. Erol's legs gave out, but the sheriff held the thin stick of a man up with his other hand, twitching but otherwise pacified. Baumgartner winced with distaste as he hooked a thumb into the waist band of Erol's wet jail uniform and pulled down his pants, revealing a skinny white ass and piss-soaked thighs. The sheriff looked away and he shoved Erol forward.

"I was just kiddin' anyway, Erol. I was never gonna let you go."

Erol began to scream. Tate had fallen to his knees, and Baumgartner heard a sound like a man chewing through a particularly fatty piece of steak. Soon, Erol's howls of agony drowned out the terrible rending of tendons and flesh.

"I don't let chomos walk. In fact, I think I may have just invented my own unique flavor of capital punishment. Like chemical castration, but without the chemical part." The sheriff let Tate feed, consulting his watch to mark the time of first contact.

He threw the now-castrated Erol back in his cell once Tate had finished with his entrée of molester oysters on the half shell.

No longer occupied with these insane experiments, his mind went inward as he returned to his office. He ignored the screams and calls of confusion from the firefighters. It sounded like they were set upon by wild hyenas. His thoughts turned to Vivian again. Of what Susannah had said. That maybe Vivian hadn't run off. But no, if she'd got taken, if the Langans had taken her... If she'd turn into one of these things...

No. That was too horrible to contemplate.

# Chapter 25

L OU REALIZED HE'D NEVER seen Jessie cry before. But when she'd rushed into the ICU and saw him lying there, his eyes half-lidded from the narcotic cloud, one side of his face covered in bandages, she let loose. Lou groaned as she went to hug him.

"Easy girl, easy," he croaked as he wrapped his arms around her and felt his own hot tears beginning to form. Not even twenty-four hours ago he was positive he was going to die in that hillbilly hellhole. Now he was clean, medicated, and embracing one of his best friends. He was going to live. Live to see his girls again. Live to eat and breathe and kiss and love. Yes, there was the fact he may never walk again, but that was a small, inconsequential blemish on this silver lining. Being tortured and forced to peel away the layers of your humanity like a rotten onion really helped put things into perspective.

"What the fuck happened to you?" Jessie asked. Lou swallowed, felt a knot in his throat. He was working himself up to begin, to recall that brief, nightmarish Chapter of his life, when Geoff walked in, and behind him a middle-aged woman with curly blonde hair and a haunted look in her eye.

"Man, you look like shit," Geoff said with a shaky laugh, going in for a quick one-armed bro hug.

"Yeah, and you look like you won't be able to jack off right for months, asshole," Lou replied, and they both laughed. He noticed the woman blushing slightly. "Damn... Almost got the whole band together. Where's Allen? I bet that sonofabitch didn't even get a scratch on him. Fucker always was like a cat." But the looks on Jessie and Geoff's faces told him that Allen had finally used the last of his nine lives.

"Your friend didn't make it, I'm sorry to say. If it's any consolation... He died quick," the woman said. Lou studied her. Despite not knowing who the hell she was, he got the immediate feeling she was holding a lot back.

"Ah, shit..." A deep pang of sadness overcame Lou. Then he had a brief flashback to when those bastards were pulling him out of the van, the smears of blood and intestine. Those insides had to belong to someone.

Jessie grabbed his hand and squeezed it gently.

"Tell us what you remember, Lou. Tell us so we can punish the fucking assholes." Jessie's voice trembled but her eyes stayed their tears. Lou looked up at her before his gaze flitted to Geoff and finally to the woman, who stood holding herself by the door.

"Who's she?" he asked, not wanting to be rude, but definitely not ready to tell his batshit insane tale in front of some stranger.

"This is Susannah. She showed up not long after we crashed. She saved my life and helped patch Geoff up. I've been staying with her the past couple of days. She's a good person, you can trust her," If this woman won over the distrustful, misanthropic Jessie, then Lou knew she had to be a good person.

"Well, that's all well and good, but what I'm about to tell you guys... it's gonna sound fucking crazy. Y'all gonna think I've lost my damn mind. I don't want her running off to tell the doctors I need to be put in a straitjacket or some shit. It's gonna be hard enough explaining this shit to the cops."

"Honey…" Susannah walked up to the side of the bed and fixed him with a deep, soulful stare, her vivid blue eyes penetrating him. "I promise you, I'll believe every word that comes out of your mouth. I've witnessed and experienced things the last few days that I can't even begin to explain. It's important I know what you went through. I have a feeling it's all related."

Lou didn't know what she meant by that, but her deep, pained gaze told him she was speaking the truth. So, he told them everything. From the man in the caves, to being thrown in the shed, to the commotion outside of it, to killing Roy with his bare hands, the fire and the things that came out of it. He left out the part about shitting himself, though. That was between him and whatever fucked-up celestial entity ran this shit show. Everything else spilled out, bringing brief bursts of catharsis and adrenaline as he relived it all. They all sat and listened raptly, the only one whose look belied incredulity and doubt was Geoff.

"I swear, man, they were drinking his *fucking blood*… it was like… it was healing them… and when I shot one of them… it-it didn't even phase it. They came out of the fucking fire. Like they were invincible." The machines Lou was hooked up to started beeping as his heart rate and blood pressure skyrocketed. A nurse came in a moment later, her face flushed, and her scrubs marked with sweat stains.

"Everything alright? Sorry we didn't come in to check on you earlier. It's a nuthouse out there." The nurse panted as she checked his vitals.

"Yeah… I'm fine, just got a bit worked up is all." Lou's voice was trembling now. He laughed, shaking his head. "Shit man. Is this what it's like, having PTSD?" he asked, but the nurse had already hurried out of the room.

"You said they brought you to a cave. Was it close to the property?" Susannah asked, her eyes fierce, searching his for answers. Lou nodded.

"I think so. It was nighttime, and I was in so much pain I couldn't think straight. But it was within walking distance of the place, they had to carry me out there." Lou paused to remember. "And... there was crosses everywhere. And the cave itself... I don't know, man, everything just felt *wrong* about the place. The guy that came out of it... He was like a fucking monster, his skin all burnt and shit. He could talk, even though he didn't sound like a human. Told his boys he needed to feed by the blood moon eclipse or he... said something about being unable to control himself. Him and that guy, Roy, had a big standoff. Something about a plan. Everything went to hell after that."

A commotion sounded in the hall outside Lou's room. Doctors and nurses ran past accompanied by the squawk of walkie talkies. Someone yelled about a code blue.

"They called him *dad*? You're sure?" Susannah asked.

"Yes, ma'am. And he—the dad or demon or whatever the fuck he was—he had friends. They came out of the forest with him."

"Oh my God..." Susannah sat heavily in one of the uncomfortable plastic chairs lining the room. "That can't be... Virgil Langan is supposed to be dead."

"Do you think whatever was wrong with those cows... It had to do with this?" Jessie asked. "That cop that went all crazy said he'd gotten bit, right? And the cows, they got attacked by—"

"Pretty sure the cop got bit by the Virgil guy. He also kept talking about his other son... Tate. Acted like the big guy was the key to something. I don't know, man." Lou shook his head.

"Okay, can I just, uhm, can I just interrupt for a minute here?" Geoff piped up. "What in the actual fuck are you guys talking about? We're supposed to be on tour man. Where's our shit at? The van? What's all this talk about fucking... *vampires*? What the hell guys? We need to get ahold of the venues, someone needs to call—"

"I took care of it." Jessie said. "There is no more tour. Lou can't walk, Allen is dead. Our shit is gone, Geoff."

"Yeah, I get that, but I mean, you guys sound like you're trying to get to the bottom of this, whatever the fuck *this* is. Like we're fucking Scooby Doo and the Mystery Mobile. No offense, ma'am," Geoff turned to Susannah, "But this... weird disease or whatever, it's got nothing to do with us, or this fucked up little hick-ass town. We got Lou back. We can arrange for medical transport, head back and lick our wounds, figure out what the hell we're gonna do about Blasphemer, and just... forget about this shitty place."

"Nah, dude. I still gotta talk to the police. I fucking killed a man. The big dumb one though, I don't know where he—"

"He's with the sheriff." Susannah said, then took a deep breath, clearly working herself up to speak. "Listen y'all. I know you don't know me from Adam, and I know three days ago you were on your way to go play your rock 'n' roll and be rock stars. I know this all sounds absolutely *crazy*, but the same thing you all got caught up in has got something to do with my son's disappearance, and if nothing is done about it... well, I think it's gonna spread a lot farther than this little 'hick-ass town'. Carter County folks don't wanna rock the boat and they sure as hell won't listen to what we have to say. They'll just put the blinders on until this thing has spread far past the point of containment. Something horrible is going on in Carter and the Langans are at the heart of it."

"What are *we* supposed to do? You heard Lou, those things sound... well, *unstoppable*." Jessie said.

Susannah rubbed her forehead, thinking hard. "The caves. We're gonna have to go down into those caves. That's where it all started. I've been having dreams about it for months now. I think someone was trying to tell me something, as absurd as it sounds. I know you feel it too, Jessie." Lou noticed the way she was looking at Jessie, a stern, motherly look. "You felt what passed between us. I know you've been having visions too. You—"

"Yeah but... what do I have to do with—"

"What the hell has gotten into you guys? Do you hear yourselves? Did the crash scramble your fucking brains?" Geoff threw up his hands and laughed. "I'm gonna go find a phone and call a Greyhound."

"*Please*. I know this sounds crazy, and I know you all don't... well, don't believe what I believe in, and that's fine. But I think we were all brought together for a reason. There's been an evil percolating in this town like a ruptured sewer line for a long time now and it's about to boil over. We're the only ones that got a clue what's going on—besides the sheriff, anyway—and we're the only ones that can do anything about it. *Please,* I'm begging you," Susannah pleaded. Her glassy blue eyes were enough to penetrate even the most skeptical soul.

"She's right, man. I don't know what good I can do since I'm wheelchair bound for the foreseeable future, but I know what I saw. Those fuckers were gonna sacrifice me to those damn things, and if it weren't for those two hillbilly brothers, Allen would still be alive. We'd still be on tour. We'd still have our lives. If this thing spreads like you all claim it does, there's no telling how many of those things are out there or how bad it's gonna get." A sense of exhilaration coursed through Lou. He worried he'd get thrown in the nuthouse the minute he told them what he saw. Instead, he felt them coming together in a way that transcended the close, cohesive bond between bandmates. The stakes weren't just money and fame anymore, but life and death.

"It's what Allen would've wanted. If there was a cause or a problem in the world people were ignoring, he'd be all over it, shoving it right in your face, *making* you care about it. Even if we can't stop it, we can bring attention to it, try and get help before it's too late." Jessie said. "That's what Allen would've done."

Lou felt tears once again pushing at his lids. Jessie was right. A sudden memory came to him. They'd played a venue down in some shithole in West Virginia, opening for Gore-Grinder and a few other mid-list national acts. The place clearly didn't host metal shows very often, especially not the kind of extreme stuff Blasphemer played. After their set, some guy—a confused bar regular who very clearly didn't listen to metal and resented being forced to bear witness to the cacophony—came up behind Lou as he was wheeling his cabs towards the van.

"Hey fella, you play pretty good for a porch monkey. I gotta say, though, you look like you belong in a jazz band." He laughed at the wit of his own joke.

Lou, dog-tired and half deaf from the performance, at first didn't process what the redneck had said to him. His ears were ringing something fierce and he'd just smoked a bowl. He was willing to give the guy the benefit of the doubt.

"What'd you just say, man?"

"I said, you goddamn ape, that you play pretty good for a fuckin ni—"

Allen was on him like a bird dog on a duck. No preamble, no chest thumping, no shoving. One minute the guy was standing there with a drunk shit-eating grin on his face. The next, Allen's fist was sunk halfway into the guy's cheek, rearranging molars.

"What the fuck you say to him, huh? Fucking inbred fuckhead." Allen growled as the man pirouetted in the gravel from the force of the punch. He managed to stay upright, putting his hands up in a clumsy fighting gesture, but Allen was already moving in. A quick uppercut followed up by a full-power roundhouse blow that saw the man spitting a few teeth by the time he slumped against the wall of the venue. "Fucking balls on you," Allen grunted in between punches.

"Whoa, whoa. Hey, man—" Lou was trying to pull Allen away. By now Jessie and Geoff had come up, wondering what the hell was going on. "No need for that, let this asshole—"

"No, fuck that, man! Assholes like this deserve to get their shit pushed in. Go on fuckwit, finish what you were gonna say, huh? Finish your goddamn sentence, I dare you." Allen barked, shoving Lou away and falling on the man once more, fists flying until venue security got involved.

*Yeah, that crazy motherfucker would be all over this,* Lou thought with a brief pang of grief.

"Shit... You guys really are into this, aren't you?" Geoff's voice was thick with apprehension.

"You think it's a coincidence a bunch of black metal atheists were stranded in the middle of the Bible Belt where some kind of fucked-up vampire plague is spreading unnoticed? This woman is right, dude. It's too goddamn absurd to be a coincidence," Lou said, replaying in his mind how he shot that thing in the face—right in its *fucking* face from point blank range—and all it did was paw at the bullet holes in its head. "Those things are strong as hell. They walked through an inferno like it was nothing. One took three nine mil hollow points to the dome and it barely fazed 'em. Hell, Roy shot his dad like six times, and it didn't stop him. How're we supposed to fight that?"

"I might have an idea," Susannah drew a large silver crucifix necklace from beneath her shirt. She rubbed it between thumb and index finger, looking down at it with reverence. The old Lou, the one who had no idea what real evil looked like or felt like, would've laughed at the woman's religious naivety. But he was no longer that cynical. He wasn't about to start going to church and singing hallelujah, no, but he had to admit whatever the fuck was going on in this miserable little part of the country defied all scientific or empirical explanation. "Do I have your word then? That you'll help me stop this?" Susannah asked.

"Shit, I'll do what I can." Lou gestured down at his wasted body.

"I'm in." Jessie put a hand on Susannah's shoulder. "I wouldn't even be alive if it weren't for you, it's only fair."

Susannah put a hand over Jessie's and smiled at her.

"Shit, man." Geoff shook his head. "Guess I don't have a choice. I better start seeing some real mind-blowing shit real soon or I'll commit you guys to the fuckin' psych ward myself."

"Trust me, Geoff, you don't wanna see these things," Lou said. "I'd give the whole sack of my family jewels to *unsee* what I saw."

"It's decided then. I'm gonna go wait in the car, give you guys some time. I'm sure having a strange old lady around is throwing off the vibes, or whatever you kids say." Susannah said with a thin grin, then walked towards Lou, fixing him with those intense blue eyes. "You've been more help than you know, Lou. You've given me a place to start looking. You've given me validation that what I'm hunting is real. I hope I can bring justice to those that deserve it. That your suffering won't be for nothing." She put a gentle hand on his arm.

Lou felt the faintest tickle in his arm where their skin met. He noticed her eyelids fluttering.

"You... You have a daughter?" she asked, her voice thick. Lou blinked, looked at Jessie, then Geoff.

"Uh... Yeah. How do you know about Lateria? Did Jessie—"

"It's a long story. She's beautiful." Susannah's expression was unreadable.

She grabbed a pen from off the foot of his bed, then scribbled something onto a corner of his medical chart and ripped it off. "That's my cellphone. If you need anything, just call that number. Keep us updated on your health." Lou stared at the piece of paper, then up at Susannah. He wasn't sure what happened a moment before, but he honestly didn't have the energy to think about it. He was damned tired.

Still, Lou saw something in her then, something that cut deeper than the strained, haunted gaze that pulled her wrinkles taut and lips into a thin line. He saw a dogged determination and felt a fierce resilience radiating off her. A stoic sense of righteousness so strong it almost filled the whole room with a cloying aura. Again, he felt that stirring in his guts, that exhilaration that his life was never going to be the same after this, and not just for the obvious, trauma-related reasons. He almost warned this woman not to go back there, to where those things were. But Lou bit his tongue. Something told him Susannah could handle herself, probably better than any of them could.

There were layers to this woman.

"I'll be in the car with Buckie when you all are ready. Take your time," she said softly and gave Lou's hand a hard squeeze before she left.

# Chapter 26

SUSANNAH FELT GENUINE HOPE for the first time in a long time. She no longer existed in a gray void of uselessness and despair, a purgatory of growing numbness with each passing day knowing her son was still gone and no one except Harold cared. It was equal parts devastating and validating, the closure Lou's testimony brought. Her boy was in those caves. But he was dead. He had to be. The thought that he might've turned into one of those things... No. He was a sacrifice. His suffering had surely ended, and he was with God now.

He had to be.

And then there was Jessie. She fit into this somehow. Her visions. The sort of epic transference that occurred between them when Susannah was giving her CPR. The godhead from her dream begging for her. What did it all mean?

Susannah knew the caves were vast and treacherous, it was the reason that unfortunate geologist had come here and subsequently disappeared doing his job, trying to peel back the layers of mystery to the caverns. She knew going down there would almost certainly be a death sentence. And yet she found herself even more determined to see this through. If it meant getting Daniel out of there, if it meant giving him a proper, Christian burial, then she would die for that. Lord, yes, she would.

She would go down there and find the source of this evil. She would put a stop to it or die trying. Again she thought of the way Anderson recoiled at the sight of her crucifix. That was all the confirmation she needed that this was a devil she knew, or thought she knew. A creature that could walk through fire and withstand gunshots like they were BBs but recoiled with pain at the sight of her crucifix was a sign that God was at work here.

And a devil, too.

As soon as she walked out of the ICU, she had begun planning. Susannah was so deeply in thought that she nearly jumped out of her skin when she felt someone reaching for her.

"Miss Paige?" a flustered-looking doctor asked. Susannah recoiled at her touch, then caught herself.

"Yes? Can I help you?"

"You're the one who brought in Miss Smith, correct?"

Susannah blinked for a second, so lost in thought she'd almost forgotten the reason she'd gone to the hospital in the first place. A pang of anxiety shot through her as she braced for bad news.

"Yes, is she alright?" Susannah remembered the girl's ashen pallor when they brought her through the door. The doctor exhibited an award-winning poker face as she talked.

"Well, yes. We finally got her sedated, but uhm, Miss Paige, I need you to be honest with me. Was Elizabeth on any kind of drugs when you brought her in?"

Susannah was so taken aback that, at first, she didn't understand.

"I... *what?* Goodness, no. I don't think Elizabeth has ever done anything harder than a wine cooler. I told you, she got bit by one of our animals. We think it might've been infected with something." She was amazed at how much lying could fit into a simple truth. "What is the mea—"

"I only ask because, well, it took a lot of anesthesia to put her under. A *lot*. To the point where it would've killed a normal person. We normally only ever get cases like that with the addicts."

Susannah moved her lips but didn't talk as she struggled to find something that could explain the obvious abnormality here, the elephant in the room. Instead, she remembered Elizabeth repeatedly assuring Susannah she'd dosed the cattle with more than enough anesthesia, yet the animals continued to writhe and rage. She felt lava churn in her stomach and course through her bowels.

"I... I don't know what to tell you, except that she isn't on drugs, okay? Test her blood if you have to." *And you'll see something in there alright, but it won't be drugs*, she left off.

The doctor nodded. "Alright. Well, what I can tell you right now is Elizabeth is fighting some kind of blood infection the likes of which we've never seen. You said she got bit by a sick animal?"

"Yes." *You could say that.*

"I'm gonna be honest with you here Miss Paige, we're running all the blood panels as we speak, and nothing is showing up in any of our virology or pathology reports. Either way, we have her stable... sort of, but she's going in and out. We're going to have to amputate the arm, it's becoming gangrenous already. I don't know how, but it is. We're hoping this will at least stop the viral load being dumped into her bloodstream. She's very close to going into septic shock."

"I see." That was all Susannah could say, afraid that at any moment the truth, in all its absurdity, would come spilling from her mouth.

"And one other thing," the doctor added, consulting the chart in her hand. She was speaking fast, her words clipped. "Do you know if she has an allergy to certain metals?"

Susannah blinked, not understanding.

"I... I don't think so, I'm just her boss, ma'am, I—"

"I ask because… Well, just look for yourself. This is violating every HIPAA law in the book, but I… You just have to see this." She took out her phone with shaking hands. Elizabeth lay sprawled on an operating table, even more ashen than before. Restraints circled her wrists and ankles. Two nurses in full biohazard gear were standing over her, one had a scalpel in his hand. "Our instruments are stainless steel. She had no reaction to those, but some of our scalpels are silver, naturally antimicrobial and antibacterial. Makes them easier to keep clean. We tried to make an incision with it, but…" She trailed off as Susannah watched.

Elizabeth bucked and let out a keening wail as soon as the scalpel touched the skin of her forearm. A small puff of smoke came up where the skin met silver.

"Christ, how is she still—" one of the suited figures gasped.

"Get her sedated, *now!*" someone yelled from the phone speaker as Elizabeth began to thrash on the table.

"That was *after* we'd given her a hundred CC's of Propofol, over three times the recommended dose for her body weight." The doctor was growing more exasperated as she talked. "Frankly, Miss Paige, I don't—"

"You should be calling her parents, telling them all this. I'm jus— I'm just her boss." Susannah abruptly felt a need to be out of this building, the walls sliding in to entrap her, to force her to bear witness to the mistake she'd made. She shouldn't have brought Elizabeth here. These doctors… Susannah had just lobbed a viral grenade in their path. The burst of confidence and virtuous courage she had convincing the kids to join her cause was gone. The urge to vomit was upon her, Baumgartner's words echoing through her mind. *Same thing you do with a rabid dog. You put it down.*

She almost wanted to scream at the doctor that they should kill her immediately, that there was no saving her, that all of them needed to leave this place *right now*, because a plague was coming, a plague biblical in its horror and magnitude. Instead, she swallowed, trying to work the spit back into her mouth.

"Excuse me, but I need to… I need to check on my dog." She fled, nearly bowling over a phalanx of nurses who were power walking somewhere with great deliberation, their clothes spattered with blood, surrounding a wheeled gurney. Strapped to the bed was a firefighter, his uniform singed and reeking of smoke, a hand clasped to his bleeding throat. *Just like Deputy Anderson,* she thought as they rushed past.

She'd left Buckie in her car with the engine running, the A/C on full blast, and a country station playing at low volume. He was on her as soon as she climbed into the SUV, sniffing and licking her face, pressing into her. He must've sensed her growing anxiety, and perhaps even the black dread welling up within her like a terminal infection spreading with rampant insidiousness. The silver crucifix around her neck seemed to grow a pound heavier with each passing second. The implication of what she saw on the doctor's phone was so awful it seemed to push her down into the car seat with suffocating force. Not only did she just bring a typhoid Mary into the one regional hospital for miles around, but her conviction about God being at work here was shattered. Tides of guilt and dread threatened to drown her. Buckie whined softly along with Merle Haggard.

One thing was clear to her now—It had nothing to do with the cross. There was no abhorrence to Christian symbolism. It was silver. It was the *metal* that these creatures detested, not the powerful cruciform shape it held. Susannah felt her resolve slipping and she held onto Buckie all the harder for it. She felt like a silly naïve old woman who was in way over her head, not some valiant crusader who'd been appointed to lead this cleansing mission by a higher power.

Time dilated and she slipped into a black hole, her heart pounding, an invisible vise locking around her head. Buckie whined continuously, and she felt even worse for stressing her poor dog out. Buckie didn't understand the abysmal horror unfolding around them. He was only trying to soak up her bad emotions, trying his hardest to make her happy. She sunk her face into his fur and released a moan of pure grief.

Susannah jumped as she heard a knock at her window. Jessie stood there, motioning for her to unlock the door. Susannah blinked, looked at the dashboard clock to see how much time had gone by, then hit the master unlock button. Jessie fixed her with a concerned stare as she made her way around the car.

"Hey, you alright?" Jessie asked as she got in. Buckie reluctantly relinquished the passenger seat as he climbed into the back. Susannah glanced at herself in the rear-view mirror and was met by a ghastly expression of hopelessness.

"Yes... I just... I think I'm gonna get all of us killed. That's all." She let out a laughing sob.

"Maybe, but someone's gotta deal with this. For your son. For Allen. For everyone else whose lives have been, and are going to be, changed by this." The assurance of Jessie's words and Buckie's ministrations made her ensuing panic attack evaporate just a little bit. She took a deep breath, trying to break the invisible iron bands around her lungs.

*Alright, so maybe God isn't the star of the show here. Maybe those dreams are just that, dreams. But she's right, I've gotta try. I know their weakness now and I can exploit that. This isn't the time to have a breakdown, woman.*

"So, what's the next move?" Jessie asked.

Again, Susannah thought of Tate Langan, who, despite being culpable in all this, had the mind and personality of a half-wit puppy. She wanted to talk to him again. She needed to know more about Virgil

Langan, about the caves, about what he'd seen down there. If he was still able to. She remembered he'd gotten bit. *Anderson and Elizabeth got bit, too, and look what happened to them.*

"We're going to the sheriff's department to talk to Tate. Maybe I can convince Baumgartner to come with us." Susannah took out her phone and called him once more. She tried twice while in the hospital, calling both his personal cellphone and the department's open line, but no one answered. She got his voicemail again.

"You really think that slimeball is going to help us? Fuck that guy." Jessie put on her seatbelt. Susannah gave a thin smile as she put her car in drive.

"Yeah, he's not the most pleasant man, but he's got skin in the game. His daughter went missing around the same time Daniel did. He swears up and down she ran off. If he truly believes that he's a bigger fool than I could've imagined. I guess old Standridge is right. We may have to go see him as well. He might have answers, as crazy as he is." They shot down the highway, the sun huge and vivid through the pallor of smoke emanating from the smoldering woods.

Susannah could tell the eclipse would be happening soon. The last time she'd seen the blood moon eclipse, the whole sky took on an odd, deeply red hue, like the sky on the cusp of sunset, except the sun still stood triumphant in the sky, the moon slowly encroaching to rob the burning star of its daytime reign.

Soon, the midnight sun would be upon this land, bringing with it odd shadows, an occulted distortion of light and shadow. She knew death would breed from that unnatural darkness.

# Chapter 27

"DAMN, THIS DISEASE, OR curse, or whatever, sounds like one hell of a way to get revenge," Lou said, thinking about what Jessie had told them about the Coldonas.

"Okay, yeah, but all that shit about Vlad, Dracula, whatever, was a bunch of bullshit. I mean he did impale people and all that, and I think he might've drunk blood once as a theatrical stunt, but all that shit about him being a vampire... It's honestly kind of racist to assume some Romanian immigrants would bring a vampiric plague with them," Geoff said.

"Yeah, but..." Lou's voice was growing fuzzy with the morphine he'd been flying high on ever since the nurse changed out his IV. "Look at psychosomatic phenomena, placebo, you know, but like, on a much bigger level. What if you get a whole village or, hell, a whole *nation* of people to believe something so strongly they eventually manifest it out of the ether? What if you believe something so fiercely, you *will it* into existence?"

"Nah, man, you're just stoned. Which sounds pretty fuckin' nice right about now," Geoff said, staring dismally at his hand. The tension of his body reminded Lou of a loaded springboard.

Lou knew he was stoned, but that wasn't all of it. His mind was wide open and receptive to even the most absurd postulations at the moment because of what he'd seen with his own two eyes. The hellish nightmare he'd survived plus the mind-numbing opiates eliminated the comforting barrier of logic he'd clung to for years. Anything was possible now.

"Vampire cows though? What the fuck, dude?" Geoff said with a laugh.

"I don't know. I guess it makes a lot of sense with what Jessie said about the caves and the mining accident." Lou suddenly felt very tired. His mind had gone through a whirlwind of emotions, and now trying to apply logic and reasoning to this problem that defied both caused the fatigue to synergize with the numbing bliss of the morphine. All he wanted to do was sleep, sleep and hope he woke up from this fucking nightmare.

"Now a *parasite* I can believe. Especially if it's something that's been growing down in those caves. You ever heard about the lead contamination this area has? Shit's fucked, man. Who knows what kind of nasty stuff has been spawning down there." Geoff was about to launch into some environmental tirade when Lou put a hand up.

"I'm tired, G-man. This is all real heavy shit. I need sleep. I need to process. I need a million things, but I need sleep the most," Lou said, fighting to keep his eyes open.

"Yeah, alright, man. You rest up. I'll keep watch. Gotta make sure I can protect you from these nurses. You think any of them have ever seen a real-life black man before?" Geoff's sarcasm brought a dopey smile to Lou's face.

"Fuck off. Give Jessie a call after a while. I worry about her." Lou's tongue was growing thicker and heavier by the second. Moving his jaw to form words took a herculean effort.

"Nah, our girl is tough as nails. Shits lightning and eats thunder. Not sure what to make of the bible thumper she brought along. But Jessie? She'll be alright." Geoff patted his shoulder, sending him off into the void.

When Lou came out of his morphine coma sometime later, the world seemed to have lost its mind completely.

# PART THREE
# A POUND OF FLESH

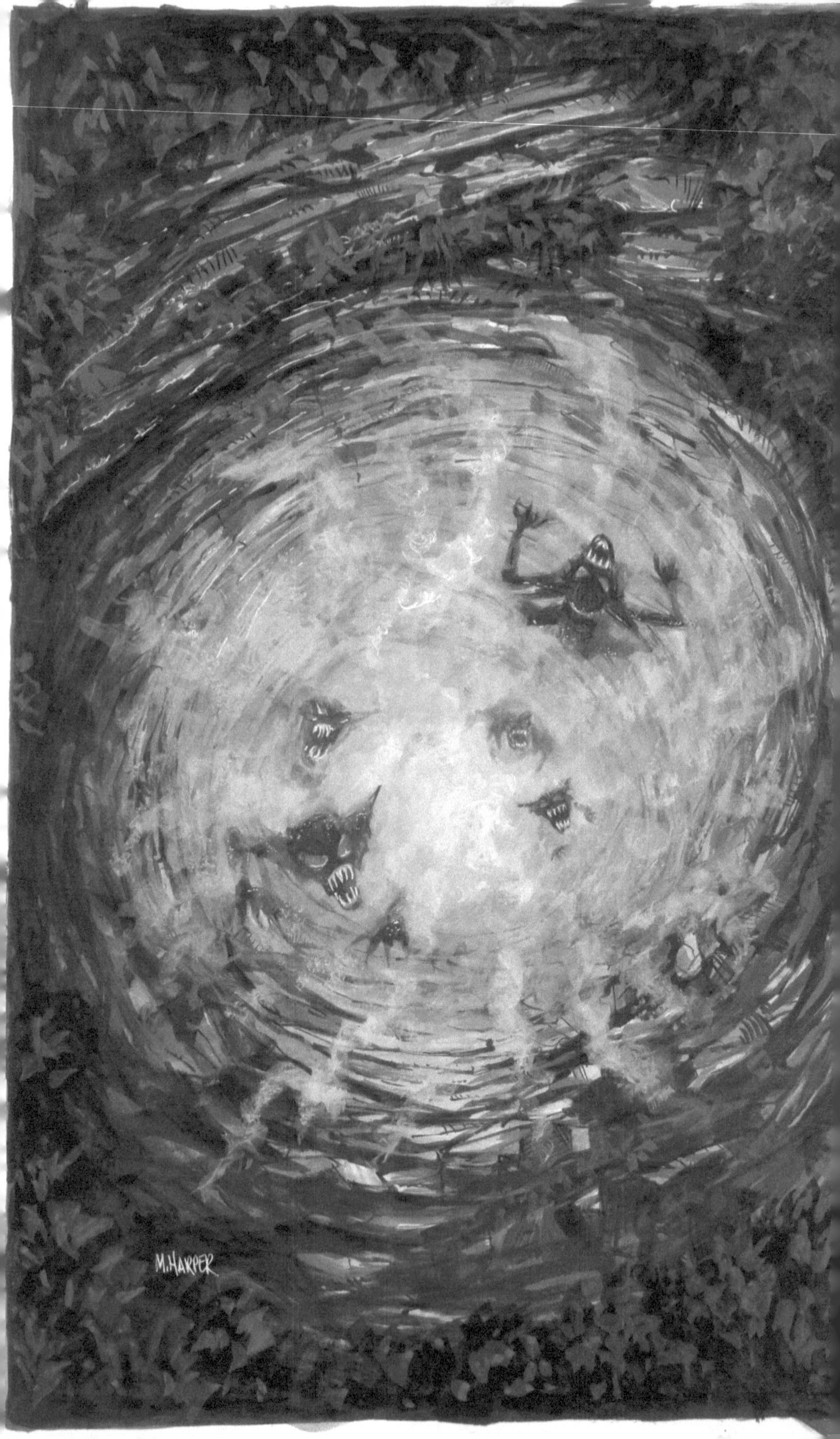
M.HARPER

# Chapter 28

T HEY MADE A QUICK stop for gas and to use the restroom. Susannah came out lugging a bag of goods: energy drinks, candy bars, a few foil wrapped hamburgers off the Hot-n-Ready tray from the Texaco's dismal food court. Jessie barely noticed until the smells of food distracted her from her research. She'd borrowed Susannah's phone and was trying to find out everything she could about vampire lore, specifically from Romanian folklore. Service was spotty, and it took some digging to get past the cheesy paranormal blogs and literature-based search results, but eventually, five pages deep into a Google search, she came upon a Smithsonian-curated website dedicated to the culture and folklore of Romania.

"You need to eat, darlin'. Let's stop for just a second and collect ourselves before we head to the sheriff's office. Something tells me once we get him involved there'll be no going back." Susannah pulled out of the main gas island and towards a side parking lot, where a row of semi-trucks sat idly, their drivers snoozing away, oblivious to the monstrosities lurking in the woods just beyond the well-lit gas pumps.

Jessie rifled through the collection of junk food Susannah had bought and felt nauseous. She knew she should eat something, but every time she thought of food, memories assailed her of the cow and the way its head exploded from its body via Susannah's shotgun. Without weed to stimulate her hunger, her appetite was non-existent.

"I'm good, I—"

"No, you're not. I can see it in your eyes. Please, Jessie, just take a few bites of something." Susannah's maternal side was coming out strong. She turned to look at Buckie, who'd been sitting obediently in the back seat, his tail wagging at the smells of food. "And *you* better thank your lucky stars, buster. Normally I'd never let you have this garbage, but I'm not driving all the way back home for your food." Susannah opened one of the sad gas station cheeseburgers and pinched off bits for Buckie between taking bites herself. Buckie eagerly took what was given to him, his tail thumping a steady tempo against the back of Jessie's seat.

"I... I don't eat meat. I'm sorry," Jessie said. If she wasn't already a committed vegan before, the sight of Susannah butchering those cattle *(vampire cows? Is that what they were?)* had forever cemented her disgust for animal flesh.

"Alright. Here." Susannah thrust a PayDay into Jessie's hand. The thought of sweet and salty did send a mild pang of hunger through her stomach. Jessie unwrapped the candy bar and took a few experimental bites while she read, looking for anything that might help them now that the horrors they were dealing with seemed firmly rooted in some form of vampirism. Lou's testimony all but sealed the deal on that. She made it through the initial introduction to the era of Vlad the Impaler and a brief historical info-dump on the area of Wallachia before finding some pertinent information on something called Febra Vampirilor, or vampire fever. Jesse read on, her mind taking in bits and pieces of information while skimming over the rest: Romanian peasants succumbing to fever, sensitivity to sunlight, sensitivity to silver. Rustic superstition ascribing magical horrors to what was most likely some form of distemper, alpha-gal, or other tick born illnesses.

"Learn anything useful?" Susannah asked as she got back in the car, having taken Buckie out to do his business in a well-lit corner of the parking lot. Jessie blinked, realizing she'd eaten the entire PayDay and had fallen into another one of her reading fugues.

"Kind of. Seems like silver has a historical basis for being used against them. That part checks out at least."

Susannah sighed. "Yeah, silver." Jessie watched her absentmindedly thumb her crucifix as they pulled onto the road.

Jessie read on and had just come to a very interesting section when they approached the police station. Several words jumped out at her before closing the screen. *Thrall. Hierarchy. Source of the Infection.* She filed these away as she prepared herself.

Jessie dreaded going to the police station. Amid all this crazy shit going on, she'd almost forgotten about the asshole sheriff who'd threatened to arrest her for the weed. She absolutely did *not* feel like dealing with him again. In her mind, going to the sheriff's office was almost as frightening as heading into those caves everyone seemed so goddamn afraid of. But Susannah seemed sure he would help. That, and one of the Langan brothers was locked up there, which Susannah seemed to think was important. So Jessie acquiesced, willing to follow this brave, stoic woman anywhere. There were a lot of terrible people in the world, but by now Jessie realized Susannah Paige wasn't one of them.

Buckie only further reinforced her aversion to police stations and sheriffs when they pulled up to the small brick building, its exterior a bleak brutalist design. The dog growled, then whimpered, before growling again. Just like he did the other night.

"Shh, shh, it's okay, Buckie." Susannah parked the car and turned to console the bristling collie, scratching behind his ears and kissing the top of his head. His golden eyes were fixed dead ahead, muzzle wrinkled in a snarl. "I know you don't like Charles. I don't either."

"I don't think it's the sheriff he's growling at. You said that Tate guy got bit too, right?" Jessie asked.

Susannah nodded and took out the Glock. "True. Let's be careful going in." She gave Jessie the .22 Marlin, showing her where the safety was and how to cock it. The PayDay turned into a squirming, cramping ball of indigestion in Jessie's stomach as she held the rifle. She almost begged Susannah not to go in, but she was already out of the car, leaving it on for Buckie, whose growls had disintegrated into a whimper as his master went towards the source of his distress. He pawed at Jessie as if to say *stop her, please don't let her go in there.*

Jessie gave the dog a quick scratch on his chest, told him they'd be back, and exited the vehicle. She felt extremely vulnerable out in the open as the day took on a preternatural darkness, the moon slowly sliding in front of the sun, casting an eerie off-kilter glow that corrupted shadows and gave everything an odd, sepia tone. From here, she could see the vast rolling hills and solid canvas of trees that extended out in all directions, bathed in an unsettling hazy monochrome from the residual smoke of the forest fire. She was pretty sure they were far from the blaze, but the smell of burned wood hung thick in the air and tickled her lungs.

A wave of surreality washed over Jessie. They were about to barge into a fucking police station like a couple of bandits, armed to the teeth, while the world outside felt more like some absurdist painting of hell than the real, innocuous world she knew.

She stood behind Susannah as the woman cautiously opened one of the double doors of the front entrance, then strode into an empty, unlit lobby. Sounds and smells met them as they crossed the threshold, the door hitting Jessie in the butt as it closed behind her. First was the cloying smell of garlic, and underneath that a coppery undertone Jessie couldn't quite identify. Then there was the sharp chemical tang of ammonia, but with a burnt rubber quality to it, faintly familiar to Jessie.

The place was a cacophony of sounds. A man yelling, his baritone raspy and raw, on the edge of being hoarse. The repeated thud of bone and flesh hitting metal. And the incessant digital chime of a phone going off somewhere ahead. It sounded like madness in here.

"The hell..." Jessie said under her breath.

"Flick that safety off, honey," Susannah whispered as Jessie heard the metallic *snick* of the pistol's safety being flipped. "Sheriff? Charles?" Susannah called, creeping behind the front desk, where light spilled from a room in the back. As they rounded the corner, Jessie saw the word BAUMGARTNER etched into a small metal plaque affixed to the partially ajar door. Susannah pushed it open with her shoe, the door squealing softly on its hinges. The lights were on, but the office was empty. What Jessie immediately recognized as a meth pipe sat on his desk, thoroughly and recently used judging by the charred look of the bowl. The ammonia tang was stronger in here, and Jessie realized it was freshly smoked crystal she smelled.

A bitter laugh threatened to bubble up out of her mouth. *Fucking dickhead acts all high and mighty about me bringing drugs into his county when he's smoking ice in his own office. If that asshole has one thing it's the goddamn audacity.*

She then followed Susannah's gaze towards the whiteboard in the corner of the room, where, on full display, one could see the frantic inner workings of a speed-addled brain. The handwriting was tight and sharp, as if the sheriff stabbed the words onto the board with the magic marker.

*Garlic: NO*

*Crosses:* ~~*NO*~~ ~~*YES*~~ *MAYBE*

*Silver: ?*

*BLOOD - LOVES BLOOD*

*SEE GEOLOGIST NOTES*

*Langan doesn't speak CHOMO does = intelligence a FACTOR (?)*

*Carter County COMPROMISED calls coming in*

Clothing rustled behind her, and Jessie screamed when she turned around and saw the huge, black circular void of a revolver pointed right at her. Susannah whirled, Glock drawn, and for a moment the huge barrel of the gun had the power to freeze time, paralyzing Jessie as they stood in a Mexican standoff. Centuries seemed to pass before the sheriff finally lowered his gun, blinking rapidly.

"Shoulda knocked. Don't like being snuck up on." Baumgartner was chewing gum, his jaw muscles bulging and flexing at a rapid pace. His eyes flitted from Susannah to Jessie, to their guns. Then he grinned. It made him look like an absolute lunatic. "Jesus, ladies, y'all coming to start a war or what?"

"Christ, Charles, what is this?" Susannah pointed at the whiteboard, then at the meth pipe. "What—"

"What I've been *doing*, is *learning*. Studying. Trying to figure out this goddamn thing's weakness. And guess what? I made some pretty good headway."

"Looks like you made a pretty good dent in your baggie of meth too." Jessie couldn't help it. *This* was the guy they wanted to join their team?

*Christ, we're fucked.*

"Now you listen here, little lady, never you mind what I do in my spare time. Susannah here likes to hit the bottle when she's lonely. You like to hit the skunk. We all got our vices, don't we, darlin'? Least when I'm on mine I'm getting shit done." Baumgartner's voice was breathy, his jaw muscles flexing rapidly as he spoke around the wad of gum. Jessie noted that the last two fingers of his left hand were bandaged and drumming a clumsy machine gun rhythm on his pant leg. Jessie's mind drifted to her kick pad, the way her beats got all herky-jerky like that before she warmed up her legs for the litany of $32^{nd}$ note kick drum parts in Blasphemer's set.

"Where's Tate?" Susannah asked.

"Mr. Langan is, uhm... well, let's just say his talking days are over. But that don't mean he hasn't been a huge help. Learned a lot from that ol' boy in the last couple of hours."

"What are you talking about?" Jessie asked, "Did you kill him?"

"No, ma'am. I sure did try though. Come see for yourself." He flashed that unhinged grin and headed out of his office. Jessie shot Susannah a miserable look, but she only shrugged and followed after the twitchy man.

"On the phone, you made it sound like Virgil was alive," Susannah said.

"Yeah. Well, I wouldn't say alive, necessarily, but he's up and kickin', that's for sure. Pretty sure that's who bit Anderson. Tate said they'd been keepin' him in the cave on their property. Said God came and resurrected him like Jesus. Can you believe that?" the sheriff said with a bark of laughter.

"How?" Susannah asked.

"I don't know. Old boy kept talking about a gypsy curse. Something about the Coldonas. You know, that old mining family that—"

"The ones killed in the cave-in." Jessie interrupted. The sheriff nodded, eyebrows raised.

"Someone's been doing their homework." He gave Jessie a wink as he led them downstairs. "I been doing my own research. And, Christ, I think that boy might've been tellin' the truth."

# CHAPTER 29

S USANNAH HAD NO IDEA what they were walking into. Charles
seemed to have lost his mind long ago. They followed him down
into the basement jail, where the smells of garlic and blood grew
stronger.

"I'm not sure if y'all have had much time to consider what it is
we're dealing with, but I've come to the conclusion—insane as it may
sound—that we got ourselves an infestation of the vampiric kind,"
Baumgartner said as they reached the bottom of the stairs. There came a
cacophony as soon as they were within sight of the cells.

"Yeah, we kind of gathered that," Jessie said flatly.

*Vampires.* Hearing the word made Susannah nauseous. There just
wasn't any way that could be it. This had to be something logical, an
illness, some viral pathogen mutated in the polluted aquifers of the caves.

"Give them to me, give them!" crowed that raspy bassoon voice Susannah heard when they first entered the department. Susannah paused,
staring at smears of drying, black blood on the concrete floor beside a
discarded bronze crucifix of Jesus Christ, the exact same kind she had in
her living room. Seeing it down there on the floor, discarded among the
blood, was almost a slap to the face, as if the Devil himself were taunting
her. *Your God holds no sway down here,* the scene seemed to suggest.

"Give them! GIVE THEM!"

"Easy now Erol, you don't wanna piss me off again, do you?" The sheriff stood in front of a cell where the blood on the floor was still fresh.

"Fuck you. Fuck you. FU... Oh..." The voice faded as Susannah and Jessie approached. Susannah blinked, then put a hand to her mouth. She clenched her jaw and stuck her tongue to the roof of her mouth, an old trick from her internship days when she had to work procedures that were particularly nausea-inducing.

"What the fuck..." Jessie whimpered as they came face to face with a stark-naked man, a gaunt wraith whose skin hung like ivory crepe paper from his sharp bones. At his center, where his manhood should be, was a ragged, vague stump of what looked like blackened hamburger, and from his groin radiated midnight black lines of infection that spread to all points of his body. Stringy hair hung in front of wide, bulging bloodshot eyes. Both Susannah and Jessie flinched back as the man threw himself at the bars.

"Her. I want her I want her her HER!" He tried to push himself through the narrow slot in the bars. Susannah could hear the metal of the bars groaning slightly as the man (no, no longer a man, but a *thing*, she reminded herself) strained with all his might, red eyes focused on Jessie, unblinking and huge with a feral need reserved only for the basest instincts of predators. His pupils dilated, and he reached a grasping hand through the bars. "I can smell it I can smell the heat off you bitch come here let me taste let me taste you LET ME TASTE YOU!" His panting turned into hoarse screams. His teeth, terribly long and jagged, snapped together in a grinding click. Susannah flinched as the .22 spoke four times in response to the man's sickening beckon.

Jessie's first shot missed and whined off the concrete cell in a ricochet, but the other three found their mark. One in the man's throat, one in his cheek and one in his left shoulder. Three neat little holes that opened up the body to reveal more blackness beneath the skin. Not red, not spurting, but black and lazily oozing.

"This one here is a sight older than what you like, Erol" Baumgartner's lips twisted up in a thin grin as he pressed the barrel of the .22 towards the ground. "Easy girl, gonna shoot your eye out with that thing."

Jessie wrenched away from him, backing up until she was pressed against the empty cell on the opposite side of the hallway, her eyes fixed on the terrible thing before her. The castrated man continued to reach through the cell, unperturbed in the slightest by his wounds. Susannah stared at the thing's mouth.

Unlike the Hollywood vampires, there were no discernable fangs or elongated canines, nothing so clean and refined, but rather the whole of the dental works were transformed into something more predatorial, something she'd only ever seen in the mouths of diseased carnivores. The old teeth had broken away, chipping into jagged, crooked rudimentary spikes, the gums eroding to reveal their ghastly length. Then Susannah remembered the cows. She swore she saw vestigial teeth trying to push through the pads in their mouths. It was as if this thing—virus, curse, what have you—was transforming each host into its most primal, predatorial form.

"Yeah, learned a lot down here with these two. But what I haven't come to figure is how to put the damn things down permanently," the sheriff said, inspecting the bullet holes in the man's body the way a sommelier inspects a bottle of wine.

"Wha-what *have* you been doing down here, Sheriff? What'd you do to this poor man?" Susannah wondered if she was having another one of her nightmares, like she was back in hell, the world becoming unhinged and surreal with its deluge of terrors. She thought of Harold's whiskey back at home and wished badly for a numbing shot.

"Me? I didn't do a goddamn thing to him. Not directly anyway. *That*," Baumgartner pointed to the glistening black stump where genitalia should be, "was all Tate. Speaking of which, come on, I wanna show you something else." He walked down the hall, giving the groping man a wide berth. "Don't get too close to him now, they're quick as rattlesnakes when they're like this."

They went down the hall and turned left. The miasma of garlic was enough to make Susannah's eyes spring tears.

"You gonna tell me garlic actually works against these things?" Jessie's voice was strained as they came to a cell at the very end of the hallway. Susannah braced for the worst, but was surprised to find Tate whole, uninjured it appeared, *completely* uninjured. Which was odd, because she vividly remembered the ghastly bite wound on his arm. Now, only mottled pink flesh, a patch of scar tissue, stood out against the eggshell white of the rest of his body.

Susannah's heart skipped a beat as the ground shook with the impact of Tate Langan's body slamming into the cell doors. His face bulged between the bars, and she heard the metal groan, louder this time, and saw that the cell doors bowed outward ever so slightly. He reached for the sheriff, who'd carefully approached the cell doors and stuck out a foot to drag away one of a dozen or so quarters and dimes that lay in a pile near the cell door, as if he'd made Tate turn out his pockets prior to becoming what he was now.

"Nope, don't do a goddamn thing to 'em. Cut up enough cloves to season a whole Olive Garden menu and all it did was make my eyes smart. Nor do crosses. Or I should say, just any cross. But—"

"Silver ones work?" Susannah asked. He nodded sharply.

"Gold star for you, Miss Paige. Took me a minute to put it together, but yeah, they fuckin' *hate* silver. Or anything with a bit of silver even in it." He held up a quarter he picked up off the ground. "Observe, a 1985 Kansas State Quarter. Date is important, because any quarters

made after 1964 only got a itty bitty smidge a silver in 'em. And yet..."
He approached the cell door, the coin thrust out before him like an
exorcising tool wielded by a priest.

Susannah noted the way Tate peeled his head back from the cell door
as the coin came near his face. It wasn't the violent revulsion that deputy
Anderson exhibited with her cross, but there was a mild repellent nature
with the impure silver.

"Now, let's see if I can do it right on the first try. Was practicing this
little number all day." The sheriff took a step back from the cell door. His
fingers trembled. The veins stuck out starkly in the back of his hands as
he raised the one holding the quarter and slipped it between his thumb
and middle finger. He squinted one eye shut, appearing to aim carefully.
Then, with a sharp, snapping motion, the coin shot from his fingers with
a soft whine and went straight into Tate Langan's hissing maw with a wet
*plop*.

Tate's gurgling hisses turned into a high animal shriek of pain as
he grabbed his throat with both of his huge hands and shot his head
forward. He made several crude, wet, voiding noises, glottal ejections
from deep within his throat, as he struggled to spit the quarter out.
Small tendrils of smoke shot out of his mouth, reminding Susannah of
the Saturday morning cartoons Daniel used to watch, where a Looney
Tunes character would eat something spicy and have steam shooting
from their ears and mouth. Tate dropped to his knees, his huge frame
shuddering.

Finally, with a whole-body heaving spasm, the coin shot out of his
smoking mouth and bounced off the floor, where it spun on its axis
before falling face up. Tate flinched and scrabbled into a corner, away
from the benign currency.

"Now, here's something *really* interesting. And very shitty for us."
Baumgartner removed one of the bandages from his left hand. He'd
sliced the pad of his pinky cleanly with a blade, and he winced as he

balled his hand into a fist. His arm muscles bulged as he squeezed, his face scrunched up in a ghastly rictus of pain. "There we go," he said through gritted teeth. A few drops of blood fell onto one of the horizontal support beams of the cell door, about face-level with the sheriff.

Tate's reaction was instantaneous. One moment he was backed up against the wall, his charred tongue thrust out like a burned slug, the next he was clambering across the room, heavy booted feet shaking the ground as he once again hurled himself at the door. A wave of surreal dissociation washed over Susannah as that blackened plump tongue shot out and lapped up the blood like a cat with a saucer of milk, panting heavily as he did so.

"That's it, boy, lick it all up," the sheriff said, as if he were speaking to a dog. Once all the blood was gone, Tate's tongue remained thrust out, eagerly searching for more, like a dying man in a desert slurping up the last drops of water from his canteen. The tongue's charred surface was slowly going back to pink, the blackened bits falling away like a discarded scab and sticking to the corners of Tate's red-smeared mouth.

"Oh my God..." Susannah whispered as she watched this unholy miracle unfold. It was just like that Lou boy had said.

"Don't know how much God has to do with it, but yeah, it's somethin' ain't it?"

"I-I..." Susannah momentarily forgot why she'd even come to this Godforsaken building in the first place. Could the sheriff really help them? That steely, intelligent gaze he had when conducting police business was gone. Instead, there was a glint in his bloodshot eyes. Some small part of him seemed to be *enjoying* this.

"So, what exactly did you wanna talk to Mr. Langan here about?"

Susannah swallowed, tried to get her wits about her.

"Can we... Can we go back upstairs, please? I can't, not with them down here. Like this." Despite her revulsion, she'd taken a step towards the cell. With a speed belying the big man's normally clumsy demeanor, Tate lashed a hand out at Susannah. Cold flesh locked onto her arm.

She didn't even have time to register the pain of his grip. The world exploded into darkness around her. It was as if she'd been thrown into an all-consuming black hole.

She sensed a hunger so terrible, so ravenous in its intensity her stomach twisted inside out with need. The crimson cloud from her flash with Jessie was back, overwhelming her, flooding into her mouth and nose, choking her. A violation that went beyond physical rape, she felt her very cells and synapses become infected with this terrible mist.

Nightmarish scenes flashed before her eyes. She was looking through the eyes of another. *Flash.* Stone walls surrounded her, the smell of wet limestone and old blood. Her body held stiff by invisible shackles as some great, unseen force imposed its will upon her. *Flash.* She was soaring through the woods, fast as a cheetah in full sprint, honing in, following the red mist. Becoming the red mist, until it came to a stop at a familiar scene. The overturned van. Susannah on the shoulder of the road. Leaning over Jessie. A golden aura exploding from Jessie's body. *Flash.* Walking through hellfire. Flames surrounding her, burning her. Roy Langan's prostrate body. *My son, don't make me eat my son, please*—The thought was quick and ephemeral before Susannah feels teeth that are not her own sink into flesh. The richest ambrosia she has ever tasted filled her mouth. It was a feeling beyond ecstasy, beyond the most powerful orgasm she's ever had, beyond—

Just when she thought she would drown in this blood-mist nightmare, the jail erupted back into her sight. She was gasping, sweating, thrashing against Charlie's big body as he pulled her away from Tate.

"Easy, Sus, easy. What the fuck was that about?" he said as she snapped out of it. She wasn't even sure she could call that a flash. It was something else entirely. Jessie was looking at her, grave concern in her face.

"I... I..." Susannah tried to find words, but her mind was still reeling from that encounter. "Just get me the hell out of here,".

"If it is the Coldonas, maybe it's like... revenge? That historian guy everyone seems to hate, he hinted that it might've been a murder. It seemed the whole town wanted them gone," Jessie said. Her eyes kept flitting back to Susannah, who tried to stifle the trembling waves that periodically came over her.

"Yep, I thought something similar myself after Tate wouldn't shut up about them, before he turned, I mean. My granddaddy said that woman, the old one from the family, she was some kind of shaman or some such. Something about a curse, all that jazz. Of course, people make up shit in small towns. Rumors about folks going missing in those caves. Guess they—just a second." Baumgartner whirled around. The phone had been going off since they'd come in through the front door, a litany of messages left by Lordell PD about a county wide emergency going on. Susannah heard snatches of the incoming dispatches. People were being attacked. Something about meth heads high out of their minds, biting people.

The intense horror of her flash was temporarily usurped by the dread that this thing was already spreading quicker than the wildfire. She had a feeling the fire had something to do with it. *Don't make me eat my son, please—*

"Aren't you... Aren't you going to answer those?" Susannah asked as the sheriff yanked the fax machine and answering machine power cords from the wall. He gave them both a thin smile.

"Not sure if you caught any of what them folks are saying, but this thing," he pointed down to indicate the two prisoners downstairs, "has spread. Tate told me they had some kind of system in place at their part of the cave entrance that kept their daddy from leaving. Well, that big ol' blaze that went off at the Langans' and spread like the plague must've destroyed whatever was holding them back. That, and something about the blood moon eclipse, which, if you haven't noticed, has come early. Now, me, knowing what I know, I understand there ain't shit that can be done about this. These fuckers can't be killed, they—"

"They can. You have to remove the head completely from the body," Susannah butted in, feeling some of her old self coming back, remembering that poor cow. How it had finally died.

"Alright, noted. So, these things are *extremely hard* to kill, and their curse, or disease, whatever, is spread through a bite. The child molester down there, Erol, took him about—" He checked a small notepad on his desk, "two hours and fifty-six minutes to turn completely. I reckon Anderson took just about as long, though I wasn't watching the clock then. Same with Tate. I've been listening to the reports. Ten calls come in so far about 'attacks' from what people around the county think are meth heads that've gone plumb crazy. No telling how many of them were killed outright and how many were left alive to be turned. You ask me, this situation is beyond a lowly county sheriff. FUBAR. I've failed my county and my people, I hate to admit. But... what can you do?" Baumgartner shrugged.

"There's a way they can be stopped though. This started in those caves. If we can find the source... maybe we can find a cure. Maybe we can find your daughter. And my son," Susannah met his eyes. He quickly looked away.

"Don't you start in with that goddamn shit about Vivian, woman. I ain't in the mood. Besides, you wanna go down in them caves? You must have a goddamn death wish. Them caves is where them things *live.* We go down there, they're all gonna be—"

"You said yourself that the fire freed them. The eclipse is upon us, and I know for a fact the sun hurts them. I'm willing to bet those caves are almost empty by now. They had to ration the bodies the Langans brought them for a long time, and now that they're free, the blood moon having whatever effect on them, they're probably out running wild like the Amish on Rumspringa, gorging themselves. Now's the best time to go, Sheriff. Right now, this very instant," Susannah said. The red mist stayed in her mind, throbbing like a poisoned heart. *The taste of blood in her mouth, washing down her gullet. So delicious.* She wanted that heart to stop beating. Immediately.

"That, and… Well, I learned there's this thing called the 'thrall' system. Hard to say if it's legit, since much of the lore with vampires seems to be 50/50 bullshit and truth. But if it's true, that might be our way of stopping this thing in its tracks," Jessie piped up. Both Susannah and Charles turned to look at her.

*"The what?"* they asked in unison.

# CHAPTER 30

"I T's SORT OF LIKE a failsafe, I guess," Jessie said, feeling herself disassociate as she spoke. She'd just shot a man, she'd just... No, not a man. Still, the way she'd automatically raised the gun and fired. Like what happened at the vet clinic with the cow. Some part of her—some hidden facet of Jessie's mind—kept taking over, guiding her through this. Despite the mental turmoil roiling in her mind, she continued, recalling the few bits of helpful information she'd found.

"Something about how, uhm, older vampires... since they can live forever, they needed something to keep the population in check. Vampire Darwinism? Fuck, I don't know. Something happened in Russia similar to what's going down here," she said, pointing to the floor. "*Upirs* they called them, I think. They'd managed to track down the first of the vampires who started the infestation. Removed the head from the body and burned the fucking things to a crisp. Apparently, right after they did that, the rest of the infected just... randomly started burning too. It killed everyone infected. It's like a-a hierarchy system. The original vampire is like the hive mind, and everyone else is sort of enthralled to them. A slave, you know?" Jessie felt stupid even saying this out loud. Of all the batshit insane mythology she'd read, that one seemed the most far-fetched. But it was something. It was an ace in the hole if it was true. "Basically, you kill the maker, you kill the monsters they made."

"Uh huh…" Baumgartner nodded doubtfully. "Well, that's all very interesting, but that doesn't change the fact y'all are crazier than shithouse rats for wanting to go down in them caves. Y'all should be like me, looking for greener pastures. Blow this fuckin' popsicle stand. I thought there was a way to fight this thing, but, well, I've been thinking about it all day, and, short of nuking this place, I don't see how that's possible." He stood, hitching his pants up. "Now, if you'll—"

*Crack.* Almost like a gunshot. Jessie didn't know what happened at first until she saw Susannah standing there, breathing heavy, a bright pink handprint on the side of Charles's surprised face.

"Now you listen here, you corrupt, pigheaded sonofabitch. You think you can just get up and *leave*? Do you lack *that* much of a spine? No. I'm not letting you take the coward's way out. *You* are the reason the Langans got away with this shit for as long as they did. *You* are the reason this county is currently under attack from hell itself. *You* and your…" She shuddered for a moment. Jessie could almost feel the tension radiating off her. "…*goddamn* refusal to rock the boat and actually put your neck out there. *You* owe me, Charles Baumgartner. You owe me and the people of Carter County big time, and you're gonna pay us back starting *right now*. You're gonna grow yourself a pair of balls, right this minute. You're gonna get your head out of your ass and you're gonna help me put an end to this. Don't you wanna know? Don't you even have an inkling of a doubt that maybe she didn't run away? Don't you at least want to check? They found her car, damnit! *Right up the road* from the Langans'. I know you're dumb, but you're not that stupid. Please, Sheriff. Help us."

Jessie and the sheriff were stunned silent by this profanity-laden speech. Susannah's voice did not waver. The sullen, miserable look Jessie had seen on her face in the car at the hospital was gone now. Righteous anger radiated from her. In that moment, Jessie felt a sort of mama bear adoration for Susannah Paige, a feeling that'd been culminating since the rugged veterinarian took her in. Though Susannah's overprotectiveness was stifling at first, remembering their unfortunate fight in the car, Jessie was once more taken by the feeling she'd follow this woman to hell and back. And though Jessie knew Baumgartner was right, it was insane, all of this was, she felt Susannah's determination, felt the courage and need to be brave flooding into her.

Baumgartner stared at Susannah for a long time, an utterly flabbergasted glare on his face. For a moment Jessie thought he would explode, try to attack her. Instead, something changed in him. Jessie watched the unhinged lunacy that pulled the corners of his mouth into a tight little grin disappear. He still seemed wired to the gills, yes, but she saw something like comprehension filling him.

"Alright now, darlin'..." Baumgartner said softly, his jaw finally ceased its flexing as he stopped chewing his gum to rub his reddened cheek. They all heard the click as the barrel of the Glock rose up to his face.

"You gonna help me? You gonna do what you're supposed to do, and *protect* and *serve* these people? Are you gonna help me find out what happen to our *children?*" Susannah's voice hitched on the last word. She was staring, unblinking, right into the sheriff's bloodshot eyes.

Things happened in the space of a whip crack as the sheriff moved with adder-like speed. He snatched the gun out of Susannah's hand and in an equally quick, fluid motion popped out the clip and pulled the slide back. The round in the chamber flew out and rolled to the floor. He handed the field-stripped gun back to Susannah, who took it, stunned.

"Sure, okay." The sheriff's voice was flat. "But you *ever* pull a fuckin' gun on me again, woman, we're gonna have problems." His authoritarian tone and brief display of finesse reminded them he was, indeed, a lawman.

"Alright," Susannah said, clearing her throat. She replaced the clip and put the gun away. "You have the materials that were found off that geologist, don't you? In evidence somewhere? Maps and stuff?"

The sheriff nodded slowly. He cracked his neck from side to side, and then did a quick little shiver, like he needed to shake off that verbal reaming and get back to business. When he spoke again, he sounded a bit saner, a bit more in control, a bit more like a sheriff.

"Yes, as a matter of fact, I was just looking 'em over. Cross-checking what he found with the county geologic records. If you woulda let me finish, I was gonna *explain* that I was trying to find a way to seal off every exit to those caves. I know for a fact the Langan entrance was connected to the major system the Coldonas mined. Thought maybe some crazy sumbitch— not me, but *somebody*—could go down and finish the job, keep 'em trapped down there forever once they all came back inside when the sun came up."

"But our children could be down there, Sheriff. We can't just—"

Baumgartner put a hand up, the gesture showing patience, not agitation.

"*As I was saying*, that system is huge, miles and miles of tunnels and entrances. If you'll excuse me, I'll show you just *how* big."

Susannah backed up, letting the sheriff stand and walk across his office. In a corner sat two brown cardboard filing boxes labelled *C. PARKER- 03/15/2017* in Magic Marker.

He lugged the boxes to his desk, haphazardly scooting various police reports and other bits of office detritus off the side to make room for them. He opened one and pulled out two rolled up sheets. He handed one to Jessie while he unrolled the other, using a paper weight and a stapler to pin down both ends.

USGS GEOLOGICAL SURVEY-1945- SALEM CAVERN SYSTEM, CARTER COUNTY, MISSOURI, said the map legend in the corner. Jessie stared down at the map, confused at first by what she saw. A giant amalgamation of squiggly lines and shaded red areas. She noticed a measurement legend on one side. For this map, two inches equaled about five hundred feet. Now that she had a scale for reference, her stomach lurched when she understood just how vast this cave system really was. The sheriff wasn't kidding. Miles and miles of subterranean passages crawled underneath their feet, pitch black, harboring unfathomable horrors within its lengthy bowels. The thought of going down there made frost form between her vertebrae. Then she thought of Allen. How he'd gone missing, or, correction, his *upper half* had gone missing.

The PayDay bar turned to nauseating lava in her stomach and she swallowed thickly as the sheriff went on. He talked fast, still had that breathy quality to his voice, but he sounded less like a meth head lunatic the longer he talked.

"This is the caverns map the last time they were surveyed. Of course, this is just a rudimentary guesstimation. These gray areas here where the caverns extend off the page are where they had to stop. Un-surveyed areas, you see. This is the Langan entrance, right here." He pointed towards the very southern portion of the map, where a gap in the dotted lines that defined the boundary of the caverns showed entrances into the caves. Jessie counted seven entrances, many of them miles apart, some of them coming out into Lordell County.

"Now, ma'am, if you would." The sheriff gestured for Jessie to hand him the rolled-up sheet.

He unfurled the translucent plastic sheet and placed it over top of the map spread out before him. It was almost identical to the '45 survey, except there were aberrations in the design, and the clear portion extended out farther than the original map, showing even more subterranean veins.

"This is the Parker survey, which was incomplete because, well, the Langans got to him, or maybe their daddy did. When we found his truck, he'd had these sonar doodads mounted on tripods that I reckon mapped out the area without ever having to go into 'em. According to his notes here—" He pulled a crumpled notepad from the other box with *United States Geological Survey* emblazoned upon it and began to flip through the pages. "These areas marked in black are where cave-ins occurred. See, when the Langans set those charges, they didn't just bring down the ceiling on the Coldona operation." He pointed towards the middle of the map, approximately four miles from the Langan property entrance. "It collapsed two more ceilings, here and here. They didn't realize how unstable the karst was with all the years of blasting they'd done." His fingers rested on two more black blobs on the clear plastic.

Jessie visualized this in her mind. The cave-in had essentially created a bottle neck that cut off one side of the system from the other.

"Now, this large area is an atrium, essentially a huge open space where many of the entrances and their veins come together." Baumgartner circled a large area just to the right of the center of the map with a red dry-erase marker. He then pointed to the Langan entrance towards the bottom. "Since we know Virgil went into this entrance and encountered these things, we have to assume they're trapped on the southern side of the cavern system. Which means there's two other ways, that we know of anyway, to access this portion of the cave system. One is on the Kurtz property, which is out of the question, since we can't just go tear-assin' on private land. There might be a few decommissioned mine shafts too. The survey didn't account for man-made entrances and what not."

"I know the Kurtzes, I could probably—"

"Nope. They're gonna ask questions, and our answers are gonna sound batshit insane. Not only that, but he's probably gonna make me bring a warrant before stepping foot on his property. Me and him... We ain't got the best rapport, Sus."

"Who *do* you have a good rapport with?" Sussanah asked, her voice flat.

"Yeah, yeah. Anyway, so Kurtz is off limits, and so is the Langans' since I heard some firefighters ran into those things up there. Not only that, but it's still probably hotter than hell up that way, even with the fire out. Which leaves one entrance left." He pointed at Blue Springs

Lake. Jessie remembered Susannah's board, where she'd marked the cave entrances and her postulations on the Langans using them to hide the bodies. Christ. She'd been right this whole time.

"Blue Springs? We'd need a boat to get to that part of the cave." Susannah said, staring at the map. "Plus, it's the farthest from the center compared to the other two entrances. At least a mile, it looks like."

"Now you can see why I gave up on the notion. That, and there's so many little ins and outs we don't know about—chutes and mine shafts and sinkholes—that collapsing the rest wouldn't be a guarantee. Even if you were able to *not* get lost down there, you gotta assume you can make it to the deepest part of the cave, where I'm assuming these things have been hiding. Who knows what's down there? If there is a mastermind, if it knows its importance to its... thrall, or whatever you wanna call it, you gotta assume it's holed up down there, dug deep. Probably keeps a few of its minions around to protect it. Same way a queen bee is usually in the deepest, most well protected part of the hive."

"That's alright, we'll just kill them. We know what hurts them. If the thing about taking off their heads Jessie was talking about is true, then we might have a way to actually kill them. Plus, I might have an idea. What do you have in your armory here, Sheriff? Got any shotguns?" Susannah asked.

The sheriff blinked.

"Well, uhm, yes. We got two Remington 870 riot guns and a couple hundred rounds of buckshot for each. But you saw how useless guns are, you—"

"With *lead* rounds, yes. But shotgun shells, you can peel 'em open and take out the shot, put silver in instead. Harold did that one time, made some homemade Dragon's Breath for a Fourth of July party." The sheriff's eyebrows shot up an inch or two. Jessie could almost smell the burnt exhaust of his drug-addled mind spinning in high gear.

"Well, for one thing, that's highly illegal. But I'll overlook that in this special instance, considering the gates of hell opening up and all. Secondly, goddamn Miss Paige. That's a good idea, but where the hell are we gonna find pure silver buckshot?"

"Maybe not buckshot, but I know a place where we can get silver tailing and cast offs. Make our own shot." Susannah opened up her phone. Jessie saw it was ten-thirty at night and had to blink in confusion. Time seemed to have taken on properties of its own since the eclipse snuffed out the last vestiges of sunlight, causing night to come early. Or perhaps the constant barrage of jarring and traumatizing events was making her brain process time differently.

"I'm calling Bernie Standridge," Susannah said. "Not only does he have that little metal smithing operation, he can probably tell us more about the Coldonas, considering he's the historical expert around here. I've treated his old basset hound a few times for gum infections. Said he would give me a discount if I ever wanted to use his services. He probably won't be too happy, and he'll more than likely have questions. Who knows how much of the stuff he writes about he actually believes, and how much he just uses to sell books, but he's gotta help. You can do what you do best, Sheriff, wave that badge around and act like you own the place."

"Shitfire woman, you're something else. Hell, that old boy will probably wanna go down into them caves with us. Put it in his next goddamn book or something." The sheriff sighed and rolled the maps up, tucking them under one sweat-stained arm. He grabbed his meth stash and pipe off the table—two of the few things he hadn't flung off to the side—and tucked them in his chest pocket. "Well, let's go bother this fella, and—"

Susannah's cellphone started ringing, cutting off the sheriff, and she stared at the unknown number.

# CHAPTER 31

*THE GARDEN SPADE PUNCHED first through cartilage, and then skull. He watched the life go out of those eyes. But before he could even register that he'd killed a man, charred hands were gripping him, blackened arms shaking him violently, those things were going to eat him, they were going to—*

Lou shot awake, forgetting where and when he was, his mind still dumping adrenaline into his body from the nightmare. He'd felt a scream boiling up from his lungs but abruptly bit it off when he saw Geoff, who was gently yet incessantly nudging him awake, trying not to jostle him too much.

"Please, Lou, get up, man. *Get the fuck up.*"

"Wha-What?" Lou mumbled. Geoff was whispering, trying to be quiet, but the sound of screaming drowned his voice. Someone a few rooms over was shrieking.

"Listen, man. We gotta get outta here. Some shit is going down. I don't know what, but some *shit*. You need to be silent, okay?" As he spoke, the scream died down into a wet gurgle. A tide of memories came back to Lou: The hellish heat of the shed, his own liquid shit cooling against his ass, the smell of his filth, killing that man. He wanted to go back to sleep, because last he checked he was in the hospital—a safe place. And yet, here was Geoff, sweaty and haggard, telling him he needed to be quiet, and, Christ, there was that terrible choking, gurgling noise cutting off the scream. No, this was just another stage of the nightmare.

It never ended, apparently.

"Wha—"

Geoff put a finger to his lips, then pulled out a blood-spattered smartphone and showed it to Lou.

"Copped this off the unlucky motherfucker who got torn to shreds outside. One fuckin' security guard for this whole hospital... I've been hiding out down here watching shit go down. Kept the lights off and the door locked. Good thing you don't talk in your sleep. It's fucked, man. All of it. Fucked."

The screen showed several grainy black and white rectangles Lou recognized as security camera footage. He saw images of hallways painted with black spatters of blood. Shapes loping through those bespeckled hallways with a familiar animalistic locomotion. The little battery sign in the upper right corner was flashing red, along with a big X where the cell-signal bars should be.

"You guys were right, dude. Some seriously crazy shit is going down, okay? But *please*, for the love of fuck, be quiet," Geoff hissed. He went away from Lou's bed momentarily to grab the wheelchair sitting in his corner of the ICU room. Technically he wasn't supposed to be moved for a month. Lou assumed he hadn't been out *that* long.

Lou flinched at the clatter of breaking glass from somewhere down the hall. Feet scrabbled against metal and glass, followed by heavy panting and breathing. He caught shadows racing across the small bar of light underneath the door that led out to the hall. Visions of those things coming out of the fire, hideous, horrible monstrosities from hell itself. Their charred skin flaying away to healthy pink tissue as they fed.

"Ah, fuck," he groaned under his breath as Geoff unfolded the wheelchair and put it flush against Lou's bed. "Hey, man, doctor said—"

"I know, okay? But all the doctors are dead or left. Not a single fuckin' person came to get us when shit started going down. So, *fuck* the doctors. I'm getting you out of here." Geoff hooked his good arm awkwardly round Lou's midsection. Despite the thick plastic upper-body cast meant to keep his spine immobilized for the duration of his convalescence, the vertebrae in the base of his spine ground against each other when Geoff shifted him into the sitting position. Lou bit his lip and, with all his willpower, tried to swallow the scream of agony that wanted to erupt from him. The feeling of someone shooting him with molten buckshot peppered his spine as pain raced up his shattered spine in hot electric currents.

He couldn't stop the whimper that escaped his lips as Geoff clumsily shifted him from the hospital bed to the wheelchair. By the time the excruciating process was over, Lou's vision was pulsing at the edges. Geoff was panting, about to unhook the two IVs in each arm when Lou shot out a hand.

"Hold on, G—" Lou reached for the bed, hitting the small red button, the one that controlled his morphine drip. He knew the button only dispensed so much regardless of how often you pressed it, but he'd been out for a hot minute. One last kiss from the opiate gods before plunging back into madness. He clicked the button five or six times, fast, listening to the machine whir, feeling the slightest burn in his left forearm. A few seconds later, the line of searing pain climbing his back had dulled to a prominent throb. "Alright, beam me up, Scottie," Lou whispered.

He didn't even register the pain as Geoff crudely yanked the needles from his arms, his spine was still the star of that show. Unburdened now, Geoff rolled him across the room and stopped just short of the door. He pantomimed silence with a finger to his lips as he glanced at the phone, making sure the coast was clear before quietly pulling open the door. Lou was thankful for the well-greased hinges as the door opened with a hushed whoosh of air and not the high-pitched squeak of every door in every horror movie ever made. Geoff stuck his head out and looked both ways like a child crossing the street. He propped the door open, kicked his shoes off and shoved them in Lou's lap, then quickly wheeled Lou out into the hall.

The lights were still on. Nothing looked out of the ordinary apart from the lack of doctors and nurses, and the occasional smears of red that stood out in stark contrast to the sterile whiteness of the walls and floors. The wheelchair sighed softly as Geoff rolled him down the hall, the pat of his bare feet barely audible over the susurration of rubber on tile.

Geoff slowed to a crawl as they came upon one of the ICU rooms. Its door stood ajar, bright surgical light spilling from it. Geoff parked Lou and crept by the wall next to the door, peering just his head in. Lou could see the words form silently on Geoff's lips: *Holy Fuck*. Geoff stood watching for another few seconds, face contorting into a rictus of horror, before shaking his head and creeping back to Lou. Slowly, glacially, they proceeded past the open door, their passage as silent as a cat's. Lou turned his head.

He expected to see charred flesh, something burnt and hellish, fearing those things had followed him from the wildfire all the way to the hospital. Instead, he saw the scrub-clad body of a nurse bent over a guy in a firefighter's uniform sans jacket, with the thick canvas pants, fireproof boots and a black shirt reading DOLVIN VOLUNTEER FIRE DEPT. Beside the nurse was another guy in firefighter digs, skin sooty and brown hair wild. They both hunched over the man on the floor, his body spasming as the sound of their desperate gulping filled the pregnant silence of the hallway, both so enraptured in the act of feeding they didn't notice the two in the hallway.

Lou and Geoff jumped when a CB radio clipped to the downed firefighter's chest squawked. The tinny, frantic voice emanating from the speaker sounded desperate.

"This is Engine 1550 requesting a personnel update. Repeat, all personnel check in, this is an all-station call. Goddamnit, this is 15— Where the fuck are you guys? What—"

The voice was cut off by a yell, followed by unintelligible noise. The feeding nurse pawed at the radio, ripping it from the suspender it was clipped to, and stared at it inquisitively before throwing it against one wall where it shattered. Shortly after, the sound of gulping continued.

Geoff wheeled Lou past the horrible scene. Once they passed the door, Lou looked forward. They were headed towards the elevator. More heavy breathing and more liquid sounds—a kid gulping a milkshake—sounded from down the hallway behind them. Geoff froze, looking at his phone, frantically cycling through the security camera feeds until he mouthed the word *fuck*. Lou saw the screen went blank. The battery had finally died.

Geoff wheeled him towards the reception desk at the end of the hall. Lou huddled, watching while Geoff crept past the desk partition to investigate. In that moment, the horror briefly faded away as Lou saw Geoff demonstrate balls he'd never known his posh, liberal arts educated friend to demonstrate.

Geoff had always been the polar opposite of Allen. He didn't stick his neck out for *nobody*. He laid low anytime there was conflict and was the first one to acquiesce to majority opinion. He had the spine of a jellyfish. The only thing Lou had ever seen him stand up for and actually fight for was the level of his guitar solos in the studio mix of the album they were currently (well... had been) touring for. Watching him take charge and do his best to get Lou out of this situation was, well, as mind-blowing as the real-life monsters they were trying to evade.

Or maybe he was just stoned, that last burst of morphine blunting his adrenaline and fight-or-flight mechanisms and letting his mind wonder about such trivial things while his life hung in the balance.

"Fuck fuck fuck..." Geoff raced back towards Lou and pushed him behind the reception desk, crouching low. Lou strained to crane his neck around the desk but couldn't see anything. Geoff shoved him in a corner, his view a giant office printer and someone's crumpled bag of McDonald's. Lou had a flashback to the shed, to the milkshake. A wave of disassociation crashed over him. *No, no, snap out of it, dipshit.* He focused on Geoff, who'd grabbed one of those vases containing fake plants that all shitty hospitals seemed to have in their reception areas, meant to give a cheery vibe to an establishment whose only business was pain and death, their fake green leaves only magnifying the harsh sterility of their surroundings.

Lou watched, confused, as Geoff took the vase and hurled it down the hall. A screech rang out. Not a scream, but a high-pitched ululation that sounded like the hiss of a cat mixed with the shriek of an incensed hog. There was a human quality there as well. Lou was reminded of that terrible war cry he'd heard back at the Langan place. Soon after, bare flesh slapped against linoleum and bodies crashed into medical equipment. Those things were racing down the hall to chase after the loud shatter of breaking pottery.

"Holy shit, holy shit—" Geoff yanked Lou around the corner of the reception desk and whipped towards the elevator. Lou braced the sides of the wheelchair with his hands to keep from being rocked around more than he already was. Every jostle made his nerve endings scream against the numbing buffer of the morphine. He heard a tinkle of glass and Geoff cursed under his breath as they dashed for the elevator. Geoff hit the call button. Ice flowed through Lou's bowels at that metallic chime. It sounded just like a dinner bell.

Geoff balanced on his right foot, his left dripping blood as he grimaced, pulling out a shard of glass from the broken window next to the elevator. Lou heard the slap of feet approaching. Time dilated to a crawl as a young woman came into view, red hair frizzled and matted with blood. Blue eyes turned slate gray and bloodshot searched the room before locking onto them.

"Shit, G—"

The woman hurled herself forward. In a blur Lou saw she was topless, her pale torso the color of a corpse. Black veins emanated from breasts whose nipples were gray and wept a black ichor. She looked pregnant as she loped forward, her body skinny and sharp angled save for the distended swell of belly that swung in a hypnotic, pendulous motion with her breasts.

Behind them, the elevator doors opened with a mechanical slide of metal on rubber.

Geoff was just starting to push Lou into the cab when the woman started running. He hurled himself out of the way as the woman leaped like a jaguar across the air and slammed into Lou causing his chair to fly back into the elevator. Lou's upper body went numb as vertebrae ground together before a thunderbolt of pain struck him. He heard the scraping of teeth against something hard, like a dog gnawing at a bone. He looked down to find the woman was doing her best to bite through his cast, bits of teeth breaking off in the gouged furrows of plastic that wrapped his chest.

"FUCK OFF OF HIM!" Geoff roared. Lou looked up in time to see Geoff slam another one of those tacky vases down on the thing's neck and back. Porcelain met bone with a solid thud before the vase shattered, bits of broken porcelain raining on Lou. The woman reared back. Flinging arms knocked Geoff to one side of the claustrophobic elevator. Light jazz Muzak spilled from the interior of the cabin, adding a level of absurdity to everything. Geoff cried out and shot his leg out in a clumsy kick. It looked like he was going to go for a groin shot, but his foot connected with the bulging mass of pale belly. The woman stumbled, a great retching sound coming from her.

Geoff push-kicked her again with an indignant feminine cry, right in the ass, propelling her out of the elevator. Just as the doors began their agonizingly slow journey to converge, the woman's ivory frame heaved. A great torrent of blood erupted from her mouth as she leaned over, vomiting scarlet. Right before the doors closed, Lou saw the nurse and the firefighter slam into the woman. Their mouths darted towards the floor, where a growing lake of red spilled into the cabin. A grotesque slurping sound echoed through the elevator as the two lapped up the regurgitated blood.

Finally, the doors shut, and Lou heard someone pounding on them as Geoff hit the first-floor button. With a lurch, they descended.

"Holy fucking shit." Geoff leaned heavily against one wall of the elevator.

"Yeah..." Lou gasped in a daze as his mind replayed that thing, what was once a woman, erupting with blood. She hadn't been pregnant. That was *blood* swelling her belly. Instantly his mind thought of mosquitos and ticks, the way they could just keep feeding until they ballooned to twice their size, the epic blood smears they left when you finally popped them. Lou thought of that half-burnt man, Virgil, from the cave, the way he talked of rationing bodies. The way he talked of the impending blood moon as though the astral event would cause them to lose control.

It was always feast or famine in the wild. Only humans had the luxury of knowing when and where their next meal would come. Wherever these things came from, the evolutionary need to gorge when the opportunity arose had only grown stronger with each iteration of this plague. Their need grew with each day they had to get by on sips and animal ichor. Somehow, in a haze of pain and pharma-dope, the sight of that bulging belly full of blood made Lou finally understand. It'd been so long since these things knew excess and indulgence. When one was let loose in the hospital, it was like letting a starving fox loose in a henhouse. They just couldn't stop themselves.

# Chapter 32

T HE FIRST FLOOR WAS all but deserted, though Geoff and Lou continued to traverse it with stealthy caution. They made a quiet beeline for the main service desk, where Lou saw an honest-to-god payphone was still in service.

"Christ, this place still uses fuckin' payphones?" Geoff began frantically searching the waiting room. He found a blood-spattered Louis Vuitton purse beside a chair and rummaged through it. He pulled out a crumpled one-dollar bill and a handful of change, pawing through nickels and dimes before finding a few quarters. Geoff took out the small piece of paper that had Susannah's number on it. As Lou kept look out, Geoff deposited the quarters into the machine, each coin dropping into the deposit basin sounding monstrous and metallic in the preternatural quiet. Lou winced at the noise. There was a pause as Geoff dialed the number, and then carried on a hushed, one-sided conversation.

As Geoff talked, Lou's eyes darted around, looking for any signs of movement. The few couches and chairs that comprised the main waiting area were either knocked over or pushed askew. The television mounted in one corner played Fox News on mute. A newscaster silently talking about something with a vapid, blank eyed stare, cutting to scenes of the nation's president, talking about some foreign policy or another. It all seemed so alien in this context, that horrible things like this could happen in the middle of a first-world country. Supernatural monsters having a fucking pogrom inside a modern hospital. People dying grotesque deaths where regeneration and recovery were promised. Reality seemed to have broken in this small rural town, and all the while this news anchor spewed on about things that seemed to take place on another planet entirely.

And where were the police? Surely, in their maddened stampede to evacuate the hospital *somebody* must've had the sense to call the cops. Yet, it seemed they were the only ones left alive. It was as if the entire world had said *fuck this place, let the bloodsuckers have it.*

"Come on, man, they're coming. Let's get out of here." Geoff let the phone hang off its hook before pushing him towards the revolving door at the main entrance. A warm, humid night awaited them on the other side. As soon as they were outside, Lou was captivated by the moon, crimson and domineering in its size as it hung over them like some feudal lord over his field of serfs. He must've missed the eclipse while he was out. Lou was mesmerized by the many craters and pockmarks of this distant celestial body in vivid clarity, getting a visceral sense of its vastness in a way he'd never been able to before.

In that moment he could understand why dogs felt the instinctual urge to howl at it, why whole oceans were moved by it, why these things, whatever biological or paranormal basis they had, were driven to a bloodlust frenzy by it. Geoff was talking to him, but he was miles away. The moon sang a silent song to Lou, and for a moment the pain and the fear and the dread left him, his pupils dilating as he took in the blood moon. It was only the distant roar of an engine sometime later that finally snapped him out of his lunar trance. That, and the distant but familiar shriek of someone who had just found more fresh meat.

# CHAPTER 33

IN PLACE OF GUM, whose last stick he'd chewed through an hour ago, and dip, which he did not have time to resupply, Baumgartner clenched his jaw and ground his teeth. It sounded like someone kneading a burlap sack full of gravel. His body was a springboard of tension. He felt at one with his Charger then, his heart revving with the RPMs as he gunned it to the hospital. Though it was late, and Highway Y wasn't much of a traveled corridor at night, he passed car after car, all of them speeding in the opposite direction. His sirens were blaring, and the Charger was doing ninety as they hurtled towards the hospital. Many of the cars did not bother yielding as he flew past. He didn't care. His official capacity as sheriff was void for the time being. He was something else now.

None of them spoke as he drove, and he was glad of it. His mind raced, as did his heart, as he rehashed the plan they'd gone over at the station. He chewed on what Susannah had said to him, burrowing right into his calloused heart and breaking down the door he'd nailed shut with booze and ice. He knew it was fucking suicidal, going into the heart of enemy territory with his only backup being a middle-aged woman and some punk runt who probably wouldn't care if those things tore him to shreds. Oh, and that mutt, who *really* didn't like Baumgartner. The feeling was mutual.

But Christ. What if Vivian *hadn't* run away? What if she *was* down there?

The questions scraped across his mind like sandpaper. Questions he hadn't even allowed himself to consider. Some headshrinker would call it a defense mechanism or a coping tactic, it didn't matter. He was facing it now, and with this confrontation a chasm opened in his heart. A pit where all the fatherly love and hopes and dreams he'd had for his only child had been locked away, Baumgartner disallowing himself to ever feel such foolish things again.

But now he felt that great ripping in his chest as a tide of suppressed emotions washed over him like a tsunami. At the forefront of that wave was the unfathomable dread that Susannah was right. He thought of when Vivian was just *Viv*, his little baby girl with luscious brown hair and dazzling eyes. Viv, whom he'd used to tickle awake for school with the hand-puppet piglet she so affectionately called Mr. Snuffles on account of the throaty pig oinks he used to make when he'd playfully attack her with it, bringing her out of even the most groggy sleep in a fit of giggles.

Viv, who wanted to be first a painter, then a writer, and then a musician. She showed such genuine artistic talent with every hobby she picked up. There were some days Charles couldn't believe this magnificent little creature had any of his DNA, or his wife's for that matter. The sweet child whose cherubic shell cracked one day with the advent of hormones and her first period, and emerged a troubled, rebellious young woman whose strongest vocation was hating her own parents.

He gripped the steering wheel hard enough that his forearms had the vascularity of a bodybuilder. What would she think of him now? An abject failure. A full-blown meth addict. A man who wallowed in his own nihilistic destruction like a pig in shit because he had no one left in his life to be a good man for. He failed his wife. He failed his child. He failed the town he swore to protect. It was as if with that bitch-slap, Susannah had forced him to face the looking glass, and he'd finally opened his eyes to what he had become: A man in the throes of a slow-motion suicide.

*So what? I told you boy, in this job you gotta have your own back. In these woods you either got the constitution to get along by yourself or you get left behind. That huffy ol' cunt is right, while you still got that badge on, you got a job to do, son, and you best do it. If them things cut you down, best do it while you're standing your ground. If they got your baby girl, then you better go give them hell. She's the only good thing to ever come out of you existing. Corrupt you might be, but coward you ain't. You wanna off yourself? Fine, but at least die doing something good, you fuckin' pussy.* His father's steely voice almost made him sob. But he wouldn't dare.

Baumgartner's mental war was abruptly forgotten as he rolled up on the hospital. It was unnerving, seeing Saint Francis empty like that, and on a Friday night of all things. Christ, everything really had gone to shit while he was holed up in his station, slowly losing his humanity while he experimented on those *things*. As Baumgartner pulled into the parking lot, he killed his lights and sirens. He spotted the hipster kid with the broke arm huddled next to the one he'd found passed out in Roy Langan's truck, covered in shit. He pulled up next to them, but just as he was getting out, Susannah made a noise, a sort of sighing sob. Then came the border collie's low growl, which turned into a flurry of barks.

"Oh, Elizabeth," she groaned.

Baumgartner flipped on the Charger's hi-beams, recognizing the once petite redhead who'd been disheveled, flustered, and doe-eyed at the clinic. Her eyes were now wide and wild and red, reflecting the light like a cat's eyes and causing her to look like some bejewel-eyed monster. Her pale body was smeared with blood and laced with black veins, her once slender form distorted by a bulging belly. She walked like something that'd once loped on all fours and only recently learned bipedal locomotion.

"Come on, let's get them in here before that thing—" he began but Susannah was already out of the car, a shotgun in her hands. "Fuck's sake, come on, girly, let's get your friends." He opened the back seat for Jessie, there being no way to open it from the inside.

"Oh, honey, oh, no. This is my fault, all my fault... Please... Remember me. Look past the sickness and remember me." Susannah was begging the girl, but she was distant, her voice growing fainter.

As he and Jessie raced towards the two boys, he heard something off to his right and whipped his gun out. A sound like a broken record skipping over the same word over and over again. Jessie looked in that direction too. What they saw froze them both for entirely different reasons.

Baumgartner blinked. The man standing before him was a ghost, come back looking even worse than when the sheriff had seen him last, on the brink of death.

Virgil Langan strode out of the trees buck naked, with what looked like a human satchel strapped over his shoulder. Five wraith-like humans trailed behind him, their skin the pallor of a well-used ash tray. It was only when the half-man dropped down and started approaching them on his hands that Baumgartner fully understood what he was seeing.

"Jessiejessiejessie," the thing muttered like an invalid caught in a thought loop. Red orbs with no discernable pupil or sclera shone in Baumgartner's Maglite.

"What the... Wha— *Allen*?" the girl whimpered.

For a second, Baumgartner could only stand there, watching stupefied as the half-man hauled himself towards her. Jessie had fallen to her knees, the pistol she carried slumped in front of her.

"Get up, girl. You're gonna have to use that thing now." Baumgartner took out his Python and aimed it at a dead man. "The fuck, Virgil?"

"Christ... She is something, huh?" Virgil said. His eyes were red too, but sunken, barely visible. He was squinting at the girl like she was the sun, like she shone with some incredible, blinding radiance. His entourage also stared, some held their hands up as if warding off some unseen force of nature.

"Jessiejessiejessie—" The thing mumbled stupidly, within a few feet of the girl now.

Jessie let out a short scream that devolved into a sobbing shriek.

"Jessie!" Lou started wheeling towards her. "Get the fuck away, that ain't Allen!" he yelled, but the girl didn't hear him.

"Allen... I..." she said between great, hitching sobs. The half-man was within grabbing distance now.

"Aww *hell*," Baumgartner grumbled and leveled his gun at the shambling abomination.

He hesitated as the world around him seemed to shimmer. Images appeared to overlay each other like transparent photo negatives stacked on top of each other. One minute he saw the monster before him—a crawling truncated nightmare—the next he was whole, a rather strikingly handsome man with a lean, muscled body and wide frame. Baumgartner blinked, wondering if maybe his brain was finally short-circuiting from all the meth. Then he heard the dreamy coo of Jessie's voice.

"Allen... Oh... It really is you—"

*"Jessie!"* Lou shouted at the top of his lungs. The shrieking voice was enough to finally shock Baumgartner from the illusion. The half-man was now on top of Jessie, his mouth only inches from hers. A drunken beam of elation lit the girl's face. Baumgartner fired on impulse. With the bark of the gun, the real world seemed to snap back into place.

Black gore spattered Jessie as Allen's noggin exploded in a way that reminded Charles of the watermelons he used to destroy with homemade m-80s when he was a hellraising teenager. She screamed then, a terrible, sustained sound of one's soul shattering.

"The fuck is this, Virgil? What are you?" Baumgartner's gun swiveled towards Virgil.

"Reborn. This is atonement, son. We're all repenting now." The old man's voice sounded about as bloodshot as his eyes.

"Come here, child." Virgil gestured towards Jessie. The girl kept screaming, watching as the half-man that should be dead flopped on the ground like a fish out of water, pale brain matter falling from his open skull. Somewhere on the other side of the road Susannah was talking to what was once Elizabeth. The dog was going hog wild in the back seat of the cruiser.

Charles's eye began to twitch. This was too much. It was all too much. He knew bullets wouldn't kill them, but he could at least slow 'em down. Two of Virgil's welcome party stepped forward, mouths open and drooling, aiming for Jessie. Charles shot first one and then the other, blowing a leg off each at the knee. They fell onto their sides but continued to crawl towards her.

"Stay outta this!" Virgil roared and charged at Baumgartner.

In that moment, rage exploded out of that raw wound in Baumgartner's chest. All that dread and sadness and mourning for his child had laser focused into an anger so pure it was a high in and of itself.

Virgil slammed into him, fetid breath hot in his face. Teeth gnashed right next to Baumgartner's ear. The sheriff, his reflexes operating on a hair trigger from the meth, spun with the blow and slammed Virgil into the cruiser.

"Where's my daughter at you *goddamn sumbitch*?" Baumgartner roared. He'd flipped the heavy Python like a gunslinger so that he held the fat barrel on one end and proceeded to club Virgil with it. The old man hissed and thrashed as his head caved in like an overripe pumpkin. Baumgartner's vision pulsed red as the butt of the gun drove like a piston, going up and down, up and down.

"Where is she? I said where is she? WHERE. IS. SHE?" He punctuated each word with a blow from his thoroughly bloodied revolver. He didn't even notice the gunshots until he felt something fall on his back.

Claws raked the flesh on his back. His uniform split open. Pain bright and hot lanced across his back. He roared like a bear as he reached one hand behind and grabbed a handful of cold, yielding flesh. It came away like a loose T-shirt in his hand. He bucked and twisted to slam himself into the patrol car. The thing straddling him screeched just as he felt teeth nick the skin at the base of his neck before dropping away.

He wheeled, aimed, and fired without pausing. The slumped creature jerked and twitched with the two shots, but was slowly getting to its feet, straining for him. At the throaty blast of one of the 870s going off, he turned to see Susannah was shooting at the Elizabeth-thing. She had leapt over the roof of the car and landed in front of Jessie, who'd been laying in a fetal position, holding herself.

"You can't save her. He'll... He'll keep comin'..." Virgil croaked from somewhere off to his left.

Baumgartner reared back his leg like it was '85 again and he was the all-star Cougar High placekicker aiming for a field goal somewhere over in Oklahoma. He kicked that girl as hard as he could in that beachball belly of hers, then blinked stupidly as a jet of red exploded from her mouth. Jessie was kicking and trying to scoot herself up against the patrol car as the blood splashed her shoes and ankles.

The remaining horde, their focus on Jessie temporarily forgotten, converged on the growing lake of red in the parking lot. Baumgartner didn't pause, but yanked Jessie up by one arm and half dragged her over to Mr. Wheelchair, who'd sat gawping at the ensuing horror.

"Come on!" he screamed loud enough to make his voice break. Jessie seemed to have finally got her wits about her and was running with the wheelchair. The gimp-armed kid stumbled to keep up as they made a beeline for the car. Baumgartner froze for just a second watching the hellish things eagerly lapping up that spilled blood. At least a gallon of the shit must have erupted from the girl's mouth.

Susannah was the only one not moving. She stood framed in the cruiser's bright spotlights, shotgun aimed in the general direction of those things.

"Elizabeth…" Susannah breathed.

"That ain't her no more, goddamnit. Now come on!" Baumgartner darted toward Susannah. But just as he was reaching for her, the Elizabeth girl's head shot up from licking up her own vomited ichor.

For just a second Baumgartner saw a flash of humanity in those eyes. He knew Susannah did too.

"Oh honey…" Susannah's eyes were huge, haunted. Elizabeth pulled herself from the horrible feast, head twitching, teeth gnashing, blood-shot eyes roving. Susannah raised the shotgun. "I'm sorry. I couldn't save you."

Just as Baumgartner detected the subtle change in the thing's posture, a sure sign it was getting ready to leap, Susannah fired. She aimed for the belly. The ten-gauge buckshot tore open the distended midsection, sending so much blood flying Baumgartner almost didn't believe it. She quickly chambered another round and fired at the girl's head even as the beasts were converging on her, too maddened by the sudden eruption of blood to attack their attackers.

Baumgartner was pulling her away even as Susannah blew the girl's head apart.

"Get in the goddamn car! Ain't nothing you can do!" He shoved her rudely towards the passenger-side door, then ran around to the other side, aware one of the creatures he'd lamed was crawling towards him. A cold corpse hand locked on his thigh as he threw himself into the driver seat. He slammed the door shut, a crunch of bone telling him he'd amputated the limb. It now sat icy and heavy in his lap. He ignored it and threw the charger into reverse.

The car lurched over one of the things. Another jumped on the hood with a thud. He slammed on the brakes and jerked the steering wheel to the left, sending the car fishtailing just as the windshield formed a starfish of cracks. A gray fist punched through before the body was thrown from the car. RPMs spiked and the tires screamed as Baumgartner literally put the pedal to the metal.

The cruiser, crammed full now, sped down the highway. Baumgartner didn't dare to slow down until he'd put a lot of miles between him and that parking lot, though he did roll down the window to toss out the truncated arm in his lap. His mind kept replaying the torrential spray of blood erupting from that girl's mouth. He felt his gorge rise but swallowed it back down.

"Jesus fuckin' Christ, that was crazy, huh?" he said, but no one in the car said anything. His eyes flitted to the rearview mirror. Jessie had a glazed-over, slack-jawed look on her face. The black feller—Lou, Louie, Lawrence? he couldn't remember—had a scrunched-up expression of pain. The other one, the one he'd interviewed a few days ago, stared impassively out the window. Buckie was crammed in the middle, ears flat to his skull, a low whine in his throat.

He then looked at Susannah. She and Jessie shared very similar expressions. He'd never seen the woman like that before.

"Sus? Susannah?" he asked gently. His voice sounded too breathy, too ragged to be sincere. He thought of reaching out to touch her, but had the feeling if he did, she would rip his hand off. Something was brewing under that cold veneer of shock. She was going to snap out of it alright, but she needed a minute or five. He'd give it to her, but he needed to know where this blacksmith fella lived. "When… You're ready, I need you to tell me—"

"South, left on Route 32," Susannah said flatly. She stared unblinking at the line of trees that seemed to separate this isolated rural burg from the rest of the world, her knuckles ghost white, clutching the shotgun like a life preserver.

# CHAPTER 34

BERNIE STANDRIDGE LIVED A few miles past the middle of nowhere, on the very outskirts of Carter County, where the winding country highway led past places that once were: a long defunct gas station, an abandoned drive-in movie theater that still presented its fading Saturday night matinee schedule from 1999 on a large wooden billboard, smatterings of double-wides, and a few churches that were no longer the house of God.

Past this was a slew of scabrous farmhouses, and then trees. Trees for miles. Trees as far as the eye could see. They eventually came to Shawnee Ridge Drive, a rough-cut tract that barely passed for a dirt road, and Susannah had to remind Baumgartner several times to take it slow here. Potholes and sharp turns made the drive arduous, poor Lou in the back kept letting out small gasps of pain with each bump. Susannah didn't notice her surroundings at all, her eyes were open, but they did not see the land passing by before her, her mind on autopilot since she'd had to put Elizabeth down.

Yes, just like a rabid dog. The way Elizabeth's midsection *exploded* with blood, the way she had burst like a plump tick. She saw small traces of humanity in those eyes, that small fleeting glimpse of Elizabeth how she used to be. Elizabeth, who fought hard to combat the profound blood lust that usurped her willpower.

Susannah absentmindedly thumbed her crucifix as they approached the house. It's once reassuring metal texture now felt cruel and fake as she worried up a blister on the pad of her thumb from the constant rubbing. What sort of God let his most devout worshippers face such horrors? What sort of God allowed such a blight to be visited upon the soil of honest, God-fearing, salt-of-the-earth folk? Was she supposed to be the next Job? Had she not demonstrated enough her unwavering dedication to Him?

She could hear Buckie's tail swishing in the backseat and a high excited whine in his throat as they came upon the small ranch house. A prefabricated shed off to the left sported a small, hand-carved wooden sign reading STANDRIDGE METAL WORKS. Her heart, which was growing several layers of scar tissue by the hour, found yet another raw ache. Her poor dog had been through enough tonight. Knowing he smelled a fellow canine—Judge, the Standridges' surly old basset hound—and had reverted back to his normal puppy state made her wish she could just leave Buckie with the old couple.

But even if she could pry Buckie away from her side, she would be worried about him all night. She had no idea how far this thing had spread. The verdant hills surrounding the Standridge property, once idyllic in its isolation, now felt claustrophobic with the many shadows the thick, unending foliage harbored.

Susannah knew she was being selfish in wanting to keep Buckie with her, but she simply didn't feel right leaving him with someone else. Especially not people like the Standridges, an elderly couple who walked slow and whose handshakes were made stiff by the arthritic gnarl of their hands. She felt Buckie was only truly safe with her, even though she was plunging right into the diseased and atrophied heart of this madness. She would die before she would let anything happen to her boy. She would die ripping and tearing and gnashing teeth if she had to, if it meant protecting him, because she was *not* losing anyone else in her family.

"Alright, let me do the talking, but I need you there looking official. If he asks, it's police business, and that's it. And for God's sake, keep your hands in your pockets. He doesn't need to see you all twitchy," Susannah commanded Baumgartner as they got out of the car.

"I ain't shakin' *that* bad." Baumgartner dropped his keys as he said this and had to fumble around in the Charger's floorboard before getting ahold of them.

"You're shaking like a leaf, Charles. Also, you're bleeding. Did you get bit?"

"Ah, shit…" Baumgartner reached to touch the back of his shoulder, his fingers coming away red. He winced as he probed his wounds.

"Dude, you get fucking bit or what?" Geoff asked from the back seat, fear tightening his voice. Jessie gazed forlornly into nothing, borderline catatonic.

"No, I ain't get fuckin *bit*. Things clawed at me is all." Despite his assurance, his voice sounded unsure.

"Let me look." Susannah shined the flashlight on her phone at his neck. Long ragged scars, like a tiger had swiped at him, extended down his back below a small little wound up near his neck. If he did get bit, it was shallow. *But is that enough to infect him?* she wondered.

Luckily, the sheriff had a spare jacket in his trunk, and put this on over his ruined uniform, even though it was a balmy 75 degrees.

Judge's rusty howl echoed from inside the house, alerting his owners someone had come in from out of the dark to disturb their quiet evening. Susannah looked at her phone and winced. It was almost midnight. She did not have the mental energy to put on an act, she did not feel like doing this song and dance. But she had to. They needed as much silver as they could get their hands on.

The screened-in door flew open with an unoiled squeal, and a bewildered old man in flannel pajamas stepped out, an ancient double barrel shotgun thrust out in front of him, rheumy eyes squinting against the Charger's headlights.

"Who in the hell—"

"Bernie, it's me, Susannah," she said quickly, putting her hands up. Baumgartner had surreptitiously placed his hand on his Python, and she elbowed him hard. He grunted before putting his trembling hands to his sides, fingers splayed in a sign of placation.

"Easy there, old timer, let's put that scattergun away before you blow my balls off." Baumgartner said. Susannah thought he was fighting hard to control the nervous jitter in his voice.

"Susannah Paige? What the blazes... Is this about Judge? I—"

"No, Bernie. I'm really sorry to be bothering you like this. I know it's late, but we have a bit of an emergency and I'm afraid you're the only one who can help."

"Me? I don't understand, I—"

"I know, and trust me, it's gonna sound crazy if I try and explain it. Look—" She took out a crumpled wad of twenty-dollar bills. "I need any and all silver scraps you can part with. I mean, *anything* you don't absolutely need. Pure would be nice, but I'll take whatever you have regardless."

"Silver? You come to my house at a quarter 'til midnight to raise a fuss about some *silver*?" His bushy eyebrows knotted together in absolute confusion.

"Police business, sir," Baumgartner said, almost robotically.

"Police business? Say, that Charles Baumgartner? Sheeeit, I knew your daddy. What's a bunch of silver tailings gotta do with the police? Y'all hunting werewolves or something?" he asked with a coughing laugh.

"Vampires, actually," Baumgartner said nonchalantly. Susannah turned on him, her eyes telling him to keep his goddamned mouth shut. Bernie laughed again, an unsure sound that withered up like week-old lettuce when he saw Baumgartner's unsmiling expression.

"Aww hell…" A look of sage knowing deepened the furrows on Bernie's face. "Y'all ain't kiddin', are ya?"

"…No, sir," Susannah admitted after hesitating.

"I knew this day would come… Two of the old families on my doorstep. I wasn't going crazy after all." Bernie shook his head.

"Bernie? What the hell is all that racket?" Missus Standridge called from somewhere in the house, while Judge continued his warbling serenade.

"Nothing, woman. Just shut that goddamn dog up and go back to bed, I'll be inside in a minute!" he hollered over his shoulder as he closed the door behind him and shambled off towards the shed. "This is about what's in the caves, innit? 'Bout them folks disappearin'? About what got swept under the rug?" he asked, a wry smile on his face.

Susannah and Baumgartner looked at each other, unsure how much to say.

"Say, Bernie… Where, uh, where'd you get all that information, about your book? And you know, about the Coldonas?" Susannah asked as they followed the old man. She expected him to take them to his shed, but he walked past it, around to the back of the house. He stopped, then turned to look at them, squinting against the Charger's headlights.

"Family records, talkin' to you folks' parents and grandparents, interviews with some folks across the pond. Depending on where you go, the Coldona name is spoken with the same fear as Lucifer. You call 'em vampires, but see, I don't think that's entirely accurate. Come on. Got something I wanna show ya." He continued around the back of the house, his own flashlight in tow.

Susannah did not like following the old man into the woods. After what happened at the hospital, she looked at every shadow and tree trunk as if some horrible human facsimile with a taste for blood hid behind it. And there were *many* trees and *many* shadows out there. Baumgartner had his hand on his gun again, his other holding the Maglite on Bernie.

The sheriff's thick neck creaked as his head swiveled like a lawn sprinkler, trying to look everywhere at once.

"Where the hell you taking us, old man?" Baumgartner's voice was tight.

"Not much farther now. See, I knew there was some merit to what happened in them caves and people talkin' about curses. My daddy was one of the workers that got disappeared down there. That's a smart man who knew them systems. He was one of the head foremen, wasn't likely to get lost down there. Everyone thought I was just plumb crazy when I started digging deep into this town's history. Found the old journals left behind by folks' parents and grandparents. Hell, Miss Paige, I remember your daddy telling me how proud he was to make that land deal, selling y'all's old tract to the Langans, only for it to go gumbo. In a way, that's where all the trouble started."

"My family didn't have anything to do with what went on in the caves. We didn't set those blast charges. That was all Langan." Susannah surprised herself with the heat in her voice.

"Oh, darlin', we all got skin in that game. It's only fitting the surviving ancestors are here to put a stop to it. Only one missing from this party is a Langan. Then it'd be a truly complete picture."

Susannah and Charles looked at each other but didn't say anything.

"Oh yeah. There was lots of talk. About demons in the caves. Stealin' folks. Turning them into monsters. EPA tried to say it was a noxious gas down there causing hallucinations. Ain't no gas down there though. I've seen the readings. It ain't even considered a Superfund site no more." Bernie continued to follow a barely discernable, rough-hewn foot trail. "Would sound plumb crazy if there wasn't so much evidence pointin' otherwise."

"That's all well and good, but we got ourselves a county-wide emergency going on, sir. We need that silver." Baumgartner said, the patience thin in his voice.

"Silver, huh? That what kills 'em, you think?" Bernie spoke without turning his head, still walking forward.

"You got another idea? You seen these things before, Bernie?" Susannah asked.

"You'll see. Not much farther now. See, I tried my hand at raisin' some chickens about a year and a half ago. Spent a fortune on the coop, the feed, the heaters. Was gonna make me a mint sellin' country eggs to them folks down at the farmers' market. But somethin' kept getting at them chickens. Somethin' strong enough to rip apart my cages to get at 'em. Put out all kinds of traps trying to catch the varmint responsible. Coon traps. Coyote traps. Even bear traps. Heavy duty kind you chain to a tree. I know we ain't had black bears in these woods for some twenty year now, but hell, I was at a loss. I kept reinforcing the cages, kept buying new chickens. They kept getting taken. Till one day... I came out here and found one of them traps had been sprung."

They were about a half mile behind the house, woods surrounded them thick on all sides. Bernie's flashlight beam went down to the ground, and both Susannah and Baumgartner froze at what they saw.

At first, Susannah thought she was looking at a mummy. Dry crepe paper skin clung to the human skeleton so tightly it looked as if the dehydrated dermal layer had been shrink-wrapped to its body. Lips and eyelids had been eroded away to reveal raisin eyeballs that still moved in their sunken, exposed sockets. And the teeth...

"My God..." She watched the thing feebly reach out for them. Its ankle was ensnared in the steel jaws of a bear trap, the trap working its way down to the bone where the beast had struggled for hours, days, to get it off. The heavy chain that was fastened to the thick oak tree was thoroughly caked in mud and blood. But what her eyes kept coming back to were the long, exposed roots and jagged points of teeth closed together lazily, a raspy hiss coming from the thing as it tried to reach out towards them.

"When I first came upon this thing, boy, he was ornery. Came upon him in the daylight, skin was all melted off his body. Didn't know what to make of him. Didn't know who to tell. I shot him a good number of times, as you can see—" Bernie pointed with one gnarled finger at puckered mounds of scar tissue on the thing's head and shoulders.

"How long—" Baumgartner began.

"About nine months now. Kept waiting for the thing to die on its own, but... Well, it just doesn't. Think it got ahold of some rabbits or squirrels that came within reach of it. Just enough for it to stay alive, but now... Well, most animals know to stay far away from here. It's been starving to death. In daylight, it'll burn up right down to the bone, though I reckon these spruce trees give it some shade to hide under. And then at night the skin grows back, but each time it's thinner, more fragile. Reckon any day now it will finally keel over."

"Jesus fuckin' Christ. Why didn't you tell someone?" Baumgartner was staring at the old man with disbelief.

"What's there to tell? Who'd believe me?" Bernie looked back at them both. Neither one had an answer. Bernie shook his head and glanced down at the pitiful thing. "So why you folks so gung-ho on silver? I've come across it in my studies, sure. Some of the Coldona clan had developed a fierce allergy to it a long time ago. They started using silver during the purging rituals, the towns they infected, but I always thought that was just some old folklore hoodoo."

Susannah took out her silver cross necklace and carefully lowered it onto the thing's eggshell forehead. The effect was instantaneous. A small gout of fire shot up, puffs of smoke burning away the thin layer of dried flesh as though it were a match head. The thing shivered violently and spasmed. Susannah shot her hand away as those teeth clacked together hard enough to send ivory splinters flying.

"I see... Huh. Woulda never known..." Bernie's bushy eyebrows shot up in surprise.

"What else can you tell us about this thing, Bernie?" Susannah asked. Bernie sighed, then looked at the two with a weary gaze.

"I know it's a curse. I followed the Coldona name all the way back from when they was just Romanian peasants. Noticed the name appeared a lot alongside dates associated with plague and famine. Seems wherever they popped up, disaster struck. Kept happenin' to the point the name became synonymous with death and disaster. So, I guess they fled across the country, across the ocean. Ended up in our backyard. But you know what they say about history repeatin' itself and all."

"Yeah. Well, what you read about the silver must be true, as you can see." Susannah clasped the cross around her neck.

"Well, alright then. Come with me. I'll get you folks squared away."

"So, what's your plan? Go down there, throw a bunch of silver pebbles at 'em?" Bernie smiled as he unlocked the door to his workshop. Judge continued to howl from somewhere deep in the house.

"No, we, uh... This girl we got with us, she's whip smart and been studying everything she can on 'em. There's a system she talked about— It's all very complicated, but basically, if we can find the source of this curse, if we can destroy the source, then—"

"Then the rest will fall. Yep. Some call it the thrall, some call it the get. That's one of those universal things you find across all flavors of the folklore, which usually means there's some truth to it." Bernie pushed the door wide. Industrious chaos greeted them. Boxes labelled with various metals and their purities. Smithing instruments and what Susannah assumed were furnaces meant for different kinds of smelting lined the walls.

"You folks are in luck. This fella was going through a nasty divorce with his wife, she's trying to wring him out for all he's worth. So, he takes her parents silverware collection. Real sterling, mind you, a full fifty-piece set, and tells me to melt it down. Says he's gonna take it to that coin shop up in Lordell, they do trades for raw ores, gold and silver and all that. Well, ol' son never picked up his smelted dinnerware. Few weeks after he dropped it off, I heard in the papers. Murder-suicide. Took his old lady out and himself with her."

"Ain't that some shit," Baumgartner said.

"Ain't it? Works out for you folks though. Now I got a couple pounds of silver tailings just sittin' around. Resale value ain't what it used to be." Bernie stepped over boxes and tools then hefted a large cardboard box that rattled when he picked it up.

"What's the purity of these here tailings?" Baumgartner asked.

"Oh, I'd say eighty percent. Some impurities, but I reckon that there dollar store cross is less pure, and you saw what it did." Bernie said, nodding towards Susannah.

"Hell, that's perfect." Baumgartner took the box from the old man.

Susannah handed him the wad of twenties, but Bernie only stuck out a hand, shaking his head.

"No, no, that won't do. If y'all are tellin' the truth, then what you're gonna do is beyond payment. And if I'm bein' honest, probably a one-way trip. Y'all is brave, but equally stupid." He nodded towards the house. "Heard on the news about that wildfire, and people saying there's some drug-crazed folks on the loose trying to bite people. I reckon this ain't got nothin' to do with drugs and everything to do with the Coldonas."

"You reckoned right," Baumgartner said.

"Hell, I guess if it's got that bad somebody's gotta do something. We been hiding things too long in this town. Only fitting you two would put a stop to it."

"Stay inside, Bernie. Keep Judge in too. If he starts howlin', get ready to fight. I think dogs can smell 'em. Least mine can, anyway." Susannah took his gnarled hand in both of hers. "Thank you, and God bless you." She looked into those rheumy eyes. He squeezed her hand in return.

"And may He watch over you. I pray you folks succeed in whatever it is you're doin'. It's been needin' to be done for a long time. *Long* time," he said before shambling off towards the house. "Ethel? Grab my shotgun. And where in the hell you put that big ol' steak knife I got? The silver one?" He hollered as he pulled open the screen door. He looked back to Susannah and the sheriff. "You all come back now, if you survive. I got another book in me yet."

# Chapter 35

J ESSIE'S HANDS CRAMPED AS she wielded the needle-nose pliers, but she did not stop. She was on her tenth shotgun shell, she and Susannah working silently to refill the shells while the sheriff drove them out to Blue Springs Lake. It had taken several gentle nudgings from Lou and Susannah to snap Jessie out of her mental fugue and get her to work. When she finally came to, she looked around confused, unsure of where she was for a moment. It was like her brain had simply shut down for about half an hour.

It was tedious work, prying up the edges of the casings, plucking out the lead shot inside and finding pieces of silver that were small enough to fit inside the shells. Often, she'd have to crimp the edges of the oblong silver pieces with the pliers into something resembling a crumpled ball, before pressing the casing back down and ensuring their payload wouldn't fall out. Susannah had shown her how to do it, and Geoff, only half joking, had called her a female Rambo as she worked.

It kept her hands busy, kept her mind on autopilot. Still, as she worked, reloading each shell, thoughts of Allen crept in. Lou kept reassuring her that *wasn't* Allen, that was just some puppet in Allen's body, that the real Allen had passed on. But it didn't matter. The sight of him, walking on his fucking hands, spine dragging along the ground.... Or, even worse, that brief illusion of him whole and alive. So visceral and real. Allen walking towards her, his crooked shit-eating grin on his face. Arms outstretched to hug her. She almost met that embrace too. Almost. Before the sheriff splattered his rotten brains all over her face, and the illusion evaporated.

*Fuck.*

She closed her eyes and bit her tongue against the rising gorge. She already threw up once on the way out to the lake. She wouldn't do it again. She felt Lou's hand on her shoulder and shrugged it off, a reflex.

Jessie tried to take some solace in the work she was doing. She was scared shitless, yes, but finally, after days of trying to comprehend the horror of everything, of simply being a witness to this unfolding nightmare, she was taking *action*, she was going to do something about her circumstances. Jessie was going to avenge Allen, who'd had more balls than any man she'd ever met. She was going to make whoever had transformed her kindhearted, virtuous friend into a hideous sideshow freak from hell pay dearly. And she was going to do it fighting alongside Susannah, who in the span of just a few days, had felt more like a mother to her than her biological mom or any of her foster moms ever had. She drew strength from the woman's stoicism and would gladly follow her into the pits of hell.

Jessie understood with a heavy finality that she was either going to die by Susannah's side or see this through to its end.

Something had changed in her when she'd shot that man down in the basement jail. She was horrified at first, disgusted with herself for giving in to emotional impulse and pulling the trigger on reflex. Conflicting emotions roiled within her like oil and water being churned but refusing to mix. Guilt at her impulsive decision to try and kill another person. But, no, it wasn't a person. Those things were no longer people, and she felt satisfaction at finally striking out at the horror that had consumed her life. What she'd done was completely normal under the circumstances. But believing that was easier said than done.

Still, the desperation with which that man reached out for her… They all seemed to *need* her. They were drawn to her in a horrible way she didn't understand. The way their leader, Virgil, and his gang of bloodsuckers could barely look at her and yet seemed to be actively hunting her. That, coupled with the sheriff's twisted exhibition of bodily experimentation had revealed something about the human condition to Jessie she'd known deep down in her soul but had never dared bring up to the conscious level. Its implication was terrible, it changed the way she viewed *everything*.

The epiphany, which settled over her like a ceremonial shroud as she sat comatose in the car, was this: Civilized humanity is a fake, fragile and hollow thing. We've conditioned ourselves to ignore our crude base impulses and exercise restraint, telling ourselves this is what makes us different—no, *better*—than the 'animals'. We hide our nudity behind clothes and hide our preternatural penchant for violence behind wars fought for seemingly noble causes. We hide our primal roots behind fashion and grooming and education and language.

But those base impulses are always there, lurking just beneath the surface of the id. A bloodthirsty, territorial chimp hides within us all, just waiting for the right combination of adverse circumstances to come out, yattering and biting. These impulses never go away, they simply become things we can control. Jessie thought of serial killers, dictators, well-known human monsters who'd shed their civilized veneers and showed the whole world the monster that lurks within us all. Though she knew the comparison was absurd, she couldn't help but feel herself slipping, tapping into her primal, animal side.

All it takes is a few alterations in our daily lives to bring out the savage within us. Jessie saw it in Lou's harrowing testimony of killing Roy Langan. She saw it in the sheriff proudly showcasing the information he'd gleaned from torturing the human facsimiles that he kept imprisoned. She saw it in Susannah when she had to shoot Elizabeth, and *kept* shooting her, until nothing was left of her head. She even saw it in Allen, or the thing that was Allen.

How easily the things that make us human can be robbed by a few simple acts of violence. These vampiric creatures served as some living metaphor to demonstrate how much overlap there is between modern humans and the screeching, shit-flinging primates we sought to distance ourselves from.

This realization settled into her bones, into her marrow, and she accepted it with numb resignation. She thought she had a firm grasp of humanity's complex condition being raised in tumultuous poverty, but that was only a small taste, the visible tip of a vast submerged iceberg. And so, she loaded the shotgun shells with their silver, because fighting these things was the objectively moral thing to do, even if their very existence and reason for being served as a reminder of man's cruelty and hubris. It was a clear dichotomy between good and evil, savage and civilized, and it made it easier to digest the fact that lying dormant within us all was a latent capacity for unspeakable cruelty.

They pulled into a large sloping parking lot, and Jessie finally looked up from her work to see the wavering reflective sheen of the lake in the Charger's headlights.

"Wish I was here under better circumstances. This place is some good fishin'," Baumgartner said, more to himself than anyone else it seemed. He perused the parking lot, swiveling the spotlight on his side of the car to inspect the lingering shadows and crevices. It appeared they had the place to themselves.

"Does Lee Williams still run those canoe rentals out here?" Susannah asked. The sheriff nodded.

"Yep, good thing we ain't trying to do this in the fall or we'd be shit out of luck." He pulled up to a small building that sat at the edge of the lake, the large white sign on its metal roof read BLUE SPRINGS MARINA in a cute, sprawling nautical font, a cartoon image of a catfish with a hook in its mouth painted next to the sign. *One of the largest spring fed lakes in the country!* a small placard boasted. CANOE RENTALS- APRIL-SEPTEMBER- $150 FOR A WHOLE DAY, SHUTTLE SERVICE PICKUP AT JACK'S FORK & ELEVEN POINT JUNCTION, a hand-painted sign informed them, with a spray-painted arrow pointing towards the back of the marina.

"Alright, let's go commit theft and possibly some property damage." Baumgartner parked the car at the edge of the concrete boat ramp, which hugged the marina on the right side. He opened the back door for Jessie. She tried to keep Buckie in the car next to Lou, but he shot out right behind her, loping after Susannah, who carried one of the big riot guns towards the back of the building. Baumgartner opened up his trunk and brought out a large industrial pair of bolt cutters before following Susannah.

Ten canoes of various sizes and styles rested on T-rack-style metal brackets. Each was fastened to the rack by padlock and chain, the rack itself anchored to the ground via concrete foundation.

"Which one should we use?" Susannah asked as they looked at the vessels.

"Biggest one holds three people with enough room for stuff like coolers and all that. Bigger the better." The sheriff pointed to the largest of the canoes by far, a fifteen-footer with a red fiberglass bottom that looked thoroughly scuffed but still durable. He put the bolt cutters to use and snipped the three sets of chain that held it in place. With its shackles undone, the three of them awkwardly maneuvered the heavy watercraft off its mount, Susannah directing them through gasping instruction to walk it down to the boat ramp.

Jessie wondered why the thing was so goddamn heavy when she saw the thick wooden oars sequestered within the hull. Gently, they lowered the canoe half in and half out of the water, and for a terrible moment Jessie looked out over the glassy obsidian surface of the lake and wondered if those things could swim. *Surely,* they had to if this was one of the ways out of the caves. She imagined hands reaching up out of the water to yank her overboard, pulling her down into those vast depths where the lake floor sunk into a gigantic underwater aquifer. She shook her head and followed Susannah and Baumgartner back to the idling cruiser.

"So... What are we gonna do about the other two?" the sheriff asked as they pulled their gear from the trunk. Two more shotguns, one for Baumgartner and one for Jessie, Parker's maps, two boxes of silver-loaded shotgun shells and a box of regular slugs, and headlamps, plus the small plastic bag filled with the remainder of Susannah's gas station haul: a few bottles of water and some candy bars. The food and ammo were shoved into a satchel bag Susannah had carried with her from the car.

"Give them the cruiser to get out in case this doesn't work. Looks like the infrastructure around here is breaking down, we're gonna need outside help. Besides, that poor Lou boy needs to be in a hospital," Susannah said as she corralled Buckie into the canoe while Jessie carefully set the gear in the middle, doing her best to even out the weight distribution.

"Shit. Don't really wanna ditch my ride, but I reckon you're right. Not like we're leaving them caves alive anyway. Speaking of which, you sure you wanna bring the mutt with you?" He nodded towards Buckie.

"Yes. I don't trust him with anyone else. Besides, pretty sure he can sense those things before we can see them. Not sure if it's smell or what, but he stays with me."

"Suit yourself." The sheriff sighed and looked at Jessie. "Wanna go tell your friends sayonara before I let them run off with police property?"

"What? No fucking way. We're not leaving you guys." Geoff was standing by the car, the sheriff holding out his keys. "Besides, what the hell you think is gonna happen when a cop sees *me* driving a sheriff's car?" He gestured at himself, a skinny-looking long-haired kid in a sleeveless Meshuggah T-shirt and jeans, tattoos on full display, one arm in a blood-stained cast.

"He's got a point, man... But, fuck, I need to be back in a hospital," Lou groaned from the back seat.

"Well, son, that's why you're gonna be deputized." Baumgartner opened the passenger door and rummaged around in the glove box, until he pulled out something that looked like a leather wallet. "Now, I ain't the most popular sheriff around here. Which is why you're gonna drive as far as that half tank gets you. Go west, towards Kansas City. In Lee's Summit there's a fella named Wayne Daniels who's chief of police up there. Me and him go back a bit. Used to be hunting buddies back when he was sheriff for Lordell." He flipped open the wallet, which had a laminated display pouch featuring a card emblazoned with CARTER COUNTY SHERIFF'S OFFICE.

Baumgartner slipped this out, then took out a pen he kept tucked in his breast pocket. "You tell him Charles Baumgartner, Carter County Sheriff, is in grave danger. That there's an emergency going on in my county and the comms are down. Don't go telling him the truth, now, or they're gonna think you're plumb fuckin' crazy and arrest you. Tell them... Hell, I don't know, tell them we got a drug cartel up here taking the town hostage. You get pulled over on the way, you show them this. It's got my badge number on the back and my signature. Tell 'em you're from Carter County, that you've been emergency deputized and to send the state troopers, the fuckin' National Guard, hell, SEAL Team Six, if they can spare it." Baumgartner slid the card back in its case and shoved it in Geoff's good hand.

"What the fuck, man, I—"

"Just go, Geoff. You guys are both injured, and it's the best way you could help. Besides, Lou needs medical attention." Jessie put aside her aversion for personal touch and wrapped her shithead guitarist in a tight bear hug. She felt Geoff tentatively put his arms around her in return, squeezing her.

"Fuck, Jessie... Just come with us. Please..." Geoff said, and to her astonishment his voice quavered. Never in a million years did she imagine hearing Geoff cry. No, no, no, that wouldn't be any good. She would start crying then too, and they did not have time for that Lifetime channel bullshit. As comforting as it felt being in his arms, having someone she knew and had lived life with holding her, she pushed him away before the waterworks could begin.

"No. I can't. I don't believe in God, but I believe in fate, and I'm positive my fate was to be right here, right now. They need my help, and I owe Susannah. Do it for me, Geoff. Get out of here and go get help. I'm gonna avenge Allen. I'm gonna go destroy the fuckin' assholes who did that to him."

Geoff only stood there shaking his head as she climbed into the back-seat and grabbed Lou's hand.

"You've always been a stubborn punk ass," Lou said with a thin grin. "Come back in one piece, J. When this is all over, we're gonna smoke the fattest blunt in the world and tell people you're a fuckin' vampire hunter." Jessie felt her eyes grow wet and she blinked away the tears.

"You got it, man. You fuckin' got it." She reached over to hug him. It felt like she was hugging a plastic garbage can with his body cast, but she didn't care. He weakly hugged her back, and then she dragged herself away, emotion overwhelming her. "Get outta here, you assholes. Before I change my mind." She walked towards the canoe, not wanting to look back. She heard the throaty roar of the Charger's engine start up behind her.

"Just a second!" Susannah called after them. Jessie turned and saw her handing Lou the Glock through the back window of the cop car. "It won't kill them, but, just in case." Jessie thought that sending an armed black man off into the world with a stolen cop car was a good way to get dead, but she didn't say anything. Susannah meant well by it.

Jessie felt a mild burst of adrenaline as they pushed the canoe into the lake, the bottom scraping against the concrete ramp. Baumgartner took up the rear, getting his shoes wet as he awkwardly jumped into the canoe. They nearly tipped over when the overladen vessel listed sharply to one side before Jessie shifted her weight in the opposite direction, paddling hard to the right.

"Easy, easy," Susannah said. She cradled Buckie to still his whimpering. Finally, the canoe leveled out as Jessie and the sheriff began paddling in tandem. She'd gone kayaking, long ago when they played a show up in Montana, but this felt way different, the canoe moved like a sluggish whale through the water, the smallest shift in her body was transferred immediately through the canoe, and she feared a small wave could tip them over. The fact they were probably a hundred pounds past the thing's weight limit didn't help the matter.

"Which way?" Jessie asked, paddling towards the middle of the lake. Her headlamp just barely illuminated the opposite bank.

"Look for a cliff with a big-ass hole in it," Baumgartner huffed as he paddled. "Go to the left just a bit... there you go." They adjusted course. Behind them, the Charger's souped-up engine roared and echoed off the lake as Geoff and Lou left all this madness behind. It was just the four of them now: a metal drummer, a methed-out sheriff, a veterinarian, and a border collie. It was like the setup to the punchline of some shitty joke. Jessie almost wanted to laugh at how crazy this was. She didn't dare though, focusing on her breathing and keeping her mass centered. Eventually Buckie quieted down, and the only sounds were the slap of water against the hull, the oars churning the lake's surface, and the clinking rattle of Susannah loading each shotgun with silver rounds.

"I'm loading these with a mix of the silver shot and the slugs. The slugs are to open them up. The silver won't have much penetrating power given the fact they're just metal shards. If you gotta shoot 'em, do it up close," Susannah said.

Something about her words cemented it for Jessie: they were *really* doing this. Adrenaline dumped into her system as they crossed the lake, and her headlamp revealed the high rock wall jutting up from the bank, a cave entrance the size of a double-wide trailer recessed into it.

Oozing from this earthen maw was the familiar, dense red cloud. Jessie's skin prickled with gooseflesh, the sudden urge to piss overwhelmed her, and for a split second she almost called out, almost demanded they turn this fucking thing around. But then she remembered Allen, and that fear quickly gave way to rage. To anger.

The red cloud was thicker than she'd ever seen it before. Tendrils of crimson mist oozed from the hole and flowed over the edges into the lake, reminding Jessie of the walk-in deep freeze at Burger Zone, the way the icy mist would bleed out into the kitchen when you opened the door.

Jessie swallowed her fear, not even bothering to ask if the other two could see it. She knew they couldn't. Whatever happened to her that night Susannah saved her from the wreck, it changed her. She had glimpsed beyond the veil of death, and something had followed her back from the ether.

# Chapter 36

T HEY BEACHED THE CANOE on the rocky shore, Jessie taking point and keeping lookout while Susannah and the sheriff began unpacking their gear. The cliff wall extended some thirty feet on either side, with dense foliage and forest lining the tops of the cliffs and circling the rest of the lake. Susannah kept looking up, half expecting to see one of those things crawling down the sheer vertical rock wall like a spider. But the night was silent and still save for their own movements. When Buckie leaped out of the canoe and onto dry land, he immediately put his nose to the ground and began to sniff, ears raised and tail tucked between his legs, a low growl in his throat, just like that night in the yard.

Those things had been here alright.

The sheriff handed her a box with the remaining shells. He'd already stuffed both chest pockets and his trousers full of them. Susannah did the same, putting two in her jeans pocket, two in her flannel breast pocket before handing the rest to Jessie, who took the box with some trepidation. The shotgun she held looked too big for her. Susannah was afraid a single blast would knock her off her feet. She took the shells all the same, sequestering them away in various pockets.

"Me and Buckie will take point. If you hear him growl, get ready for a fight." She whistled and Buckie shot to her side. "Stay close, boy, you hear me? Stay close." She knelt down to wrap an arm around him and kiss his forehead. He grunted in acknowledgement. "You all ready?" she asked the others, chambering a round into the gun. Jessie and the sheriff nodded in unison. With that, she began to climb the steeply graded trail leading up to the cavern entrance.

As they neared the entrance, the smell of wet limestone and old pennies wafted up from that great stone gullet. Susannah double checked to make sure she had a round in the chamber. Unlike a normal 870, the riot gun's extended tube magazine held 7 shells instead of the normal 3. She made sure the first round in the chamber was a deer slug. Poor Buckie, she thought. The loyal dog was probably going to be deaf if they managed to get out of this alive, but he was no stranger to gunshots. Harold had done enough target shooting in their backyard to normalize him to such things, so she knew he wouldn't run off once the lead (and silver) started flying.

Susannah pulled out the red bandana she'd had in her back pocket since they'd left the house and waved it in Buckie's face. She had no idea why she would need Daniel's old bandana, the one he used as a makeshift sweatband to work on his car out in the driveway during the summer, but something deep in her gut, an instinctual pull, told her to grab it from his room. She hadn't been able to bring herself to wash it, and the material was stiff and musty from months of accumulated sweat. Buckie's pink little nose wiggled, and his nostrils flared as he took in the scent of his long-lost human companion.

Neither she nor Harold had ever tried to ingrain any tracking or hunting training into Buckie, so she didn't know if her plan would work. But something, a nudge, a mental tingling, told her to let the dog find his way. For all she knew Daniel wasn't even in the cave, he could've been one of the ones out there running loose and terrorizing the county, or he could've been killed outright. But as she approached the cave, the tingling grew stronger, and, validating that deep maternal tidal pull that led her into this stone abyss, Buckie immediately put his nose to the ground and started forward, slowly but steadily.

The cavern soon narrowed from a passage big enough to drive a bus through to a claustrophobic limestone throat with maybe three inches of clearance from its roof to the top of Susannah's head. She knew Baumgartner was probably having to crouch-walk behind her. His boots scuffed the stone floor along with the occasional rasp as his broad shoulders scraped off the side walls. But he didn't complain. None of them dared speak as Buckie led them down, the stone floor beginning to take on a definitive downward slope.

Finally, they came to a junction, a small atrium with three branching passageways, one tunnel so tight they would have to get on hands and knees to traverse. As Buckie stopped and snuffled, his head darting about as he tried to catch the scent, Susannah shrugged off her backpack and pulled out the Parker maps. The other two huddled around, their headlamps converging on the topographical map.

"Okay... I see..." Susannah whispered. She took a red Sharpie and put an X on the portion of the map that showed where they were. Two of the passageways—the one on the very left and the center one—had been charted, their pathways shown as narrow winding veins on the map that eventually converged. The small tunnel on the right, the one Buckie was pointing his nose into, showed up as a blank spot on the paper. "Buckie, you sure that's the way, boy?" She asked him. The dog chuffed and ran up to her, pawing at her jeans before running back over to the tunnel. The message was clear.

"Ah hell..." the sheriff groaned quietly. "I don't even know if I can fit in there."

The sheriff took point this time, the logic being if he got stuck or if the tunnel turned out to be a dead end, he wouldn't be blocking their way from behind and they would have an easier time trying to pull him out than trying to push him from behind. Susannah's nerves sparked like downed power lines as they crawled forward, knowing if one of them got attacked while they were in this tight crawlspace it would be disastrous. Her arms and knees ached from scraping against the rough stone floor. A global sense of dread worked its way into her as she imagined one of those things coming up on them and trying to get away from all those gnashing teeth in such a small, claustrophobic space.

That's when she heard the sheriff gasp. His big body froze stone stiff.

"What the—Viv?" the sheriff asked, his voice going high and squeaky. It didn't sound like Baumgartner at all.

"What is it, Charles?" Susannah asked, confused. The thin air felt supercharged, the fine hairs on her arms and neck standing stiff as if she were about to be within spitting distance of a lightning strike. It reminded her of the episode in her backyard, and she struggled to breathe. Peering over the sheriff's shoulder, what she saw made her heart stutter step in her chest.

"M-Mom?" Daniel asked. Susannah blinked. Daniel stood there. Skin that same healthy end-of-summer tan, blonde curls illuminated by her flashlight.

"*Daniel?*" Susannah gasped and shoved the sheriff forward. "Daniel, I'm here!" Both she and Charles ran ahead, stumbling, entranced by the sight of their children. As Susannah watched, Daniel retreated further into the tunnel, disappearing abruptly.

"Vivian? Viv? Where'd you go?" Baumgartner yelled as he rushed forward. Susannah stumbled after, not paying attention to the sheriff. Her trance was only broken when Buckie started growling. That wasn't right. Buckie should be *excited* to see Daniel. The growls turned into a flurry of barks before something pale and hissing and baring teeth exploded into the headlamp's range. Baumgartner fired. Susannah yelled, recoiling instinctively. The muzzle flash temporarily blinded them. When they got their vision back, the tunnel was empty. Susannah blinked stupidly.

"He's fuckin' with us," Baumgartner grumbled.

"What's going on up there?" Jessie called from the back.

"Nothing, hon. Just... Nothing." Susannah said, feeling flustered. Her nerves stretched to the breaking point.

They continued on, the tunnel just wide enough for the sheriff's bulky frame to squeeze through. Susannah could hear ethereal whispers bouncing off the cave walls. It was Daniel's voice.

"Ah shit, drop off ahead," Baumgartner grunted over his shoulder. His voice echoed strangely in the vast stone throat.

"How much of a drop off?"

"'Bout six or seven feet, but the ground here is steep. Can't see what it rolls off into." His voice was breathy again, but Susannah didn't think it was from exertion. In the harsh light of her head lamp, his face was unusually ghastly and sweat rolled off him. She told herself he was just coming down from the chemical cocktail he'd been flying high on all night, but her mind's eye kept coming back to the small wound on his neck. She didn't want to draw attention to it, but she couldn't help but try and sneak glances as they traversed the tunnel, searching for black infection lines.

"What should we do? You wanna head back?" Susannah asked. The thought of having to crawl backwards through that quarter mile of narrow rough stone made her want to groan with misery.

"Nah, think if I just... Shimmy out a bit. Lower myself." He panted as he slowly pulled himself out over the opening, splaying his legs wide and shoving his boots against the walls of the tunnel to anchor himself. Susannah saw the circular opening ahead, the sheriff's upper body disappearing as he cautiously tried to pull himself out. In that moment she wished they would've thought to bring some rope, but they simply didn't have time to get everything they needed.

"Sumbi—"

Baumgartner lurched forward. Another shotgun blast roared across stone.

"Charles!" Susannah grabbed at his boots as they shot forward. She clawed at his pantlegs, feeling the body heat radiating through his trousers. Something was pulling him forward.

"Goddamn motherfucker!" Baumgartner roared. Then Susannah heard what sounded like a branch breaking. A pained hiss came from something on the other side of that circular void, before Baumgartner slipped forward again.

She tried to hold on, but the sheriff was two-hundred-sixty pounds of good ol' boy losing a tug of war with gravity. Susannah felt herself sliding with him, her shoes scraping against the tunnel wall.

"Guys? What's going on?" Jessie's voice echoed from behind. With Buckie's fluffy butt in front of her she probably couldn't see what was going on.

"Goin' down, honey!" Susannah almost yelped as she felt herself being pulled over the edge of the opening and down into darkness. As she fell, she heard Buckie begin to growl, followed by a scream from Jessie.

# CHAPTER 37

J ESSIE HAD BEEN WALKING, now crawling, in a red haze since they'd entered the caves. The mist compounded her claustrophobia tenfold, and it was taking all of her willpower to not scream and breakdown as visages formed out of that scarlet fog. Allen came to her, fully formed, then as his true half-man self. *This is your fault, Jessie. You could've saved us. He wants you, Jessie, he wants you so bad. Look what he did to me, just to get at you.*

She fought for each breath tooth and nail. Each step forward was bought with a profound amount of mental fortitude. She ignored the ghastly images, the mental taunts. She knew both Susannah and the sheriff were facing their own mental demons, and she hoped they could see past the illusions. Still, it was becoming increasingly harder to see the veil between reality and the twisted tricks of whoever reigned supreme down here. So, when first the sheriff, and then Susannah fell forward, leaving her alone with the dog in the manhole-sized tunnel, she officially freaked out.

"Guys?" She called out. Buckie scrabbled directly ahead of her, looking for his master. "Shit. Shit." She pushed forward, but her shoe caught on something. She kicked. That's when she felt something tighten like a vise on her foot. *It's just a trick. It's more mental magic bullshit*, she tried to tell herself, until a sharp pain shattered that comforting notion. She started to thrash, panic seizing her as she tried to look behind to see what the hell was going on with her foot. Buckie, whose smaller frame could turn around in the tunnel, pivoted back towards her. His snout wrinkled up in a snarl. His barks, loud and shrill, echoed in the narrow space.

Between the dog barking, the sensation of being pulled back into the stone tube she'd so painfully crawled through and deeper into the crimson haze, and the feeling of the stone walls closing in to swallow her, her existence converged into a solid wave of primal fear. Jessie couldn't stop the scream from bubbling up and erupting from her throat. She kicked out with her other foot, feeling her stitches give way as she bucked and writhed.

"Get... the fuck... OFF ME!" Jessie kicked as hard as she could, banging and scraping her knees against the stone walls. Walls that closed in tighter like a convulsing diaphragm with each passing second. Walls that wanted to swallow her. Her other shoe slammed into something as solid as a bowling ball, and the painful grip on her foot eased. Using her elbows and her knees, Jessie shot forward, not caring that she was shoving the dog ahead of her. Not caring that she was tearing the skin off her knees. With a cry, Buckie fell over the edge. Jessie flung herself forward, not even pausing to look as she pulled herself past the lip of the opening, preferring to fall to her death than be pulled back into that stone throat.

She was vaguely aware of falling onto a heap of limbs and fur instead of the hard, unforgiving stone she expected. She heard a canine yelp, then a heavy grunt of pain from Baumgartner, followed by the smell of death as something bony and leathery fell on top of her. A ragged inhale of foul breath, like the blast of a jet engine, rasped right in her ear. The clacking gnash of teeth, loud and terrible. She screamed again as those teeth sank into the cartilage of her ear. Hot pulsing pain erupted from the side of her head as the thing bit and sucked. Wet sounds of chewing, like a starving man attacking a fatty piece of beef gristle, filled her ear.

Hot liquid and a sickening sensation of fullness flooded her ear canal as her hearing muffled. Jessie shot out an arm, her shotgun getting caught up in a tangle of limbs and her own clothing.

"FUCK!" she screamed in a full panic now. She shoved the thing off of her. Her headlamp came off in the struggle and rolled down the slope. Something grabbed her from behind and dragged her away. She fought to break free until she realized it was Susannah and Baumgartner.

"Sonofabitch," the sheriff breathed as he got to his feet. The sound of his shotgun as he racked a round weakly reverberated in Jessie's sundered ear. He kicked at a still-twitching body somewhere off to their left.

His headlamp illuminated a figure that reminded Jessie of the pictures she'd seen from concentration camps. It was so far gone, so emaciated that it was androgynous. Its genitalia long ago ripped away to a black crusted stump. Gray skin, mottled with scar tissue, clung tightly over sharp bones. It raised a trembling hand, the fingertips worn to ivory nubs, to shield itself from the light.

"H-Hungry... Please," it rasped.

They froze, shocked silent that it could speak. Jessie pictured Allen's face superimposed over the thing, saw it chewing on something gristly. It slowly crawled forward, the joints of its wasted frame flexing beneath its crepe paper skin as it tried to advance on the sheriff. It was clear it had been starving, the very antithesis of the macabre gluttony they witnessed at the hospital. Its pale tube of a throat bulged as it gulped and swallowed the huge chunk of Jessie's ear, licking its lips clean with an ash-gray slug of a tongue. The greedy sucking sounds it made were nauseating. *You taste so good, Jessie. How come you never let me taste you before? We had so many opportunities...*

Jessie didn't flinch as the gun barked twice more. The deer slug took off the top of the thing's head before the sheriff was already ejecting the spent shell and blasting a silver round into its chest. In the headlamp's harsh light they could see smoke rising up from the holes. The chest cavity rapidly eroded with a crackling, spitting sound until nothing was left but ash, the silver eating through the wraith until they could see stone floor beneath. It was then that the gears finally turned in Jessie's mind. She ran a finger along the grizzled nub of her ear and pictured the chunk of her cartilage in its stomach. It had *bit* her. The brief wave of sickening horror from the Allen-illusion evaporated as this realization sunk into the marrow of her bones.

"I've been bit. I've been bit. Holy fucking shit—" Jessie was hyperventilating. Fear seized her like a giant iron fist.

"Jessie, calm down, honey. You're having a panic attack—" Susannah was holding her tight, whispering a calming chant of *it's gonna be okay, it's gonna be okay,* but all Jessie could think was that she was going to be one of *them,* one of those wretches who drank themselves so full of blood their stomachs literally burst open with gallons of gore. Or maybe she'd become something like Allen—a reanimated puppet, a cipher for other's nightmares.

"Bit me it fucking bit me oh my fucking god oh my—"

Her words were cut off as neatly as a knife through butter as the sheriff slapped her.

"Shut up and breathe, girl. *Breathe.*" Baumgartner pantomimed big breaths. Temporarily shocked out of her panic, Jessie ripped in a huge hitching breath, letting it explode out with a sob. All the careful composure and sense of bravado she'd tried to inherit while watching Susannah stoically handle this unfolding nightmare drained out of her like water through a sieve. She was a scared young girl now, terrified of the monster she was doomed to become.

"Listen to me, honey, we can stop it, we can stop this. If we find the Coldonas, or whoever's at the center of this, and destroy them, then we can put a stop to this. You told us yourself," Susannah said into her good ear.

"She's right." The voice came out of the darkness. Baritone in register and ragged in timbre, it floated up out of the surrounding dark like a disembodied god. Baumgartner and Susannah both looked around, their lights converging on the figure.

# CHAPTER 38

"CAN YOU BELIEVE IT, man? Me, driving a fuckin' cop car," Geoff said as the Charger lurched around the winding country roads. The guy's driving had never been great, but having to rely on his bad arm now, Lou thought he'd seen freshman permit students drive with more finesse. Lou slammed back in his seat as the V8 roared. "Goddamn this thing has some go," Geoff wailed, high-pitched with excitement.

"Just focus on the road, Dale Earnhardt." Lou closed his eyes. Funny how he, a black man from rural Kentucky, had never once found himself in the back of a good old boy's cruiser. Now here he was, riding in the prisoner's suite while one of his best friends drove like a maniac and the other was probably facing some unfathomable hell down below.

Thoughts of Jessie temporarily distracted him from the burning line of pain traveling up his back. Shame burned deeply in Lou. He was no more than a helpless side note in this epic and fucked up journey. He should be down there with her, facing whatever godless horrors lurked underneath that little town. Jessie didn't deserve this shit. Lou had heard her life story when she'd finally felt comfortable enough opening up to him, a milestone in their relationship he'd cherished dearly. The woman was more deeply guarded than the Desert Storm vets he'd worked with on the road, tight-lipped and glassy-eyed. She'd had a hard enough life, and it seemed Blasphemer was her one true stable constant in life, despite the chaos of touring. In his own way, Lou thought of her as a little sister, and though she was tough as nails, he felt responsible for her.

"Turn right at Y junction," the calm, cocktail conversation voice of the onboard GPS told them.

"You got it, babe. Man, this thing is sweet." Geoff took a sharp turn, his cast accidentally knocking some switch. The red and blue swirl of jackpot lights joined the wail of the siren. "Ope, cherries and berries."

"Quit fuckin' around, man. They're relying on us to call in the cavalry," Lou snapped, itching to bitch-slap Geoff up the side of the head. No longer the valiant, brave soul who'd navigated him through the hospital, the old Geoff was back in full force. Lou didn't know if this was a good or a bad thing.

The Charger lurched around a steep curve, revealing a road choked with abandoned fire engines, their red and blue lights still swirling. Great pools of dark liquid coated the road. Just as the cruiser began to hydroplane, Lou realized it was blood. They were hydroplaning in fucking blood.

After everything he'd lived through these last few days, this realization didn't even faze him.

"Turn into the skid." Lou tried to tell Geoff, but the one-armed NASCAR wannabe lost control and fishtailed. They narrowly avoided colliding with one of the fire engines. After pulling a full 180 in the road, Lou worried he was going to throw up. The sudden motion and the pain made his brain swirl in his ears.

"Holy fucking shit, is that—"

"Yeah, reverse and get the fuck out of here." Lou stared into the blackened husks of the trees lining the roadway. Those fucks had to be close. Panic seized him as he thought of the shed, of the things coming out of the fire. They must be near the Langan property. The realization made sweat pop out and everything from the waist up tingle. "Go, Geoff!" he yelled.

"I'm trying, man. Fuck!" Geoff clumsily threw the car in reverse, executed an elaborate ten-point turn, and finally got the Charger reoriented, all while the GPS was losing its mind, firing off ad-libbed directions. When they finally got straightened out, someone was standing in the middle of the road a hundred or so feet ahead. Lou noticed the canvas pants of a firefighter. His torso was bare and distended. He knew what that bulging belly was full of. The nausea came on again.

"Ram that fucker," Lou gasped. The once firefighter began to walk towards them, not moving with the speed of the ones in the hospital but shambling like a zombie in a Romero flick.

"You sure?" Geoff said. The V8 purred at idle as if agreeing with Lou's command.

"Yes." Lou grabbed the oh shit handle by the window and braced as the car shot forward. By the time the Charger slammed into the firefighter, they were going almost sixty. A wash of red coated the windshield reminding Lou of a birthday party he'd been to as a kid. They'd had water balloon fights, except the balloons were filled with dyed non-toxic stuff so when they burst it was in shades of blue, green, and red.

"Jesus, fuck." Geoff turned on the windshield wipers. The body thudded up over the roof then fell behind them as the wipers cut neat semi-circle portals through the gooey red. Lou knew then they would never make it to this place the sheriff told them about. He imagined some family driving along the highway and watching as a blood-smeared sheriff's cruiser roared past, a couple haggard-looking metalheads behind the wheel. He started laughing.

"What's so fuckin' funny?" Geoff asked.

"Nothin', man. Just drive," Lou said, shaking his head.

They occasionally passed a state trooper or even a goddamn low-flying helicopter on their way out of the county. Lou was shocked no one tried to pull them over. He assumed someone must've got word out that some seriously wicked shit was going down in Carter, the anomalous cruiser was the least of their concerns. When they finally got on the Interstate, Lou felt himself entering a sort of waking dream state as the wide-open road stretched out before him, the great two-lane corridors almost completely empty. According to the dashboard clock it was almost three in the morning.

Eventually, the gentle lull of motion, the hypnotizing strobe of the sodium lights above and the fatigue brought on by everything he'd experienced sunk him into something beyond sleep.

"Hey, uh, Lou. Lou? Wake up, dude." Geoff said. Lou peeled open his eyes. His world was a wash of color. Red and Blue. Red and blue.

"What... the... fuck—" Lou groaned as he looked around, rubbing the gummy sleep from his eyes, not remembering where he was. He tried to get up. The ground glass of his shattered vertebrae shocked him awake.

They were still on the interstate, that much he could gather. They were in some city now, the bright dazzle of lights and modern buildings seeming like something out of a dream after days of nothing but trees and shacks and hills. Then he looked behind him, blinking stupidly at what he saw. The interstate was now a freeway, five lanes to each corridor. Their side, the northbound side, was lined with police cruisers tailing behind them. All had their sirens on.

"PULL OVER IMMEDIATELY! PULL OVER NOW AND COME OUT WITH YOUR HANDS UP!" some great, amplified god-like voice told them from everywhere and nowhere.

"Geoff—"

"Listen, I wasn't stopping for shit, okay? First it was just one guy, he tried to pull me over, hailed me over the CB and everything. But we were so close. We're only five minutes away from the station, dude. They arrest us, we can't help them. So I just kept driving."

"They're gonna fuckin' *shoot* us if you don't stop, motherfucker!" Lou spotted a police roadblock up ahead.

"Shit. Shit, shi—"

"Hold up. I got an idea," Lou said, shaking his head at the absurdity of it. Before they left, Susannah had given him a Glock pistol, fully loaded. He looked at the cage divider of the cruiser, marveling at how much the rural police skimped on stuff like this compared to inner-city cops. No plexiglass, bullet-proof divider here, just a wire mesh cage with holes big enough to put a skinny wrist through.

As the cruiser crawled to a stop, and the state troopers swarmed the car, Lou kept his head down. He pointed the barrel of the Glock through the cage.

Geoff turned around, eyes going dinner-plate big.

"Bro, what the fu—"

"Just play along, man, and don't fuckin' move," Lou breathed. The cops, fully decked out in riot gear battle rattle, froze at the sight of the two men. Lou could detect the sea change in the gung-ho officers as word spread this was now a hostage situation.

"Lou, what the fucking fuck? I—"

"Shut up!" Lou got into character. Just then he heard the *thump thump* of a helicopter fly overhead, Lou spotted the tail end of the rotor. It was a news chopper. *Janel, if you seein' this, I can explain*, Lou thought wildly as two men approached, Bushmasters raised.

"Crack your window," Lou hissed. Geoff did as he was told, whimpering now. The sharp smell of piss filled the car and Lou sighed. "You'll be okay, you jackass. *I'm* the one that's gonna get shot here." Lou got ready as the window went down.

"One more step and I blow his fuckin' head off!" he roared. The excruciating pain caused from having to lean forward nearly made him drop the gun. To the officers it probably looked like Lou was coming down off a crack binge with his wide, bloodshot eyes and unhinged, sweat-streaked face. Good. Let them think he was wild. Let them think he was a loose cannon.

The officers stood, rifles trained on the cruiser. One of them was radioing something in clipped cop jargon.

"I got demands!" Lou said stupidly. He tried to recall any and all action blockbusters he'd seen. What would the bad guys say in this situation? He'd seen *Die Hard* over ten times, yet he couldn't think of a single thing Hans Gruber said. One of the officers radioed in something, and for a long, *long* time they just stood like that: Lou pressing the gun to Geoff's head, them with their pants-shittingly military-looking rifles trained on him. An Eastwood standoff if ever there was one. Lou looked around wildly, making sure no sharpshooter was drawing a bead on him. Surely they knew the windows were bulletproof, or tempered glass or whatever shit they had in cop cars these days.

"You're fuckin' crazy, man." Geoff kept his hands raised in the air.

"You're goddamn right I'm fuckin' crazy, little punk ass bitch!" Lou roared, doing his best to sound like a mean, street-chewed drug dealer and not some farm boy from eastern Kentucky. "You fuckin' pigs better give me someone to talk to or I'm ventilatin' this dude!"

"Turn your channel to 301!" one of the officers shouted. "We have a negotiator on the line for you."

"Do it," Lou said to Geoff.

"I don't know how to fucking work this thing, man. You drove trucks, not me."

"Just turn the knob—I mean, turn that fucking knob, you dumb-ass punk. Just like that!" Lou thought he should get an Oscar as Geoff scanned through the CB channels until it came on 301. "Pick up the receiver, bitch!" Lou's throat was getting raw from yelling. He was sweating so bad the Glock's textured grip was slipping in his hands.

"Is this Squad Car 38, Carter County Sheriff's Department?" A cool, calm voice came over the radio. Lou motioned for Geoff to pick up the receiver, showing him how to press down the talk button.

"Uh... Yeah, this is us," Geoff said stupidly.

"Alright. Let me tell you my name, son. I'm Dallas Clark with Lee's Summit Special Operations. I'd like to know who I'm speakin' with and why I got a stolen cop car from a pissant county causin' such a ruckus in my city." The man spoke with the calm assurance of an airline pilot informing his passengers they'd be touching down soon. Geoff held down the talk button, but Lou spoke before he could.

"Listen, dude, we need to speak to Wayne Daniels. He's chief of police up your way," Lou said, dropping his thug accent.

There was a pause. "Wayne Daniels? What the hell—"

"Just put him on. Tell him Baumgartner sent us."

# Chapter 39

B AUMGARTNER SAT ON A three-foot wide ledge beside Susannah and the girl, staring down where the ground sloped sharply to a narrow crevice. Standing propped up against one large stalactite pillar was a man, one half of his body mottled pink and wrinkled, the other half corpse gray. He winced as the lights converged on him, the scarred half of his face twisted up into an ugly permanent snarl, the cheek burned away to reveal wicked ivory blades embedded within his gums. The scars where the sheriff had shot him only hours ago stood out in puckered keloids of flesh.

"You again. Goddamn. How'd you... I—" The sheriff trailed off as Virgil approached.

"Get that fuckin' light out of my face, boy," Virgil Langan hissed, putting up an arm to block the high intensity head lamps converging on him. The sheriff racked another round and aimed the thick barrel right at that half-burned face. "Boy, I can smell that silver. Y'all finally wisened up, huh?"

"Why ain't you dead? Huh? You're supposed to be dead. Twice over now," Baumgartner said through clenched teeth.

"Yeah, and so is Liam Coldona, but lo and fuckin' behold." Virgil squinted against the harsh light.

"I-I don't understand. If you're like the others, why aren't you—" Susannah began, scooting away from the man, dragging Jessie with her.

"I ain't like the others. The ones you came across earlier, those was the young 'ns. When the thirst first takes hold, you turn into an animal. Your body don't even know how to process what's going on. I was like 'em once, couldn't speak, couldn't walk right. Just wanna feed. Woulda ate my own boys right down to the marrow if they hadn't been wearing them goddamn crosses. You learn to control it eventually... a bit anyway. I don't know. The big hoss made me different than the others, He can do that. Control the change. Atonement and... *Ah, hell*." He looked at Jessie. "You got bit?" The horror on his face made it even more ghastly, somehow.

"What's that matter to you? You just want our blood, don't you?" Susannah was holding Jessie protectively.

"Yeah, but her... Lordy, she's special. She got something in her none of y'all do. I was gonna use her..."

"Why are you jawing with us? Why ain't you tryna make like a tick and get at us?" Baumgartner said. After seeing the feral savagery of the other vampires, watching Virgil Langan calmly compose himself made Charles's brain hurt. It was like witnessing a dog speak perfect English.

"I can control it... barely." Virgil's rough voice had a strain to it. "Like I said, He made me different. And He wanted *her*." A corpse finger pointed at Jessie. "I was supposed to get her for Him. He was gonna sip on her, like a fine wine. See if He couldn't absorb what she has. 'Cept I was gonna use her as bait, same way He done up her half-man friend as a lure. Wasn't gonna let Him have what He wanted. Motherfucker needs to die. This all needs to end."

"Wait... what?" Susannah asked. Baumgartner's overtaxed brain pan sizzled as he tried to make sense of Virgil's behavior. Virgil acted like he was a free agent in all this.

"What're you talkin' about, you burnt fuckin' hotdog?" Baumgartner said.

"I was His servant. I guess I still am. Once you get turned, it's like He's got a hook in your brain."

"The thrall," Susannah muttered.

"Sure. 'Cept He cursed me with just enough smarts to realize what was bein' done to me. Made me use my boys to get food for Him. He promised me a new chance. He promised me Tate could have the girl. Start a family. Keep the Langan bloodline going. He played me though. Like a fuckin' fiddle. I shoulda kn—"

"What girl?" the sheriff asked. Virgil only stared at him, the wince curled up into a knowing grin. "What *fucking girl?*" Baumgartner barked. The shotgun started to waver in his hands.

Virgil's fists clenched. The sound had a disturbingly wooden quality to it. "Don't you fuckin' get it? Your folks and mine, this *county*—we supposed to pay for what we did. Full circle. You go down there, you face Him, you're gonna find what you're lookin' for."

"If you're so goddamn in control of yourself, how come you bit Anderson? You're the reason this whole fucking shit show started!" Baumgartner flared with anger as he remembered Anderson bleeding out in his cruiser, remembered the savage hatred in those eyes when the deputy stood up from the clinic table, looking at that cross like it was the most terrible thing in the world. Virgil nodded, then sighed again.

"I didn't want to. I mean, I *did*, obviously, but we got ways of con-servin'. There's ones we keep alive to sip on, like a good whiskey. But *He* insisted. No more hidin', He said. Wants *everyone* to pay. 'Twas His doing, me losin' my mind and lashing out like that. Haven't done that since I was first turned, a pup... but He's got that hold on us. He wanted me to kickstart the spread." Virgil took a step towards them.

"You stay right there, hoss. One more step and I'll open you up like a Thanksgiving turkey." Baumgartner said.

Virgil laughed and shook his head. "Hell, if I knew that would kill me for good, I'd invite you to shoot me here and now. Besides, I can smell it on you too. We better move on, or else half your crew is gonna turn." He eyed Baumgartner with a terrible grin.

Charles instinctively put a hand to his neck, where an hour ago he felt those teeth scrape along his skin. *It just nicked me*, Baumgartner thought. *Just fuckin' nicked me.* Apparently, that was enough. Still, the lethal implication of that paled in comparison to what Virgil was hinting at. A desperate, sucking void filled the sheriff's stomach at the thought of Vivian down in this subterranean hellhole. God knows what was being done to her. It almost made him want to shoot this walking Lazarus if not for the fact he seemed bent on helping them.

"What's your endgame, Virgil? Are you trying to help us or what?" Susannah asked from behind the sheriff.

"I'm here because I want this to be done. This is hell, ya see. I've been stuck in these caves for... hell, I don't even know what time is anymore. We are all slaves to Him, it's our atonement. He made me live through His torments. Made me feel what His family felt. He got both my boys. Made me... made me feed on my Roy. That's when I knew it was all lies, what He told me. The Langan bloodline is dead in the dirt now, and I reckon at first, that's all He wanted. But that anger's been a-growin' in Him like a weed, it's been infectin' us, and now, with the moon, it's like a fuckin' match to the powder keg. The urge to rip open your throats... It's there alright, and it's taken every ounce of willpower not to do just that. We've had to conserve, you see. Live off the land, takin' what animals we could. But it ain't the same, animal blood. It sees you through, but barely. He wouldn't let us go out and hunt for ourselves. Now it's a goddamn free for all."

"Who's 'he'?" Baumgartner asked.

"Liam Coldona. You wanna end this? You end Him. I'll take you to Him, but I can't promise you won't get slaughtered along the way. It's

His world down here, remember that. Me? I just want it to end. Livin' every day with this fuckin' pain in my gut. A feelin' of starving so intense that no amount of feedin' ever makes it go away. You know what it's like to starve for years on end? He got his wish. He killed off all the Langans. I was stupid to think I could bargain with Him. But now it ain't good enough. He wants the whole town. Don't matter if they come from the old families or not. Please... put an end to this fuckin' madness."

"You know for sure killing him will end this? Will cure her?" Susannah asked as she cradled Jessie, who'd gone silent, almost catatonic.

"I honestly don't know. All I know is when you turn, you get the knowledge that comes with the Curse. Six hundred years of sufferin'. Rape. Starvation. Murdering. Fire. *Lot* of goddamn fire. I did not know such a misery could exist until Liam Coldona found my half-dead ass and turned me all the way."

The man-thing looked eternally tired then, reminding the sheriff of his grandaddy's old international harvester truck, over sixty years old, scabrous, belching oil smoke and lurching along the county roads against all odds.

"It's a poison, y'all. A poison brewed from years of hatred for humanity, filtered down like sour mash until only the blackest, purest hate is left. There's some old magic in there too. Witchcraft or something. I don't know. All I know is He's made me live through it every day. Every *goddamn day.*" Virgil leaned against a rock, clearly not used to speaking so much.

"But, why?" Susannah asked.

"A viper poisoning one of its own eggs... the mongoose that steals it gets the shit end of the stick. This all started... Liam's mama. The minute He died in these caves and... His mother watched her house burn— she... she knew the time had come to unleash that poison. Whether it leaves when you kill the bastard..." Virgil trailed off, his voice growing rougher "Better hurry. I can feel that sumbitch worming His way into me. He-He's wonderin' where I'm at. He can tell that girl there is close, and, lordy, does He want her." Even as Virgil spoke, Charles noticed the old man's body stiffening, like he was resisting some great force, bracing himself against an invisible gale force wind only he could feel.

Just then, a red mist erupted from the various tunnel entrances honeycombing the walls. To Baumgartner, it looked like when the great steam engines blew smoke through their stacks. His shotgun swiveled wildly, anticipating a fight. The sheriff believed he was prepared for all manner of horrors after the day he had. He was wrong.

They flooded out of the mist like roaches from an overturned pizza box. Dozens of ash-white bodies, crawling along on all fours, more animal than human. As they got closer, Baumgartner saw Vivian. He saw her face in all of them.

"No... What... No. No fuckin'—"

"Don't let him fool ya, son," Virgil said, but his voice was small. It was far away, unimportant.

"NO!" Baumgartner roared as they converged on him.

*Why'd you let me leave, daddy?*

*It's all your fault, daddy.*

*I always knew you were a failure.*

*Had to leave before I turned out just like you.*

*Look at what you let happen to me.*

*"No!"* Baumgartner screamed, his voice cracking. The shotgun roared with him. Round after round pumped into the Vivian clones. Each one evaporated into a poof of crimson mist.

"Charles!" It was Susannah, but he ignored her.

*Please, daddy. Pleaseeee,* one said as she began to crawl up his leg. Baumgartner fell and scooted on his ass, trying to get away from this hideous corruption of his daughter. Then Susannah was in front of him, slapping him hard. Stars and stripes roared across his vision.

"Snap out of it!" Susannah screamed. Baumgartner reached for his shotgun but found Susannah had wrenched it from his grasp. When the sparkling floaters finally dissipated from his sight, he saw it was just them again, the good old Peanuts gang.

"Told ya," Virgil said with a shake of his head. "Can't trust nothin' you see down here."

Baumgartner's mind felt like it was boiling. The various fuses in his brain were winking out like blown lightbulbs. *Just shoot him, shoot him right now and shoot every goddamn thing that ain't human. Get to your girl,* a part of him said. *It all makes sense. You should listen to this rambling asshole. He might be the key to getting out of this alive,* another part of him contested. He blinked. His eyes felt like they'd been given a good scrub with 60 grit sandpaper.

Virgil's eyes—one milky white, occluded by scars and the other obsidian black with no discernable pupil—fixed on him, unblinking.

"If you gonna shoot me, boy, you best do it now. Otherwise get your fuckin' shit together and follow me. And keep your eyes open, the weak ones are down here. They fed off the reserves, but it's not enough. A few drops a day is only torture, just enough to ignite the flame in your gut. They ain't that tough, but with Liam playin' His mind games on you—" Virgil shook his head. Then he finally blinked, staring to the right of Baumgartner. "What the fuck is a dog doin' down here?"

Buckie had sidled up, his white paws at the very edge of the slope, hazel eyes glaring at Virgil. The dog's growl was low, almost silent in his throat, an unsure sound. Baumgartner could tell the collie was trying to make sense of this thing before him. *You and me both, buddy,* he thought.

"Yeah, he's part of the A-Team. Crazy, I know, but so is the rest of this goddamn shit show. About your blood buddies, can't you just—"

"Nope. We are *thrall,* we are all thrall to *Him.* It's a miracle I even got this much control. I was supposed to ambush y'all, see. Had to carry that feller with me this one here was supposed to know. Liam's got the power to do that, sculpt us like fuckin' clay. He went through a lot of effort to lure you in, girl." He pointed to Jessie, who'd once again slipped into a doe-eyed, catatonic daze. "But that was too much trouble. I knew y'all would be bullheaded enough to come down here."

"My boy… Daniel, is he—" Susannah began.

"Just come on," Virgil said, not looking at Susannah. He crouched to all fours and spider-walked down the slope. "Better stay close."

Charles looked back at Susannah, his mind too frazzled by what he'd just seen to lead them. She nodded as she slowly got to her feet, helping Jessie, who cupped her bleeding ear, a dull, distant expression glazed her face.

"Come on, honey, you gotta help us. You hear what he said? We can stop this," Susannah said to Jessie. The girl nodded, but it was a slight gesture, imperceptible. Charles thought she might be going into shock, which, hell, he couldn't blame her. His own mind was coming unbuckled at the seams.

Together they walked to the edge of the slope, with Baumgartner going first. He slid on his buttocks, the wet karst proving to be a gritty slip and slide. He did his best to proceed gracefully down the slope, using the butt of the shotgun as a makeshift ski-pole to keep himself from rolling end over end.

Still, by the time he reached the lip of the narrow canyon, he'd rolled onto his side and flopped four or five feet into the narrow passageway. Virgil was down there waiting for them, staring impassively as the sheriff groaned, his hip taking a nasty thump in the fall. He picked up the two shells that slipped out his shirt pocket and tucked them back in before staggering to his feet. "Thanks for the help, asshole."

Virgil just stood there like a statue, waiting for the others to come down.

"You feelin' it yet?" Virgil asked as the others made their way down. "Feel that pull in the back of your—"

"Shut the fuck up." Baumgartner snapped, not wanting to hear it. Because he *did* feel it. He'd been ignoring it since they got into the caves. The fever breaking out in his body. The vise grip on his brain tightening the further they descended. How terrible it would be to finally find his daughter, to show her how much he truly loved her, only for him in the end to... *No. Nope. Huh uh. Stomp that shit down right quick.*

"Lord." Susannah shook herself off after her own clumsy descent, double-checking her 870 to make sure it still worked. A distant whine sounded above them. Buckie was still up there, pawing at the edge of the slope, reluctant to follow his master. "Come here, boy, come here, Buckie!" Susannah said, her voice going high and sweet. Baumgartner thought it was far too pleasant a sound for such a dark, fetid place. Buckie whined pitifully once more and then took a step. He slid, then let out a yip as he began to backpedal, but his hairy paws caught no purchase. He tipped over and then rolled, thrashing as he tried to right himself. "Oh boy..." Susannah sighed, trying to anticipate where the dog was going to end up.

At the last minute she sprang to the right and caught him just as he was rolling over the edge of the canyon wall with a yipping howl. She grunted as the sixty-pound animal slammed into her. They both fell to the ground, Susannah landing flat on her ass.

"You're heavier than you look, buster." She got up from the ground and checked Buckie over. He shook himself off, limping slightly, but was otherwise okay.

Jessie descended last, the most graceful of them all as she wordlessly slid down the embankment on two feet and caught herself at the gap, landing on her feet. Baumgartner wondered if that grace was entirely her own, thinking of the way Virgil carried himself.

With that, Virgil proceeded into the darkness, not bothering to see if they followed.

# Chapter 40

An inferno raged through Jessie's veins, like liquid fire instead of nourishing blood. Each heartbeat pushed the conflagration further throughout her body. It spread from the side of her head, slowly traveling down to her shoulders, a marrow-deep burn that numbed as it blazed. She barely registered the fall as she glided down the side of the slope, her body moving of its own accord despite her haggard condition.

Jessie stared at this one—Virgil. Somehow, in some inexplicable way, she felt connected to him. She did not want to sense the invisible thread that bound them like twins in a womb sharing the same umbilical cord, growing more solid and substantial with every minute that passed.

Together they followed after him. The once solid void of darkness bled away until everything was a varying grayscale of light, the headlamps on Susannah and Baumgartner's heads transforming into mini supernovas that burned her retinas with hellish brightness.

The valley went on for some time, walls narrowing until they had to sidle through some sections. Even the dog just barely fit through some of the stone crevices. As they went on, Jessie kept her eyes forward. Things stirred in her peripheral vision. Voices from her past called to her. *Jessie, Jessie, Jessie. Come here, little Jessie. Papa has got a gift for you. Severe attachment issues, we don't foresee her taking well with any foster parents.*

*Jessie, Jessie, Jessie. You're not our real daughter, you're just a freeloading runt. No need to tell anyone about this, right Jessie? This will be our little secret. Jessie, Jessie, Jessie.* Allen moaned, trailing along on his hands, the phantom scraping of his spine against stone grating at her ears. She knew they were just apparitions, but still, they wore her down, eroding away at her sanity bit by bit.

Then they entered another large open area. The walls were honeycombed with holes and tunnel passages where at one time bats might've roosted in these great expansive chambers. Red mist oozed from every crack, ghostly limbs from nightmare specters bleeding out of each. She could hear the others collectively losing their sanity in the sharp intake of breath from Susannah and Baumgartner. Even the dog was not immune to the horrors. He whined pitifully and clung close to his master's side. Virgil didn't hesitate, leading them down the leftmost tunnel to a steeply sloping cavern with high ceilings whose pointed stalactite growths protruded like earthen fangs from above.

Jessie sensed others, their bodies like glowing coals in the darkness ahead. She could feel the burning desire within them, a pulsing current of savage need directed at her. She knew it was Him. The red haze was a manifestation of His desire. Whatever happened when Susannah brought her back, whatever she inherited from the ether... *He* wanted it. At that same moment, Buckie began to growl, loud and clear. They all froze, except Virgil, who took a few more shambling steps before stopping to look back at them.

"Up ahead," Jessie said. She was at the end of the group. Away from the others. Just in case.

"Where, honey?" Susannah asked.

"Close," was all Jesse could say, rasp really.

"She's right..." Baumgartner hissed and chambered a round. "Fuck... I think I can feel the bastards. That's not good, huh?"

"Better watch where you're shootin'," Virgil said.

"Then keep your head down." Susannah said flatly as she shouldered her gun at the sound of the cry, which bled through the air encompassing all that dark and permeated it with the anticipation of bloodshed. The high keening wail of a starving animal rapturously announcing a feast. To Jessie, the sound was more heartbreaking than disturbing. She sensed the thrall's desperation as they clambered forward. One swung from the cave stalactites like a monkey from tree to tree. Another darted in from behind, slinking and stumbling down the narrow cavern, so weak was it.

Jesse whirled, training the shotgun on the imp that crawled towards her. She sensed the bond with this one too, a connection that simultaneously disgusted and intrigued her. Her finger tightened on the trigger, watching as Allen—*no, not Allen*—shambled towards her, telling herself she could pull the trigger, telling herself she could sever this bond, because her connection to this thing was that of corruption, another link in the chain that slid her one step away from humanity.

"One above you," Jessie warned the others. She felt the one from the ceiling drop down in front of Susannah and the sheriff just as the one that had crawled up from behind surged forward in a final desperate burst of speed. She gritted her teeth and closed her eyes as Allen, whole, perfect, muscled Allen closed in. Her finger tensed. The gun roared like some great mythic beast of the heavens and bucked in her arms. She was knocked into Susannah, who cried out as she and the sheriff fired at the same time. Buckie was barking now, his voice lost amidst the gun reports as chaos broke out.

A vacuum-filled silence rushed in as the blasts of the shotguns finally faded through the caverns. Jessie was faintly aware of pieces of cave ceiling raining down on her neck and shoulders. She stared down at the twitching body at her feet, a large hole blown through its chest cavity. An anomalous imp—most definitely *not* Alan. She knew the next shot would be silver and she dreaded it. But she racked the slide and pulled the trigger anyway, watching as the hole widened even further until a cavernous, glistening maw opened the thing up, its insides spitting and hissing as the silver shot buried itself within foul meat and gristle. The ethereal umbilical was fading between her and this once human thing, and she was glad for it. But others were closing in, their chains sinking into her.

The sheriff was shoving off the emaciated body of the runt that fell on him from the ceiling. Gelatinous black goo covered his already stained uniform. For the first time, she sensed the faintest link to him too. Virgil was right.

"You sure you ain't just trying to lead us into the mouth of the beast, old man?" Baumgartner snarled, combing gore from his thinning hair.

"I am, but wasn't that your goal anyway?" Virgil said and continued walking.

The path stretched on, growing steeper, going deeper, until all of them had to half scoot on their butts as they descended. Jessie knew she was nearing some great and throbbing presence, distinct from Virgil and the others. This one had an aura that seemed to push into her very brain tissue, a throbbing pulse that drew her like a distant but powerful magnet calling to every grain of fine metal that floated in her bloodstream. This pulling terrified her. She felt drawn to it, the way a cold body is drawn to the warmth of the sun. Like she *needed* it. How long did the sheriff say it took for his prisoner to turn? Two something hours? It'd been about thirty minutes for Jessie, and already she was feeling the changes. And what about the sheriff himself? How long before he turned on them?

Soon they came to a large cavern with a perfectly flat stone floor and rounded dome walls, conspicuously man-made. A thousand faces peered from those stone walls, faces made of red mist. All opening their mouths and screaming. Jessie recognized every one of them, each visage stolen from various low points of her life, every one belonging to someone who'd made her suffer. Jessie did her best to ignore their pleas and accusations. Susannah was looking pointedly down at the ground, breathing heavily. Baumgartner was muttering to himself, eyes darting around wildly, and she knew they were all enduring the same hell. Liam truly was a god down here. They saw exactly what He wanted them to see.

"And here's where the shitshow all began." Virgil pointed to his left. A massive pile of jagged stone and boulders filled the otherwise smooth and architectural space, as if the earth itself were pushing in on this man-made defiance of its inner bowels. "We're getting close. I can feel Him. Not long now before it's outta my hands. So someone best be watchin' me." His voice was turning strained, breathy.

"I've decapitated some of them. If you want death, I think—" Susannah began. Virgil just laughed. It sounded like a death rattle.

"Nah, it puts a stop to the body, and to some of our senses, but we're still alive. It's like a chicken with its head cut off. It don't kill us all the way. Makes us blind and deaf and slows down the healin' a bit, but it ain't true death." Virgil let out another rusty hinge of a laugh. "Ain't nothing can truly kill us when we're like this, not even the silver. Unless you find some way to totally destroy the body. Otherwise, we come back. We, what's the word... *regenerate*," Virgil said as he began to walk down the mine shaft.

"...Oh..." Susannah sighed. It was a very tired sound.

Dread suffocated Jessie. Before, she took some small solace in knowing if she *did* turn all the way, Susannah could grant her a mercy kill. But apparently even *that* was off the table. All possible respite was being robbed from her.

"What about Liam? How do we kill him... completely?" the sheriff asked, following the twitching and shuddering Virgil at a distance, his shotgun at hip level, ready to fire. Occasionally the barrel twitched to the left and right, indicating he too endured more manufactured nightmares.

"Save some of that silver for Him. Decapitation oughta work. Destroy the head completely. But silver definitely. Maybe both… I think."

"But you just said—" Susannah began.

"The rules ain't the same for Him. Hard to explain. Just know He looks old and weak but He's tougher than a sun-dried cat turd. Now quit making me talk. Gettin' hard to-to… concentrate. Jus-just keep going straight." Virgil fell to his hands and knees. *"Fuck…"* he growled.

"You good old man?" The sheriff stopped, taking a shooter's stance.

"Oh, hell… Haven't… been good… in a minute… son," Virgil said through clenched teeth, his torso heaving with ragged breath. "Better do it now… I can smell it in you. It smells so goddamn good. So…"

That's when he shot to his feet and charged the sheriff.

Baumgartner was ready. The gun spoke twice, delivering first a deer slug that blew off the top of Virgil's head in a large spray of black jelly and bone, then a blast of silver shot that peppered his neck and upper torso.

"Goddamn…" Baumgartner said, but Jesse could barely hear him over the tinnitus singing in her ears. "Come on. Let's get this shit over with,"

Jesse followed after; her body now fully ablaze with that corrupted infection. She was a woman afire, ready to do anything to extinguish the flames cooking her from the inside out.

# Chapter 41

S USANNAH DID NOT WANT to go any deeper. She did not want to face this madness anymore. But she knew she must. She had to see her Daniel. Even if what she found shattered her mind into a thousand tiny irreparable pieces, even if it turned her soul into a festering, black void, she had to see this through. The cattle, Elizabeth, those men in the prison cells, her son, the sheriff's daughter, every innocent bystander that got swept up in this hurricane of horror—all spawned from the agony and misanthropy of one terribly blighted family.

And now poor, sweet Jessie was at risk of succumbing to this earthly hell. Susannah couldn't help but acknowledge the deep maternal bond she shared with her. She barely knew the girl, but they'd been through more together in the last few days than most people would in a lifetime. Susannah didn't know if she had it in her to shoot Jessie. Especially knowing what she knew now.

*Oh, God... Elizabeth... I thought I put you out of your misery...*

A raw sob wanted to explode out of her throat, but she bit it back. She would not think about that. She couldn't. Not now.

Again, the cross around her neck seemed to take on an almost un-bearable weight. It grew heavier with the growing disillusionment she felt with her God. She had to wonder if a God that could allow such horrors to be visited upon His people was worth worshipping. But the thought of abandoning Him terrified her. Without His constant guiding light, what use was there living in a world such as this, where unholy manifestations like the Coldona Curse were allowed to fester? To be utterly alone and autonomous in her convictions and morals against such evil?

Susannah was no longer doing this in the name of any god, she realized. She was doing this for *her*. She was finding her son for *herself*. She was putting a stop to this for *her* town. And she was going to die for them, the innocent, naive townspeople of Carter, if it came down to that. The sheriff was right.

It was time to end this or die trying.

They took their time reloading their weapons, wanting to be fully prepared. She ignored the hellish visions. A naked, emaciated Daniel crawling towards her on hands and feet, pawing weakly at her. He wept tears of blood as he begged her to end his suffering. Other visions of Daniel as a healthy, ravishing young man sporting an obscenely large phallus, speaking Oedipal obscenities that no boy should ever say to his mother. Susannah ignored these all, though she could not ignore the scars forming on her soul. Susannah grimly helped Jessie load her gun. The poor girl's hands shook too much, and Susannah needed a distraction.

"How are ya, kid?" She placed a hand on Jessie's bare shoulder. It was almost painfully hot to the touch, the flesh wasting from beautiful alabaster to a sickly gray. She ached to hug her, but... she wanted to keep eyes on Jessie's mouth. She didn't trust those teeth. There was no telling when or if Jessie beould turn, and then there was the sheriff... Yes, as much as she wanted to embrace Jessie and banish some of this hopeless dread, Susannah would keep her distance.

"Feel like shit. Feel like I'm in a living fucking nightmare. How're you?" Jessie groaned, sounding like Harold a week deep into the worst flu of his life. His voice had sounded just like that; breathy, delirious, wrenched raw with fever.

"Facing a bit of an existential crisis. I feel like Hell has come upon this earth and that the Devil holds more sway down here than God does. Otherwise, I'm just peachy." She let out a squeaky, unstable laugh.

Baumgartner stood off to the side, staring at his shoes, rubbing his neck. He seemed to mentally clock out while the ladies talked. Sweat poured off him, soaking his already ruined uniform, the stink of him pungent. Buckie continued to sniff and guide, and wordlessly they began to follow the dog down the tunnel, picking up where Virgil had unceremoniously left off.

Eventually they passed two huge sinkholes. Each held the discarded husks of countless fauna—rabbits and raccoons, deer and squirrels, more than a few mummified human corpses—all piled high, nearly brimming over the sides. Skins and coats clung to the skeletons like shrink-wrapped plastic, the eyes reduced to cloudy marbles that hung in their sockets like a lone raisin in a cereal bowl. It reminded Susannah of the thing chained in Bernie's back forty.

They trudged past the macabre graves in silence, continuing on towards damnation. They found two more of the 'weaklings' as Virgil called them. These were so far gone they weren't much of a threat. Buckie growled, but it was a halfhearted noise. They simply crawled along the ground, reaching feebly as they grew closer. Like before, they seemed to converge on Jessie. Baumgartner lowered his gun to one of them, but Susannah stopped him.

"Don't waste ammo on these pathetic things." Susannah took out her cross and with one hand pulled the thin metal chain over her head. She let it dangle and placed it on the head of the nearest emaciated soul. With her other hand she held the head in place. Susannah didn't even think about the flashes she would receive from one of these things. But as soon as her hand touched that cool, eggshell skull, it was like being thrust into a vacuum.

Susannah couldn't breathe. Unbearable weight crushed her from all sides. She realized why as she looked at the fifty tons of rock that sat atop her. A man in overalls stuck half out of a debris pile, his mouth open and his esophagus prolapsed from the immense pressure of the crushing rocks.

Susannah let out a little yelp and fell back on her butt, scooting away as she dropped the crucifix on the imp's forehead.

The sheriff looked at her questioningly. "You okay?"

"Fine," she said curtly. The thing let out a hoarse shriek as she grabbed the cross and pressed it more firmly against his eggshell skull. The skin burned away to reveal the skull plate underneath. For a split second, she pitied the thing, understanding it was one of the original mine workers trapped down here all those years ago.

Then she thought of Daniel, stuck down here, just another of these poor, hideous things. An abrupt spark of indignant rage washed over her. Susannah grabbed the cross like a knife and jammed the bottom shaft into the thing's head, the large cross now doubling as not just a holy symbol but a weapon. The skull gave like a pumpkin rind, cracking slightly as she pushed, encountering some resistance, but nowhere near the density of healthy bone. Clenching her jaw, she sunk the staff in further, until the thing's entire body was racked with violent spasms. The foul smell of burning rotten meat permeated the earthy must of the cavern.

The imp's sunken eyeballs swelled and ruptured like two grapes under a foot, and still Susannah buried the cross deeper, metal scraping against bone until the two horizontal branches of the cruciform halted its progress. She then yanked the crucifix out, taking pieces of the skull with it. Susannah was sickened as boiling brain erupted from the hole like gray oatmeal from a dolphin's blowhole. At the same time, a savage, primal satisfaction overtook her. It was a raw feeling she'd never encountered before. She shook her head, horrified by what she'd just done and the satisfaction she gleaned from it.

The sheriff was busy slamming the butt of his shotgun against the skull of the other wasted vampire, until only a pulpy, sludgy black mass remained above the stem of its neck. Jessie stood there, staring off into some abyss only she could see while they dispatched the monsters, wavering slightly on the balls of her feet like a sunflower in a gentle wind.

Wordlessly, they trudged on, Buckie sticking close to Susannah, looking up at her. Surely he sensed something changing within his master, a sort of callous hardening of the pure caring soul she was. She kept the chain of the cross wrapped tightly around her knuckles as she held her gun at port arms, waiting for a warning from either Buckie or Jessie. But they only continued on until the tunnel widened, eventually opening to an antechamber, then beyond to a vast cavern, the biggest one they'd seen yet. What Susannah saw down in that vast pit was terrible enough to bring her to her knees.

Crude scrawl lined the antechamber walls. A repeating phrase in a language Susannah did not know, though if she had to guess, it was some Eastern European language. Slavic. Russian. Romani.

*Fie ca ei să sufere veșnic.*

The phrase was etched on every surface: the floor, the sloping walls, not a single inch of rock was left to spare. It glowed red and wept red. Occasionally the foreign words morphed and changed into English.

*Terrible mother.*

*His blood is on your hands.*

*All your fault.*

*You failed him.*

Then the mocking phrases would morph back into the mysterious script.

"May they suffer eternal," Jesse moaned.

"You know what that says?" Susannah asked.

"I-I don't know how I know," Jesse said, shaking her head. "God, it's like... it's like pieces of someone else's life keep pushing into my brain. Fuck—" She squeezed her eyes tight. "He's close. I feel Him, like a hot iron poking into my head."

"Oh, my sweet fuckin' Jesus. Vivian..." Baumgartner stood at the edge of the antechamber, his headlamp bleeding out into the huge atrium which looked to be the size of a football field, if not bigger. A narrow stone passageway led down from the antechamber to a circular plateau of rock some twenty feet in diameter. Water that glowed a shimmering teal encircled the rock formation. Their headlights reflected off the water and cast a brilliant scintillating pattern on the cavern walls. The ghastly sight upon the rock island contrasted almost painfully with that natural beauty.

"Oh my god... Daniel..." Susannah breathed as she stood beside Baumgartner. The two clung onto each other, setting aside differences to share that cohesive bond of parents who've faced the worst fears any family unit could. Together they beheld the awful sight.

On the rock, at its center kneeled a thing that barely resembled the human he once was. He was like the others: thin, emaciated, eyes shrunken deep into a gleaming hairless skull. But that is where the similarities ended. He had no ears. His skull had eroded away to reveal a recessed twin canal where a nose had once been, glistening with red-tinged mucus. His lips had long ago withered away, displaying teeth that would've looked more at home in a shark's mouth than a human's. Only his were not jagged, crooked shards of ivory. They were uniform blades, their sole purpose to part flesh with horrific efficiency.

The thing raised its head towards them, stretching out disproportion-ately long arms. Skeletal fingers grasped the black tentacle tethers that extended from either side of his body. These thick, onyx pulsing veins bound him to the two figures that hung from wooden cruciform struc-tures positioned on either side of him. One woman and one man. Both completely naked, both in similar states of emaciation. Their heads hung limply, arms extended outwards, a perverse mockery of Jesus Christ.

Despite his wretched state, despite his once healthy tan skin now thin and ashen, despite his once golden blonde hair having gone the color of old straw, Susannah recognized her son.

"DANIEL!" Her voice carried, amplifying in the vast space. Her an-guish and her rage and her relief swelled into a heart-wrenching rever-beration. Daniel's head tilted up. Once vibrant blue eyes, so like her own, now dimmed by a year in pitch-black darkness and what she knew must be a slow, methodical bloodletting, gazed back at her. She found no recognition in that gaunt visage, only confusion, and pain.

"Viv..." Baumgartner whispered, so quietly that Susannah wouldn't have heard him if he hadn't been inches away.

The thing that must be Liam Coldona stood, towering above the two wooden platforms, and flexed his arms, causing the tethers to pulsate. Hidden devices within their bindings caused blood to trickle down the arms of both prisoners. Neither made a sound or any acknowledgement of their injuries. Liam strode towards Daniel, then licked the blood that lazily dripped down his arm, an almost sensual maneuver that made Susannah's rage blacken and fester into something feral. Her whole body thrummed with a renewed energy to destroy that which hurt her son. If she hadn't been so disillusioned with her faith, she would've thought it was the Holy Spirit flooding her, preparing her for battle.

*YOU HAVE COME AS I KNEW YOU WOULD. YOU HAVE BROUGHT THE VESSEL, BUT SHE IS CORRUPT. SO I WILL TAKE THAT WHICH IS MINE,* the thing boomed. His voice projected not aurally but mentally, so modulated and penetrating that Susannah could feel it in her chest like the report of Harold's high-caliber deer rifle. *PAIGE, BAUMGARTNER, THOSE WHO HAVE SOWN THE SEEDS OF THIS SUFFERING. REAP WHAT YOU HAVE SOWN.* He flexed his long, twig-like arms. The tentacles pulsated violently, and both Daniel and the woman who must be Vivian twitched. Blood wept from their wounds.

"*What have you done to my girl, you bastard!*" Baumgartner screamed and ran down the stone pathway towards the circle. Susannah followed, both of them fueled by that super-human adrenaline boost that comes to parents in times of most dire need for their children.

A tide of human imps emerged from those cerulean waters and oozed out of the honeycombed passages like pus from a cyst. They came by the hundreds, the thousands.

"Charles!" Susannah cried out, trying to grab him. But Baumgartner was already halfway down the stone path, charging headlong towards this monstrous being and his stone pedestal of abhorrence.

"There's too many of them!" she tried to warn him, but Baumgartner was on the warpath.

"They're not real!" Jessie screamed from behind. Susannah looked unsurely at Jessie, then back at the horde of creatures bearing down on the sheriff. She flinched as more of them converged on her, leaping with jagged nails and bared teeth. Nothing happened. They were just facades, apparitions. Jessie was right.

In a sudden flurry of emotion, her brain switched fully to fight instincts. Susannah charged headlong beside the sheriff. By the time they reached the stone island, Liam had disengaged from his two human blood banks, both Daniel and Vivian going limp with the disconnect. The wraith-like thing that was all sharp angles and thin dimensions exploded with a fury of motion. Twin shotgun blasts roared. Susannah and Charles were shooting so fast, so furiously that their gun reports bled into one long, continuous dragon's roar of firepower.

Slugs tore away chunks, while silver shot peppered small sizzling holes into that thin body, which, as they drew closer, Susannah realized was much bigger than she'd initially thought. That, or Liam had somehow managed to puff himself up as another defense, like pufferfish or cobras flaring their skull-vents. Or perhaps it was just another cruel illusion.

Susannah didn't even see the black tendril flailing at her like a black rat snake lashing out. It struck her across the face like the pop of a cold leather belt before ripping the gun from her hands. Meanwhile, the sheriff struggled with the other jet-black appendage, managing to fire off a shot and sunder the left-most tentacle.

Liam shrieked with indignant rage, an unintelligible burble of syllables. Susannah unfurled the cross from its chain and swung it in a circular motion like a medieval warrior wielding his chain-mace. She lashed out once, closing the distance between her and that terrible face and daring to near that huge gaping maw and its rows of teeth. The effect was awesome, much more volatile than before. Perhaps there *was* some esoteric spiritual hand at work, Susannah thought when a violent fireball exploded from his side the instant her cross hit his arm.

Liam reared back in disgust and smacked Susannah aside with one of his long spider-like appendages. Susannah went flying, but not before grabbing at the thing and managing to pin the tendril between her ribcage and arm.

Her hand clutched at the tentacle, feeling as if she'd just wrapped her hand around a boa constrictor, and instantaneously she was transported.

Flames engulfed her. Before her eyes ruptured from her skull from the heat, she saw dozens of dirty faces, pointing and cursing and shouting, behind them the awesome snow-capped peaks of the Carpathians. She screamed as she was buried alive, silver shackles binding her wrists and ankles together seared like carbolic acid against her flesh. The cold, bitter earth flooded her mouth as more peasant visages peered down at her from above, looks of abject disgust and hatred on their faces.

She felt that terrible, immense pressure again as the world collapsed around her. The black sky of cavern roof rained stone upon her, crushing every bone and rupturing every organ before the Curse infused her mangled body with terrible life.

Susannah had screamed herself hoarse by the time she was in the cabin, watching girls she did not recognize but thought of as family roasting alive, cherubic faces blackening, flesh boiling and crisping.

These flashes of suffering, more vivid than any Susannah ever encountered before, slammed into her one after the other, dominoes of agony falling into each other. Soon, she was wrenched back to the present, coming to in mid-air and having just enough time to register that she was in the fight before rolling towards the edge of the water, the wind knocked out of her. The potent reek of human excrement and unwashed skin nearly caused her to retch. Susannah looked over and saw that Daniel had been forced to stand in a growing pile of his own waste. His older deposits formed a black hardened crust that mired the base of the cruciform. Fresher layers of shit, not that much brighter, covered his feet up to the ankles.

She would have screamed if Liam hadn't wrapped his bony fingers around her throat, then hauled her up like she weighed no more than a newborn kitten.

*THERE IS NO MORE HIDING. NO MORE COWERING IN THE DARK. WE WILL BE THE BLACK TIDE THAT WASHES OVER THE WORLD. WE WILL BE THE BELLS OF ATONEMENT FOR A SPECIES MIRED IN ITS OWN HUBRIS.* The words drilled into her brain with sharp stabs of pressure. The black tendril slammed into her side, latching on with its puckered leech mouth. Susannah felt a revolting suction, like someone had just stuck the end of a shop vac nozzle to her love handle.

She watched the onyx tube swell, a bolus of her own blood traveling down the fleshy vein towards Liam's body. He sighed contentedly as he ingested her blood. The craters of wounds they'd just inflicted on his body immediately closed up and disappeared. He took another drink of her, the suction growing more intense. Her kidneys ached and her heart fluttered with the sudden loss of blood as he kept a choking vise lock on her throat. She kicked and thrashed, but Liam held tight, even as she pressed the cross against the burning, sizzling hand clutching her throat. By the second, his form began to fill out. The slate gray pallor of his skin slowly darkening, his eyes glowing brighter, nose and ears reforming. Vitality flowed into him.

*HOW LONG IT HAS BEEN SINCE IVE SUPPED WITHOUT RESTRAINT?* The voice that drilled into Susannah's mind was thick with orgasmic bliss. The rate of consumption increased until Susannah began to feel weak, the lack of oxygen and her rapidly depleting blood making her vision wash gray at the edges.

"Hey, motherfucker!" Baumgartner shouted.

Liam didn't acknowledge him. His vibrant eyes burned into Susannah's, intent on witnessing the life be sucked out of them. A shotgun roared, and finally Liam's attention was diverted as a slug tore through the snake-like appendage in mid-gulp, ripping the tendril in two. A spray of Susannah's blood fanned across his face. He dropped Susannah. The ground slammed up to meet her with a jarring impact, inches away from the pile of her son's fossilized shit. She began to gasp, holding a hand to her throat to stop the steady seep of blood. Pure adrenaline the only thing keeping her going.

# CHAPTER 42

B AUMGARTNER FIXED HIS GAZE on the demon before him, know-ing the minute he glanced at Vivian up close he would shatter. He would want only to run to her, to comfort her, to fix her. He had to deal with this monstrous motherfucker first. He walked slowly, aiming his shotgun at the thing's head. He fired once, sending a round of silver shards into Liam's face. Just as he ejected the spent shell and loaded a deer slug, Liam shot out his free tentacle, striking Charles's arm just as he fired again. The slug, meant to hit Liam square in the forehead, instead grazed the side of his temple.

A fleshy vise locked onto the sheriff's arm and yanked him forward. He flew some six feet and landed on his side. Somehow, he'd managed to hold onto his gun, trapping it between his body and the ground. Liam yanked again, dragging him along the stone floor. The flesh on Charles's face and arms scraped away. Then one of those stick-like legs, deceptively powerful, kicked him over onto his back. His headlamp caught Liam full in the face, which caused him to flinch just long enough for the sheriff to draw the shotgun up between them. Liam's mouth closed on the barrel of the gun instead of Charles's throat.

Liam bit and gnashed, his teeth breaking off with a sound like a kid biting into rock candy as he attempted to bite through the metal barrel. Charles's arms shook as Liam pressed against him, his frail body possessing incredible strength now that he'd had a fresh meal. Charles saw Liam was about to try and wrench the gun away from him when a golden white blur shot across his peripheral vision. Suddenly Liam's eyes, which he'd kept squeezed shut against the headlight, shot open. A roar of pain escaped that horrible mouth.

Buckie had joined the fight. His muzzle clamped down on the other feeding tube. Charles understood then, staring as the dog held onto the appendage with an iron grip, blood spurting out and coating the collie's beautiful coat and muzzle, that he needed to destroy those things. They couldn't allow this bastard to consume another drop of blood, or they could empty an entire armory of ammo into the motherfucker and it'd be like shooting BBs at a grizzly bear.

*"Buckie!"* Susannah screamed as Liam snarled and flung himself at the dog. Bony fingers sank into fur and his mouth opened wide. Buckie let out a high-pitched yelp as razor-sharp teeth sank into his scruff. Just as Liam was rearing back to take another bite, the sheriff kicked out as hard as he could. A size 12 boot connected with the back of Liam's knee. The beast fell back, dropping the dog. The sheriff tossed his large pocketknife across the way to Susannah, who was clambering to her feet.

"Cut the bastard! Cut his tube thing off!" the sheriff snarled. He came up behind Liam and hooked the gunstock against his throat, crushing it towards his body, using his old high school wrestling training to keep the bastard pinned down while Susannah hacked. It was like trying to keep a rabid tiger down. Liam thrashed and struck out with claws, digging into the sheriff's arms and sides, gauging out large chunks of flesh with long, ragged nails gone yellow and black at the edges. Charles gritted his teeth and bore through the pain, and through the pulling sensations in his mind. Blistering waves of heat throbbed through his body. With each scorching tsunami he felt that tug in his mind, invisible hooked fingers cracking open his skull to get at the vulnerable lump of gristle and gray matter inside. He fought against the creature desperately trying to enthrall him. His back molars cracked as his jaws clenched hard with the effort of resistance.

This was his repentance, this was his atonement for failing his daughter, for failing his town. He would make his daddy proud, he would give honor to the Baumgartner name, and he'd save his daughter before he died. He held onto the thrashing demon, using the last of his strength to keep it restrained. He would bear whatever pain this sonofabitch could give him. He wasn't letting go.

Susannah stumbled over, crying now but still fighting, her side covered in blood as she plunged the knife into the second flailing tentacle. The appendage had sought out Buckie's torn scruff and was trying to find purchase through thick fur. The dog was lying on his side, heavily panting, likely going into shock. Susannah hacked and slashed and screamed as she plunged the small knife up and down like a piston, working with frantic speed to sever the limb. Liam's thrashing intensified tenfold. He rolled and got to his feet with the sheriff still clinging on, hanging off the vampire's back like a child riding piggyback. Charles was intent on crushing the fucker's windpipe, but there was no give to the monster. It was like trying to crush the throat of a bronze statue of David.

Then he felt Liam reach around. Those long spindly sharpened bone nubs that passed for fingers poked into the sheriff's side, finding his kidney, and squeezed it like a festering pimple. A thunderbolt of pain shot through his side and robbed him of breath. Black sparks shot across his vision. Charles finally let go, collapsing to his knees as he hugged his side.

He clenched his jaw and tried his hardest to fight through the pain. Meanwhile, Liam turned towards Susannah, grasping her hand to stop the bloody knife at its apogee. The once lowly lead miner turned demonic manifestation raised his tentacle-limb towards Susannah, her knife hand pinned in place by his own. But the appendage spasmed and flopped uselessly. It'd been nearly torn in half, only a thin membrane of gristle keeping it connected. The other—the one the sheriff had blown away with a deer slug—flailed about like an unattended fire-hose at full blast, spurting black sludge from its severed tip.

Liam opened his mouth to bite, bits of Buckie's fur and blood caught in those spectacular teeth, when Susannah shot out a fist. Light glinted off the silver chain of her cross necklace wrapped around her hand like brass knuckles. She landed a beautiful roundhouse right to the toothy asshole's kisser. Needle teeth flew and a small plume of smoke rose up from the thing's face. As Liam backpedaled, Susannah stomped on the appendage, pinning it in place with her foot so when the monster backed away his sundered tendril was separated from his body with a wet *snap* as the last bit of gristle and sinew tore free.

Leaking gore from his severed limbs, Liam stared at them both with absolute hatred and threw his head back. What sounded from that throat was the very chorus of hell itself. The voice of every soul who has ever died in agony emerged from that singular maw. It was hell's own choir, calling out to their morning star. Pieces of cavern ceiling began to fall, splashing into the water and falling around them as Liam unleashed his scream. The sheriff raised his gun. His eyes watered and his vision began to waver from the sonic onslaught which called out to the deepest part of his soul.

For a split second, reverential awe washed over him. Rage and disgust burned away and the need to serve briefly overtook him. His vision went red. His arms trembled violently. Only a sliver of his mind was still his own and allowed him to peel one hand off the gun and punch himself hard in the nose. The shock of cartilage and bone shattering was enough to jolt him from the imminent grip of enthrallment.

"*Fuck you!*" Charles roared as blood dripped from his nose. He took careful aim and pulled the trigger, targeting not the thing's head but the throat, intent on silencing the beast once and for all.

The gun kicked against his shoulder, but the mighty roar of the 870 was all but a whisper compared to the screeching caterwaul that threatened to bring the whole chamber down. The slug tore through Liam's throat in a spray of flesh and gore. His ear-splitting cry sharply cut off as it devolved into a gurgling hiss.

Liam clasped his own throat with spindly hands. Teeth gnashed at empty air as he tried to continue his cry. He collapsed to his knees, black sludge seeping out from between his fingers. Susannah and the sheriff closed in on him, both of their ears ringing from the intense vocalization. But just as they were going in for the killing blow, intent on taking the beast's head off, they heard the muffled blast of Jesse's shotgun from far away.

Despite the sheriff's silencing shot, the scream had been enough to draw those creatures who were lingering throughout the cave system like plaque in arterial walls, returning from a night of prolific slaughter to rest and hide from the encroaching sun. These were no illusions. The thrall had finally been called home to feed.

Their headlamps darted around the black spaces of the cavern, highlighting Liam's diaspora as they boiled up from holes and tunnels like maggots from a festering wound. Four converged on Jessie, who was holding them at bay with the shotgun, but the sheriff knew they had to act quick or they'd be overwhelmed.

He lowered the barrel of his gun and aimed for Liam's legs. He shot twice, both rounds almost at point-blank range. Silver shot tore through the back of Liam's right leg and nearly blew it off, while the slug took his left one off cleanly at the knee. Liam fell and began to thrash on the ground, his wounds no longer magically healing.

The sheriff returned the favor from earlier and kicked Liam onto his back before standing over him with the barrel of the gun pointed at his head.

"Pry his goddamn mouth open!" Susannah screamed, coming up on the other side of the thrashing monster. Charles gladly obliged, shoving the thick black gun barrel into the mouth, breaking away teeth as he wrenched the blood-smeared jaws open. Black eyes stared at them with unfathomable hatred. Susannah took the necklace from her hands and shoved it down Liam's throat. Smoke erupted from between shattered teeth. Liam thrashed hard enough to wrench the barrel free. The sheriff ejected his spent shell and pulled the trigger.

Nothing happened. He looked down at his gun stupidly and realized he hadn't been keeping count of his shots.

"Shit!" Charles fumbled for the two remaining shells in his pants pocket, not bothering to see if they were slug or shot. Susannah flung herself atop Liam, the sheriff's pocketknife glinting in the headlamp's light as she hacked at his throat, screaming in defiance. Just as he'd managed to load the second round into the gun, something jumped onto Baumgartner's back and latched onto him like a monkey. Teeth bit at the nape of his neck, right where the other had clamped on earlier. Agony seared through him as teeth tore away flesh and muscle, finishing what the other had started. "*Fuck!*" he roared as he tried to buck the thing off.

Then something was grabbing at his legs, biting at his ankles. "*Susannah!*" he screamed, shocking her out of her bloodlust. Black ichor covered her up to the elbows. He tossed the shotgun to her with the last of his strength. "*Finish it!*" he roared before yet another body with teeth and claws fell upon him.

Time slowed to an adrenaline-dilated molasses crawl as Charles spun, finally allowing himself to behold his daughter. Her body was paler than he'd ever remembered it being. She was always a petite girl, but her frame was wholly wasted, rib cage flared and clearly visible, eyes half-lidded, deep circles under them. Her black hair hung in sweaty clumps. She seemed oblivious to what was going on around her.

The pain assaulting his body from every point was gone. A penetrating grief so intense it numbed the parting of his flesh and the teeth scraping against his bones like some terrible analgesic.

*Get her out of here alive, Susannah. My baby girl, be that artist or musician you always wanted to be. Fall in love, see the world, do everything your daddy couldn't.* For the first time in years, tears sprung to his eyes. He blocked out the multiple points of agony on his body and hurled himself towards the water, trying to lead them away from Susannah. He took great handfuls of cold, slick flesh in his hands, grabbing onto as many of the bastards as he could, crushing them to his body so they'd sink with him.

Charles Baumgartner did not feel fear or terror as the cold acidic water closed in around him, setting his wounds afire and flooding his lungs. Instead, he felt a great contentedness, a solace in knowing he did everything he could for his daughter. He prayed that she would live to know his sacrifice and perhaps learn to love him in her own way again.

He was not a good man, he accepted this, but he would not die a coward. As he felt his jugular rip open and the last of his breath was robbed from him, he let this singular thought comfort him in death. That his daughter would live on.

It was all he wanted.

# Chapter 43

J ESSIE KNEW SHE WAS going to run out of ammo long before she could fight off the things that swelled around her. She felt as though she were being tied up by a hundred red threads, all of them growing stronger the more they swarmed her. Those threads bled into the red mist and drew strength from it, like steel being tempered in a blazing furnace.

What was worse was the urgency, that *need* to attack when she heard Liam Coldona's blood-curdling scream. Her body thrummed with infection. Her limbs felt alien, and her mind seemed to come untethered from her body. Her original purpose for coming down here—*to stop him, to stop that bastard*—was now unclear. *Why* was she trying to stop Him? *Why* try to extinguish this beautiful radiant aura that she wanted to give herself completely over to, this warming presence that filled the void in her soul like the missing puzzle piece of life itself? That crimson cloud she'd failed to see the utter beauty in until now?

No, she would *not* be enthralled to him. She would not turn. She would die completely before letting herself be turned into one of these goddamn things.

And so she made a run for it, charging through the bodies with the last of her strength, using the shotgun as a battering ram as they clawed and bit at her, scratching and biting and ripping pieces of flesh from elbows and calves as she fought her way through. They were sluggish and bloated from their biblical slaughter. Many of them, confused by her advanced stage of turning—not quite human and not quite them—didn't fall upon her with the same zeal as normal bipedal cattle. She kicked one that blocked her path square in its distended gut and ignored the fountain of gore that erupted from its maw, ignored that delicious umami scent of blood, no longer cloying and coppery but rich and savory in her nostrils.

Every once in a while, her body craved meat. Yes, some days, usually during her period when she was running low on B vitamins and despite her ardent veganism, she craved a huge, medium rare New York strip. What she felt now made those cravings seem infinitesimal in comparison. God, how her mouth watered and her stomach *burned* with that need to consume things red and dripping and raw.

*YES, COME TO ME. LET ME FEED OF YOUR AMBROSIA. GIVE ME THIS LIGHT THAT SHINES SO BRIGHT WITHIN YOU. COME TO ME COME TO ME COME—*

Something snapped within Jessie as three more of the imps jumped on her, bringing her to the ground. She felt herself on the cusp of death. Maws snapped at her, licking her bleeding wounds, making sounds of rapturous bliss as their tongues came into contact with her oh-so-special blood. All the while Liam's voice drilled into her head, boiling her gray matter with its insistence. Her heart palpitated violently as it did when Susannah had brought her back when her heart stopped on the side of the road. She had the sensation of leaving her body once more. A most visceral déjà vu flooded her.

She clung to consciousness long enough to witness Charles Baumgartner make the ultimate sacrifice. He'd tossed his shotgun to Susannah and was using himself as a magnet to draw the thrall horde away from the woman.

In that moment, the nihilistic misanthropy that clung to Jessie's soul like a caul after her experience in the jail vanished. Years and years of encountering the worst of humanity had left her soul jaded. Her view of humanity as a whole was that of a parasite. But Susannah had shown her that even in this day and age, human beings could still be virtuous and genuinely altruistic. And the sheriff's display of bravery, an exhibition of courageous selflessness from a most unexpected source, cemented this sea change of perception.

There was still horror in this world, yes. And human monsters would always abound. But there were also pure souls among the species, those who sought to heal and thrive rather than destroy and corrupt.

*Humanity was worth fighting for.*

With that realization came a sensation of doors slamming shut, of heavy nuclear-blast-proof doors thudding closed. Jessie came back into herself. The blast-furnace heat of her infection had burned away. The vile urge to drink blood by the gallon, to eat raw, still twitching flesh was gone. The horde clambering over themselves to get at her exploded away as if invisible hands yanked at unseen tethers, flinging them away as Jessie answered Liam's bone-rattling caterwaul with a shout of her own.

Whatever force had been imbued within her on the side of that county road now came to a boil as she called it to the surface. Jessie's war cry was her answer to Liam's summoning shriek. A renunciation. He was not the only titan down here now. Her whole body thrummed with an energy not quite her own. She no longer feared the monstrosities surrounding her.

Imps now cowered before her, confused and frightened. Jessie saw with uncomprehending awe that she exuded her own aura—a bright, wavering gold that emanated from her arms and legs like an ethereal second skin. The red mist that bathed the whole cavern dissipated with each step she took.

Jessie ran headlong towards Susannah, who straddled Liam and was plunging the knife, over and over and over, screaming *why won't you die!* at the top of her lungs. Buckie lay in a panting heap beside her, blood coloring his thick coat, while the two human kegs slumped inert against their crucifix bindings. Baumgartner was gone.

Jessie came up beside Susannah and kicked aside Baumgartner's shotgun. She knew now that no earthly weapon could banish this abomination. Susannah paused mid-plunge, her blue eyes reflecting the golden silhouette of Jessie as she turned to behold this walking star of light.

"Oh... My God... What—" Susannah began. Jessie gently pulled her away from the still-thrashing Liam. His head and neck were a vague pulp of bone and blood and gristle, yet still he thrashed with terrible life. Susannah simply went on staring, shocked out of her bloodlust by the sight of Jessie's transformation.

Jessie looked down at this man, this poor, everyday working immigrant who'd been forced into living the very prophecy he'd tried to escape. In that moment, knowing what she had seen of the Coldona Curse, understanding the generations of hatred and racism and human poison they'd had to endure, she found it in herself to pity this foul thing that had once been a good, honest man.

Even with his head a ruinous heap of torn flesh and bone, Liam raised his caved-in skull and hamburger face to Jessie, one eye remained in its shattered socket, looking up at her, hateful but pleading, hungry, *needing* this light that grew inside of her, *needing* this elemental force that, through some unknowable divine converging of paths, had been endowed into Jessie's soul with the help of a woman pure of heart. Needing that hope, that whatever it was blossoming inside Jessie could fix him, could undo what his mother had done all those years ago.

She understood then that she was a vessel for the cure. It was the light to his darkness. It was the pure essence of humanity, of love and empathy and the human condition. It was the antithesis to the black poison that comprised the Coldona Curse.

Jessie made a fist and reared back. Liam's black eye widened, his blown open throat making desperate whistling, gasping sounds right before she plunged her fist into that razor-maw of shattered teeth.

*YOU DON'T DESERVE THE GIFT. YOU HAVE NOT ATONED LIKE I HAVE. I DESERVE THE LIGHT. I DESERVE TO BE HUMAN AGAIN I—*

"You want this so fucking badly? Huh? *This what you fucking want?*" Jessie screamed, her voice carrying with it the preternatural loudness of the force that surged through her body and into the thing that cowered underneath her.

The ground shook as she plunged her fist into his head, punching him hard enough for her knuckles to punch through skull and hit the rock floor beneath Liam's head. Pieces of cavern fell around them. Liam's body began to inflate like a balloon as Jessie felt this transference of energy, she the anti-venom and he the festering snakebite. She the light and he the darkness.

Brilliant shafts of light began to eat through the patches of pulled-taut skin as Liam continued to inflate, almost comically now, into a bloated Macy's Thanksgiving Day Parade float version of himself. Ruptured sockets bled forth twin columns of light as brilliant as the sun at high noon. She didn't feel his teeth sink into her as light spilled from his mouth. In that moment she didn't feel anything, except a cleansing warmth.

Then came the flash. Susannah screamed. A hellish chorus of imps cried out, their voices modulating into a hideous tri-tone of pain and agony as the infection was burned from their bodies. Jessie felt the warmth deepen from her skin to her bones as Liam exploded into a ball of pure, red energy.

In an instant, her connection to Liam and the others was sundered. Threads snapped with whip-like violence, like guitar strings popping back after being tuned too high. The aura was vanishing, and with it that burning tidal wave that churned and roiled within her.

Jessie collapsed to the stone floor. Everything fell away. What she felt went beyond exhaustion. It was like being dead while still drawing breath.

"Jessie, honey, please, come back to me," Susannah pleaded. But in her daze, Jessie didn't know who the poor woman was talking to.

After some unknowable amount of time, Jessie finally ripped in a great, raw breath of stinking air. Her heart gave one powerful lurch before returning to a normal, albeit fast rhythm. She finally managed to open her eyes and saw the ten or fifteen remaining vampires, once human beings, once people just like her, falling to their knees. Jessie had a hard time seeing them, her vision was no longer the cat-eye gray scale that let her navigate effortlessly through the obsidian void of this hell hole. Now she only saw what Susannah's floundering headlamp saw, and in that blessed beam of light bodies began to rapidly decompose, steam rising from their corpses as at long last, these tortured souls were allowed to move on from this hellish world.

She turned to face what remained of Liam Coldona and blinked, for what she saw her mind could not comprehend. A hovering, glowing red ball, a mini-scaled dying sun, the very essence of the Coldona Curse distilled into its raw essence. With an abrupt burst of movement, the basketball-sized sphere exploded into brilliant streamers of pure light before dissolving into nothing.

It was as if the invisible vise grips that had clamped onto Jesse's lungs, brain and very soul were released. The pain from her physical injuries throbbed back to life, yes, but compared to what she'd just endured, these barely registered. Slowly, shakily, she got to her feet and rushed toward Susannah, who was desperately attempting to free her son from his bindings, hacking away the lashings with the gore-caked knife.

Daniel collapsed, muttering nonsense, his frail, emaciated body falling into his mother's arms.

"Oh, Daniel, my sweet baby. Oh my God... Oh my God—" Susannah cried as she held her son tightly, pushing matted hair from his brow.

Jessie went to Vivian, this woman who looked nothing like her father. Though she was still in shock from the mind-blowing transcendental episode she'd just lived through, though her body felt like a spent, hollow shell of itself, Jessie was still able to feel a brief pang of intense melancholy as she looked around and saw the sheriff was no longer with them, remembering his final act of selfless bravery. How the love for his daughter had helped him become something of a noble man in the end, and yet he didn't even live to see her rescued.

"Hey... Can you hear me?" Jessie asked as she began to untie the bindings. One arm, and then the other fell limply as she unbound the woman. The reek of unwashed flesh and human waste was incredible, but Jessie forced herself to bear through it as the woman moaned deliriously. God only knew what these two endured while down here. What horrors they saw and experienced.

Jessie found the discarded backpack, took out a granola bar and a bottle of water, and offered them to Vivian who snatched both with surprising quickness.

"Easy now, don't... gulp that," Jessie said as she heard the water glug down in four quick swallows.

"Where... Where am I?" Vivian asked, clarity returning to her eyes. Jessie had assumed whatever mental powers Liam used to create those horrid illusions could also be used to obfuscate a person's sense of self, a loathsome hypnosis that kept one in mental limbo.

"It doesn't matter, we're getting you out of here." Jessie removed her sweaty blood-soaked shirt, long past the point of caring if anyone saw her in her bra, and handed it to Vivian, who gratefully wrapped it around her frail, naked body.

Next, Jessie knelt beside Buckie. His once plush fur was now matted with blood, his golden eyes wide with fear and shock; reduced to a scared puppy.

The dog whimpered softly while Jessie cradled him in her arms, then rose to her knees. Susannah met her eyes as she hefted her son's arm around her, both of them beyond words.

"Can you walk?" Jessie asked Vivian.

"I... I think so." The girl's voice was raw and weak. She stood on trembling legs, stumbled for a moment. Jessie thought she was going to fall, but the woman caught herself. Veins and tendons stood out on her thin legs.

On the other side of the platform, Daniel was leaning heavily on Susannah, and together they began to walk, retracing part of their path on the way in. With the dog in Jessie's arms, Susannah with her son limping beside her, and Vivian trailing close behind, they traversed the caves in total silence.

With the Curse eradicated, the cave systems were a hollow, dead thing. They saw no subterranean fauna. No bats. No lizards or newts. Just miles of unending rock.

Though neither woman could explain the force that led them, there was a definitive, unseen hand guiding them through the maze of tunnels, nudging them this way and that, sending them down passageways they'd never been down, an instinctual gut feeling telling them which way to take. They gave themselves over completely to this ethereal force, letting it guide them through the bowels of this poisoned earth, until finally the peach-colored light of dawn greeted them at the end of one tunnel.

# EPILOGUE

J ESSIE STEPPED OUT ONTO the porch with Susannah's laptop, knowing if she heard much more of the waterworks going on in the next room she'd start crying too. Harold Paige had just come home, and the intense reunion was too much for Jessie.

Her emotional state had been a fragile one since the cave incident, and she knew this was a symptom of PTSD. Some serious therapy was in her future, though she didn't know how to talk about the things she'd seen, what she had *become*, and the things she'd done without the first psychologist she spoke to immediately arranging for her to be put in a straitjacket. She didn't want to end up like the sheriff's daughter.

No, she would worry about that later. Right now, she was convalescing, not in the corporeal way Daniel was doing in the back room, but in a spiritual manner.

She stared out at the verdant surroundings of the backyard. The complete peace and tranquility of this little area had been healing for her. It'd been two weeks since the battle at the cave, and every morning since, she'd sat out here disassociating and letting her mind be untethered by the forest sounds. In that trance state, she let her mind crawl over the things she'd seen during her change. The old man with half a face had been right. Each one who had succumbed to the thrall inherited that agony, that generational suffering that followed the Coldona family name the way stink follows a corpse. Gently, she had to let her mind examine the various things she saw, like a tongue probing carefully at an abscessed tooth, exploring the enamel, finding the cavities.

The images came to her in waves, with their vividity and accompanying senses: Heat, the smell of burning flesh, the reek of carrion rotting in the sun, the coppery scent of fresh spilled blood. These were not sequences from a dream, which one could hold at a comfortable, abstract distance, content in knowing they weren't real. No, these were *memories*. Someone had lived through them, someone had carried that pain and that complete grievous devastation, and they harbored it until it became a poison. One that could be spread down the line, a volatile, weaponized suffering that had brewed and been distilled into something real and physical, then turned into something that could be harnessed with eons of old magic.

Then there was the matter of her... transformation. That was really the only apt word she could think of. She had to ask Susannah several times, confirm she'd seen it too. Susannah attested to the "angelic glow" that emanated from Jessie in the cave. Jessie took Susannah's explanation for what it was: relying on her religious beliefs to ascribe a holy quality to Jessie's inexplicable transcendent state. Yet, despite the incredible, paranormal and wholly extraordinary things she'd seen and endured in the last two weeks, Jessie wasn't quite ready to start believing in gods and angels just yet.

But if she refused that explanation, there was the trouble of just what the fuck *had* happened to her. What was that elemental force she'd inherited when Susannah brought her back to life? What was it inside of her that Liam Coldona cherished so badly? A force so profoundly powerful that it had vaporized the poisonous curse like Alka Seltzer in a vat of battery acid, saving Jessie from turning at the very last minute and vanquishing Liam to whatever realm lay beyond this one.

Part of what triggered her random panic attacks was that burning, unknowable question of what and why. Why her, why choose her body as the vessel for that power? And what was it that inhabited her and allowed her to defeat such profound evil? The fact she couldn't answer that question kept her up more nights than not. She sipped her coffee, letting the morning sun warm and comfort her, the throbbing of her bandaged ear a corporeal reminder of her epic odyssey.

*Speaking of coping with your traumas*, she thought as she begrudgingly opened up the internet browser on Susannah's laptop.

Jessie had made it a point to avoid any and all internet and social media during this time of healing and recuperation, knowing she was too fragile to deal with the outside world. But it'd been two weeks, and her morning therapy of coffee on the porch, listening to the animals run through the forest, and smelling the many rich earthy smells of rural living had done her some good.

She checked her email. The first thing she saw was a message from Lou:

*Hey girl, hope you're doing alright. Thought you'd wanna see this. Fuckin' hilarious, but I guess they had to spin it some way that didn't sound batshit. Anyway, thought you'd get a kick out of that. Come see me when you're ready, the old woman's got me on bed rest for the foreseeable future, and I'm gonna go cray-cray if I don't see someone soon who isn't Geoff. Fucker has a bug up his ass about writing some songs about this shit, can you believe it? Anyway, take care, stay alive out there in that redneck Riviera. –L*

Jessie smiled, then clicked on the links Lou had sent her with the email. It was good knowing those two assholes made it out alright. She'd gotten a phone call from Geoff a few days after the showdown. It was hard to make out over his breathy, excited talking, but according to him, they were gonna be celebrities. After a state-wide police pursuit that made national news, the police detained both Geoff and Lou, who showed up to Lee's Summit PD at four in the morning with a stolen cop car after Lou had apparently taken Geoff hostage, demanding to speak to the chief of police. That in itself was enough to make Jessie laugh with incredulity.

According to Geoff, both men had been incarcerated, with Lou under supervised medical care. Someone over at Lordell County PD had finally decided to call the big guns in to Carter County after scared shitless dispatchers reported calls that corroborated what the crazed kid with the broken back and the jacked sheriff's cruiser was going on about. When the National Guard finally rolled down Route Y, full of piss-scared reservists not knowing what in god's name they were about to get into, they found a town in chaos. Mummified corpses that looked like they'd been dead in a vacuum for hundreds of years. Other corpses, fresh ones, completely exsanguinated. Some brutally mauled as if by wild animals. Tales of people going crazy, of taking a full clip of rounds to the head and torso and not going down. Of these same seemingly invincible folks randomly dropping dead for no good reason, all at once.

Bath-salt-laced meth. That was what the special investigators had determined.

One of the articles Lou had sent her quoted Missouri Highway Patrol Lieutenant Lance Myers, "I know it sounds crazy, but we had something just like this happen a few years ago in Saint Louis. Some guy walking on the highway naked as a jaybird at four in the morning. Some good Samaritan stops to help him, and the guy eats his face off. Toxicology said he had a snoot full of that bath salt shit you can get at the gas station. You put that crap into a widely distributed drug like methamphetamine, and, well..."

Jessie almost laughed out loud. Lou had been right. That sure was one hell of a way to spin it. She clicked on the other link.

**Corrupt Local Sheriff Poisons Town: A Special Report**

A small cramp twisted her stomach when she saw Baumgartner's name. The sheriff had been "missing" since the brief epidemic had started, and when state patrol went into the sheriff's office to investigate, they found two dead bodies in the jail and a baggie of meth on his desk.

Jessie felt conflicted. The man she had once hated took the rap for what happened to the town. He could be a psychotic asshole, yes, but in the end, the sheriff demonstrated real courage. He had given his life for his daughter. They couldn't have defeated the monsters without him luring them away. He may have been mildly psychopathic and a tad bit narcissistic, but he didn't deserve this hit job.

Jessie remembered the way he'd plunged into the water, his body covered in those corrupted human vessels like lampreys to a shark's flank. He took them all down with him.

He died so they could succeed.

He died so his daughter could live.

She shut the laptop as thoughts of Allen came unbidden to her mind. Allen, a pure soul who ended up road pizza, his remains locked away in some pissant rural cold box, being handled by some indifferent coroner, while the other half of him lay undiscovered in a cave somewhere. *Jessiejessiejessie*, she could still hear that jabbering idiot moan as he dragged himself towards her. Despite the warm sun and muggy morning humidity, she shivered at the thought.

Jessie stared once more at the tree line, focusing on her breathing exercises. Susannah had said she could stay as long as she liked, she could even live there if she wanted.

Jessie at first balked at the idea. How could she, a young woman who'd lived a life on the road, her home no permanent place but rather the ephemeral shifting of van bench seats and stranger's basements, feel at home in such a banal and boring place? A Christian home in the middle of the boonies? Ridiculous.

And yet, as she sat on the porch, letting the silent tears streak down her cheeks, she realized she'd never felt so at home anywhere else before. The Paige house radiated stability, it radiated safety, it contained within it strong, noble people who would do absolutely whatever it took to keep their family safe. Jessie felt permanence and familiarity here, the very antithesis of her previous life.

She leaned back in the canvas porch chair and closed her eyes to stem the flow of tears. She listened to squirrels chittering. She heard the soft sounds as they chased each other through leaf litter and up trees. She heard the splash of fish in the pond. She smelled wild juniper and the green, loamy perfume of the surrounding Ozarks as the morning breeze kicked up.

Yes, she would let herself heal here awhile yet. And perhaps even allow herself to plant roots here.

Perhaps.

# About the Author

Richard Beauchamp has been publishing fiction since 2017. His short stories have appeared in many critically acclaimed anthologies and collections, including the "SNAFU" series by Cohesion Press, the "Negative Space" anthologies from Dark Peninsula Press, and "2017 Year's Best Body Horror" by Gehenna and Hinnom Publishing. His short story collection, "Black Tongue & Other Anomalies" was a 2022 Splatterpunk Award nominee for Best Fiction Collection. His story "Sons Of Luna" was a 2018 Pushcart Prize finalist.

Richard lives on the eastern cusp of the Missouri Ozarks with his wife, their dog, and too many cats. He can often be found traversing those low mountains, living off the land when he can, and spending time outside when he isn't stuck in his office abusing a word processor.

<u>**Other Works by Richard Beauchamp**</u>

*And They Will Suffer* (Anatolian Press), a novel

*Black Tongue & Other Anomalies* (D&T Publishing), a short story collection

*Triptych: Three Tales of Frontier Horror* (self-published), a short story collection

*Horror In the Highlands: Collected Horrors From the Ozarks* (Bell Mountain Press), a short story collection

Learn more at my website: http://www.richardbeauchampauthor.com

# Acknowledgements

I have several people to thank for the creation of this novel.

First and foremost, my wife, Sierra, who's been my number one beta reader and biggest supporter throughout my journey as a horror author.

Second would be my close friend and developmental editor, Korey Dawson, who helped reshape the earliest version of this manuscript and give this story the depth it needed to be ready for submission.

Third, our dog Helios, who serves as the archetype for "Buckie" and helped change me from a staunch cat-person to a lover of both species.

Finally, I want to thank the fine folks at Grendel Press for helping me bring my vision of *Thrall* to life. None of this would be possible without them.

www.ingramcontent.com/pod-product-compliance
Lightning Source LLC
Chambersburg PA
CBHW061337310726
48974CB00001B/82